RED STONE SECURITY SERIES

BOX SET VOLUME 4

KATIE REUS

Cover Art by Sweet 'N Spicy Designs
Editors: JRT Editing & Julia Ganis, JuliaEdits.com
Digital Formatting by Author E.M.S.

Red Stone Security Series Box Set Volume 4/Katie Reus. — 1st ed.

ISBN-10: 1942447736
ISBN-13: 978-1942447733

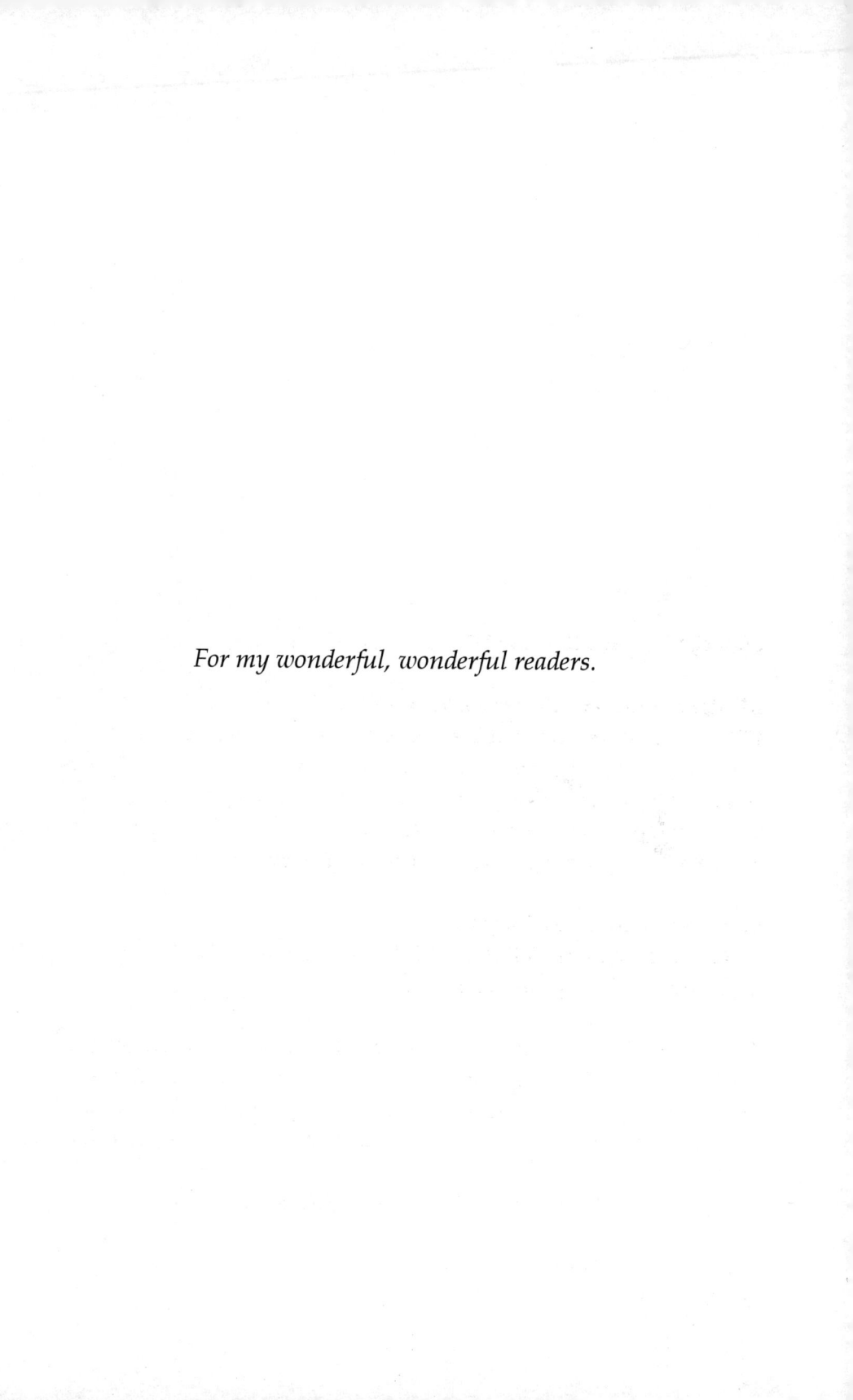

For my wonderful, wonderful readers.

PRAISE FOR THE NOVELS OF KATIE REUS

"Sexy military romantic suspense!" —USA Today

"...a wild hot ride for readers. The story grabs you and doesn't let go." —*New York Times* bestselling author, Cynthia Eden

"Has all the right ingredients: a hot couple, evil villains, and a killer action-filled plot. . . . [The] Moon Shifter series is what I call Grade-A entertainment!" —Joyfully Reviewed

"I could not put this book down. . . . Let me be clear that I am not saying that this was a good book *for* a paranormal genre; it was an excellent romance read, *period*." —All About Romance

"Reus strikes just the right balance of steamy sexual tension and nail-biting action....This romantic thriller reliably hits every note that fans of the genre will expect." —*Publishers Weekly*

"Prepare yourself for the start of a great new series! . . . I'm excited about reading more about this great group of characters." —Fresh Fiction

"Wow! This powerful, passionate hero sizzles with sheer deliciousness. I loved every sexy twist of this fun & exhilarating tale. Katie Reus delivers!" —Carolyn Crane, RITA award winning author

"You'll fall in love with Katie's heroes." —*New York Times* bestselling author, Kaylea Cross

CONTENTS

DEADLY
FALLOUT

PROLOGUE

Zoe Hansen slipped her earbuds into her ears, the soft classical music drowning out the typical hospital sounds as she stepped out of the elevator. It was four in the morning and time for her required break from the ER rush since she was working a double.

Normally she took her breaks with friends, but this morning, she actually needed some alone time. One of her fellow surgeons had been harassing her lately. Subtle stuff at first; innuendos in front of co-workers, trying to make it sound like they were a couple.

Please.

First of all, the guy was married so there was no way in hell she'd ever date or sleep with him. And second, he was twenty years older than her and definitely not her type. The age thing actually didn't bother her much, it was his douchey personality and God complex.

But tonight things had gotten even weirder. He'd sent her two dozen red roses and made a point to ask her about them in front of some of her co-workers. It had been incredibly embarrassing and unprofessional. She needed to decompress and go over her options because she wasn't letting this crap continue any longer.

As soon as her shift was over, she was talking to someone in the HR department. She understood the annoying politics of the hospital and that she shouldn't 'make waves' but she'd never put up with anyone's crap and wasn't about to start now. Especially not with this kind of creepy behavior.

When she reached a room she knew was often unused, she ducked inside. After checking the bathroom to make sure it really was empty, she flipped the lights off, letting the illumination from outside the two big windows guide her. Sighing in relief, she eyed the bed and the bench by the window. If she got in the bed she'd pass out and her break was too short for a real nap. Heading to the window, she stretched out on the padded cushion and leaned her head back against the wall. Since she was petite she didn't have to scrunch her legs too much.

Before she closed her eyes, she set her phone alarm to go off in twenty-five minutes. The buzzing would jar her awake if for some reason she dozed off.

"Finally, peace," she murmured to the empty room. The bright city lights of Miami weren't even a distraction as she let her eyes close. She'd had so many back-to-back surgeries yesterday and early this morning that nothing could distract her now.

Sweet rest edged her consciousness as the soft music helped calm her frayed nerves. When she felt her phone buzzing in her pocket, she shifted against the seat. Had she actually fallen asleep? Opening her eyes, she fished into her pocket and looked at her screen—and sighed. Only a couple minutes had passed but there was an emergency. Of course. That's what she got for trying to sneak away for a few minutes.

As she swung her legs off the bench, a slight movement in the shadows on the other side of the bed made her freeze. Heart pounding, she pulled her earbuds out. Holding her breath, she paused, listening and watching.

A curtain had been pulled back from the uncovered bed, but she could swear she saw movement. Or maybe it was her imagination going crazy because she'd been so tense lately. She'd felt as if she was being watched, possibly even followed.

Squeak.

Shit. Blood rushed in her ears. "Who's there?" she demanded, glad her voice came out strong. This floor wasn't as busy as the ER but it wasn't devoid of people. It was too damn dark to see behind the curtain. With no light from the bathroom behind it, it was like a dark abyss.

When Braddock Klein stepped out of the shadows, ice flooded her veins. Him being here after his weird behavior lately was *not* good. "I'm glad you could sneak away so we could spend time together," he murmured, his voice low and probably what he thought of as seductive.

Sneak away? Her heart rate kicked up again, the staccato beat going overtime. "What are you talking about?" She kept her voice even as she took a step away from the bench. She tried to keep her movements small, not wanting to give away that she was trying to make it to the door.

He was in street clothes, dark slacks and a business casual Polo shirt. He was tall and dark-haired, with a distinguished face. In his fifties, he was a handsome-looking man in a country club, preppy sort of way. Or he would be if it wasn't for the fact that he was clearly deranged.

"I know you come up here sometimes," he said, moving to the end of the bed and effectively blocking her escape.

Almost no one knew she used this room for downtime so he had to have been watching her *closely*. Zoe took a step away from him and toward a rolling cart. It was in the opposite direction of the door, but she needed a weapon if things escalated. Because the look in his eyes was creepy as hell and she wasn't ignoring her instincts.

"Why are you here?" Her voice shook.

His head tilted to the side a fraction and he looked at her as if her question was stupid. "You know why. I don't understand why you keep playing so hard to get. Everyone here already thinks we're a couple."

"You're married," she said, even though that wasn't remotely the point. She just wanted to get his focus back on reality.

Klein made a weird tsking sound and stepped closer, rounding the bed now. "You're mine, Zoe," he growled, his face turning feral as he lunged for her.

Zoe dove for the rolling cart and grabbed a metal bedpan on the bottom shelf. She'd barely grasped it in her fingers when Klein tackled her to the bed, his big body pinning her face-down. The pan fell to the floor with a clatter.

She slammed her head back, trying to break his nose, but he twisted to the side, avoiding what would have been a hard blow.

"Bitch," he snarled.

She let a scream rip free as she tried to scramble over the bed. The door was so close, just within her grasp. Her feet hit the floor but before she'd taken two steps he tackled her again, slamming her against the wall and cutting short her cries for help.

The pain jarring her entire body barely registered as he hissed in her ear, his breath hot as it rushed over her skin. "You're going to learn your place." His thick arm wrapped around her neck as he tugged her back against him.

Struggling to breathe, she clutched his arm as he lifted her off the ground. Oh God, she couldn't breathe!

His hand clawed at her crotch over her scrubs. Tears stung her eyes at the violation. She kicked back with one of her feet, barely clipping his shin—

The door opened and lights flooded the room.

Instantly he dropped her. Without thinking Zoe sprinted for the door. A female janitor looked at her in surprise as she rounded the small entryway. The cleaning cart blocked Zoe. On instinct, she turned back toward Klein, ready to defend herself. But he just stood there, adjusting his shirt, tucking it into his pants. Except for his ruffled hair, he looked completely unaffected.

"Is everything okay?" the woman asked.

Zoe shook her head. "No. Come on." She shoved at the cart and forced the woman back into the hall. She didn't care how rude she was being, she needed to get the hell out of the room and away from him. As they spilled out into the hallway, she pointed toward the elevators. "Get off this floor now." She didn't have time to explain herself to the woman and Zoe wanted her out of harm's way.

As the woman hurried in the other direction, Zoe raced for the nearest nurses' station to get help. She risked a glance over her shoulder as she ran and saw Klein strolling out of the room. He was smoothing his dark hair into place, his movements unhurried.

Fear battled with outrage inside her when he winked—actually winked—and turned away from her, heading toward the elevators as if he didn't have a care in the world.

CHAPTER ONE

Seven months later

"You about out of here?"

Zoe looked up at the sound of her new boss, Gerard Fernandez's voice. "Yes. Seriously, I can't believe I didn't know how great private practice could be." After leaving the public hospital months ago she hadn't realized what a toll the hours and stress had been taking on her personal life. Now she left work every day between five and six, could actually take days off and had her own office. She grabbed her jacket off the back of her leather rolling chair and slipped it on as she rounded the desk.

A grin tugged at his mouth. "You're preaching to the choir. Come on, we're the last two here. I'll walk you to your car."

"You don't have to." Gerard knew what had happened to her at the hospital and Klein's subsequent threats, but that wasn't why he was walking her to her car. He walked every woman who worked at his family practice to her car when they got off work. He was like a throwback to a different era. Just one of those truly good men she was glad to call her friend.

He simply snorted. "That line's getting old, Hansen. Besides, isn't *he*…getting back in town soon?"

Throat tight, Zoe nodded and found her voice. Her gaze automatically went to the wall calendar, as if she didn't know the exact day that freak show Braddock Klein was returning from his six month Medicine Without Borders stint overseas. "Yeah."

"You told your family yet?" he asked as she turned her lights off and stepped out into the hall with him.

Zoe scowled. "Remind me again why I told you about all this?"

He just snorted again because they both knew the answer. After Klein's attack, the whole thing had turned into a he-said, she-said type of situation. And since the psycho had been—unbeknownst to her—laying the groundwork at work so that everyone thought she was in some type of relationship with him, her work life had basically imploded. Apparently it was much easier for her co-workers to believe that she was just some slut hooking up with a married doctor and had then decided to press charges against him for 'fill in the blank'. She'd heard all the rumors after everything had gone down and they'd all horrified her. He'd refused to leave his wife for her, so she'd decided to cry would-be rape. It shouldn't shock her so much that people she'd worked with hadn't seen the truth, but it did. At least she'd been able to get a temporary restraining order against him—unfortunately permanent ones were almost impossible to get.

Of course hindsight sucked. There were signs that something had been wrong with Klein, but it had all been little stuff. Unfortunately it all added up to a grade A psychopath who'd become insanely focused on her.

And now said psychopath was returning to the States in a week. "I'm scared," she finally said into the quiet as they strode down the hallway that led to the door that emptied into the waiting room. They always left out the front door after dark because there was better lighting.

"You've taken all the right precautions, but you need to tell your family," he said as they strode through the small waiting room and into the lobby.

It was already dark outside, the lights from the parking lot bright through the wall of windows. "I know. I will." But she hated the thought of worrying them. Her brother was now blissfully engaged, her two sisters had busy lives and big families, and her mom would just worry. It didn't matter that she and her mom butted heads more often than not, Zoe didn't like upsetting her mom. And Klein had left the country months ago so there'd been no reason to make her mom worry needlessly. Especially when there was nothing she could do about it.

Gerard shook his head and made a disapproving sound, likely because he'd heard this before. She really was going to tell them, it was just...hell, if she said it out loud, it became real. This whole, horrible situation became real. Not to mention that if she admitted it, it almost made her feel weak. Like she was admitting that she'd become a victim in this mess.

Sighing, she nudged the glass door open with her hip and shoved her hands in her jacket pockets. Her phone and keys were in one and the pepper spray she always carried now was in the other. She'd actually gotten a concealed weapon permit but simply couldn't carry a gun around. It felt too weird. The chilly December air rolled over her, reminding her that she still needed to buy Christmas presents for her huge family. Of course her put-together sisters would have already done their shopping months ago. Not Zoe, she saved everything until the last minute. It worked for her.

Gerard began locking up the exterior glass door. She knew from watching him do it a hundred times that he would set the alarm remotely once the building was locked up tight. Instinctively, she scanned the parking lot—and froze when she saw Klein leaning against the back of her two-door car. *No.* Her throat tightened as fear scraped across her skin.

"Gerard," she rasped out, wondering if she'd lost her mind and was now seeing things.

She heard the snicking of the deadbolt sliding into place before he said, "What's..." Suddenly Gerard was standing in front of her, moving incredibly fast as he started striding across the parking lot with determination.

That was the only thing that moved her into action; seeing her boss taking action. Because the truth was, the sight of Klein terrified her. She'd always been so sure of who she was and what she wanted to do with her life. From the time she'd been a kid she'd wanted to be a doctor and no matter what, with everything else going on in her life, the hospital had always been her safe haven. She'd loved it there — and he'd taken that feeling of security from her.

No more.

Gripping her pepper spray tight, she pulled her hand out of her pocket and hurried to catch up with Gerard. Her boots clicked softly against the pavement as she fell in step with him, her stride unwavering. There was no way she was letting this monster steal the new job she'd made here. She wouldn't let him force her to move jobs or move away out of fear.

Klein pushed up from her car, a smug look on his face as he eyed her. For a brief moment, when he glanced at Gerard, Zoe could see his mask slip a fraction. His expression was one of barely concealed rage, as if the monster inside him was clawing to get free, but just as quickly, it was gone, replaced by a charming-looking middle-aged man.

"You're on private property. Leave before I call the police," Gerard said, his voice clipped.

Damn, he got right to the point. Right now Zoe was grateful she'd bared her soul to the man.

Klein's eyes narrowed a fraction, but he didn't move any closer to them. Zoe remained where she was, about fifteen feet away from him, her legs simply refusing to work any longer. It didn't matter how angry she was, or how many times she'd played out this scenario in her mind, she was fucking terrified of this man. It was the deadness in his eyes. Now that she looked at him, truly looked, there was nothing inside his soul.

That was scary.

"Are you fucking her too?" Klein asked abruptly, his gaze narrowing on Gerard.

Damn it, no. She didn't want this psycho's attention on her friend and boss. Anger detonated inside her, shoving her fear out of the way. "Well, 'too' would imply that I've fucked you and we both know I haven't. And never will."

Aaaand, that did it. Klein's attention was back on her, that laser-like intensity unnerving. But she stood her ground. She refused to cower in front of him, not when she knew he craved it. He took a menacing step in their direction. Zoe tensed, her grip on her pepper spray tightening.

Gerard jerked a thumb behind him. "Our security cameras send an automatic dump to an external server every few minutes. So you being here has been recorded. Even if you decide to be stupid and try to attack us then break in and erase the history, you'll never be able to cover anything up. So why don't you get the hell out of here and never come back? Because if I see you again, you won't get a warning." There was something deadly and serious about Gerard's voice. A tone Zoe had never heard before.

Klein's entire body drew taut as he went impossibly still, his dark eyes intent on her until just as suddenly, he relaxed and let out an eerie laugh. "Just wanted to stop by and see you, Zoe. Now that I'm back in town, I'm sure we'll be seeing more of each other." Turning away from them, he headed across the parking lot, his gait steady and unhurried.

Just like when she'd seen him leaving that hospital room months ago.

A shiver snaked down her spine. She kept her gaze on Klein until he got into a dark luxury sedan and steered out of the parking lot. As he sped away, she released a pent up sigh of relief and turned to Gerard. "That was an impressive threat." He was always so mild mannered and easy going. She felt as if she was seeing a different side of him.

"I don't like bullies." Jaw clenched tight, he finally looked back at Zoe when Klein's car pulled out of sight down the road.

"I'm filing a restraining order tonight," she said before he could continue. She'd filed a temporary one right before Klein had left, but it had expired a month ago. With him out of the country, she hadn't attempted to get it extended, mainly because she'd moved and she didn't want to list her new home address on it. Not when she'd gone to great lengths to hide where she was now living.

He nodded. "Good. I'm going with you."

Her first instinct was to argue that it wasn't necessary, but she knew that look of determination by now and the truth was, she didn't want to go alone. Instead of arguing she nodded. "If you're sure it won't affect you getting home in time for dinner?" Because she knew he loved having family dinners with his two teenage daughters every night. Especially since his wife had died a couple years ago.

Half-smiling, he shook his head. "My sister is with the girls. They're fine."

Palming her keys, she nodded, already feeling stronger. "Let's do this then."

Zoe stood in front of the security desk at her friends Mina and Blue's high rise luxury condo. After filing a restraining order against Klein, she'd been too wired to go home. Well, and scared. Terrified that Klein had found a way to follow her, she'd checked her car for freaking trackers. She'd felt stupid doing it, but was relieved once she'd finished her inspection and found nothing.

After leaving the police station she'd driven around aimlessly for what felt like forever until finally she'd decided to come here. Their building had the best security she'd ever seen. The couple could certainly afford it and Blue was security-minded by nature, especially since his new wife had just inherited her father's billion-dollar empire, and he worked for Red Stone Security.

The twenty-something aged man behind the desk smiled politely at her as he placed the phone back in its cradle. Zoe was on their approved list of guests, but it was still late, and security didn't let anyone up without verbal approval. Not workers, friends, family, no one.

"You're cleared to go up, Ms. Hansen," he said, nodding toward the elevators where another two security guards stood like Roman sentries.

And these weren't typical security guys, not like the type they'd had at the hospital. Every single man or woman she'd seen here had a distinct military bearing and they were all visibly armed. Probably had hidden weapons too. Strangely, the sight of those guns actually made her feel safe.

A couple minutes later she stepped out into the lobby of the penthouse floor and found two more armed guards. She didn't recognize them, but knew they must work for Red Stone Security, the same company Blue and her brother worked for.

They nodded at her in that same polite way as the guard downstairs. Completely professional, but it was clear they were looking at her as if she might be packing heat or something. Before she'd taken two steps, the front door of the condo flew open.

Both men turned and went to stand in front of Mina protectively but she brushed past them, her arms outstretched. "Zoe! This is such a pleasant surprise."

And the woman meant it. The welcoming note in her voice did something to Zoe. She hadn't cried over the entire mess with Klein, not after her attack and not after the hospital treated her like garbage, forcing her to leave a job she loved. But seeing Mina opening her arms to her, Zoe lost it.

She burst into tears, clearly taking Mina off guard. Well, she'd taken herself off guard too. God, she hated crying—because it was embarrassing and she was an ugly crier. Ugh.

Zoe was vaguely aware of Mina wrapping her in a hug and ushering her into the plush place as tears blurred her vision. She should probably be more embarrassed but Mina was her friend and she knew she could be real with her.

"He's back," Zoe blurted as Mina led her to one of the couches in a spacious living room that overlooked downtown Miami. The city lights below were a kaleidoscope of bright colors, all blurred by the tears in her eyes. "I parked across the street but was careful not to be followed," she added, wiping the wetness on her cheeks away as she managed to get herself under control.

Mina just snorted softly. "This place is a fortress, don't worry about that. So...you're sure he's back?" she asked as she sat next to her, turning her body to face Zoe's.

She nodded. "Oh yeah, he showed up at my work." Just thinking about that made her shiver.

When Mina let out a surprising curse, Zoe smiled, the small action loosening something inside her chest.

Her friend stood and moved to the small mini-bar by the window, grabbing two glasses and a bottle of red wine before sitting back down next to her. "Tell me everything."

Twenty minutes later Zoe had unloaded everything that had happened, including her trip to the police station and that she'd finally told her brother about what was going on. He was in California on a job now so she felt even worse that she'd unloaded so much with him out of town. He'd been pissed that she'd withheld something so important, and in typical Vincent fashion, he'd threatened to kill Klein. She wouldn't admit it to anyone, but that was the real reason she hadn't told her brother before.

As a former SEAL, Vincent wouldn't have a problem defending her against a psycho. But she didn't want him to do something he couldn't take back, something that could affect his career and the rest of his life. He'd worked so hard to get to where he was and she couldn't ever be responsible for him ending up in jail.

Mina leaned back against the couch, wine glass in hand, her finger idly tracing down the stem. Zoe noticed that Mina hadn't actually drank anything, but didn't comment as her friend set the glass down on the table next to her. "So the restraining order bars him from coming to your work?"

Zoe nodded. "Yes. And I'll be making copies of it for everyone at work and including his photo so they know who he is." She just hadn't listed her home address on the order. Considering Klein knew where she worked, which wasn't a surprise since people she used to work with were aware of her new job, she hadn't wanted to make it easy for him to find her house in case he didn't know yet. Because a piece of paper wouldn't stop him from coming after her. It would certainly get him in trouble with the law if he broke the order, but if he decided to attack her, she'd still be injured or dead, piece of paper or not.

After his attack at the hospital, he'd been smart about harassing her, making sure nothing could be traced back to him, but she knew he'd slashed her tires, stolen her mail, and sent her too many anonymous, vile texts from a burner phone to count until finally she'd changed her phone number. The police had actually believed her. But believing her was one thing. The State's Attorney wouldn't press charges against someone like Braddock Klein—upstanding citizen with a lot of politically powerful friends—without hard evidence. The justice system was so broken it made her want to cry. Or punch something.

Mina started to say something when a soft chime filled the room, the alert letting them know someone had entered the front door.

"Mina? Is Zoe here?" Blue called out from the front of the condo as Mina stood.

Zoe followed suit and realized she still had her jacket on—and still felt cold despite the warmth in the room. It was a bone-deep kind of chill, one that had nothing to do with the temperature.

A second later Blue and another man entered the living room, both dressed in suits. It took Zoe a moment to recognize the guy. Dark hair, piercing green eyes, about six feet of raw muscle that a suit couldn't hide. Sawyer McCabe. Navy SEAL, or maybe former, if he was working with Blue now. The last time she'd seen him, he'd punched her brother in the face.

Zoe withheld a groan. Just freaking great. She had enough to deal with without some jackass who'd tried to hurt her little brother being present to hear all her drama.

CHAPTER TWO

Braddock Klein wrapped his fingers around the glass tumbler, trying to temper the rage burning inside him as he stared out at the Atlantic Ocean. The spectacular view from his lanai normally soothed him, but nothing could do that now. He couldn't believe the way Zoe had spoken to him after all the time they'd been apart, and in front of someone else no less.

Dr. Gerard Fernandez was a prick. Braddock had met him at different functions over the last decade and couldn't stand the guy. So self-righteous about everything. It wasn't like Fernandez did any pro bono or charity work, not like Braddock did. Something Zoe should be able to clearly see. Why couldn't she see how good they'd be together? How right they were for each other?

After spending six months in South America working for Medicine Without Borders, he'd come back ready to start something with Zoe. He knew she was angry at him for what had happened at the hospital, but she shouldn't have played so hard to get with him. She should *know* that she belonged to him. He'd made his intentions clear long ago and she'd seemed receptive, always so friendly at work. Until that night when she'd completely overreacted to his advances.

He'd even left his wife for her. Right before he'd gone to South America he'd started the divorce proceedings. His lawyer was brilliant and everything had gone smoothly. He was paying out the ass for the divorce but it was worth it. Especially since he knew he could be paying a lot more.

For some reason his ex-wife hadn't fought him at all. She'd just taken what was owed her in their prenuptial agreement and walked away without a fight. She'd tried to leave him once two years ago but he'd made it clear that no one walked away from him. Ever since then she'd done nothing but try to please him. It had been so tiring. Being rid of her was one of the best things that could have happened to him.

Now he could focus all his attention on Zoe. Like she deserved. She was a smart, talented woman and deserved to be with someone like him. She was knowledgeable about their industry, could hold intelligent conversations with their peers, and was an incredibly calm surgeon. She'd never gotten rattled during surgeries, had always been cool and focused. That alone was a turn-on. Plus she was beautiful so he could take her anywhere. That nonsense from the hospital would blow over eventually. It was just a misunderstanding and he would forgive her for embarrassing him. Of course he'd have to punish her, but he wouldn't hold it over her head forever.

When he realized his tumbler was empty he started to stand— only to discover he wasn't alone. As he faced the glass doors that led to his living room, he frowned at the tall, lithe woman standing there with her hands on her hips.

"What are you doing here?" His gaze went to the Scotch bottle in her hand and his frown deepened. He hated it when she made herself feel at home. He'd barely been back in the country and here she was. Annoying him.

With a tinkling laugh, she glided toward him, her hips swaying seductively. Despite the cooler temperature and the breeze coming up off the ocean, she wore a skin tight neon purple dress that accentuated all her curves. The puffy jacket she wore looked as if it was for fashion, not warmth. She had a tight body, one she worked hard to keep, but strip it away and there wasn't much underneath. She'd been a good fuck, nothing more. It was deeply disturbing the way she kept trying to insert herself back into his life. All those emails and phone calls while he'd been away. He knew she wasn't that bright, which was one of the reasons he'd originally hooked up with her, but she was clearly persistent.

"I heard you were back in town and couldn't believe you hadn't called." Her lips pulled down into a faux pouty frown and he noticed she wasn't wearing her normal bright red lipstick.

How the hell had she known... Damn it, fucking social media. He'd gotten an alert that the hospital had posted something about his return. He'd wanted to fly under the radar for a couple weeks, but he should have expected that someone as important as him wouldn't go unnoticed for long. Well, if she was here, maybe he could get something out of her visit. He tilted his head at the bottle in her hand before he sat back in his chair. "Is that for me?"

Sighing, she moved toward him, her heels clicking on the tile as she opened the bottle. She poured him a glass before spreading her legs and straddling him. Her puffy, feathery jacket brushed against his face as she sat on him. "You're in a mood. Did the South America trip not go well?"

His gaze dipped to her mouth as she spoke and he started to get hard. The woman could give some serious head. He wondered if she'd blow him then leave. No, that would be too much wishful thinking. She'd want to stay and talk afterward. "It was fine. I'm just tired after traveling."

She shifted slightly over him, her dress riding up on her thighs as she rubbed herself over his growing dick. "Is that for me?" she murmured, leaning down to nip his ear between her teeth.

He slid his hands around her, letting them settle on her hips. Pushing out a sigh, he leaned his head back. "I'm not really in the mood." He knew if he said that, she'd give him what he wanted and he wouldn't have to do any work. And after he got what he wanted, he'd make up an excuse about having to get up early tomorrow and kick her out.

She leaned back then, her dark eyes flashing with anger. One of her hands tightened on his shoulder and the other slid around to the back of his neck. She usually liked it rough, maybe he'd make time for her tonight after all.

"Not in the mood? Could've fooled me," she snapped.

Damn, time to placate her. "It's not that. I...my divorce is just final and I've been in a shithole for the last six months. I'm exhausted and you know what I need." He dropped his voice, sounding apologetic.

Her lips pursed. "If you're so exhausted how did you have the time to go see Zoe Hansen tonight?"

He jerked in his seat, sitting up straighter. Alarm surged through him. He hadn't told anyone he'd gone to see Zoe. "How the hell did you—"

A sudden, sharp pain pierced his neck as she sliced across his jugular. He lurched forward, his hands on her hips tightening as blood sprayed everywhere, covering her face and clothes. *Blood?*

That was when he saw the flash of metal in her hand as she slid off him. Crimson stained her stupid jacket as she laughed crazily, a knife gripped tightly in her fingers. He slapped a hand to his neck, trying to stop the gushing. He stood, his legs wobbling, but he forced himself to remain upright.

She took a step back, watching him gleefully, her eyes completely crazy.

His knees shook, but he had to stand, to get help. Sitting would accelerate the blood loss. Help. He had to call for help. He fumbled in his pants pocket and grabbed his phone. It slipped from his fingers because of all the blood. As it landed on the tile, she laughed again.

"That's what you get, stupid fuck," she spat, turning on her heel and stomping toward the open sliding glass door.

He took a step after her, but fell to his knees, the impact jarring him, but he barely felt the pain. The blood was spurting out, not leaking so the bitch must have cut an artery. He opened his mouth, trying to speak, but a rush of pain overwhelmed him as blood gurgled up from the wound. He tried to hold his wound but his hands were too slick and his vision was turning dark.

No! This stupid bitch couldn't have killed him. He refused to die like this. No, no...

———————◦•◦———————

Sawyer tried not to stare at Zoe as she smoothed a hand down the front of her wool coat and made her way around the couch to hug Alex. Or Blue, as almost everyone else called him.

But hell, it was hard not to watch her. Petite and compact with smooth mocha skin and intelligent dark eyes, nothing got past that woman. He vividly remembered the last time he'd seen her and inwardly cringed. He didn't regret punching her brother, but he did regret doing it in front of an audience. Especially since she'd been there.

He'd only met her a couple times before that encounter and each time he'd been too damn nervous to talk to her. Big, bad SEAL couldn't talk to a small woman with luscious curves and a smart mouth he'd had way too many fantasies about. Her hair was shorter now, the corkscrew curls bouncing everywhere. Years ago she'd worn it long and straight. He liked this version of her too.

He jerked out of his haze when he realized Blue was talking to him. "Sawyer, this is Zoe Hansen, Vincent's sister."

Sawyer started to say they'd already met before when Zoe held out a hand, her expression polite. "Nice to meet you."

What the fuck? She didn't remember him? That shouldn't annoy him as much as it did. Talk about a blow to his ego. He gritted his teeth and tried to force a polite smile as he returned her handshake. God, her hands were soft too. That was when he realized how red her eyes were, as if she'd been crying. He frowned. "You okay?"

Just like that her polite expression went completely blank. "I'm good, thank you." Then she cleared her throat and looked pointedly at Blue.

His friend gave a short nod before looking back at Mina and Sawyer. "We're going to be in my office for a few minutes but make yourself at home."

"Come on, I'll get you something to drink," Mina said, smiling and motioning to the mini-bar. "How's this week gone?"

Tearing his attention from Zoe's retreating backside, he turned to Mina and smiled as she poured him a bourbon. "Good. Learned a lot."

Laughing lightly, she shook her head and handed him the drink before dropping onto one of the couches. "Such a succinct answer. You're as bad as Alex."

"You really want to hear about the protocol review and training exercises we did?" After a twenty-year Navy career, he'd recently retired at thirty-seven and had taken a job with Red Stone Security heading up one of their East Coast divisions. And this was his last week of training under Alex.

It was still too soon to decide, but Sawyer was going with his gut that this was the best damn move he could have ever made career-wise. He'd been offered jobs by multiple government agencies, but the political bullshit he'd have had to deal with had held him back from accepting. When Porter Caldwell, one of the owners of Red Stone had contacted him, he'd internally jumped at the offer. He'd made Porter wait for his answer because he'd wanted to negotiate his hiring terms, but taking this job had been a no-brainer.

Mina pursed her lips together. "Well, I don't need *all* the details." She started to say something else when a soft bell dinged.

He knew from being invited over here on multiple occasions that was the timer for the oven. They had a chef who came by four or five days a week and prepared dinner for them. Since he hadn't seen or heard their chef, he assumed she'd gone home for the evening. Sawyer automatically stood. "I'll get it... What did Marcelle make tonight?"

Smiling, Mina stood. "Herb-roasted lamb with a side of potatoes, butternut squash soup and a spinach salad. And you don't have to get anything."

He just grunted. "You shouldn't be doing anything anyway." A week ago Alex and Mina had told Sawyer that Mina was fourteen weeks pregnant. He didn't know anything about pregnant women but she probably shouldn't be lifting stuff.

"Seriously, don't even start with me," she muttered, nudging him out of the way with her hip. "I only get nauseous in the mornings and I think I can handle pulling a glass pan out of the oven."

Ignoring her, Sawyer headed into the kitchen and took the oven mitts left on the counter before opening up one of the ovens. Their kitchen was one of those state-of-the-art types with commercial grade appliances that probably rivaled the best restaurants in the city. Especially the stainless steel double oven with a sixty inch range and a built-in broiler with a raised griddle. He'd learned to cook at a young age—thanks to his mom, he and all his brothers had—and found it was something he enjoyed immensely. Good thing too, since he'd been single most of his life. He'd love a spread like this.

"You always look at that oven like you want to marry it," Mina said lightly.

Snorting, he pulled out the giant pan and set it on the stove top before turning it off. "I don't know if I'd go that far," he said, lifting the lid to the soup. The rich scent was perfect. "I can leave this simmering or turn it off, depending on how long Zoe and Alex will be?" He phrased it as a question because, yeah, he was digging for information. He hadn't liked the sight of Zoe crying at all and he wanted to know what was going on. And he wasn't above fishing.

Crossing her arms around her middle, Mina leaned against one of the counters next to a covered tray of assorted cheeses Marcelle must have left out. "I don't know how long they're going to be."

"Something going on with your friend?" Screw the subtle art of fishing.

Mina bit her bottom lip. She glanced at the entryway, then back at Sawyer, her dark green eyes filled with worry. "Yes. I don't think it's a secret either." She fidgeted with the hem of her sweater before sighing and continuing. "She has a stalker. The guy's been out of the country for the last six months but he's back a week early and stopped by her work tonight to harass her. It really rattled her."

That hadn't been what he'd been expecting at all. "She has a stalker and Vincent hasn't...taken care of the problem?" At one time Sawyer and Vincent had had some issues but no matter what Sawyer thought of him, Vincent was the type of guy to take care of his family, by legal means or otherwise. No way he'd let some asshole harass his sister without doing something about it.

"She only recently told Vincent. As in, earlier tonight." Sighing, Mina headed for the stainless steel refrigerator and pulled out a bottle of sparkling water. "Alex has been monitoring the guy as best he could, but obviously he got back into the country without him knowing. I'm sure he's trying to figure out what happened as we speak."

"What's the stalker's name?" Sawyer asked before he could stop himself. This wasn't his deal, had nothing to do with him, but...fuck. If Zoe had a stalker and hadn't even told her brother about it until today, someone needed to look into this guy further. It might as well be him.

Mina paused and for a long moment he thought she wasn't going to tell him. Finally she sighed and sat down at the center island, exhaustion he was pretty sure was from her pregnancy, on her face. "Braddock Klein."

Braddock Klein. Sawyer filed that name away and vowed to put a stop to Zoe's stalker situation.

CHAPTER THREE

Zoe stepped into Blue's office. Instead of the giant, masculine furniture she'd expected it was all wood, glass and sleek looking décor. And of course paintings by Mina graced two of the walls. The third 'wall' was all windows, overlooking the city, and the last was lined with built-in bookshelves.

"So, how far along is Mina?"

Blue shot her a surprised glance over his shoulder as he made his way to his glass-topped desk. He picked up a remote control and pressed a couple buttons. A soft humming sound filled the room as blinds descended from the top of the windows, covering the floor-to-ceiling length expanse. "How'd you know?"

Zoe shrugged, glad she'd guessed right. They'd make great parents. "She didn't drink her wine tonight and I've been around enough pregnant women to know one when I see one. She kept holding her stomach almost protectively."

Blue's face split into a wide, unexpected grin. Zoe had known him for a long time thanks to his friendship with Vincent and the man was always so damn serious. Until Mina. She'd definitely been the best thing to ever happen to her friend. "It's unexpected and we haven't told many people, but fourteen weeks."

"How's she doing? Any morning sickness?" It was an outdated term since pregnancy related nausea could happen at any time of the day.

"She's good but gets a little nauseated in the mornings. Her doctor said that's normal though?" He phrased the last part as a question, a thread of panic invading his voice.

Smiling, she nodded. "Totally normal. Who's her OB?"

When Blue named the best obstetrics doctor in not only the city, but probably the East Coast, she nodded her approval. "Good."

Blue motioned toward a sleek, but comfortable-looking leather couch near the now covered window. It was angled in between the window and one of the bookshelves and had a throw blanket and Mina's ereader on it. Zoe guessed her friend relaxed in here while Blue worked sometimes. The thought made her smile, despite the turmoil surging through her. He slid the stuff to the side as they sat.

"Tell me what happened," Blue said quietly, all business.

Zoe launched into another recap of the evening, feeling stronger the second time she recounted what had happened. When she was done, Blue's jaw tightened as he stood and snagged his laptop from his desk.

Wordlessly he turned it on and clicked away until finally he stopped, frowning. He shook his head then shot her a concerned look. "I've had Lizzy tracking Klein—I didn't tell her the reason— and I've received no alerts that he's used his credit card or other accounts at any foreign airports or back here in Miami. The use of any of his accounts would have alerted us he was on the move. Not even his cell phone pinged..." Sighing, he cursed under his breath. "Never mind. Lizzy's system just sent an alert that his phone reactivated in Miami an hour ago."

Zoe didn't care how he'd returned undetected, she just cared that he was here and a big problem. "He could have paid all in cash and he probably flew in on a medical flight. I'm pretty sure he came straight from the airport to see me. God, it was so creepy seeing him again. I was just starting to feel normal." And she wasn't going to let that psycho take that away from her.

"We're going to stop this guy." His voice was serious, making her feel a little better.

"I've got a good alarm system and I took your advice. I've been going to the gun range every week without fail."

"If he violates his restraining order the police will actually have something against him, but...he has no priors and he's got a lot of powerful friends." Blue's expression was grim.

Zoe knew how broken the system was, especially after working in the ER for so many years. It was how she'd developed friendships with a lot of Miami PD officers. It would have been impossible not to with her job. She knew more than most how things worked. If Klein violated the restraining order, he'd get in trouble, but he wouldn't end up doing any jail time. Not with his lawyers. Not unless he actually hurt her. And he was too smart to overtly violate it. Last time he'd sent so many disgusting texts, but they'd all been from burner phones and there had been no way to track them back to Klein as the purchaser.

She wrapped her arms around herself, fighting off a chill. After six months of peace she'd almost forgotten how tense and stressed she'd become before Klein had left the country. Now the ugliness was all rushing back.

"I'd like it if you'd sleep here tonight. We've got a big guest room and—"

"Okay."

Blue blinked in surprise. "Thought I'd have to convince you more."

"Seriously?"

He lifted one big shoulder. "You can be stubborn sometimes."

She knew he was referring to her not telling Vincent, but that wasn't really stubbornness so much as watching out for her brother. But okay, she *could* be stubborn. "Not about my safety. If that psycho came to see me immediately after getting back into town, I'm not risking anything. And thank you, I really appreciate the offer. I'll have to go home in the morning before work, but the thought of going there right now alone is a little terrifying." She hated Klein for making her so scared. Soon she wanted to take all that power back from him. She just needed to figure out how.

"I'm going to have one of my guys follow you home tomorrow and make sure you get to work safely. I'd do it myself but I've got a big meeting in the morning. A potential new Red Stone client." His expression was apologetic.

"I should probably say you don't have to do that but... I'm taking you up on your offer." Because she wasn't gambling with her life. "Thank you, again. I—"

He shook his head. "I don't want your thanks. I just want you safe."

"I know." Her eyes started to well up again, but she quickly blinked away the tears.

Blue stared at her like a deer caught in headlights. Probably because he'd never seen her cry. She normally took everything in stride, had been doing it since she was a kid. Her dad had been like that and she was glad she'd gotten that personality trait. It was one of the things that made her a good doctor. She cared for her patients but she was able to compartmentalize her emotions. Until now.

Now she was like a leaky faucet and she didn't like it. Soon enough she was going to take back the power from that psycho Klein. She just had to figure out how.

Zoe finished zipping up her black slacks and smoothed a hand down the front of her sweater. Mina had given her something to sleep in last night, but she was wearing the same clothes she'd left work in yesterday. Not that she cared. After a steaming hot shower this morning and a peaceful night's sleep, she felt more focused about everything.

And her hair looked amazing, which she knew was a stupidly small thing in all this, but for some reason, it gave her confidence a huge boost. She had a lot of hair, but it was incredibly fine. Luckily Mina had pretty much every beauty product imaginable, including what Zoe needed to tame her mass of curls. When Zoe had been younger she'd hated her curly hair. It had taken a lot of trial and error to figure out what worked for her, but now she loved it.

Today, it was part of her armor as she faced the world again. The world which her crazy stalker had waltzed back into.

Shaking her head at herself, she picked up her coat from the bed and headed out. Her feet were silent against the hardwood floors as she made her way down the hallway to the kitchen. She was surprised to hear a male voice since she knew that Blue had said he was leaving early this morning, but then remembered their security. For the most part Mina's daily security wasn't inside her condo with her until she started working in her art studio. Then they took up residence in the condo. But Mina was so sweet she probably invited them in for coffee every morning.

As Zoe entered the kitchen, all the breath left her lungs in a whoosh. *Sawyer McCabe.* Damn that sexy man, what was he doing here?

"Zoe," Mina said, smiling warmly at her. "How'd you sleep?"

She stepped farther into the room, a smile pulling at her lips. "Surprisingly good. I was going to strip the sheets, but then just made the bed since I wasn't sure what you wanted me to do, and..." She shrugged nervously. *Oh my God, stop rambling,* she ordered her frazzled brain. She always did that when she was feeling out of sorts and being around Sawyer put her on edge. She wasn't exactly sure why, but it probably had to do with the way her body heated up just being around him—even though he'd once punched her brother in the face. The reaction was so visceral and so unlike her and she didn't like wanting someone whom her brother didn't like. She was thankful her bra covered her hardening nipples.

"It's fine. You remember Sawyer from last night." Mina nodded at Sawyer, who was intently watching Zoe now.

Forcing her mouth to work, she found a polite smile and nodded. "Yes, nice to see you again."

Instead of a suit, today he wore dark gray pants and a black sweater that couldn't hide his strong physique. Even though he leaned casually against one of the counters in Mina's gorgeous kitchen, holding a cup of coffee, he looked anything but relaxed. His body was pulled taut, alert, as if he was ready for danger at any moment. Her brother was the same way. Definitely a SEAL thing, though she'd learned from Blue last night that Sawyer wasn't in the Navy anymore, but now worked for Red Stone Security in a management position. She knew it was pretty rare for someone to be hired on directly to management with them so this guy had to have a seriously impressive résumé.

"You too. There's coffee if you want to grab some before you leave or we can stop somewhere." That warm, honeyed voice rolled over her, making her fight off a shiver.

Until it registered what he'd said. Frowning, she looked between him and Mina, then back to him. "You're coming with me?" she asked.

Nodding, he headed toward the sink where he started rinsing out his mug. "I thought Blue told you that you'd have an escort today."

"He did, but..." She cleared her throat, not sure how to continue. Blue had told her that he was sending one of his guys with her to her house, but she'd assumed it would be one of his normal guys who stayed with Mina.

"Oh, Sawyer is highly trained. He was a SEAL, just like Vincent," Mina said, clearly misinterpreting Zoe's hesitation.

"Thank you," she said, because really, that was all she could come up with at the moment. There was no way she could explain her hesitation. "And I don't need coffee. I'll just grab some at work." Right about now she was really thankful it was Friday and that she wasn't one of the on-call doctors this weekend.

Sawyer turned from the sink and looked at her with an unreadable expression and nodded. "Do you need to get anything else?"

She shook her head before focusing on Mina. After hugging her and saying goodbye, she found herself alone in the custom-made, wood-lined elevator with Sawyer. "Thank you for coming with me." Normally she didn't need to fill silences, but she desperately felt the urge right now.

He nodded once, his posture alert and perfect as he stared ahead at the closed doors. "You're welcome. We've met before, by the way." His voice was tight, controlled.

"I know," she blurted before she could stop herself.

He glanced down at her, real surprise in his green eyes. "You remembered?"

She nodded and felt a blush heating up her cheeks. "I was embarrassed yesterday and just...reacted poorly I think. I didn't want anyone else to see me like that. Blue and Mina are fine, but you're virtually a stranger and I just... I'm sorry." Because what else was there to say?

His expression softened and he turned toward the doors as they opened up. "Well, I'm sorry the last time we saw each other that I punched your brother."

Despite the tenseness humming through her, she snorted and stepped out into the lobby with him. "Somehow I doubt you're actually sorry about punching Vincent." While she wasn't sure what had gone down between the two of them, Sawyer didn't seem like the type of man to regret things or to attack someone lightly.

"I'm sorry I did it in front of you," he amended, not looking at her as he scanned the lobby and sitting area. Bright sunlight streamed in through the glass windows and doors, illuminating the crystal and chrome chandeliers overhead, making the entire space sparkle beautifully.

His response lightened her mood even more. Not completely, because nothing could do that. Not when she was in the position that she needed an escort simply to go home and to work. She did feel incredibly safe with Sawyer though.

Vincent was still out of town but was going to try to come home early. Even though she didn't want to affect her brother's job, she was truly glad he'd be returning to Miami soon. He might be the baby of the family but he'd always been a rock for her and her sisters after their father had died.

"I would deny this under torture because I love my brother, but... I'm betting it wasn't completely unprovoked."

Sawyer looked down at her as they reached one set of glass doors, his eyebrows drawing together. "He didn't tell you what it was about?"

She shook her head. Vincent had seemed almost embarrassed by it and she hadn't wanted to push. Not when he'd been dealing with so much back then.

Sawyer didn't respond, just opened the door. Instead of letting her go first, like she'd expected, he moved outside in front of her, using his body as a barrier as he scanned the relatively quiet street. Two women jogged by on the sidewalk, both with earbuds in as they pounded the pavement. Then an older, white-haired man walking a small dog with white-and-black fur strolled by carrying a Starbucks cup. Nothing seemed out of the ordinary.

Sawyer must have agreed, because he gave an almost imperceptible nod before looking back at her. "First we're going to get your car. I'm going to scan it for any tracking devices or...anything. Then you're going to drive me to my truck, which is just a block from here—I couldn't find a spot any closer. From there, I'm going to follow you home. Blue's filled me in on what's going on so I'd like to shadow you at your work today, see if that fucker shows up. He's going to be notified of the restraining order, probably already has been so if he's pissed enough, he'll show up at your work. If we can document that, it's a start."

His words made her chest tighten as she realized she had no choice but to face her new reality head on. She wouldn't have an escort every day, but for now, she was glad to have someone on her side—someone trained—who had an idea how to tackle today. She still needed to make copies of her restraining order and give them out to everyone at work, but today suddenly seemed manageable with Sawyer by her side.

"Thank you for doing this."

"I don't need your thanks," he said brusquely before turning toward the road and glancing both ways.

Oh right, this was just a job for him. Well, job or not, she was still damn thankful for his presence.

CHAPTER FOUR

Sawyer parked his truck behind Zoe's two-door car, automatically scanning the exterior of her house and neighbors' homes. It was eight a.m. so some people were already leaving; parents with kids and others dressed in business attire. No one appeared out of the ordinary and no one looked like Braddock Klein.

Blue had sent him a detailed file on Klein last night after Sawyer had more or less volunteered to shadow Zoe today. His friend had planned to use one of Mina's security guys to trail Zoe, but Sawyer was having none of that. His training was officially over today and he started with his new team on Monday. They could put someone else on her then if necessary. But he wanted to look out for her now and over the weekend, and he wasn't going to examine why too closely. He just knew he wanted her safe. He also knew that had nothing to do with a sense of duty because she was Vincent's sister and everything to do with her specifically. The woman intrigued him.

Shutting his door behind him, he met Zoe as she was getting out of her car. A breeze blew up and her curls bounced softly in the wind. An unbidden image of what it would feel like to run his fingers through her hair while she was naked and under him entered his mind, but he locked that down. He was on the job and her safety was more important than his fucking libido.

"Did it seem as if anyone was following us?" she asked, an anxious frown creasing her brow.

"Nope." He was good at locating a single tail, but if someone was working with a full team or in tandem with a partner, then it became more difficult. Since Klein seemed to be a one-man stalker, Sawyer was almost certain they hadn't been followed.

"Thank God," she muttered, glancing around nervously.

Yeah, what Sawyer wouldn't give to kick this guy's ass. Seeing fear on Zoe's face sliced at him. He'd spent most of his adult life fighting terrorists and when you got right down to it, they were nothing but psychotic bullies who wanted the world to see everything their way. Now everything about Zoe's life was being affected by a bully with an ego. That brought out all his protective instincts whether he wanted it to or not. "You set your alarm yesterday, right?"

She nodded and palmed her keys. "Yes, so if it's off..." She trailed off, not needing to finish.

After they entered her house, the insistent beep of her alarm sounded and he could see the tension leave her body as she pressed the code into the keypad. He locked the front door behind them then ordered her to stay put. Her eyes widened at his tone, but he didn't have time to reassure her. He needed to sweep her house.

Withdrawing his SIG, he held it at his side as he methodically swept each room. She had a three-bedroom, two-bath home in a higher end part of town and close to the practice she worked at. Her neighborhood had lake access, though her house wasn't on the water and from the file Blue had given him, they had twenty-four-seven security driving around or sitting in the guard house he'd seen when they'd entered the subdivision. But it didn't appear to be actually gated, something he hadn't liked. He planned to ask her about that later.

Once he was certain the house was secure he found Zoe standing in her foyer next to an oversized floor vase, her arms crossed over her chest. "House is secure."

"Thank you. And next time, if there is one, *ask* me to stay put, don't order me around."

He'd taken plenty of orders in the Navy, but for the most part he'd given them, especially on missions. His instinct was to tell her that he'd just been doing his job, but he could stand to use some finesse, especially where Zoe was concerned. "My apologies."

She blinked, her arms dropping. "Really?"

He lifted an eyebrow. "You want me to argue?"

"No, I...it's nice to be talking to a grownup, that's all." She gave him a real smile then, a megawatt one that lit up her face and it was all for him. The sight was a kick to his chest, stealing all the breath from his lungs. "I already showered so I just need to change then snag a cup of coffee. I have one of those one-cup machines so if you want, feel free to brew yourself a cup. Or we can just grab some at my work."

He nodded and started to respond when a sharp knock on her front door had him straightening. He turned, blocking her body with his as he reached for his weapon.

"Miami PD, open the door," a loud male voice said.

Sawyer's first instinct was that this was a trap. He moved to the peephole and peered through, aware of Zoe right behind him. There were three men, two wearing police uniforms and one man wearing a suit and tie. Two cruisers were parked at the curb out front. "Show some ID," he demanded. Sawyer had no clue how devious Klein was and he wasn't taking any chances with Zoe's safety.

The man in the suit straightened and faced the peephole directly. "Zoe, you in there? Answer me." His tone was concerned.

Zoe's hand on Sawyer's forearm made him look down. "It's okay, that's Carlito Duarte. He's a detective with the police department." She turned from him and unlocked the door. When she opened it, Sawyer knew immediately that whatever was going on, was bad.

All three men looked grim, especially the detective. The man looked at Sawyer and assessed him before focusing on Zoe. "Zoe Hansen, I have a warrant for your arrest for the murder of Braddock Klein."

"What?" she gasped, reeling back a step.

Klein was dead? Well that solved one of her problems, but this was just fucked up. Sawyer wanted to haul her back from the men, but knew he'd just make the situation a hell of a lot worse if he got in the way. Because this had to be a setup, no doubt about it.

The detective with bronzed skin, gray eyes and a GQ thing going on, nodded. "You have the right to an attorney and I'm telling you to exercise that right and not say a fucking word. Got it?" he asked her, his expression tight. Sawyer could tell the man hated doing this part of his job with Zoe.

Zoe's expression was one of horror and shock. She looked up at Sawyer as if he could somehow fix the situation. And hell if he wasn't going to try.

"Don't say a word," he told her. "I'm calling Alex and your brother right now. Where are you taking her?" he asked, turning his attention to the detective.

"Down to the station."

Sawyer nodded and looked at Zoe again as one of the officers stepped forward with handcuffs in his hand. *Fuck, no.* He didn't want to let her go and it was clear the detective didn't like this any better than she did. The sight of the cuffs made Zoe jerk with shock, but she didn't try to resist.

"Tell my brother to call our family lawyer and my mom," she blurted. "And call Gerard Fernandez. He's my boss. Alex has his information. I don't know what's going on, but he was with me before I went to Blue's last night..." She trailed off as Duarte stilled the man in uniform with the restraints.

"We'll cuff her in the cruiser and her hands go in front," he said quietly.

Not much, but it was a small show of courtesy, telling Sawyer all he needed to know about the detective. "I'm following you right now and making those calls. You're not going to jail so just stay quiet until your lawyer gets there, okay? I'm not kidding. Not one *single* word."

Swallowing hard, she nodded, her big brown eyes wide with fear as she let the officers escort her to the waiting police cruiser. What the hell was happening? If Klein had been murdered that was damn fast police work for them to have a suspect already. And there was no way in hell they'd have shown up on Zoe's doorstep and actually *arrested* her without physical evidence. Sawyer had a decent understanding of civilian law, more so now because of his new job, and it was too soon for the police to be here without concrete proof.

Something else was going on and Sawyer was damn sure going to find out what it was and make sure Zoe got out of this mess.

The only silver lining in all this was that her stalker was no longer a problem.

———————◆●◆———————

"She's going to be okay," Sawyer said to Tanice Hansen, Zoe's mom, who was pacing nervously at the far end of the rectangular, cheap wood table.

They'd been taken to a quiet conference room at the police station, courtesy of Detective Duarte, whom Sawyer had recently discovered was friends with a lot of guys from Red Stone Security and had interacted with Zoe frequently when she'd worked at the hospital. Mina and Blue were both in different rooms being questioned by detectives to corroborate Zoe's alibi. And Sawyer knew that Blue had already had the security feeds from his condo sent over to the police for analyzing.

"I just can't believe anyone would think she'd even be capable of taking a life. She took the Hippocratic Oath and that means something to my girl. And I still can't believe she didn't tell me about any of this." A pop of anger sounded in the petite woman's voice. She was the same height as Zoe with flawless, darker skin. She looked decades younger than Sawyer guessed she had to be. Right now worry was evident in every taut line of her body.

"It's normal in a situation like this to keep what happened private from those closest to her." And Sawyer had already been in contact with Vincent who was currently on his way back to Miami.

Tanice frowned and swiveled toward him, hands on her hips. "How is that normal to keep something so big from her mother?"

"I'm just guessing, but Zoe probably felt ashamed, possibly embarrassed. She probably tried to think of all the different ways she could have seen this sooner, maybe prevented it from happening." One of Sawyer's guys had been stalked years ago and had been in a state of denial that it was happening to him, especially since it was another male doing the stalking. He figured Zoe had probably been in denial for a while too, made easier since Klein had been out of the country. It was a normal, human reaction.

Tanice's eyebrows furrowed together. "That makes no sense, she couldn't have prevented some crazy from focusing on her."

"We know that and intellectually Zoe knows that. But self-blame is a common effect on stalking victims." He was just impressed how well Zoe had been holding up.

Losing her steam, Tanice pulled out a chair and collapsed into it. "You'd think that once your kids were out of the house and had families and lives of their own you could stop worrying. But you never do." Her eyes started to well with tears, but she looked away from him, angrily swatting at the wetness. The action reminded him so much of Zoe.

Realizing she didn't want him to see her upset, he stood from his chair and headed for the door. "I'll grab us some more drinks." He'd had way too much coffee the past couple hours while they waited so he'd be grabbing water.

"Thank you."

The door opened before he'd reached it. Zoe, Blue, Mina and Duarte stepped in. Zoe's eyes were red-rimmed, but she also looked relieved. Okay, that was a good thing. As she rushed toward her mother who'd already jumped from her chair, Sawyer looked between Blue and the detective. Zoe's attorney wasn't with them, which surprised Sawyer. Maybe the guy was filling out paperwork or he wasn't needed anymore.

Duarte shut the door behind him so they all had privacy.

"She's free?" Sawyer asked, needing to hear the words.

Duarte and Blue nodded at the same time. "Yes, thanks to a rock solid alibi," Duarte said. "If she hadn't stayed with you guys last night..." The man shook his head, his mouth still pulled into that grim line.

Sawyer only knew the basics at this point. That Klein had been found dead at his home, his throat cut. Zoe's fingerprint had been on the knife, but nowhere else at the scene. "So what happened?" he asked, not bothering to wait until he was alone with Blue. He figured Zoe's mom needed details now too.

"Someone called in an anonymous tip that Klein had been murdered late last night. They gave a description of a woman leaving his place who looked a lot like Zoe. Since she'd just filed a restraining order against him last night...well, Klein had powerful friends so there's a push to get this solved. Since she was a viable suspect, the techs ran her prints from the hospital against the single print on the knife and it's a match. Luckily there's no DNA of hers at the scene and her alibi is airtight. And the single print is...interesting."

Sawyer didn't respond, but he understood the man's meaning. One single print and no DNA at a crime scene? Unlikely. Someone planted that print.

"The time stamps on the security of her arriving at Alex and Mina's and witness statements from both of them are hugely helpful. The State's Attorney won't be pursuing criminal charges and we're now hunting for the real killer."

Sawyer had a lot of questions, like had they started looking for who'd called in that anonymous tip, but he wasn't in law enforcement and Duarte likely wouldn't tell him anyway. The important thing was, Zoe wasn't a suspect. "So she's free to go back to her life?"

Duarte nodded at him, then looked at Zoe. "Yes, but someone planted that knife and called in a tip that someone who looked like you was seen leaving Klein's residence. And since you can't think of anyone other than the deceased who would have done something like that, the killer's still out there. Framing you could have been an opportunity because Klein has enemies and you were an easy person to blame, or...his murder might have been an attempt to hurt you. You need to be careful."

"I will be," Zoe said, her arm wrapped around her mother's shoulders as she faced the detective.

After speaking to Blue and Mina for a few more minutes, the detective left the room. Zoe was still talking quietly to her mom and Sawyer felt suddenly awkward. He didn't want to leave Zoe but he knew she probably wanted to be with just her friends and family right now.

Sawyer cleared his throat and looked at Zoe. "I spoke to your boss and he was really understanding, but you probably want to call him and let him know you're okay."

"I will, thank you. Thank *all* of you," she looked around the room, tears welling in her eyes. "This is all so awful, I just can't..." She shook her head and wiped away the wetness tracking down her cheeks. Then she took a deep breath. "Dinner at my place tonight. All of you are invited. You too, Sawyer," she said, giving him a watery smile.

He just nodded as she continued.

"I'm sure Vincent will be back by this afternoon so I'll call—"

"I'll take care of calling your brother and sisters," Tanice said firmly. "And I'll make sure they don't hassle you for keeping us in the dark." She gave her daughter a firm squeeze around her middle, never taking her arm from around her daughter.

Zoe's eyes widened. "You will?"

"Yes. Sawyer explained why you felt the need to keep this a secret from us and I—" Her voice broke as she pulled Zoe into another hug, murmuring how thankful she was that Zoe was okay.

As Zoe hugged her mom, she gave Sawyer a grateful smile over Tanice's shoulder. The sight did strange things to his insides, just like when she'd given him that bright smile this morning. In that moment he realized just how easily he could fall for this woman if he wasn't careful.

CHAPTER FIVE

Zoe slipped into her room and shut the door behind her with a quiet click. She twisted the lock in case someone tried to come in because right now she needed just a couple minutes to herself. Voices and music from the living room and her back porch were a steady hum of activity.

She was so damn grateful to be here and surrounded by people she cared about and who cared about her in return, but today's events were finally crashing in on her and mental exhaustion crept through her veins, weighing her down. That third glass of wine probably wasn't helping her emotional state either.

When she heard running water coming from her bathroom, she straightened, that familiar tension punching through her—until Sawyer walked out.

He looked surprised, then almost sheepish to see her. He ran a big hand over his dark hair, his arm muscles flexing slightly with the movement. Her gaze trailed down the length of all those sinewy muscles. "There was a long line for your guest bathroom and I've had a couple beers. Figured I could sneak in here unnoticed and your mom said it'd be fine."

She stepped further into her room. It was weird having him in here, but she also kind of liked it and found herself thinking how good he'd look splayed out on her king sized bed. That thought was a jolt to her system. The man was gorgeous, but she hadn't thought lusting after someone would even be on her radar right now. "After what you did today, you don't have to apologize for anything, ever. My mom thinks you're a saint. Whatever you did to keep her sane at the police station, thank you." She sat on the end of her bed and fidgeted with the light blue and brown comforter. It still felt surreal that she'd been freaking arrested this morning and was now celebrating with friends and family since she was free and clear.

Half-smiling, he stepped closer, moving with that predator-like grace that made her entire body alert with awareness. Not only had he stepped up today and just taken over, calling everyone necessary, he'd been so sweet to her mom. It wasn't like he'd had to stay at the police station. Sure, he was insanely sexy, something she was finding impossible to ignore tonight. He had on dark slacks and a dark green sweater that made his piercing eyes pop even more against his tanned skin. The sweater sleeves were pushed up his forearms, showcasing muscles she wanted to trace with her fingers and lips. Looks aside, the man clearly had an honorable streak—and that was the sexiest thing of all.

He sat next to her, reaching out a hand as if to squeeze her leg, but pulled back at the last second and placed it on the comforter instead. There wasn't much space between them and she swore she could feel his body heat. His scent was purely masculine, subtle and made her think of springtime. Being this close to him sent a shiver of pure delight down her spine.

"How're you holding up?" he asked quietly.

"Great!" she said a little too brightly, then winced. "Okay, how fake did that sound?"

Sawyer's chuckle made butterflies take flight in her belly. "Pretty bad. It's okay to *not* be fine."

"I know, I just don't want anyone to worry."

"Well, you don't ever have to fake it with me," he said quietly.

God, this man. Her gaze dipped to his lips almost against her will. When he made a rumbling, sort of growling sound, her eyes snapped up to meet his. Pure fire simmered beneath the surface of his gaze as he watched her.

She sucked in a breath at the visible lust. Oh yeah, no denying that. Any other night under any other circumstances she'd have over analyzed this to death, like she always did, but not now. Not when her stalker was dead and she felt like she could get back to living her life, to feeling normal again. But she didn't want normal and boring. She wanted a taste of Sawyer.

Without thinking, she leaned forward and brushed her lips over his, softly. He stiffened slightly and she wanted to die of embarrassment. Maybe she'd made a mistake, misread the—

Sawyer crushed his mouth over hers, moaning into her mouth like a starving man.

She clutched his shoulders and suddenly found herself flat on her back on the bed, one of his thighs between her legs as they kissed. He was huge and she loved the sensation of being pinned down by all that raw strength. Kissing seemed like such a dull description for the way he was devouring her. She felt like she was a teenager again, making out for the first time, and that was insanely hot.

He tasted like coffee and chocolate, rich and sweet and she arched into him, sliding one hand down his back. She wanted to touch every inch of him. He held the back of her head in a solid grip as his other hand grasped her hip. He wasn't making a move to do anything else other than kiss.

Normal Zoe wouldn't make the first move, especially not with a man she'd only had a couple conversations with. Normal Zoe wouldn't even think about sleeping with someone she hadn't gone on at least half a dozen dates with, probably more. And by then she usually lost interest.

Normal Zoe could take a hike right now.

She slid her hands up the front of Sawyer's shirt, shoving at it, wanting to see and feel all of him. Every muscular inch he was trying to hide under his clothes. She felt almost crazed with the need.

When he pulled his head back, breathing hard, he stared down at her. "How much have you had to drink?"

"Not enough to regret this."

He started to respond, but she was having none of it. Reaching down, she grasped the edge of her fitted purple sweater and tugged it over her head. Before she'd pulled it all the way up Sawyer made a sexy-as-sin growling sound.

"Fuck," he murmured, his gaze tracking over her exposed chest and torso. "I was going to say this is too fast."

"You sure about that?" she murmured.

"I don't want to take advantage," he continued, his voice strained as he sat up, staring down at her as if he didn't know where he wanted to start.

Reaching behind her back, she unsnapped her black bra and let it slide down her arms as she sat half up. "Then let me take advantage of you." She had no idea where the bold words came from, but she felt as if she was on fire right now. New Zoe celebrated. A burning heat simmered inside her and was only growing hotter. The only thing that could ease her ache was Sawyer.

He made another strangled sound before his head suddenly dipped toward her breasts. She gripped his head, urging him on. He sucked on one hard nipple, palming the other with a surprising gentleness. The way his tongue laved over her sensitive bud had her arching into him, demanding more. She hummed with energy, as if she could crawl right out of her skin for how good he felt.

Gently, he pressed his teeth around her nipple and flicked his tongue over it, back and forth, as he rubbed his thumb over her other one. The dual sensations were making her crazy, heat building in between her legs like—

Knock, knock. "Zoe?" She froze at the sound of Vincent's voice.

Sawyer's head snapped up. "Is the door locked?" he whispered, not worry on his face, but clear discomfort.

She nodded at Sawyer as she called out, "I'll be out in just a sec, V."

"Okay, just making sure you're good. A couple people are asking about you, but take your time." He sounded so sweet and sincere, she had to smother a laugh. He wouldn't be telling her to take her time if he knew what she was doing in here.

Sawyer made an almost inaudible groan and laid his head against her breast bone. "We don't have enough time to do everything I plan to do to you anyway," he whispered.

She slid her fingers through his dark hair and bit back a groan of her own. Her entire body was primed for an orgasm but there was no way in hell they could finish what they'd started. She had guests anyway and just couldn't stay in here ravishing Sawyer, no matter how much she wanted that. But that didn't mean she wasn't disappointed. It was probably better this way though. Things might have gotten awkward—wait, what had Sawyer said? "Are you still planning on…doing those things?"

His head lifted and his eyes connected with hers, the intent in them clear. "Oh yeah."

A shiver rolled through her and she fought the sudden urge to kick everyone out of her house so she could find out exactly what he had planned. After the number her ex had done on her, she hadn't dated much in years—not that what she and Sawyer were going to do would be considered a date. Work had also prevented much of a social life so tonight she was going to make up for all those times she worked instead of having fun.

* * *

"Are you sure you don't want anything to drink?" Mallory Tate asked, twisting her slender fingers together in her lap.

"I'm good, but thank you," Detective Carlito Duarte said, briefly scanning her sparse living room. There weren't many personal touches and he knew she hadn't been living in the waterfront condo more than a month. "You've already been eliminated as a suspect so you can relax. I just want to know more details about your husband."

"*Ex*-husband." Then she seemed to remember herself and cleared her throat.

It was late Friday night but the woman had been willing to talk to him. Not that Carlito had given her much of a choice. He'd told her he could meet her now or bring her down to the police station for questioning. Since she'd already been questioned while her alibi was being confirmed he knew she had no desire to go back to the station.

"Sorry, *ex*. So tell me a little more about him. What he was like as a husband." Often it was better to let people just talk instead of giving them specific questions, especially in a situation like this. She was more likely to be honest this way.

"He was..." She looked behind him, her pretty face tensing for a moment before she met Carlito's gaze again. "I'm sorry, it's hard to believe he's dead."

"I'm sorry for your loss," he murmured, even though he wasn't sure he was sorry at all. Not after the report he'd read from Zoe Hansen.

"I'm not." Mallory's voice was so quiet he almost didn't hear her. In her late thirties, she had long, honey-blonde hair and long, lean limbs. She was conventionally attractive but there was an almost regal air about her. The type of women he so often came into contact with in Miami from the upper crust had a plastic quality about them. Not Mallory Tate. She was the kind of woman who would definitely age gracefully.

He raised an eyebrow. "I take it that it wasn't a happy marriage?"

"At first it was. Or I thought it was." She tucked a strand of hair behind her ear, her fingers trembling. For a brief moment he saw a flash of fear in her gaze, the type he'd seen on the faces of countless battered women before.

Well, hell. She'd never filed any reports and there'd been nothing in his measly information file on her to suggest Klein had abused her. She hadn't said much when she'd been at the station earlier, had let her attorney do most of the talking. "Nothing you say has to leave this room. Just let me know what's on the record and off."

His words seemed to trigger something in her because she straightened. "I don't care who you tell. I'm tired of being afraid of him. I...know people thought I married him for his money or status, but it's not true. I loved him. Well, the version of him he let me see when we were dating. His previous wife seemed so vindictive and he convinced me she'd say anything to keep us apart, that she just didn't want him to be happy. Now I wish I'd taken the time to listen to her, but I was just so blinded, so in love. He was very charming but about a year after our marriage that veneer started to crack. I won't bore you with details because I'm sure you've heard the same, tired story a hundred times before." She laughed, the sound brittle and self-deprecating.

"I want to hear your story." He meant it. After speaking with her at the station he thought he'd had her pegged. He'd been wrong. It didn't happen often.

She gave him a wry smile. "He changed, or I guess he just started showing his true colors. It was little stuff at first, nothing I did was good enough. Or I embarrassed him at a hospital function—which was complete crap considering he was the one who always got drunk, but that's not the point. At a fundraiser I caught him fooling around with a woman I know. We're not friends, but we belong to the same country club. I was angry and went to see a divorce attorney that week. I tried to leave him but…he made it clear I'd never be allowed to do that."

Bastard. "How?"

She swallowed hard and glanced down at her hands, clenched tightly together in her lap. For a moment he thought she wasn't going to answer. Then her voice came, quiet and sure. "He drugged me and raped me. More than once. He kept me drugged up for a week. I was too weak to fight him but I was aware of what he was doing the entire time. At the end of the week he broke one of my arms. He made it clear that if I tried to leave him again, my punishment next time would be worse."

Carlito clenched his jaw, anger pulsing through him. He was supposed to stay objective during all cases, but it was hard to care that Klein was dead. Everything he heard about the guy was bad, that being an understatement.

"From that point he started monitoring my spending, accounts, everything. It was like living in a prison, until… I can't know for sure, but he must have started seeing someone because he started paying less and less attention to me. It was a godsend. I was able to start siphoning money away and I was getting ready to run when he left on that medical trip overseas." She snorted at that, bitter amusement on her face.

No wonder she'd been glad to see him go. Only years of

experience in law enforcement allowed Carlito to keep his expression impassive.

"He divorced me before he left and it was the best thing that ever happened to me. Like being released from prison. I heard about what happened to Doctor Hansen later, from a friend whose husband works at the hospital, and I believe every word of what she said that he did. Braddock has—had—a God complex in the worst way. He would have been ballsy enough to attack her at the hospital and think he could get away with it. What's worse, he *did*." She shook her head, disgust clear on her face.

After taking note of the names of the two women she'd mentioned; the one she'd caught her ex-husband with and the friend with ties to the hospital, Carlito talked with her for a few more minutes before letting himself out.

It wasn't case-breaking evidence, but it was a start. He was going to find out who'd killed Braddock Klein, and more importantly, who'd tried to frame Zoe Hansen for it.

CHAPTER SIX

Sawyer glanced up from scanning the news on his phone and set it on Zoe's island countertop as she walked into the room, a silky multicolored robe cinched loosely around her slender waist.

"Coffee," she rasped out, blinking blearily at him before stumbling to her one-cup maker.

He bit back a smile and waited for her to get what she clearly needed. Last night hadn't gone remotely how he'd hoped. After their scorching kiss, the party had gotten louder and busier and people had stayed until almost three. Finally Tanice had politely cleared everyone out because Zoe had been barely staying on her feet from exhaustion — and some drinks.

While he'd wanted nothing more than to pick up where they'd left off, Zoe had had a few more glasses of wine and a couple shots from friends so he'd carried her to bed. Clearly she was feeling the effects now.

"Oh my God," she muttered, after taking a sip of her coffee. "I haven't done shots since I was twenty-two. What was I thinking?"

He snorted. "That you weren't in jail."

She grinned and pulled out a seat next to him. "Well, there is that. I can't believe you're still here."

He lifted an eyebrow. "You're really surprised?"

"Yeah. I was clearly not able to, you know…" Her cheeks flushed prettily as she trailed off and raised her cup to her mouth.

A mouth he'd had plenty of fantasies about before he'd finally dozed off in her guest room. There'd been no way he could have left her last night, not after everything she'd been through.

"Thanks for tucking me in last night. That was sweet." Before he could respond her eyes widened and she softly groaned. "Does Vincent know you stayed over?"

Sawyer stilled at her question. Her brother was the last person he wanted to think about right now. "Would it matter if he did?"

"No. Not for the reason you're thinking. Or I think you're thinking. Gah, I need more coffee." Glancing down, she took great interest in focusing on her drink.

Nope, he was having none of that. Reaching out, he snagged an arm around her waist and tugged her onto his lap. She let out a yelp of surprise, but moved willingly, settling across his thighs as she turned to face him.

"I just don't want to explain to my brother about whatever is happening between us. I'm a grown woman, but he's still my brother. And you two have a history."

As long as she didn't want to hide him. "Fair enough. Why were you surprised I was still here?"

Her cheeks flushed again and he had to bite back a groan. Seeing her like that brought up thoughts of what she'd look like naked, face and body flushed from pleasure. "I just thought, well, you know."

"That I'd bail because we didn't fu—end up in bed together?" He was used to talking bluntly, but he didn't like the thought of what he and Zoe would hopefully share soon as simple fucking.

"Yeah?" She lifted her shoulders slightly.

His jaw tightened but he didn't respond. They didn't know each other well enough for him to be annoyed about her assumption, even if it rankled him. "Go out to dinner with me tonight?"

She blinked, probably from the sudden change in subject, but nodded, smiling softly. "I'd like that. And, not that I don't like this position but, if you get between me and my coffee this early in the morning, we might have words," she murmured, reaching out to grab her mug.

"Duly noted." His lips twitched as she took another sip of the hot drink then let out an orgasmic-sounding sigh. He couldn't believe she woke up looking so fucking sexy. Her hair was wild and curly even though she'd tried to tame it back into some sort of clip thing. It didn't matter, the corkscrews bounced everywhere. Visions played in his mind of what it would be like to see her hair around her face and shoulders as she rode him, her back arched and her breasts bared for him to hold, kiss, lick.

"So how did you end up working for Red Stone?" she asked after another sip followed up with one of those sexy sighs.

God, those sounds were making him hard. He shifted uncomfortably, hoping she didn't notice. He'd always been in control of his body. Except around her apparently. "It was sort of a perfect storm of things. I'd hit my twenty year mark in the Navy—"

"Twenty?" Her eyes widened then she winced. "Sorry, didn't mean to interrupt."

"Interrupt all you want," he murmured, tightening his grip around her. "And yes, twenty. I joined when I was seventeen so I'm thirty-seven, if that's your way of asking."

"I wasn't, but I was curious. So, it was a perfect storm..."

He grinned, loving the feel of her sitting on his lap, in his arms. This light banter with a woman was new territory for him. It had been years since he'd been in a relationship and even then, his last one had been all physical, something he hadn't realized until too late. "It was just one of those things. The job offer came in and I had to take it."

"You were in California for a long time though, right?"

He nodded. "Yeah. I wasn't home often but that's where I was stationed for the majority of my career."

"Do you miss it?"

San Diego was beautiful, but bases were pretty much the same wherever you went. And the Navy had been his home, not a city. "I miss my men and I miss the structure, but I'm adaptable. A nomad, my mom always says."

Zoe raised an eyebrow. "Your mom?"

"Well I wasn't spawned."

She snorted. "I just meant are your parents, or your mom, still alive?"

He nodded. "Yep. They run an alpaca farm in Missouri with two of my brothers. They're starting to downsize this year, but I don't know that they'll ever give it up completely."

"That's pretty interesting. So how many brothers do you have?"

"Four total." He loved all of them, but never could have stayed in Missouri. He'd wanted to see the world too much and the need to protect his country had been an almost inborn thing. There'd never been another option other than the military for him and he'd known it since he was a kid.

"Let me guess, you're the oldest."

He shook his head. "Middle child. What about you? Oldest?"

"Nope. Two older sisters and you know Vincent is the baby."

Sawyer snorted at that. "I'm sure he loves being called that."

A smile played on Zoe's full lips and she shifted slightly against his lap. When she did, her hip brushed right over his erection—and she froze, her expression turning to one of surprise.

"You're really surprised?" he murmured.

Her eyes grew heavy-lidded as she watched him. She shook her head and ran her tongue along her bottom lip, almost nervously as she set her coffee cup down.

He didn't bother fighting his groan as he watched her moisten that full lip. "What are you thinking right now?" he whispered.

Her gaze narrowed on his mouth and she leaned forward, gently brushing her lips over his. "What do you think?"

Sawyer didn't want to screw things up with Zoe by going too fast, but damn, the woman was making it impossible not to. When she playfully nipped his bottom lip between her teeth, he knew this was a battle he was going to lose because no way was he turning away from her. From this.

But he *was* going to take control of the situation. Wrapping his hands around her hips, he lifted her off him until she was sitting on the edge of the island. Her silky robe parted, revealing a light pink slip thing he was pretty sure was called a chemise. Her cheeks were flushed with arousal and he could see the outline of her hard nipples through her clothes.

Keeping his gaze on hers, he slowly slid a hand up her inner thigh. Her breath hitched, growing ragged, and he didn't stop until he teased the edge of her panties.

He couldn't see them yet, but his imagination was going wild as to what color they were. "I want to kiss you here," he murmured, cupping her mound as he leaned in to cover her lips with his. Her legs spread under his hold and he shifted so that he was perfectly in between her thighs. The blinds in her kitchen were still closed, but plenty of natural light streamed in through the cracks in the slats, letting him see her every expression.

She nodded and made a moaning sound he felt all the way to his cock. Touching her was making him crazy. Last night had been a tease of what was to come and now he wanted to see all of her.

When he feathered kisses down her jaw, she arched her back, letting her robe fall farther open. He slid it all the way off, letting it glide to the countertop without a sound.

Her fingers trailed over his chest as he made his way down to her shoulders, nipping at her skin. Impatient to see her breasts again, he pushed the straps down, letting the silky covering pool around her waist.

He had to pull back just so he could stare. Dark brown nipples and perfect, pert breasts just a little more than a handful. Her abdomen was flat and toned, as if she worked out or ran. "You are built for sin," he murmured, looking up at her as he spoke.

Her dark eyes glinted wickedly as she reached for the hem of his shirt. "I could say the same thing about you."

Instead of letting her do it, he tugged his shirt off then dipped his head to one of her breasts. Just like last night, she let out the sexiest moan, her back arching into him as she clutched his head with one hand, holding him close. Her other hand moved to his back, her fingers digging into his skin.

He could have stayed where he was all morning, teasing both her breasts, working her into a frenzy, but he wanted to taste between her legs, wanted to see how wet she was, to push her over the edge the way he hadn't gotten to last night. Reaching between them, he tugged off her panties—black Brazilian cut, he noted—and gently pushed her backward.

"Lay back," he ordered.

She paused, and he could tell this was a test for her. From the little time he'd known her he understood she liked to be in control. Right now, he hoped she'd let go. When she finally did, he bent down between her legs and sucked in a breath at the sight of her. Completely bare. Her skin was soft and smooth and just the hint of her clit was peeking out from her lips. "You wax?" he rasped out.

"Mm hmm." She shifted slightly, moving closer to the edge of the counter, as if nervous or maybe just anticipating.

Hell, he couldn't hold back any longer. Leaning down, he felt fucking barbaric as he inhaled her scent, wanting to imprint it in his mind. God, the woman was sweet. Everything about her. He slid his tongue up the length of her slit and didn't bother hiding his groan when she jerked against his face.

She moved her feet from the edge of the counter to his shoulders, digging her toes into him as he began teasing and licking. Each time he stroked against her slickness, she let out a strangled sound and arched herself right against his face.

When she tried to clamp her legs around his head, he pressed on one inner thigh and chuckled against her. At the motion, she jerked even harder than before, making his dick ache. He was going to slide into her soon, but first he desperately wanted to taste her release on his tongue. The need was damn near primal. He wanted to see her completely undone because of him, to see her lose control.

Right about now he wished he had four fucking hands because he wanted to touch her everywhere. As he slid a finger inside her, she grabbed onto his head, her inner walls clenching tight around him. All he could think about was how amazing it would feel to have that tightness wrapped around his cock. But first... He sucked on her clit, the action making her cry out in surprise and desire.

"Just like that." Her voice was a shaky whisper.

He could barely hear it over the sound of blood rushing in his ears. Years ago, he'd endured twenty-five weeks of BUD/s—the most intensive training in the world, and become a Navy SEAL. His skill set was vast, he could survive on pretty much any terrain on the planet and could navigate practically blind in the dark ocean. He had a sixth sense about things, as did most guys in special forces, but right now, if someone walked up behind him with a weapon, he wasn't certain he'd sense them coming because all his focus was on Zoe.

Her pleasure.

Her taste.

The sounds she was making with each stroke of his tongue.

The woman was making him insane, his erection pulsing insistently between his legs. He slid another finger inside her and she came apart underneath him, jerking and moaning incoherent words. Sucking harder on her clit, he increased the pressure when he could tell she liked it and started thrusting his fingers, in and out.

Each time he stroked inside her, her walls tightened harder and harder around his fingers as her orgasm punched through her, her toes digging into his back as her fingers did the same to his head.

When she fell limp against the counter, he slowly pulled his fingers out of her. With his gaze on her heavy-lidded one, he slid his fingers between his lips. It was like the action set something off inside her. Her eyes sparked with pure hunger.

No longer lax, she pushed up and grabbed for the buckle of his pants, her breathing erratic. *Yes.* As she worked it free, he pulled a condom from his back pocket. Before he could think about opening it, she snagged it from his hands and tore it open.

As she did, he shucked his pants, his erection springing free, a heavy club between his legs. When she sucked in a breath he saw her looking at his hard length, eyes wide. Just as quickly she grinned and reached for it, ready to roll the condom on.

He stilled her, grasping her wrist before she could. "Next time." Because he was on a razor's edge right now. He wanted to feel her gentle fingers wrapped around him, but he wanted her tight body even more.

Taking it from her, he quickly rolled it on, his hand shaking—actually shaking. The counter was too high, something she seemed to realize at the same time he did.

"Living room." Her voice was breathless as she reached for him, linking her fingers behind his neck and wrapping her legs around his waist.

He locked his arms around her and tugged her close, savoring the feel of her breasts rubbing against his chest as he crushed his mouth to hers. Teasing her lips open, he flicked his tongue against hers, her taste making him crazy.

From the party, he knew the layout of her house so he moved quickly across the tile—until she lifted up against him and impaled herself on him.

He sucked in a breath, his head snapping back from hers. Groaning as he filled her, she arched her back against him, her nipples stroking his chest with the movement. They weren't going to make it to the living room. "Wall or floor?" he managed.

"Wall." He loved that she didn't even pause in her answer.

He barely made it to the nearest kitchen wall before pulling out and thrusting back in, hard. Using the wall to brace them, he held onto her ass and began a steady rhythm, pounding into her. "Can you touch yourself?" he managed to rasp out. Because he wanted her to come again while he was inside her.

Her breathing was erratic as she reached between their bodies and started strumming her clit. It was insanely sexy that she was so comfortable with her body, the sight of her touching herself making him harder if that was even possible. His balls pulled up tight, the base of his spine tingling as the buildup increased. God, he was close. With her tight body wrapped around him like satin, it wasn't going to take long. Not this first time.

Dipping his head to hers, he kissed her again before blazing a path down her jaw to where her neck and shoulder met. He tilted her head to the side as he raked his teeth over her skin. When she shuddered he realized how sensitive she was there.

"Come for me," he murmured as he pulled out of her again,

almost fully, before sliding back in with a groan. She was so damn tight. "I want to feel you coming on my cock."

It was like his words set something off inside her. Her breathing hitched and her inner walls, which had already been incredibly tight around him, started rippling. She buried her face against his neck and bit down lightly, groaning against him as she found another orgasm.

That was all he needed to let go. With a cry, he climaxed, emptying himself, thrusting into her over and over until he buried himself completely inside her sweet heat. Breathing erratically, he stayed where he was, not inclined to leave for a while.

Eventually she shifted against him, making a soft groaning sound. He managed to pull his head back from hers to find her looking completely sated, her dark eyes filled with warmth.

She grinned that smile that held the power to bring him to his knees. "We're so doing that again."

Hell yeah. "Are you on birth control?"

She nodded and he found himself grinning right back at her as he imagined sliding into her heat without a barrier. "Good." He was clean and figured they could have that conversation later but if she was on the pill he knew it wouldn't be long until they got to that point.

Slowly he pulled out of her and disposed of the condom. When he turned back from the garbage he found her sliding the silky straps of her nightgown back up her shoulders. In their haste she'd never taken it completely off, just let it pool around her waist.

Next time, it was coming off. He wanted all of her bared to him. "Are you hungry?" he asked, picking up his discarded pants.

"Starving," she murmured, stepping toward him. He pulled her into his arms, loving the way she leaned into him, kissing along his chest as she wrapped her arms around his waist. "Want to order something or head out? There's a cute little Cuban restaurant not far from here that serves breakfast."

Her curls tickled his nose as he kissed the top of her head. "I'll cook for you," he said. She had enough in her refrigerator he could easily whip something up for them.

"That's the hottest thing you've said all morning, and that's saying something." She groaned slightly as if she didn't want to pull away from him before snagging her fallen robe from the floor. As she did, her doorbell sounded. They both paused and a frown tugged at her lips. "I'll get it," she said when he went to go with her. "Seriously I've got my alarm set and I'll look through the peephole. It's probably just a neighbor."

Sawyer didn't like it but he also didn't want to come off as a domineering jackass and insist on going with her to answer the door. But... Fuck it. Technically he wasn't guarding her anymore via Red Stone, but that didn't mean he wasn't going to stop watching out for her. There was no way in hell he could just turn off this part of himself, not when it came to Zoe's safety. "I know you're capable of taking care of yourself but whoever planted that knife is still out there."

Zoe looked as if she wanted to argue, but just nodded. "It might be overkill but okay."

It went against all his instincts not to just take over and look through the peephole, but he let her go first. When the bell sounded again, she grumbled under her breath as they reached the door. Lifting up on her tiptoes, she looked through, then let out a real curse.

Her mouth pulled into a thin line as she looked at him. "It's Vincent."

Perfect damn timing. Sawyer looked down at himself and grimaced. "I'll put my shirt on," he said quietly, striding toward the kitchen as she disarmed her alarm system.

It was going to be awkward enough with him being here this early in the morning and he didn't think Vincent would appreciate seeing him half-dressed. Not that he really cared what the other man thought.

The only one whose opinion mattered was Zoe.

CHAPTER SEVEN

Before opening her front door, Zoe glanced in the mirror above her foyer table and winced. Her lips were slightly swollen, her cheeks flushed and her hair was a little out of control. Which wasn't exactly out of the ordinary but she released her hair from her clip and tried to finger comb the curls so she didn't look as though she'd just had sex against the wall. It was no use.

Setting the clip on the table, she took a deep breath and opened the door to find her brother there scowling. What was wrong with him? "Hey, Vincent. Kinda early for you to be here. Everything okay?"

"Is that Sawyer's truck in your driveway?" he demanded. He wore running shorts, sneakers and a long-sleeved Nike Dri-Fit shirt he loved so much, as if he'd planned to go jogging.

She didn't bother looking past him to see the offending vehicle. "Would you like to come in, have some coffee?"

Vincent just growled and stomped past her, his expression dark. "Where is he?"

"Seriously, on what planet do you think I'm going to let you come in here and go all caveman about my personal life?"

Vincent's pale blue eyes that looked so much like their deceased father's flashed angrily. "Personal life! You just had a big scare yesterday, Zoe. You're probably feeling emotional and vulnerable and he's taking advantage."

"Emotional and vulnerable? Okay, what happened to my brother? Because he doesn't use words like those."

His jaw tightened. "I'm serious."

"So am I. And I'm a big girl so if this is the only crazy reason you stormed over here this morning, then you can go right back the way you came. I appreciate your concern, but..." She trailed off when Sawyer appeared in the arched entryway of the dining room. The dining room was connected to the kitchen so he'd have heard everything clearly. She inwardly winced.

Silence stretched out as the two men stared at one another, Vincent's hostility seeming to grow each second that passed. She wasn't sure what to say that wouldn't set off her brother's normally long fuse. Before she could figure it out, Sawyer stepped farther into the foyer.

He held up his palms in that universal sign for peace. "Look, Vincent—"

"Is this about Audrey?" Her brother's voice rose with each word, his body vibrating with anger.

Sawyer's lips pulled into a thin line, his expression tense. She couldn't read what he was thinking other than he seemed annoyed by Vincent. "Are you kidding me?" His words were clipped.

"Who's Audrey?" Because she wanted to know whatever had happened between these two. It shouldn't surprise her that a woman was the reason for their past issues. Still, a strange sense of jealousy settled in her bones. After everything that had happened with her ex-boyfriend, she didn't like the sound of this.

They both ignored her.

Sawyer's expression was frustrated as he looked at Vincent. "You think it's impossible that I could be attracted to Zoe, a smart, beautiful woman?"

"No, my sister's a fucking catch, I just don't like you sniffing around her."

Okay, Vincent calling her a catch was kinda sweet, but what the hell? Sniffing around her, like what, she was a bone and Sawyer was a dog? Sweet Lord, this was ridiculous. "Vincent—"

"And I don't like your timing," Vincent continued, taking an angry step closer to Sawyer. They'd both been in the Teams but they'd never been on the same one as far as Zoe knew. Still, whatever had happened must have been bad for this kind of reaction from her brother.

"Timing?" Sawyer's jaw tightened and he took a step forward too. Not exactly menacing, but it was clear he wasn't going to back down to Vincent.

Uh, oh. She didn't think they were big enough jackasses to fight, not at their age, but...she stepped forward so that she was semi in-between them. Not that she could actually stop them if they decided to brawl.

Sawyer noticed her move and gave her an apologetic look.

Vincent still ignored her. "Yeah, timing. She's got all this shit to deal with then you just stroll in like a fucking knight in shining armor. What kind of game are you playing?"

"Oh my God! Vincent, enough!" Zoe stepped in between them fully now, hands on her hips as she faced off with her brother. She wished she was wearing more than a robe and slip and had on some damn heels so he didn't tower over her so much, but she'd never put up with his crap before and she wasn't about to start now. No matter how good his intentions were. Because she knew he was just looking out for her. Too bad he was going about it all wrong.

She held up a hand when it was clear he wanted to start his tirade on her. "Whatever this thing between Sawyer and me is, it's none of your business. *None.* I'm a grown woman—older than you. I actually can't believe you're here doing this." Vincent had never given her grief about any of the guys she'd dated in the past. Of course she'd never brought anyone around the family before, but still. The way he was acting was over the top and so unlike her brother. "It's not like Sawyer had anything to do with me having a stalker or said stalker being killed. We're attracted to each other, we're both consenting adults, get over it." He opened his mouth again, so she stepped forward and pressed a finger into his chest. "And if you say one word about me being vulnerable, like I haven't been handling this shit for the last six months all by myself, I will call Mom right now." It was the best threat she had.

Vincent's jaw tightened again, his pale blue eyes flashing fire.

Finally he spoke again. "I know you're capable of taking care of yourself. I'm just not convinced Sawyer has your best interests at heart."

A sliver of worry wormed its way through Zoe. Vincent had never reacted about anyone like this. "Why's that?"

For a moment Vincent looked almost embarrassed or even ashamed. He scrubbed a hand over his face and sighed. "After Jordan left, I was in a dark place."

Zoe's entire demeanor immediately softened. When his now-fiancée had suddenly left him without a word seven years ago because she'd gone into WITSEC, Vincent hadn't handled it well. That being the understatement of the century. "Yeah, I remember," she said softly. She still remembered when Vincent had confessed everything to her, how Jordan had just disappeared on him without a trace. Now he knew what had happened to her and they were a strong couple, but back then, he'd been a mess with her gone. Once he'd realized she'd left him, he'd lost it.

Vincent shot a quick look over her shoulder at Sawyer, then focused on Zoe again. "I slept with a woman he was seeing. To be fair, I didn't know they were together, but...after I found out, I was a dick about it to him."

"Jeez, Vincent." She frowned, wanting to cut him some slack, but it was hard to. If Vincent was actually admitting he'd been a dick, it must have been bad. And it sounded like Sawyer had more right to be pissed than Vincent about the whole incident. "Mom and Dad raised you better than that. *You're* better than that."

He held up his hands. "I know! It was a long time ago and that's not the point."

"So what is the point? You think because you did something douche to him that Sawyer is sleeping with me to what, get back at you?"

"You're sleeping with him?" His voice kicked up again.

She covered her face with her hands. "So *not* the point," she groaned before looking back at him. "You need to leave. Now." Because this was ridiculous and embarrassing. She was in her thirties and a professional, not someone trapped on a bad talk show—even though that was what it felt like at the moment.

Vincent looked incredulous. "You're kicking me out of your house?"

"Um, yes. Because this is childish." She narrowed her eyes at him as another thought occurred to her. "Does Jordan know you're here?"

He got that sheepish look she was very familiar with. "Not exactly. I told her I was going to grab breakfast—which I am."

Zoe snorted. "I bet she told you not to bother me about Sawyer."

That sounded exactly like Jordan. When she and Vincent had gotten back together Zoe hadn't been the nicest person to her because she hadn't known the circumstances of Jordan's disappearance. Now Zoe deeply regretted it. She hadn't been awful, but she *might* have called Jordan a bitch the first time they met. "You want me to call her *and* Mom? I'll do it."

"You're mean," he muttered. Vincent's lips twitched as if he was fighting a smile so she knew they'd be okay. He let out a sigh, shot Sawyer a dirty look that basically said 'this isn't over' before giving Zoe a kiss on the forehead and a hug and leaving.

Once he was gone she turned around, dreading to see Sawyer's face. Unfortunately his expression was that blank one she couldn't get a read on. He'd already been with her when she'd been arrested. Sure she hadn't done anything but he must think she was a drama magnet. "Sorry about that," she muttered.

"You don't have anything to apologize for." He still didn't reach for her, so she wrapped her arms around herself, feeling insecure. After everything they'd just shared it was like a chasm was growing between them and she couldn't stop it.

An awkward silence stretched between them. She wasn't sure what to say and maybe he wasn't sure either. Finally she decided to just ask the question. "Is there any truth to what Vincent said?"

If anything, Sawyer's expression became even more unreadable, and that was saying something. "You really have to ask that?" There was a bite to his words.

She realized he thought she meant the part about Sawyer possibly using her to get back at Vincent. "No, I just meant the whole thing that happened between you guys. Is that how it played out?" Because there was always more than one side to a story.

"More or less." His jaw tightened once before he continued. "I...loved her. We hadn't been together that long, but things were getting serious. Or I thought they were. Then she slept with Vincent—and threw it in my face."

Something told Zoe there was more to the story but right now, she didn't want to ask. It wasn't like she'd been expecting forever from Sawyer, but this cast a dark shadow on what they'd shared, whether it was fair or not. Her only serious boyfriend had still been in love with his ex when he'd been with Zoe. Something Zoe hadn't known until he'd dropped the bomb on her the day after they'd graduated from med school. Deep down she'd always wondered if Rubin hadn't gotten over his ex, but had never pushed it. She'd wasted two years with him.

She wasn't going to go through that again, not for anyone. "I'm sorry for what happened between you two and for what happened with your ex." She pushed out a breath. "Listen, a lot's happened in the past couple days and I've got a lot of stuff I need to do today. I know we were going to do breakfast but maybe we can take a rain check?"

She was simply feeling too raw to deal with him right now, even if her actions were unfair.

His jaw tightened as he watched her. "You shouldn't be alone right now. Whoever planted that weapon with your fingerprint is still out there."

"I know." The knowledge hadn't been far from her mind. But she couldn't cower and hide.

Blowing out a sigh that sounded a lot like frustration, he rubbed the back of his neck. It was clear he wanted to argue with her. "I don't like leaving you."

"I've got an alarm system, a gun and pepper spray." Not that she ever wanted to have to use either weapon.

There was a long, heated silence as he just watched her. Oh yeah, he did not like this at all. Before guilt completely suffocated her, he spoke. "You'll lock your doors and set your alarm when I leave?"

Gritting her teeth, she nodded. She didn't mind a little over protectiveness, but she could take care of herself. "I've got errands to run and stuff to do but I'll set it when I leave."

He paused and she guessed he was probably annoyed she'd be leaving her house, but seriously, she wasn't going to stop living her life. If she started down that path, she could get sucked into a life of fear and she refused to let anyone control her like that. "Are we still on for dinner tonight?" he finally asked.

"Yeah." The word was out before she could stop herself. She needed some time to herself, especially after everything that had happened the past couple days—months, really—but she still wanted to see him again. And she wanted to ask him about his ex, to find out if there was more to the story—if he still had feelings for the woman.

After he gathered his few belongings, she walked him to the front door and opened it. To her surprise, he pulled her tight against him, his big hands clutching her hips in a way that sent tingles straight to her toes.

And when he brushed his mouth over hers, stroking his tongue sensually against her lips, demanding entrance, she melted against him, holding his shoulders for support until finally she pulled back.

His breathing was uneven, his green eyes seeming darker as he looked down at her. "Tonight. Seven o'clock, I'll pick you up. And be careful."

"I will." Breathless from their kiss, she shut the door behind him and immediately locked it. He clearly wanted to see her again tonight, or she assumed he did. God, what if Vincent was right and he'd only made a pass at her because of—No. She wasn't going to let her mind go there. She wasn't going to obsess about him at all.

Not today when she had her freedom in more ways than one. She was going to do something she never did for herself—go to the salon and get the works done. Sawyer had left her feeling incredibly confused and if they were going out tonight, she was going to look like a million bucks when they did.

———————•|•———————

She wrapped her fingers around the hilt of her knife as she watched the tall man leave Zoe's home. He scanned the neighborhood, pausing at different intervals before finally he got into his truck and left.

She remained where she was, hiding in plain sight on the sidewalk across the street. She had one foot propped up against one of Zoe's neighbor's trees as she bent toward it, stretching. With yoga pants, a zip-up fleece hoodie and earbuds from her mp3 player in her ears, she looked like a mid-morning jogger, perfectly blending in with her surroundings.

So, Zoe had a lover? Or maybe this was a new boyfriend? The bitch had had a party last night when she should have been in jail. Instead she'd been celebrating that Braddock was dead. Of course she wouldn't have come out and said that was why she'd had the party, but it had to have been the reason. If it had been big enough, she'd have gone inside, but she hadn't been invited and while she knew Zoe, they weren't friends.

The whole situation wasn't right. Zoe should be suffering. It was her fault that Braddock was dead even if Zoe hadn't been the one to cut his throat. If he hadn't wanted Zoe so much, been so obsessed with the idea of her, then Braddock would have been with her. She could have made him forget that bitch.

But he'd been a fool, wanting what he couldn't have. So now he was dead and Zoe was next. Killing her would be tricky though, especially now. Since Zoe hadn't been arrested, the police must have figured out the doctor hadn't done it. Planting that knife with her fingerprint had been a long-shot, but it had been worth it. Unfortunately it hadn't worked out.

That was okay. Toying with Zoe would be so much more fun than just killing her. Once the truck was out of sight, she continued jogging, looping back around the neighborhood multiple times. On her third time around, she saw Zoe's car pulling out of her garage.

Her heart rate kicked up. Zoe was leaving. This was perfect. She knew the bitch had an alarm system, or she at least had stickers on her windows and a sign in her yard that said she did, so she wouldn't bother breaking in. No, she was going to leave Zoe a present for whenever she returned.

Her entire body heated up as she thought about the expression on Zoe's face when she found it. Unfortunately she wouldn't be around to see Zoe's horror, but she could still fantasize about it. Though it killed her, she didn't slow down as Zoe left, just kept jogging, kept her pace even. When she reached the end of the road, instead of looping back the way she'd come, she crossed the street and headed back down the sidewalk toward Zoe's house.

Once she reached it, she glanced around casually, keeping up that steady pace as she headed up the driveway then the stone walkway to Zoe's front door.

On the front step, she pretended to ring the doorbell as she pulled a small package out of one of her hoodie's pockets. Since it was so cold out she was wearing gloves and wouldn't look odd, which made this so much easier. She'd been careful not to leave any prints on the package or the wrapping.

The wrapping itself was a bright silver and green with little snowflakes on it. An early Christmas present for Zoe.

Laughing to herself, she set it right on the front stoop, propping it against the door. The present was small but the contents inside would be very effective.

It was just a shame she wouldn't be able to see Zoe's face when she opened it.

CHAPTER EIGHT

Zoe shut one of her desk drawers and looked up as Gerard stuck his head in her office.

His mouth pulled into a frown. "What are you doing here?"

She held up her hands in mock self-defense. "Not working, I swear. Just had to pick up a few things." She'd gone to the salon and felt like a new woman. She was about to head home but had needed to stop by work first.

He leaned against the door frame and stuck his hands in his pants pockets. "Hair looks good."

"Yeah?" Zoe self-consciously ran her fingers through it. She'd had it straightened for a little change. Once she washed it, the curls would return but she'd wanted something different for the next couple days. Almost like a cleansing of all the drama from her past — and if she was being completely honest with herself, she wanted to look amazing for Sawyer.

"Why the change?"

She narrowed her eyes at him. "I thought you said it looked good."

"It does. But…something's different about you."

Her cheeks flushed as she thought about what she'd done this morning with Sawyer, then she cursed herself. It wasn't like Gerard could read her mind. "I have no idea what you're talking about."

He started to say something but was cut off by a familiar female voice. "Gerard?"

Zoe rolled her eyes but Gerard just sighed. Viola, tall, willowy and beautiful, the physician's assistant had been crushing on Gerard for a while and couldn't seem to take a hint that he wasn't interested. It had placed him in a weird position and Zoe knew he was starting to feel uncomfortable about the woman's attention. Zoe understood all too well what that felt like since her stalker had been like that with her.

"Want to head out with me?" Zoe murmured quietly. Before he could answer, Viola appeared in the doorway.

She gave Zoe a tight smile that didn't reach her eyes.

Well the feeling is mutual, Zoe thought. At least the woman was good at her job, very organized, one of her only redeeming qualities.

Without giving Zoe another glance she turned to look at Gerard, already crowding his personal space as she leaned closer, practically shoving her breasts at him. "What are you two doing here? I didn't think you came in on Saturdays, Zoe," she said, still looking at Gerard. There was an almost accusing note in her voice.

Zoe didn't bother answering. Just locked her top drawer as Gerard cleared his throat. "Just catching up on some paperwork, but we're heading out now." He gave Zoe a pointed look.

She resisted the urge to smile as she slipped her coat on. "Yeah, Gerard owes me dinner." A complete lie but she had no problem covering for him.

Viola frowned and glanced at her slim, silver watch. "This early?"

"Gerard likes to get the early bird specials. Especially at his age." Zoe snickered now, unable to contain her laughter.

He just shot her a dirty look as Viola's pink-painted lips pulled into a frown. She stroked a hand down his forearm, an action that could be considered casual, but the possessive glint in her eyes was anything but. "I'm heading out to get some drinks before dinner with friends in a couple hours. Do you guys mind if I tag along?"

Zoe couldn't think of a polite way to say no. Viola might annoy her but she couldn't be all out rude to her. It was weird that she'd stopped by the office though when clearly she hadn't done any work since she'd just arrived. Good Lord, was she really here simply to see Gerard?

"Of course not," Gerard said smoothly and Zoe wanted to kick him as she stepped toward them. She didn't even want to go to dinner, not when she had plans with Sawyer in a couple hours.

They both moved back and she shut her office door and started down the hallway with them. As they walked, Viola continued chatting. "So where are you guys going?"

"We haven't decided yet—"

Zoe was cut off when Gerard let out a frustrated curse.

"What's wrong?" Viola asked as they reached the front door.

"Nothing. Just an issue with my sitter," he said, looking at the screen on his cell phone. Which hadn't buzzed or dinged. His expression was apologetic as he looked between the both of them.

Zoe knew he was just pretending that he'd received a text, but Viola seemed to believe him. The woman made a lame excuse why she couldn't have dinner with Zoe and hurried toward her car as Zoe and Gerard locked up.

"Guess she didn't want to have dinner with just me," Zoe murmured.

He scrubbed a hand over his face after locking the door. "I don't know what to do about her. I've been careful not to be alone with her, but..."

"But you can't keep working like this. Sit down and talk to her and if that doesn't work, let her go."

"Yeah, I'm going to. I want you in on that meeting though."

Zoe nodded. "We'll record it too." Because she wanted to make sure her all her boss's bases were covered in case Viola tried to accuse him of something. Zoe wished he'd just fire the woman but knew Gerard would try to make things work first.

"How're you feeling after...everything?" he asked as they headed to their vehicles.

She shrugged, not sure about anything at the moment. Zoe didn't want to say out loud that she was glad her stalker was dead, but she was certainly happy she wasn't looking over her shoulder anymore. At least not because of Klein. It still freaked her out that a weapon with her fingerprint had been planted at the murder scene. Luckily she'd had a strong alibi. "The whole thing is still surreal. Last night was fun though."

He snorted. "I saw that. What time did everyone finally leave?"

"Three o'clock."

He let out a low whistle. "Apparently I really am a senior citizen."

"Whatever. You left at a normal time. I can't believe how late everyone stayed."

"What about your friend Sawyer? How late did *he* stay?" Gerard's look turned speculative as they reached his Lexus SUV. Grinning, he pressed the keyfob to unlock the doors, waiting for her answer.

"Why do you ask about him?" Zoe didn't think they'd been obvious last night. Not that she cared what anyone thought. She was single and could do whatever she wanted.

"The man couldn't take his eyes off you last night and something is really different about you this morning. Besides the hair."

"I'll let you know if anything interesting develops between us." She considered Gerard one of her closest friends but didn't want to tell him more about Sawyer until she knew where things were headed between them.

"All right. Just don't..." He trailed off.

A cool breeze blew up over the parking lot and she tightened her coat belt, fighting off a shiver. "Don't what?"

Gerard lifted his shoulders. "Maybe don't push him away or come up with reasons he won't work out?"

She started to defend herself, to insist that she didn't do that, but bit her bottom lip. Damn it, she did *exactly* that. Pretty much all the time. Sighing, she shook her head. "You're annoying when you're right."

He just chuckled, his breath a faint cloud in front of him as he gave her a brief hug.

Once she was on her way home, her boss's words rolled around in her head. Gah, she did push people away. Men at least. Relationships were so much work and took up so much damn time that she just couldn't fit one into her schedule.

At least that's what she told herself whenever someone asked her out. For years she'd just gone out with men who she considered low maintenance. Men who were in a profession similar to her own and therefore worked insane hours and were okay with her limited involvement in their lives. And vice versa. Ugh, thinking about it in those terms was depressing.

After Rubin left her she'd taken it hard. Harder than she'd admitted to anyone, even her brother, who'd been open about his own heartbreak years ago. It had been too much to admit that she hadn't been enough for her ex. On paper they'd been the perfect couple. Smart, successful, attractive people in the same field with the same views on politics and religion.

Okay, now *that* was depressing as hell too. Those things were important but she'd seen what her parents had. Their marriage hadn't been perfect but their love for each other had been. And they'd disagreed on all sorts of things, especially religion and politics. Her father had left a lush lifestyle to marry her mother. His wealthy, elitist parents had been blinded by anger when he'd fallen for a poor, black Jamaican, second-generation American. Zoe wasn't sure what they'd hated more, her mother's skin color or her status as a resident. Not that it mattered to her or any of her siblings. Zoe hadn't talked to them in years. They'd reached out a few times after her father's death, but she couldn't be bothered with them. She'd seen what a good marriage was supposed to look like, what a loving family meant and she wasn't going to let those assholes into her life. Not when they'd flat out rejected her mom. Screw them.

As she steered into her driveway, she mentally shook herself, knowing exactly why she was thinking about her parents' marriage. She pressed her garage door opener but didn't pull through when she saw something shiny sitting on her front stoop. Getting out of the car, she hurried along the stone steps, her breath catching in her throat at the next gust of cold that rolled over her.

Smiling when she saw a small gift sitting there, she scooped it up. Probably something from one of the neighbors. Next weekend they'd be doing their annual gift exchange and party. Thankfully this year she wasn't hosting it at her house.

As she headed back to her car, movement from out of the corner of her eye caught her attention. Zoe hid a wince before she let her true feelings show. Letty Nieves was the same age as her and a beautiful woman.

She was also one of the most annoying neighbors Zoe had ever had. Zoe pasted on a smile, thankful her sunglasses covered her eyes, as the woman approached.

Wearing black yoga pants, a black long-sleeved T-shirt and a bright pink puffy vest zipped up over it, Letty smiled as she jogged up the driveway, though the smile was more of a baring of teeth—like a shark. "Hey, Zoe. Everything okay over here? I saw the police here yesterday."

And there it was. Letty was going to pretend she hadn't heard from the neighbors what was going on. "Everything's good. Getting ready for Christmas? Your light show is great this year." Zoe was the queen of avoiding and deflecting. She'd spoken to a few neighbors about what had happened, but Letty wasn't one of them. And she wasn't going to be one of them.

The tall woman with dark hair gritted her teeth, her smile growing sharper. "Thanks. I put a lot of work into it. You're sure everything's all right?"

"I'm sure."

Letty's gaze narrowed on the gift in Zoe's hand for a moment before she looked at her face again. "Saw a lot of people over here last night."

"Oh, yeah, just some people from work and family friends. Last minute get together type of thing." Zoe inwardly cringed. Maybe she should have invited Letty? No, last night had been a celebration and she hadn't wanted to have anything ruin that. And it wasn't like she'd invited the whole neighborhood or anything.

"Okay, well, let me know if you need anything. I'm here for you." Her voice dripped with a saccharine sweetness that raked over Zoe's senses.

Seriously, she had no idea why this woman didn't like her. She figured Letty was just one of those women who didn't like other women.

Whatever, Zoe didn't have time to worry about that now. Once she was securely inside her house, she reset her alarm and dropped her purse and coat onto the center island in her kitchen. She wasn't even going to pretend she could wait to open the gift.

Carefully peeling back the delicate paper, she opened it without tearing any of it. As she lifted the top of the small gold box off, it took a moment to register what she was seeing.

Her stomach lurched and she automatically dropped the square top. It fell to the counter with a soft click. A Polaroid of a gruesome scene—Klein's dead body, his throat slashed, blood sprayed all over his lanai—

The photo was covering...something underneath it. She could just see the tip of what looked like... No. It couldn't be.

Swallowing the bile in her throat, she grabbed a pen from her desk on the other side of the kitchen. Chills skittered up her spine that had nothing to do with the cold as she carefully moved the picture out of the way.

A severed finger with dried blood on the stump was nestled on a bed of white stuffing paper.

She wondered if it was Klein's finger or someone else's. Klein was clearly dead as that picture showed so who the hell could have done this? Grimacing, she pulled her cell phone out of her purse and called the police.

CHAPTER NINE

Sitting half inside the front passenger seat of Carlito's police-issued SUV, Zoe wrapped her arms tighter around herself. Her legs were half out of the vehicle as she sat sideways, taking in the scene in front of her.

Still trying to process the fact that someone had sent her a finger, probably Klein's, though it hadn't yet been confirmed, and that horrific photo was going to take time. She kept racking her brain, trying to figure out anyone in her life who could have done this. She came up blank. Once Klein had started stalking her she'd done research on the stalker mindset and knew that stalkers were often someone in your life. Definitely not always so this could be random, but...it felt *really* personal.

"Have you already talked to Vincent?" Carlito asked as he approached the vehicle, tucking his cell phone back into his jacket pocket.

She slid out of the SUV and nodded. "Yeah. I called Vincent and my mom and they're going to let my sisters know. My mom's actually going to stay with one of my sisters for a few days. And everyone is going to stay locked down in their houses tonight." Just in case whoever had targeted her decided to go after her family.

Carlito snorted. "Bet Vincent didn't want to."

Despite the situation, a grin tugged at her lips. "No, but he's got Jordan to look out for and you're here. He knows I'll call him when I leave and that I'll be getting a police escort to his place." Even though she really didn't want to go stay with her brother and Jordan. Not because she didn't love him, but they were newly engaged and planning a wedding. Zoe didn't want to get in the way of all that. For a brief moment she'd entertained the idea of calling Sawyer but things were new between them and she wasn't going to ask to move in with him—that would be insane. Plus she was really unsettled by her growing feelings for him.

"Did you finish the list of people—" He glanced to his left, frowning for a moment, then pulled out his radio.

She followed his line of sight. Police cars and two fire trucks lined the front of her house, blocking off most of the street. She'd always thought it was strange that fire trucks came to the scene of crimes but didn't care now. Red and blue lights flashed intermittently, creating the perfect 'crime scene' atmosphere. Zoe couldn't see whatever it was that still had Carlito frowning.

Gah, she rubbed her hands over her face. She just wanted to get out of here.

"It's some of your neighbors, they're across the street and want to talk to you, make sure you're okay." There was a questioning look in Carlito's gray eyes, as if he would let her go talk to them.

Zoe shook her head. "I'll call them later." She really appreciated their support but didn't have the energy to see anyone else now. Her house had been searched by the police even though as far as she knew no intruders had been inside, and she'd answered a hundred different questions.

"We're almost done here." He started to say more but his phone buzzed in his hand. Turning away from her, he said, "Yeah? Okay, yeah, he's good. I called him." Ending the call, he faced her again.

Zoe leaned against the side of the SUV, counting down the seconds until she could get inside her house. "I finished the list of people who I've ever had any sort of issue with in the last year. It's all there," she said, nodding to the open passenger door of the SUV where the pad and paper were. "I can't really see any of them doing this though."

"You'd be surprised," he murmured.

Before she could respond, Sawyer appeared from behind one of the fire trucks. She pushed up from the vehicle and was surprised when Carlito waved him over.

The expression on Sawyer's face was almost angry. But that couldn't be right. Why was he even here? She'd texted him to cancel their dinner plans tonight and had planned to call him once she was free and explain what was going on.

"Thanks for coming," Carlito said as Sawyer approached.

Though it was impossible, as he came to stand next to her, she could swear she felt his body heat wrapping around her. Wait—her head snapped back to Carlito. "*You* called Sawyer?"

The detective nodded, but his attention was on Sawyer. "I've gotta take care of something but I'll be back in a few minutes."

A couple uniformed police officers were in the nearby vicinity, hovering by Carlito's SUV, but all Zoe's focus was on Sawyer as the detective left them alone. "I'm confused, Carlito called you?"

"Yep." Sawyer's jaw was clenched tight as he raked a gaze over her from head to toe. The look was completely clinical—mostly. "You're sure you're okay?" Real concern laced each word as he met her gaze again.

Feeling unnerved by his presence, Zoe shoved her hands in her jacket pockets. The thick, winter coat had a fleece lining, warming her hands immediately. She hadn't called Sawyer for a reason. He'd already been witness to so much happening to her, she didn't want him getting even more tangled up in this mess. "I'm good. I just don't understand why Carlito called you."

"What I don't understand is why you *didn't*." There went that sexy jaw clench again. The man was definitely angry.

At her.

"You're mad at me?" she blurted.

"Hell yeah, I'm pissed." He took a deep breath and glanced around their surroundings, as if trying to contain his anger. When he looked back at her again, all she saw was a simmering annoyance.

"But why? I was going to tell you everything once I got over to Vincent's house." Because no way was she staying here tonight. And she'd planned to give Sawyer a watered down version.

Reaching out, as if unable to stop himself, he ran his hands down her arms before pulling her close to him. A shudder slid through her, his presence warming her from the inside out. "Why didn't you call me about this? I would have been here."

Oh, crap. That was hurt in his voice. Which was way worse than anger. "I...didn't think you'd want to come down here for any of this. You've already done so much, I just..." She trailed off, feeling lame and guilty even though she'd never meant to hurt him. They might have had intense sex earlier that day but they weren't in a relationship. She didn't expect him to take on any more of this nightmare. It would be unfair to ask him.

Sawyer was silent, watching her with green eyes that seemed darker tonight. Instead of responding, he pulled her into a tight hug, wrapping his arms around her. She didn't even hesitate, but leaned into him, holding him tight. God that felt good. He'd come here to be with her, something that struck her deeply. She just wanted to get wrapped up in the strength of him and never let go—and that terrified her.

"How're you doing, really?" he asked quietly.

"It was awful." Her voice cracked, her words coming out muffled against his chest.

He rubbed a soothing hand down her spine, helping ease some of her tension. Not much but enough that she didn't feel like she was about to split apart at the seams.

"Come away with me for a few days," Sawyer murmured, his chin resting on the top of her head.

Surprised, Zoe pulled back so she could look up at him. "What?"

He fingered some strands of her hair before sliding his hand around to cup the back of her neck. "Instead of going to your brother's place. Let's get out of town. I know somewhere we can go. You can get some distance—which I think you need after Klein's death and your arrest anyway—and take a fucking break. The police can do their job and you can actually rest. Unless you really want to stay with your brother?"

The truth was, she didn't want to be around her family because she didn't want to inadvertently put any of them in danger. She knew they'd never worry about that because family was family and she'd feel the same if one of her siblings was in trouble. But…getting out of town sounded perfect. Still, she couldn't ask that of Sawyer. "You just started a new job."

"I know." His intense gaze never wavered.

She didn't know how to respond to that. He couldn't take off time right now. Or he shouldn't. And she wouldn't ask that of him. But his offer touched her on such a deep level it left her speechless for a moment. She must mean more to him than just hot sex, right? Or maybe he was just that honorable and didn't want to turn his back on someone in trouble. She bit her bottom lip, feeling way too indecisive.

Before she could respond, Carlito returned. "We're clearing out of here now. They've dusted the place for fingerprints just in case, but after the party you had, I doubt we'll get much. And there's no evidence he or she was ever inside anyway, but I want to cover all bases. Zoe, whatever's going on here is fucking personal. It's why I called Sawyer. Everyone in your life needs to be aware of this. And it wouldn't hurt for you to get out of town. I know you're going to Vincent's, but—"

"We're heading out of town tonight," Sawyer said, his voice commanding.

"Good. I've got a list of everyone you work with, the hospital staff you and Klein both worked with, your personal list and some other names we're going to be looking into. We *are* going to find this person but if you get out of Miami, I'll sleep easier." A harried-sounding male voice came over his radio, dragging his attention away again. He gave them an apologetic look and held it up to his mouth as he strode a few feet away.

"We're leaving tonight?" Zoe's eyebrows lifted as she turned to face Sawyer.

"Yes."

"Did you plan on asking me?" She wished she could put some heat behind the question but she was all out of steam. And the idea of getting away with him for a few days sounded like heaven.

Sawyer didn't back down, his expression hard. "Can you take time off work?"

"Yeah." Gerard wanted her to take off anyway. Once he heard about this, he'd likely pull rank and insist.

"Then no, I'm not asking." He glanced around, then lowered his voice before focusing on her again. "One of my brothers has a beach house in Saint Augustine. It's safe and not linked to either of us. We can be there in five hours."

"You're very bossy," she muttered.

"Where your safety is concerned? Yeah." His expression was like granite, hard and unforgiving.

"Wait, what about your job? You can't just take time off when you just started."

"It's not an issue." His voice was clipped.

"Sawyer—"

"Trust me. It's not."

She knew she should probably be annoyed by his tone and high-handed manner. She'd never put up with that from anyone before. Otherwise she wouldn't have gotten to where she was in life. But if she was being honest, it was nice to let someone else take over right now. And not just anyone, but Sawyer. She might still have no clue where they were headed relationship-wise, but she trusted him with her life. And the idea of leaving the city was so appealing, the answer fell from her lips without pause. She just hoped he wasn't putting his job in jeopardy. "Okay."

Normally she analyzed stuff to death, but not with Sawyer apparently. It was like he'd brought out a different side to her.

He nodded once. "Good. I've got a call to make then we'll talk to Carlito about where we're headed."

"I need to call Gerard too." Everything was happening so fast and she hated that she'd have to pass off some of her appointments, but she was terrified to stay home right now.

———————◦•◦———————

Across the street from Zoe's house, she blended into the shadows, careful to keep her body language neutral. She didn't want the glee on her face to show. Not that anyone was paying attention to her right now. She looked just like any other woman out for an evening stroll, curious about the police presence in such a quiet neighborhood.

She'd only gotten to see Zoe briefly when the bitch had been talking to a uniformed police officer. It wasn't enough. She wanted to see Zoe suffer, to see her expression of pain and fear. Just the thought made her entire body heat up with glee. A feeling similar to arousal swept through her. Her nipples pebbled against her bra and she shifted against the sidewalk, her sneakers silent on the concrete.

The more she thought about messing with Zoe, the more joy it brought her. That bitch deserved it more than she'd ever know. She just took and took and thought she could have anything she wanted. *Anyone* she wanted. Well, no more.

When a sexy-looking man in casual slacks, a jacket, and a police badge on a chain around his neck strode out from behind an SUV and waved at another man, her heart rate kicked up a notch. She recognized the man approaching the policeman.

Tall, muscular, dark hair, a hardness about him that was impossible to deny. He was definitely sexy, in a rough-looking sort of way. Not her type, she liked her men polished, but she could see the appeal. It was the man Zoe had been with before. Now he was here? Oh yes, he must mean something to her.

Probably here to support poor, pitiful Zoe. Too bad no one would be able to protect her for very long. It didn't matter where Zoe went, she had a way to track her. There was nowhere she could run. And if her lover got in the way, she'd end him too. Maybe she'd hurt him anyway and make Zoe watch.

CHAPTER TEN

Carlito sat on the edge of the seat in Letty Nieves's kitchen. Another uniformed police officer was with him, standing near the door that led into the backyard. Zoe had given them a list of people in her life who she didn't get along with. Since the Nieves woman lived in her neighborhood, he was starting with her.

It made it easier to pretend that he was just asking everyone in the neighborhood questions instead of subtly interrogating her. "Thanks again for agreeing to speak with us. Everyone in the neighborhood has been so helpful."

She smiled in a way he'd seen far too often, openly flirty. "Of course, Detective."

He bit back a sigh even though he could use this to his advantage. He'd used charm on many occasions to get suspects to loosen up. "Have you seen anyone around the neighborhood who looked out of place lately? Odd hours of the day or night?"

Letty shook her head, her dark hair swishing around her shoulders. In her thirties, she was a stunning woman, but something about her was plastic. "Not that I can think of. Well, yesterday I saw the police at Zoe's house, but I'm sure you already know that." There was a questioning note in her voice.

Deciding to be civil, he said, "Zoe's helping us with an ongoing investigation."

The woman's smile turned brittle, but she quickly recovered. "That's wonderful."

"Can you tell me about the rest of your neighbors?" Sometimes it was best to ask open-ended questions. People tended to hang themselves if given enough rope and in general, people loved to hear themselves talk. He hoped that was the case with Letty Nieves. So far he didn't have a gut feeling about her one way or another. It was too soon to tell. If she wasn't involved, hopefully she'd seen something that could help them.

"Of course." She clasped her hands in her lap and told him about both neighbors on either side of her, two across the street, and finally she got to Zoe. He had the feeling she'd been holding off on talking about Zoe when Letty's face tightened just a fraction as she mentioned her. "Now, I'm sure Zoe is helping you with your little case, but she's not the best neighbor."

Carlito straightened at that. "How so?"

She leaned forward, almost conspiratorially. "Trash comes on Thursdays early in the morning. *Before* she leaves for work. And she doesn't bring her trash can in until after she gets home."

He blinked, waiting for more. When he realized nothing more was coming, he fought his disappointment. This woman didn't like Zoe but it seemed to have more to do with her as a neighbor. He was sure people had killed for less, but after hearing Letty complain about every single one of her neighbors, she just seemed like an unhappy woman in general. He cleared his throat. "I see."

"And it's not just that. Last year she didn't take her Christmas lights down until January tenth. *Tenth.* Everyone else had them down a couple days after Christmas or by the first at the latest. Zoe was apparently too busy with her job." The woman sniffed haughtily and continued complaining about how Zoe's gardener had once left a tool in her front yard.

Carlito resisted the urge to massage his temple. He didn't have time to be a personal sounding board for this woman. When he'd been on patrol he'd gotten calls for the most ridiculous things; people called the police because their cable went out or because they wanted him to tell their eight-year old he'd arrest them if they didn't go to school. Because that wasn't going to scar them or anything. He'd thought when he became a detective it would be different, but nope. People were the same.

He smiled wanly and glanced over at the female officer standing guard. It was clear she was fighting a smile as she glanced out one of the kitchen windows to avoid his gaze.

Carlito cleared his throat again, and attempted to get back on topic. He needed to wrap up this conversation and move on to the next person on Zoe's list. Because whoever had left that finger for her to find was incredibly dangerous and he wanted them off the streets.

Sawyer steered into the driveway of the quiet beach house, using the high beams to sweep the front yard and foliage on either side of the home. Not for Zoe's current threat, but any threat. It was close to two in the morning and this house was unused about six months out of the year. Luckily his brother had someone who came by and cleaned bi-monthly and just checked on the place but still, he was more alert and vigilant than normal right now.

That 'gift' Zoe had been left was incredibly violent. Which said all it needed to about the person who'd left it. When he pulled up under the house, he inwardly cursed that they didn't have an enclosed garage. None of the houses on the water did though, because of hurricanes.

As soon as he turned off the engine, Zoe jerked awake, her eyes popping open, a tinge of fear visible in them, even under the muted moonlight. Her breathing was slightly erratic but quickly evened out as she gave him a nervous half-smile. "We're here?"

He nodded, his gaze raking over her for what felt like the hundredth time in the last few hours. She'd fallen asleep two hours into their drive and even before that she hadn't been much for conversation. It was clear she was scared and he'd wanted her to get some rest. He was going to make sure she felt safe tonight. If she let him, he knew exactly how he was going to help her take her mind off things. "Let me grab our bags and we'll head in. My brother texted me a couple hours ago, said we'd have the basics like milk and orange juice but later this morning we'll go grocery shopping."

Zoe gave him a real smile. "As long as there's a soft bed, I don't care about food."

At the word bed, all he could envision was her splayed out under him, her hips lifting to his mouth the way he'd been fantasizing about. That one time against her wall wasn't nearly enough. It had been raw and frantic and he wanted a whole lot more, especially after he'd gotten a taste of her. The woman could easily become an addiction, something he didn't mind.

For now he shut that thought down and quickly got out of the vehicle. After retrieving both their bags from the back, he led her out of the open garage and up the stairs to the next level. Like most houses on this stretch of beach front property, they were all raised at least fourteen feet higher than sea level. The stairs led to the wraparound porch and front door. As they ascended it, a cold breeze from the ocean whipped over them.

He heard Zoe make a shivering sound behind him and hurried to unlock the front door. Once inside he disarmed the code—his parents' anniversary date—then reset it and secured the door. "Tomorrow I'll show you around the house and we'll explore the beach."

She nodded, glancing around the foyer and connected living room curiously.

"You want the tour of the house now?"

She lifted a shoulder. "Yeah, I'd kind of like to know the layout of where we're staying in case... Well, in case of anything."

His eyebrows raised at her line of thinking. He'd be here to protect her, but he found her awareness of her surroundings fucking hot. Nodding to their left, he said, "This is the living room." His brother's wife had decorated the place in soft earth tones and most of the art anywhere in the house were black and white photos of ocean life or the beach. A giant ship's wheel hung above the fireplace, with other nautical-themed trinkets on the shelf under it. The tour of the house was as quick as possible with the living room, dining room, kitchen and office downstairs and four bedrooms upstairs. The place was huge for a beach house.

Once they reached the last bedroom, the master suite, he said, "You can take this one. It's big with a lot of privacy and your own bathroom."

She blinked, seemingly surprised by his offer. "Are you sure?"

He'd been hoping she'd ask him to join her but... "Yes. You've been through a lot. Plus I'll hear anyone coming up the stairs. No one will make it to your room without getting through me."

At his words, she wrapped her arms around herself and swallowed hard. Her newly straightened hair was windblown and tousled around her face from their short walk up the stairs. Right now she looked impossibly beautiful and scared. Shit. Maybe he shouldn't have said anything.

"Not that anyone's going to find us here." Screw it. He'd been trying to maintain distance between them because it seemed clear that was what she wanted, but he wasn't going to bother anymore. Not comforting her went against his nature and she clearly needed it. Besides, he hated the invisible wall she kept trying to put between them. He crossed the hardwood floor to where she hovered near an oversized trunk at the end of the king-sized bed. When he went to place his hands on her hips, to pull her close, she set a hand on his chest and shook her head.

"Don't."

That one word made him freeze. "Don't what?"

"Touch me right now." Her voice cracked on the last word before she swallowed hard again. "If you do, I'll invite you to join me in bed and I don't think that's the smartest thing right now."

"Why not?" he asked bluntly. Because getting naked with her sounded like a damn fine idea.

Her eyes widened at his question. Clearly he'd taken her off guard. She nervously cleared her throat. "Well, it's just not. After everything that happened with you and my brother and then with me being targeted by some maniac, I don't know. Sleeping together just doesn't seem like a good idea right now."

It was clear she was grasping at straws. The shit that had gone down with her brother was long-buried and had nothing to do with how he felt about Zoe. The feelings Zoe brought out in him were raw and a little primal. He just wanted to claim this woman, to taste every inch of her and then start all over again. She made him feel off-balance in the best way possible. Of course saying that out loud wouldn't be a smart move. She was trying to keep her distance.

He'd let her. For tonight.

But tomorrow — or later today — was a different story. They were under the same roof so he had plenty of time to prove to her that he wasn't into her for whatever bullshit reason Vincent seemed to think. The thought of using a woman that way made him sick.

He let his hands drop and nodded. "Okay."

Her dark eyes narrowed slightly. "Okay?"

"You want me to argue?"

Her lips pulled into a thin line. "No, you just have this...look in your eyes right now."

Sawyer raised an eyebrow. "Look?"

"It's very mischievous."

He snorted at her word choice. "Mischievous is for little boys. Something I am not," he murmured.

For a moment her eyes grew heavy-lidded as they strayed over the length of his body, down to his feet, pausing right below his belt on her upsweep, before she seemed to remember herself and focused on his face. "No, you're definitely not," she said softly.

Those words made his dick ache. Damn it, he wanted to say more. So much more, but he didn't. He knew if he pushed her right now he could get her naked and underneath him, begging for more. But he didn't want her like that, not when she was so vulnerable and not when he had to push. He wanted her to come to him.

Rubbing a hand over the back of his neck, he nodded toward the doorway. "Come on, let's get our bags and get settled in." Then he wanted to do another sweep of the house. But he didn't say that out loud since she was already nervous enough.

Unfortunately they'd be sleeping in separate rooms.

But come the morning, all bets were off. He was going to show Zoe all the reasons they should be together.

CHAPTER ELEVEN

Zoe stared at the ceiling of her room. A gauzy canopy draped over the four-poster bed but it was sheer and she could see through it. Twinkle lights lined the head of the bed and across the back part of the canopy, but she'd unplugged them, finding them distracting.

Each time the wind whistled up over the ocean, she nearly jumped out of her skin, then wanted to curse herself. She was in a new place, hiding from a deranged maniac and had a sexy man down the hall who'd made it very clear what he wanted from her. At least physically.

She grabbed a pillow and put it over her face, groaning, before tossing it off her. She could be naked and wrapped up in strong, warm arms right now. Deep down she knew she was just being a coward where Sawyer was concerned. The man was walking, talking sex appeal, but more than that he was honorable and simply put, a good man.

If he just wanted casual he wouldn't have brought her here, protected her. Right? It didn't make sense. She guessed he could have gotten her out of the city out of a sense of duty, but that didn't feel right. Not when she had family to stay with. No, he'd gone the extra mile in a way most people wouldn't have. He'd even put off his first official week of work to bring her here. That was…pretty incredible. He hadn't wanted to tell her either, but she'd gotten the details out of him on the drive here.

The more she thought about him, the more elusive sleep became. She was too caught up in her own thoughts, letting her past experiences mess with her potential future. God, she really was a coward.

Rolling over, she looked at the bedside clock. It was five in the morning and she wasn't going back to sleep. Definitely time for some coffee. She doubted Sawyer would be up, not when he'd driven them to Saint Augustine and she was almost certain he'd still been up after she'd fallen asleep last night.

Wearing long, green and white striped pajama pants and a matching spaghetti strap top, she dug a cardigan out of her bag and slipped it on before leaving her room. The heat was on, but there was still a chill in the air.

The floorboards creaked beneath her when she stepped out of the room and she winced at the over-pronounced sound. A long Persian runner ran the length of the hallway and another down the wooden stairs so she kept to it so her feet wouldn't get chilled.

She'd barely taken three steps when Sawyer appeared in the doorway to his room. Her heart jumped in her throat at his sudden appearance. When she saw the gun in his hand, her eyes widened. She knew he'd brought at least one, but seeing it put her on edge. It was just a reminder of the danger she was in.

"Hold on," he murmured, before disappearing back into the darkness of his room. A second later he was back, sans gun. "Everything okay?"

"Yeah." She nodded, her gaze straying over his bare chest. He had on loose drawstring pants that she had a feeling he was only wearing because of the situation. Something told her he was a commando kind of guy.

He placed his hands on the frame and she followed the action, drinking in the lines and striations of his muscular arms. Was he doing that intentionally, trying to distract her with his sex appeal? If so, it was working. When his hands tightened suddenly, his arm muscles flexing, she met his gaze to find him watching her intently. *Hungrily.*

"Did I wake you up?" she asked, resisting the urge to wrap her arms around herself. She wasn't scared of him—never that—just a little nervous.

He shook his head, his green eyes practically smoldering. She wished he would say something. Instead he just watched her, the heat simmering there undeniable. He was making it clear what he wanted from her without saying a word.

She cleared her throat, resenting him a little for making her feel nervous and out of sorts. No one had ever had this effect on her body, not even her ex. But it was like Sawyer was just attuned to her. She had to keep her distance or else she'd never be able to resist him. "I'm going to make some coffee, do you want some?" Amazingly, her voice sounded normal, nothing like her quaking insides.

His gaze landed on her lips. "That's not what I want this morning," he murmured, his voice a lower octave than she'd ever heard.

Heat pooled low in her belly and her nipples automatically pebbled. "What do you want?" Why was she asking? She knew the answer. Some part of her desperately wanted him to say the words, to spell out exactly what he wanted. Seeing him like this, knowing he'd dropped everything in his life to help her out when he didn't have to, was one of the biggest turn-ons she could have ever imagined.

He dropped his arms and stepped out of the doorway, his prowl reminding her of a predator on a hunt. "I think you know."

"Say it," she whispered, surprising herself.

"Take off your sweater." His words were a quiet order, the demanding note behind them increasing the warmth between her legs by a hundred degrees.

Without pause, she shrugged it off, letting it fall to the ground in the hallway. What was going to happen between them—again—was a foregone conclusion. She could try to keep her distance but spending time alone with Sawyer pretty much made her lose all self-control. And she was okay with that. The payoff would be worth it if their first time together was any indication. She might be nervous about how things would play out between them but he was worth the risk.

"Now your top." His gaze was still intent on hers, those dark green eyes pinning her in place.

She was so damn slick between her legs it was almost embarrassing. He hadn't even touched her and she was ridiculously turned on. This time she did pause, just for a moment, before peeling the thin pajama top off. He'd seen her naked, but that had been fast and furious in her kitchen. She hadn't even taken her chemise all the way off, it had ended up bunched around her waist.

Now things had slowed down and it was nerve-wracking. Her top joined her sweater on the floor. Before he could give her another order, she strode past him into his room.

The drapes were pulled back but the blinds were shut, letting in very little light. She could see enough to make out the queen-sized bed and blue and white French country décor.

She hadn't made it past the threshold before he was behind her, *on* her, his big hands clutching her hips as he tugged her back flush to his torso. His skin was hot against her back. The skin on skin was too much and not enough.

He let out a soft growl as his hands slid up her hips, spanning her waist and stomach before cupping her breasts. He didn't touch her nipples though, just held her gently. She had curves but she wasn't exactly overflowing up top. Not that Sawyer seemed to mind.

Leaning down, he nipped her earlobe, his breath warm on her face. His erection pressed insistently against her back, but he seemed to be taking his time. Which was fine with her.

"I'm not walking away from this thing between us, Zoe," he whispered darkly, his words sending a shiver through her. She didn't know what to say and he surprised her by continuing. "If you're thinking of using me for sex this morning, fine. But it's not just about fucking for me."

His words sent a thrill through her. She loved the way he was so honest about everything. After dealing with a maniac who couldn't take no for an answer, who didn't understand the difference between reality and his crazy fictional world, being with someone as blunt as Sawyer was a breath of fresh air. He said what he meant and she knew that if she told him to stop, even if he was inside her, he would. No questions asked.

She trusted him implicitly. Above all, that was so freeing.

"What is it about?" The question came out as a whisper. In the mostly-darkness, with her back to him, it was easy to be brave, to say what she wanted.

He stilled behind her for a moment and she wondered if he'd respond at all. Slowly, he took her earlobe between his teeth, pressing down on the sensitive area just as his hands fully cupped her breasts, his thumbs swiping over her nipples. Too many sensations twined through her as she arched into his hold.

"I want you to remember the feel of me inside you even when I'm not with you." He dropped one hand from her breast to sweep her hair out of the way. Slowly, torturously, he kissed a hot path along the back of her neck. Her head fell forward as he teased her, both with his mouth and his hand, which gently stroked over her nipple in soft little circles.

Knees weak, she leaned back into him. His other hand snagged around her waist, pulling her tighter to him. His thick length pressed insistently against her and her inner walls clenched, unfulfilled. She desperately wanted to feel him inside her.

"It's about you trusting me," he continued, surprising her.

She'd been so caught up in how he was making her feel she'd forgotten she asked him a question. "I do."

He stilled again for a moment before he continued his slow dance of kisses, now along her shoulders. She shivered and reached back to hold him. There wasn't much she could grab other than his behind and that was fine with her. When she dug her fingers into him, he made a sexy, growling sound against her skin.

Before she knew it, he'd moved them to the bed and she was flat on her back against the tangled sheets. The second her back hit the covers, his hands were on the waist of her pajama bottoms, tugging them and her panties down. Her toes curled into the sheets as she was completely bared to him.

He still had on his drawstring pants, something she wanted to remedy soon. She reached for him, ready to push them down, but he moved lightning quick, his hands grasping her wrists.

"Shit," he murmured, his gaze hot on hers.

A small sliver of alarm twisted through her, her heart rate increasing. "What?"

He gritted his teeth. "No condoms. I fucking forgot them." Self-loathing pulsed off him.

She'd already told him she was on birth control so... "I'm clean."

Crouched above her, his big body so beautiful she wanted to stroke every inch of it, he rasped out, "Me too."

That was that. If it had been anyone else, under any other circumstances, she'd have waited to do tests but she trusted him. "Okay."

He sucked in a shallow breath and his eyes dilated, the hunger there so damn palpable she could reach out and touch it. When he looked down again, his laser-like focus narrowing between her legs, she fought the urge to squirm under that intensity. She really wanted to taste him—all of him—but it was pretty clear what he had in mind.

And she definitely wasn't going to stop him.

Reaching out, he slid a finger down her slit and let out a groan. "You're so damn wet," he murmured. In her kitchen, he'd been unsteady. Not now. Now he was in control. His jaw was clenched tight and the tendons in his neck kept flexing, telling her he was barely holding onto that control, but this was different than before. She loved it.

Slowly, gently, he slid a finger inside her and they both groaned as she tightened around him. "Fuck, Zoe. You're going to kill me."

She shifted lower against the bed, forcing him deeper inside her, her breathing erratic and unsteady. His gaze snapped to hers, a wicked grin spreading across his face before he dipped his head down between the apex of her thighs, his mouth zeroing in on her clit as if he knew exactly what she needed.

And he did.

The man apparently forgot nothing about what she liked. His tongue teased against her pulsing bundle of nerves, the rhythm of his thrusting finger perfect. Almost alarmingly so. Without warning he slid another finger inside her, her slick body welcoming him as his tongue and teeth continued stroking against her.

She slid her fingers through his short hair, her back arching off the bed as she grinded against his face and fingers. He made her feel so amazing it was hard to be self-conscious as she immediately started to build higher and higher to climax.

All her muscles pulled tight, her body tensing for what she knew was to come. It should be too soon but she'd been primed forever, just lying in bed thinking about Sawyer. The man was her walking, talking fantasy come to life.

Rough around the edges, protective, smart, sexy as hell, and didn't worry that she was some delicate flower between the sheets. He was a very unique man, one she didn't plan to let get away. She'd be insane to do that.

"Come for me," he growled against her clit. The desperateness in his voice was what pushed her over the edge.

Letting go, her orgasm punched through her, slamming into all her nerve endings as he continued teasing her clit. It finally got to the point where it bordered on painful. She tightened her grip on his head and tried to move back, but he beat her to it.

He withdrew his fingers and sat up before he quickly covered her body with his. His mouth crushed over hers, his tongue demanding entrance as he wrapped his arms around her.

She loved the feel of him covering her, his huge body one protective embrace as he rolled his hips against her, his erection rock hard. She reached between them and slid her hand down his pants. No boxers, just commando.

Groaning into his mouth, she wrapped her fingers around his thickness. He made a strangled sound and thrust into her grip, letting her stroke him up and down until finally he tore his mouth from hers.

"I want to take you from behind." His words were guttural, sexy, and he was sort of asking.

She could see that raw look in his eyes. He wanted to just flip her onto her knees and pound into her. If they'd been a couple or had been dating longer, she knew he'd have done just that. But he was holding back. Probably because he was worried about her after the crap she'd dealt with recently.

Well, he didn't need to worry. Without pause, she rolled over and pushed her ass back to him. That seemed to set him off. "Fuck," he growled, the sound raw and strained. She looked over her shoulder, watching his hands shake as he stripped off his pants.

Then he was back on the bed, one of his big hands smoothing down the length of her spine as the other guided his hard length to her entrance.

When he pushed inside her, she let her head fall forward. He filled her completely in this position, her inner walls molded around him as if they'd been made for each other. For how she felt right now, maybe they had. The man had gotten under her skin in a way no one ever had.

The chemistry was almost too much. And at the same time, not enough. She simply couldn't get enough of him, wondered if she ever would.

When he pulled back and slid into her again, she moaned his name. "Sawyer."

Her clit was pulsing, begging to be touched again. Feeling bold, she reached between her legs and started stroking herself as he began thrusting.

"Oh yeah, touch yourself, sweetheart. Come on my dick," he rasped out, his voice a bare whisper.

His words set her entire body aflame. Her breasts felt heavy, her nipples tingling, as he grabbed one of her hips. He found a delicious rhythm that had her inner walls growing tighter and tighter around him. When he reached up and cupped one of her breasts, unexpectedly tweaking her nipple between his thumb and forefinger, she cried out.

Another climax slammed into her, the pleasure more intense than before. Maybe it was because he was inside her, completely filling her, hitting that very important spot. Whatever it was, she clawed at the sheets, moving her body back to meet his with each intense thrust as she pushed over the edge.

He had to feel her coming around him, her inner walls tightening out of control as she called out his name again. Or she tried to. It was hard to think let alone speak straight. Her words were a garbled mess.

When one of his hands tightened almost painfully on her hip and he dropped his other hand from her breast, she knew he was about to let go too.

Just like that, he did, his thrusts erratic as he cried out, releasing himself inside her in long, hot streams. It seemed to go on forever as they lost themselves with each other.

As he came down from his high, he let out a protesting groan as he pulled out of her. Her inner thighs were sticky with both their juices, but she was glad when he didn't rush to grab something to clean up.

Instead, he turned her over, which was good because her limbs were useless noodles right now. Covering her face in sweet kisses, he pulled her close, his big hands sliding up and down her back and settling on her ass as he rolled onto his back, pulling her on top of him.

Spent, she laid her head on his chest, her arms loosely wrapped around his neck. She could feel his heart beat against her chest, the staccato rhythm steady, if a little faster than normal. "That was amazing," she murmured, feeling lethargic and satisfied, glad they had nowhere else to be today. Because they were definitely doing that again soon.

After a few minutes passed, he rolled his hips once, his cock already half-hard against her lower abdomen. "Feel like taking a shower with me?"

She grinned against his chest without looking up at him. "You're a monster," she muttered.

"You like it."

That was true. She should be too damn tired but...who was she kidding? If he was up for another round, she was taking full advantage.

CHAPTER TWELVE

She looked around the grocery store parking lot, making sure no one was paying any attention to her before turning her attention back to Zoe and her new lover. She'd tracked Zoe to Saint Augustine, right down to the beach house she was staying at. It had been so easy, tracking Zoe. All she'd had to do was use the ADM—android device manager—linked to Zoe's phone. It was Zoe's own fault for being so stupid, for leaving her email open at work and giving anyone access to her personal information. After that, now she could track Zoe anywhere as long as she had her phone on her and turned on since all her accounts were synced.

So far she hadn't been able to properly scout the house without getting caught because the street was a dead end and the houses were so far apart she'd be spotted easily if someone looked out a window. She could have gone jogging down the street, but she hadn't wanted to risk being recognized. Not when she'd come so far.

Instead she'd parked at a gas station at the end of the road where the house was—and waited. It'd been long and tedious to just wait but she didn't mind being patient. And making sure Zoe paid for all she'd done was worth sitting in her car all day. She wasn't going to drag this out much longer, not when she had more pressing matters to deal with back home.

With Zoe out of town, she could kill two birds with one stone. Eliminate Zoe and focus on her next love interest. Now that Braddock was dead she needed someone else to fill her bed. Someone better than him. Someone kind and not so narcissistic. While Braddock had had many wonderful attributes, what with being a renowned surgeon and so wealthy, he'd lacked so much emotionally. Her next lover wouldn't be like that. No, he'd be happy to have someone like her in his life. But only if Zoe was gone.

Now it appeared she'd have the chance to get rid of her sooner than she'd hoped. Just as she'd been about to head back to her motel, she'd seen Zoe's male friend pulling out onto the street. Now the bitch and he were at a grocery store. Instead of following them inside, even though she desperately wanted to get a peek at Zoe's face, to see if she was stressed or scared, she wasn't going to pass up this opportunity.

She knew exactly where they were, and would have a limited time to check out the exterior of the house and come up with a game plan. Well, she didn't have to decide now. Steering out of the parking lot, she could barely contain the thrill that punched through her.

Soon justice would be done. Zoe would be gone forever. She just needed to decide how she was going to kill Zoe. She'd played out too many fantasies in her head. The one thing she was certain of, she'd have to shoot Zoe's lover. Maybe not kill him first though. A gut shot so he'd bleed out while Zoe watched. Maybe even make it look like Zoe had killed him then killed herself.

That thought brought on a rush of pleasure. She'd have to make sure she cleaned up all her DNA if she did that, make it appear as if she'd never been there. Once she scouted the house, she'd be able to figure out her exact plan better.

The only thing certain right now was that Zoe was going to die, but she'd watch her friend go first.

Sawyer looked out the glass sliding door leading to the lower back deck, a frown tugging at his mouth. The sun was now setting and ever since they'd left the grocery store that morning, he hadn't been able to shake an uneasy feeling. Not the kind where someone was looking at him through a sniper scope, but the kind where something bad was on the horizon.

He could just chalk it up to the whole situation of being in hiding, but something tickled his senses.

"You look way too tense," Zoe murmured, her arms coming around him from behind as she laid her head on his back.

He covered her arms with his own, linking his fingers through hers. She'd been impressive today, not complaining once that they hadn't been able to leave except to get groceries. Not that he'd expected her to, but he knew how civilians could be, especially after his last month of training for Red Stone Security. People didn't like feeling as if they were caged, even if the surroundings were nice, and it could make them react poorly. Not Zoe. "Sorry we couldn't hit the beach today."

She laughed lightly against his back. "Stop apologizing for protecting me. Besides it's cold outside and I've had a lot of fun in here with you." Her voice took on a seductive quality, her grip around him tightening.

Grinning, he reached up and pulled the curtains into place over the door before turning to pull Zoe into his arms. They'd definitely found ways to occupy their time. He'd already fallen hard for this woman. The sex was part of it; their chemistry undeniable, but it was more. Way more. Once they returned to Miami he wanted something serious with her. Hell, he wanted serious right now. "So what did your brother and mom say?" She'd gone up to her room—which he was now sharing with her—to call her family.

"Vincent wants me to come home but my mom's glad I'm here with you. She likes you a lot." Zoe paused, watching him carefully, as if debating something.

He liked her mom too but decided not to respond when it was clear she wanted to say more. He'd noticed that she did that sometimes, was silent while she gathered her thoughts. When she didn't continue, he chose to break the silence, tightening his arms around her waist. "What is it?"

Zoe bit her full bottom lip, her dark eyes filled with too many complex emotions for him to sift through. One of her hands was on his hip but she placed the other on his chest. "You don't have to say yes, but…if it's safe enough by then, my mom wanted to invite you over for Christmas dinner. But only if you don't have plans, don't feel obligated or anything," she rushed to add.

Her invitation warmed him, telling him she really did want him in her life. Not just physically. The invitation might have come from her mom, but Zoe wouldn't have mentioned it if she didn't want him there. Still, he wanted her to ask. "Your mom invited me? What about you, do you want me there?"

Her cheeks flushed red. "What do you think?"

"I think I want to hear you say the words."

"You are maddening," she muttered, a grin pulling at her lips. "Fine, I would like to invite you over for Christmas dinner—and Christmas Eve. It's not a big deal, but on Christmas Eve we all get together to open one present and play dirty Santa." For just a moment, a raw vulnerability bled into her gaze before she quickly covered it.

"I'd love to," he murmured, dropping a soft kiss on her lips. He hadn't planned to go home this year because it would have been too much travel after just starting a new job, but especially not now when things with Zoe's stalker were still up in the air. Sawyer had spoken to Carlito a couple hours ago and they were still running down leads. He knew they couldn't hide out forever and would have to head back to Miami for Christmas no matter if the guy was caught or not.

Her eyes lit up for a second, but then she frowned. "You're sure? I don't want you to feel pressured."

"*Zoe*," he rasped out before crushing his mouth over hers in a swift, claiming kiss. Though he hated to, he pulled back, his heart rate already kicking up at the simple taste of her. "I don't feel pressured. I want to date you—and only you." While his experience with real relationships was limited, he figured he needed to make this clear since it apparently wasn't.

She watched him for a long moment, her beautiful eyes unreadable. Finally she pressed against his chest. "I've got hot chocolate in the kitchen—instant, so don't get too excited," she said, a smile tugging at her lips before her expression turned serious. "Let's drink it while it's hot and... I need to tell you something."

His gut clenched at her words and worried expression. He told her that he wanted to date only her and her response was that she wanted to tell him something over instant hot chocolate. That did not sound promising. "Okay."

Once in the big kitchen she took a seat at the center island, waiting for him to join her before she picked up her mug. "I didn't know if you wanted marshmallows," she said, nodding at the open bag. He noticed she'd added a ton to hers.

"Thanks." He tossed some in, letting them melt while he waited for her to say whatever it was she needed to get off her chest. He just hoped it wasn't that she didn't want to see him, because he wasn't sure how he'd deal with that.

"I've only had one serious relationship, which is probably pretty sad, but there it is. I was with Rubin for a couple years. We had a lot in common and... Well, that's not important." Her cheeks flushed slightly as she continued. "We were serious and heading for marriage. Or, I mistakenly thought we were. The day after we graduated from med school, he..." She swallowed hard, but didn't take her gaze from Sawyer. "He ended things because he was getting back together with his ex. He said he'd wanted to wait until after exams to end things because he didn't want to affect my finals—which was actually really nice of him. The thing is, he was a decent guy. I wish I could talk trash about him and say how awful he was, but... I guess what I'm trying to say is I had the perfect guy on paper and it didn't work out because I wasn't enough—"

"Bullshit," Sawyer snapped out.

Her eyes widened. "What?"

"The fact that you didn't work out with him isn't because you weren't enough." He scowled, the very thought pissing him off.

"Well, whatever the reason, we didn't work out because he was still hung up on his ex. I really like you, Sawyer." God he loved it when she said his name. "I'm falling for you faster than I imagined possible to fall for anyone and, I just..." She trailed off and it took him a few seconds to understand what she was saying—or wasn't saying.

Hoping he wasn't completely in left field with his assumption, he took her free hand in his. "I'm not still hung up on Audrey." Even saying her name after so long felt odd. He hadn't thought about her in years. Zoe stiffened slightly but didn't pull away and for that he was glad. "I loved her, or thought I did. Back then all I did was travel and as crass as it sounds, she was someone to come home to." Things had been purely physical between them, he just hadn't been able to tell the difference, something he didn't think Zoe needed to hear right now.

"I was in a different place then, gone out of the country more often than not and...if you're worried that I'm settling or that you're second to *anyone*, that's insane. What I feel for you is different than anything I've ever felt before. I can see a future with us." Putting that out there made him feel so damn exposed but he needed her to know, to understand.

She pushed out a long breath, as if she'd been holding it, before a real smile broke out over her face. The kind that made his entire body react. "I can too."

Thank God. "Since we're in confession mode, you should know that I followed you yesterday. After you told me to leave and ran your errands... I was fucking worried and tailed you to make sure no one else was watching you. Once you made it to your street, I headed home." Now he wished he'd just followed her all the way to her driveway considering the 'present' she'd been left on her doorstep. "After what you've been through, I just want it out there."

Her eyebrows raised a fraction. "You followed me to the salon and everywhere else?"

He nodded.

She let out a short laugh. "I think I'm more embarrassed than anything that I didn't even notice."

"If you had noticed then I need to find a new job," he murmured, thankful she didn't seem angry at him.

Shaking her head, she smiled then leaned closer to him. His whole body tightened as he moved in to cover the distance between them. His cell phone rang, making them both pause. Zoe let out a soft groan and sat back in her seat, plucking her hot chocolate from the counter. "You better see who it is."

Even though he didn't want to, he pulled his phone from his pants pocket. When he saw Detective Duarte's name on the caller ID, he answered immediately. "Yeah?"

Zoe straightened, watching him carefully.

Carlito's voice came through crystal clear. "Everything's fine, just calling to check on you guys and to let you know I've put in a call to the Saint Augustine PD to let them know what's going on and to give them your address. If you see a patrol car drive by more than once tonight, that's why."

Sawyer's eyebrows raised in surprise. "Thanks. I'll let Zoe know. Any news?"

The other man sighed. "Nothing solid. Klein's wife gave me a list of possible women her ex either had an affair with or was possibly still having one with. She hadn't talked to him in months and isn't sure he was sleeping with all of them, but she had her suspicions. It's pretty extensive for one guy." He sounded disgusted.

"You want Zoe to look at it?" Maybe she knew one or more of the women, which might not mean anything at all, but it could be a help if there was some connection to Zoe and Klein that intersected somewhere.

"Yeah, I've just emailed it to her but wanted to give you guys a head's up in case she wasn't checking often. You sure you guys are doing good?"

"Yeah, locked down tight. Security system's top of the line and I'm armed."

After a few more minutes of small talk, they disconnected and he relayed the message to Zoe.

She slid off her seat, barely concealed hope in her eyes. "I'm going to grab my phone and check my email."

"I'll head up with you. Once you've read it, we can use the hot tub on the upper deck." Because even if someone was using a high-powered rifle with night vision—from a boat on the ocean—they were still safe on the upper deck. He'd already scouted it out and the layout gave them privacy from the beach. His brother had had the house built that way, so they could still use the hot tub in the winter and be blocked from the ocean wind. Of course the two heaters in the hot tub alcove would keep them warm too.

Her eyes glinted with lust as she nodded. "Sounds like a plan to me."

He might hate that the situation was so bad Zoe was forced into hiding, but he was glad things between them had moved so fast. He didn't plan on slowing down either. He wanted everything from Zoe and convincing her that he was in this for the long-term was going to involve a lot of naked time together if he had anything to say about it.

CHAPTER THIRTEEN

Z oe slid into the hot tub, embracing the heat as it enveloped her. Sawyer had been right, this was a great idea. The alarm on the house was set and unless someone used a grappling hook, they weren't getting to the upper deck. Even though it was on the second floor, it was technically three stories up because the first level was on stilts so she wasn't worried about someone climbing up to attack them.

Since Sawyer wasn't either, she was letting herself relax. As much as she could anyway. The day spent with Sawyer had been therapeutic.

"What are you thinking?" Sawyer asked, stepping into the water and sitting next to her. He'd slid his gun under one of the towels, keeping it close just in case.

Which was fine with her. She shifted and turned sideways, putting her feet in his lap, thinking that they would be naked in a few minutes. She wasn't even sure why they'd bothered with bathing suits. "That this is a weird kind of vacation but there's nowhere else I want to be right now."

He gave her one of those boyish grins that made butterflies take off inside her. Sawyer was all man, with a rugged face, sharp lines and striations showcasing all his muscles, but sometimes when he smiled he looked a decade younger. The man was sexy and adorable at the same time. "I agree."

"You sure you're not going to get in trouble at work for this?" She held up her hands when he frowned, his expression darkening. He'd already reassured her, but she still felt bad that she'd pulled him away from a new job. "I'm just making sure. Taking a management position with Red Stone is a big deal."

He sighed but nodded. "Trust me, it's fine. I explained everything to Porter Caldwell and he was more than happy to let me off to help you."

"Happy?" Zoe had met all the Caldwell brothers and they were pretty intense. So was Sawyer, but still, she couldn't imagine Porter being 'happy' to let Sawyer take time off so soon after starting.

Sawyer nodded. "Apparently you helped out Red Stone not too long ago when one of their agents was kidnapped. Got them access to the hospital's security feeds without involving law enforcement?"

"Oh, right." She hadn't forgotten, but she hadn't realized Porter Caldwell had known about it. Though she should have. "I had to go on a date with someone for that," she muttered, remembering how annoyed she'd been at the time. And relieved when everything had worked out.

Sawyer laughed. "I take it everything ended up okay?"

She nodded. "Yep. The woman doesn't work for Red Stone anymore and as far as I know, she actually freed herself from the kidnapper, but things definitely worked out since she's now blissfully married to an honest to goodness billionaire." Her brother had gone to their wedding over the summer.

Sawyer let out a low whistle.

"I know, right?"

Sawyer started massaging one of her feet, his knuckles rubbing over her arch, his eyes going heavy-lidded as he watched her. "So, you don't mind breaking the rules just a little bit, huh?"

Grinning, she started to answer when Sawyer stilled and dropped her foot. He turned, going for his gun when she heard, then *saw* the problem.

Viola was standing in the doorway to the bedroom, a gun pointed directly at Sawyer's chest.

Zoe's heart felt as if it stopped as she watched the other woman step out onto the deck, her normally sleek black hair a tangled mess around her pretty face. Her blue eyes were glassy and her black jacket and jogging pants were shredded in places. *What. The. Hell.*

"Don't move a muscle!" Viola snapped, her hands shaking. She couldn't know Sawyer had a weapon hidden, or Zoe didn't think the woman did.

Zoe felt frozen, unable to look away from the barrel of the gun. As a surgeon, she'd seen firsthand exactly how deadly they could be, what a bullet could do to someone's insides. And right now a maniac was pointing one at the man she'd fallen for. Her stomach roiled.

"No one's moving," Sawyer said, his voice incredibly calm.

That was what tugged Zoe out of her frozen state. She cleared her throat and focused on Viola's rage-filled face. "Viola, what's going on?" Somehow, her voice didn't shake.

The woman's gaze and weapon trained on Zoe. "It's all your fault he's dead!"

Next to her Sawyer stiffened a fraction, but he didn't make any sudden moves. Zoe swallowed hard, trying to remain calm. "Who is dead?"

"Braddock, you idiot." Her voice and hands shook again, making Zoe tense.

"I didn't kill him."

Viola's jaw clenched. "I know that. I did, but it's your fault. He was happy with me, had even left his wife, but the second he strolls back into town he had to see you. It was always about you," she spat, her eyes glittering with surprising tears.

Zoe stared at the woman in confusion and terror. It sounded a lot like her stalker had had a stalker of his own. And Viola was clearly certifiable. Zoe was terrified but knew she needed to keep Viola talking, anything to keep the woman focused on her and not Sawyer. "Why did you get a job at Gerard's practice?" Because Viola had started working there after Zoe had. That couldn't be a coincidence.

Next to Zoe, Sawyer shifted a fraction. It was subtle, the movement barely discernible over the bubbles of the jets.

Her blue eyes narrowed angrily. "To keep an eye on you. I knew you were after Braddock but I thought maybe you'd moved on when you quit at the hospital, when you realized you couldn't have him. That he was *mine.*"

Zoe forced her expression to remain bland, not to reveal her 'what the hell' face to Viola. That was when it hit her. What she'd just read in that email from Carlito. "Your first name is Courtney." There had been a Courtney *V* Rice in the list of names Detective Duarte had sent her. Viola Rice. It was too much of a coincidence that a woman with the same last name of Rice was on that list. Zoe wished she'd figured that out sooner, but it probably wouldn't have done her any good because Viola had somehow gotten into this house past the security system undetected. Zoe couldn't figure out how.

When Viola didn't respond, Zoe continued. "Do you need medical help?" Zoe motioned to the scrapes and cuts visible where her clothes were ripped. Had she gotten cut with glass?

Viola snorted. "Don't act like you care. Get up. Both of you!" She whipped her gaze to Sawyer, but kept the weapon trained on Zoe.

A surreal iciness filled Zoe's veins as she looked at Sawyer. He nodded and slowly stood with her.

"What do you plan to do with us?" Sawyer asked, his movements glacially slow as he stepped onto where he'd been sitting.

Zoe couldn't tell if he was going to go for the weapon or if he was just moving slowly because he didn't want to startle Viola.

"Maybe a murder-suicide." She laughed, the eerie sound bouncing off the walls of the small alcove, the wind whistling over the ocean creepy background music.

"No one will ever believe that," Zoe said, stepping up onto the seat too.

"And you're never going to do anything with the safety on," Sawyer said, derision in his voice.

Viola frowned and turned the gun to the side to inspect it. That was all the distraction Sawyer needed.

Everything seemed to happen in slow motion as he dove for the towel covering his gun. Instinct kicked in as Zoe jumped in the opposite direction over the hot tub ledge. Staying separated would make it harder for Viola to shoot them both.

Viola screamed and swiveled toward Zoe, gun raised. There was nowhere to go.

Pop. Pop. Pop.

Bracing for the pain, Zoe cringed, all the muscles in her body pulling taut as she landed on the wooden deck with a thud. Viola just stood there, staring eerily at Zoe.

Her heart beat out of control. Had she been shot? Too stunned to move, she flinched when the gun tumbled from Viola's fingers, rolling along the ground before hitting the water with a splash. That was when Zoe saw the hole in the woman's forehead. Eyes wide but not seeing anything, Viola fell to her knees before falling onto her face. The other two shots she'd heard must have hit her in the chest, but it was impossible to tell with all that black clothing.

Just like that, the slow motion seemed to speed up like a video fast-forwarding.

"Zoe!" Sawyer was around the big hot tub before Zoe had fully stood, gathering her into his arms. He held her shoulders and raked a gaze over her body from head to toe, inspecting her for a wound that wasn't there.

She had a dozen questions, like how the hell that maniac had gotten into the house or even found them, but she didn't care about *any* of them right now. Sawyer was alive and so was she. If only she could stop shaking. Her teeth chattered out of control and she was vaguely aware that shock was seeping into her system.

Oh, God. They'd almost died. If it hadn't been for Sawyer, she'd definitely be dead. Sobbing, she buried her face against his chest, letting him comfort her as she soaked up all his strength. Her nightmare was over.

CHAPTER FOURTEEN

One week later

Sawyer glanced up from snagging one of Tanice's sugar cookies, then paused when he saw Vincent entering the kitchen. Tension seemed to follow, but Sawyer just ignored it.

Zoe had sent him into the kitchen to grab another bottle of champagne and it had been impossible not to eat another cookie before leaving. She might hate to cook but her mom sure could—and had promised him years of home cooked meals. As if he needed a reason to stay with Zoe. He nearly snorted at the thought.

Vincent opened the refrigerator and grabbed another bottle of champagne, but kept his gaze on Sawyer. "I think we're going to need two."

Sawyer nodded. Things were still awkward between him and Vincent but after he'd saved Zoe's life the other man had seemed to realize he wasn't going anywhere. Which was good, because he wasn't and he didn't want strife with his future brother-in-law. Not that he'd actually asked Zoe to marry him yet, or even told her he loved her, but it was coming. He felt it in his bones.

Vincent shut the door but didn't make a move to leave the room. "Listen, I was a dick—back in California and at Zoe's house—and I'm fucking sorry."

"Your mom make you apologize?"

Vincent let out a bark of laughter and shook his head. "No, but she would if she knew what I'd done." He scrubbed a hand over his buzzed hair. "Seriously, man, I really am sorry. It's obvious Zoe cares about you or she'd have never brought you to meet the family and I just want her to be happy."

"I do too." More than his next breath.

"Yeah, I kinda figured that." He paused, watching Sawyer intently. "So how serious are you two?"

Sawyer picked up the champagne bottle he'd left on the counter and two cookies for good measure. He didn't need to tell Vincent anything, but he was Zoe's brother and despite their history, a good man at his core. Besides, as a fellow SEAL, even if they hadn't been in the same class, they'd always be part of the same brotherhood. And Sawyer didn't want any tension between them so he went for honesty. "I don't know about her, but she's it for me." Though he hoped she felt the same way about him.

After what had happened in Saint Augustine, he was grateful to be able to hold Zoe in his arms, to see her every day. The fact that a woman had managed to break into the beach house—using a small, high stained-glass window from one of the downstairs guest bathrooms as her point of entrance—still gave him nightmares. He'd checked the entire house multiple times and he'd known that window hadn't been linked to the security system—because no one should have been able to get through the damn thing. But Viola Rice had clawed her way through it, not caring that she'd sliced herself up to get to Zoe. And the police had eventually figured out that she'd tracked Zoe using a locator program on her phone. Fucking technology.

Vincent's eyebrows raised the slightest fraction then he nodded once, as if in agreement. "Good."

Zoe strode into the kitchen then, looking gorgeous in a red and gold dress that accentuated all her curves. Without pause she moved into Sawyer's side, wrapping her arm around his waist as he slid his arm around her shoulders. She narrowed her eyes at Vincent. "You giving my man a hard time?"

"We're bonding."

She snorted and swatted at him. "Well you better get in there, it's almost dirty Santa time."

As soon as Vincent had left, Zoe turned into Sawyer's embrace and lifted up on her toes. "Was he bothering you?" Her expression was fierce and loving—and he loved that she actually worried about him, even if he didn't need it. He couldn't remember the last time anyone other than his parents had done that.

"No..." He ran his fingertips down the side of her cheek. "I love you, Zoe," he blurted, not wanting another second to pass before he told her. He didn't care how soon it was or that they hadn't known each other that long. For the past twenty years he'd made life and death decisions on a daily basis and he didn't often second guess himself. And he wasn't going to start now. He loved this woman more than he'd ever loved anyone and he wanted her to know.

Zoe's bright smile nearly blinded him. "I love you too." Pulling a sprig of mistletoe from behind her back she held it over her head, her grin turning playful. "Now get down here and kiss me."

Relief slammed into him at her words. He'd thought she felt the same as him, but to hear her words—it was the best Christmas present he'd ever received. He hadn't realized he'd been worried what her response would be, but hearing her say she loved him too nearly brought him to his knees. Covering her mouth with his, he knew his life was never going to be the same now that Zoe was in it. Until her he hadn't realized anything had been missing but now that she was in it, he was never letting her go.

EPILOGUE

Two months later

Laughing, Zoe collapsed into Sawyer's arms, using him for support. After dancing the last hour in high heels, she was pretty much done. "I need a drink and to rest."

"I thought you'd never ask," he murmured, ushering them off the dance floor, his big hand placed firmly at the small of her back in a proprietary manner she absolutely loved.

It took a while to make it to one of the open bars because the reception after Vincent and Jordan's wedding was packed.

Zoe had known it was going to be big, but she hadn't realized just how crowded it would be. They'd decided to do an outside wedding at a place right on the water. Twinkle lights were strung up everywhere, the sparkly atmosphere exactly what Jordan had wanted. Even though it was the tail end of winter, it was Florida and the weather was already moving into spring. The entire night had been perfect, something both her brother and Jordan deserved. Now that the newly married couple had left the reception to head out on their honeymoon, Zoe was ready to leave and get some alone time with Sawyer.

For the last two months, they'd spent pretty much every second they could together. Since they both worked a lot, it wasn't as much as she'd like so when he'd asked her to move in with him—two and a half weeks after they'd returned from Saint Augustine—she hadn't had to think about her answer. Coming home to him every night was a kind of perfection she was still trying to adjust to. Part of her was worried she'd wake up and realize all this wasn't real. But she knew it was.

"What's going on in that pretty head of yours?" Sawyer murmured, picking up two champagne glasses for them.

Just like always, her entire body flared to life as his voice rolled over her. "That I'm blessed to have found you," she said, taking one of the glasses.

He gave her one of those unreadable looks before he tilted his head in the direction of a pavilion right on the water. "Walk with me?"

Nodding, she fell in step with him, unsurprised when he slid his jacket around her shoulders. She wasn't even that cold, but he hadn't missed her slight shiver. Because he never missed a thing. "You're going to spoil me."

"Good." As they stepped up into the pavilion, an icy wind blew up over the Atlantic.

She handed him her glass and slid her hands into the sleeves, wrapping her arms around herself. Okay, maybe it was colder than she'd thought. As she tucked her hands into the pockets her fingers touched a small box.

At the same moment, Sawyer got a deer-in-headlights look. It took her all of two seconds to figure out why. Or at least make an educated guess.

Surprising her, he sighed and pulled her close, his big hands resting on her hips possessively. "Pull it out," he said, almost resignedly.

With trembling fingers she did, her eyes widening when she saw a small red box. She supposed it could be earrings but... "What is this?" she whispered, her gaze fixed on his.

He swallowed hard, the vulnerable side of him he so rarely showed shining through for a fraction of a moment. "I wasn't going to do this here, but..." He took it from her hands and got down on one knee. When he opened the box to reveal a marquis cut diamond engagement ring, her breath caught in her throat. "Marry me, Zoe."

Tears blurred her vision as she nodded. "Yes," she rasped out, glad she'd managed to find her voice. Like there was a doubt what her answer would be. It had happened way sooner than she'd expected but surprisingly there was no hesitation in her. Sawyer was one of a kind and he was all hers.

She loved him more than she'd ever thought possible. He was a strong, honorable man and she couldn't wait to spend the rest of her life learning everything about him.

SWORN TO
PROTECT

PROLOGUE

Quinn Brody scrubbed a hand over his face as he exited the empty squad room. He'd transferred to a new shift within the Miami PD less than a month ago and wasn't sure he'd fit with his new team. The guys were nice enough but something was off about their team leader. Nothing he could put his finger on, but Quinn had never ignored his gut.

Hoisting his duffel bag onto his shoulder, he headed down the quiet hallway toward the private exit. This part of the building was practically deserted this time of day. At least this way he wouldn't have to see any civilians or deal with any bullshit on his way out. He could head straight home, crack open a cold beer, watch whatever game was on, then crash. Heaven.

At a soft squeaking sound, he turned and saw Suzanne White, his team leader's wife, stepping around the corner. Her blonde hair was down in soft waves around her face. He'd only talked to her a handful of times and she was always so skittish. Maybe that was the reason he had a problem with his team leader. In his experience cops' wives didn't tend to be so damn jumpy all the time. He couldn't help but wonder what the reason behind that was. Especially since she was wearing sunglasses inside.

Quinn lifted a hand in greeting as he turned back around. "Hey, you looking for Glenn?"

She nodded and started to backtrack, taking two steps away from him. "Yes, but I'll find him." The words came out in a rush and he could hear the worry in her voice.

What the hell? He was a big enough guy, but Glenn was bigger, broader, so Quinn didn't think it was his size. Quinn's instinct propelled him forward, his gut telling him to talk to Suzanne. His legs ate up the distance of the hallway in seconds. "He's in one of the gyms, I'll walk with you."

She shook her head forcefully. "No, it's fine. I know where the gyms are." She took another step away from him. It was subtle, but hard to miss when her body language was screaming she didn't want to be near him.

When she shifted her purse against her side and winced ever so slightly, alarm bells went off in his head. Maybe he was overreacting, but...he was going to go with his instinct. "Your eyes bothering you?"

She glanced over her shoulder toward a set of elevators and a door that marked the emergency staircase. All the desks in the bullpen were empty since everyone was gone. It wasn't like that anywhere else in the rest of the building, but his team was on call the next four days and didn't have to be at the station so it was like a ghost town down here.

"I'm okay," she whispered, a tremble lacing her voice as she turned back to him. "I just...you don't need to come with me." The hint of desperation in her voice punched him right in the gut.

She was afraid. Of him? Maybe. But Quinn didn't think so. He let his bag drop and leaned against the nearest desk, shoving his hands in his pockets so he looked smaller or hopefully less threatening. "What's going on? Is someone...hurting you?" Because those damn glasses made no sense. Combined with everything else, yeah, something was off here. Unfortunately he had a sick feeling he knew exactly what it was.

She swallowed hard, then to his surprise let out a bitter laugh as she took another step back in the direction of the elevators. "Don't bother. I know how things work around here, how you all stick together. Do me a favor and don't talk to me again. Don't even look at me." Before he'd pushed up from his perch she was moving away from him at a fast clip, her sandals snapping against the tile floor.

He shoved up and beat her to the elevator, covering the nearest call button with his hand. "I'll do that if you really want. But I don't think you do… When I was about thirteen my aunt came to live with my family. She'd been in an abusive relationship and at the risk of blowing this out of proportion, so are you."

When she didn't answer, just stood there staring up at him with those sunglasses so all he could see was his own reflection, he continued. "If you need help, we'll head out one of the side doors and I'll take you somewhere safe." He was dead serious. The thought of any woman being beaten on made him feel sick.

She snorted and he was glad for the bit of attitude.

"I'm serious," he continued. "It's safe. I'm not even allowed past the gate because of my gender but I know the woman who runs the place. She can help you. We both will."

Her shoulders drooped and even though he couldn't see her eyes Quinn could imagine the hope draining out of them. "He'll find me," she whispered, dejection in every line of her slight frame.

"Not there he won't. I only know about it because I helped two women escape their abusers about a year ago and the owner approached me." After vetting him, Quinn later learned. His words were quiet but maybe Suzanne sensed the truth in his statement. Or saw it on his face. Whatever it was, he knew the instant she decided to take a chance.

She stepped closer to him now, pushing her sunglasses up on her head to reveal two black eyes. One was darker than the other, as if it was an older bruise. He contained his wince but he couldn't contain the surge of rage inside him. What. The. Hell.

"Normally he avoids my face but he's been getting more violent the past couple weeks. I…don't why. He thinks I'm cheating on him with pretty much any man that looks at me." She sighed, the sound so miserable and ragged it sliced at Quinn.

He remained silent, swallowing back his rage as he let her talk. He didn't want her to sense his anger and think it was directed at her.

"I just want to go to sleep at night and not worry that I'll wake up by being slapped or punched. I just…" Her voice cracked as tears streamed down her face. But she didn't break his gaze. "I just want to be free to live my life without fear."

Throat tight, Quinn nodded. He didn't touch her, just motioned that she could come with him. "You'll have to leave right now, with just the clothes on your back. We'll get your things later." He'd deal with that fucker Glenn later too. Quinn was going to report him no matter what. Just because Glenn wore a uniform didn't make him above the law. If anything, he had more of a duty to respect it.

"Okay." She nodded and placed a hand almost protectively against her flat belly.

It was a move Quinn had seen numerous times from pregnant women. In that moment a sense of new urgency spilled through him. He needed to get her to safety fast. They were silent as they hurried across the bullpen to the adjoining hallway. He wondered why Suzanne was accepting his help when he was virtually a stranger, but he figured the pregnancy, if she was indeed pregnant, had something to do with it. She'd have to be desperate now. Quinn planned to make sure her husband never hurt her again.

When they reached the exit door at the end of it, Suzanne placed a gentle hand on his forearm, the touch so light he barely felt her fingers skimming his skin. Her blackened eyes were full of shadows no woman should ever have to endure. "He'll kill you if he finds out you helped me."

Quinn held back the rage inside him, not wanting Suzanne to see it. She needed to feel safe right now. And if Glenn tried anything, Quinn would take pleasure in pummeling him. Let that bastard see what it was like. Beating on a woman half his size was weak, pathetic. Coming at Quinn wouldn't be so easy.

CHAPTER ONE

Six years later

"**I**'m telling you, the only guy I've dated since moving back to Miami freaked when he realized I was a virgin. From his reaction you'd have thought I said I wanted to set his dick on fire." Athena ran her finger up the stem of her wine glass, unable to hide a grin as her cousin Belle practically snorted out her champagne. It was hard to get Quinn out of her head, even two months later.

"Set his dick on fire, I like that." Belle shook her head and picked up her own glass as Grant, her husband of about a year, walked into the kitchen.

"Hope you're not talking about me," he murmured, moving straight for his wife like a heat-seeking missile.

If Athena didn't love her cousin so much she might be a little sickened by their constant displays of affection. Okay, not sickened, more like a teeny bit envious.

"You know I'd never hurt that part of you," Belle murmured, nuzzling Grant's chest.

"All right, enough of that while I'm in the room." Athena's voice was light as she took another sip of the bubbly cocktail. It felt good to hang with her cousin and relax. After two years of pretty much straight traveling for work, she was thrilled to be living back in Miami and surrounded by her huge, insane family. Especially Belle. She always felt like the two of them were the only somewhat-normal ones of the Manikas clan. Mostly. Belle was only a couple years older and they'd always clicked.

Grant just wrapped his arm around Belle's shoulders and leaned against her as he turned his focus on Athena. She and Belle had been sitting at the island in Belle's kitchen, chatting and drinking while waiting for everyone to arrive.

"So, whose man parts are you setting on fire?" he asked, quirking an eyebrow.

Almost two years ago, before he'd met and married Belle, Grant had been in an explosion that had left him scarred. Faded red marks covered the left side of his face and neck and from Belle, Athena knew he had more on his left arm and back. It certainly didn't take away from the raw power the man exuded. Plus he was a fighter—and would do anything for her cousin, something Athena adored about the man. For a moment she felt bad for joking about setting someone on fire but he didn't seem upset. Still, she needed to remember not to say anything like that in the future. "No one. I was just telling Belle about how I need to lose my virginity."

Aaaaand, that did it. He froze, his arm dropping from Belle's shoulders as he took a not very subtle step toward the entryway. "I need to get the door."

She picked up her tulip-shaped glass, fighting a grin. "I didn't hear the doorbell."

He ignored her and Belle's snickers, mumbling something under his breath as he hurried out.

"That was so freaking mean," Belle said through laughter.

"I know." Athena didn't bother to hide her own laughter now. "Your husband looks like a linebacker but the word virgin scares him? Seriously, what's wrong with men? I just want to get to the good stuff and have non self-induced orgasms. But I can't seem to get that first time out of the way." She had a vibrator, but an orgasm from a toy wasn't as satisfying as she knew it could be. In addition to seeing sex everywhere in the media, she had enough big-mouthed female cousins to know that. And while she wasn't looking for marriage she didn't want her first time to be with just anyone, someone she'd regret moments afterward. Maybe it was the way she'd been raised, but there it was.

Before Belle could respond, the doorbell actually did ring. There was an array of voices and when her new boss at Red Stone Security, Harrison Caldwell, stepped into the kitchen moments later with his beautiful wife on his arm, Athena slid her champagne glass to the side. She thought she'd been subtle but when he laughed she realized she hadn't been at all.

"You're not on the clock and I'm not here to work. But I am looking forward to your presentation on Monday." He shot her a quick grin before kissing Belle on the cheek and heading for the back door. Athena knew where he was going, too.

And if the expression on Mara's face was any indication, she knew what he was doing as well. "Men and their toys," she murmured, smiling at Athena as she followed her husband.

Grant, who was also Harrison's younger brother, had just gotten a new addition to his already ridiculously large grill that was apparently drool-worthy. Or something to that effect. Athena didn't really know or care. She was just as bad at cooking as Belle—much to her mother's continuing disappointment—and a grill was a scary thing.

"Is there anything you want me to do?" Athena asked Belle as she slid off her chair. They'd had the party catered—though Belle wasn't telling anyone but Athena that—so all the food and drinks were arranged artfully in the kitchen and on the lanai. And there was a full self-serve bar set up by the pool.

"Yes, enjoy yourself," she said as Lizzy and a slew of other people spilled into the kitchen.

As Belle started greeting guests, tall and gorgeous Lizzy, who also worked for Red Stone, hooked her arm through Athena's and dragged her toward the back door. "I know there's a bar out there and I'm kid free and done breastfeeding. I need a good drink."

"I'll make you something fun," she said, allowing herself to be propelled outside, laughing at her friend's enthusiasm. "Where's Porter?"

"With Grant, looking at a new gun." Lizzy shook her head as she spoke.

That was a little weird to Athena, but she knew the Caldwell brothers and pretty much anyone who worked for Red Stone Security owned more than one weapon. Most of the men and women in the security department anyway. They were all former military and it was like a thing with them. And they really liked to compare weapons.

She'd recently been hired as an event planner of sorts at Red Stone and her first official day was Monday — though she'd technically been working from home for the past three weeks to get ready for her first day. She was helping out with an event in Vegas in a little over a week and had needed to communicate with various companies out there. Coming into the office hadn't been necessary and she'd liked the freedom to make her own schedule these past weeks.

"Are you nervous about Monday?" Lizzy asked as they rounded the pool. It was filled with multicolored floating candles.

"A little bit. Not about the job, but the presentation itself I guess." For the last two years she'd done contract work as an event coordinator all over the world. Not local wedding type stuff, but big things — tradeshows and festivals. She taken her first job the week after she'd graduated college and because of her willingness to travel — and a lot of freaking hard work — she'd landed a lot of contract jobs. Some better than others. She'd majored in hospitality and minored in public relations, both of which had been an asset to her career.

In the beginning she'd had assistant positions but for the last year she'd taken on bigger projects solo. She shot Lizzy a look when she didn't say anything. Athena could read into the silence. "Okay, I'm nervous about the job too."

"You're going to do great," Lizzy said as they reached the mini Tiki bar. The air was cool in the high fifties and the scent of various meats on the grill filled the air. Even though they'd had the party catered, apparently Grant had insisted on grilling some things himself. "I wouldn't have recommended you apply for it otherwise."

Athena ducked behind the bar and grinned at the array of bottles and other garnishes. She'd been friends with Lizzy the past couple months and knew her friend's tastes by now. As she started mixing up their drinks she said, "If I fail, hopefully they won't blame you."

Lizzy just snorted but eyed the drink mix curiously. "Purple?"

"Just wait. You'll like it." She rolled the rims of the martini glasses in sugar as she spoke.

"Where'd you learn to do this?"

"I bartended a little in college and there were a few occasions on the job where I had to assist because staff called out sick for an event." There'd been a huge festival in Madrid she'd helped out with a year ago where three of the staff had gotten food poisoning, so in addition to everything else she'd been in charge of, she'd had to help with drinks on and off. That had been such a chaotic, ridiculous job.

"At least you'll have something to fall back on if you do fail," Lizzy teased.

"I seriously hope not." She set the two glasses on the bar and strained the purple concoction into them. With the twinkle lights strung up around the lanai and the ones glittering in the pool, the sugar seemed to sparkle around the rim. "This is called a wildcat."

"You have to make me one of those too!" The unfamiliar female voice made Athena look up.

Her eyes widened as her gaze locked with Quinn freaking Brody, the too-sexy-man with an aversion to virgins. He was with the tall woman who'd just asked Athena to make a drink. But she had eyes only for Quinn. Her heart about jumped out of her chest. What was he doing here of all places? At least he looked just as surprised to see her.

She ignored him because she knew if she stared into those dark eyes she'd lose the ability to speak and then she'd inevitably embarrass herself.

The tall, built-like-a-goddess woman with pale blonde hair he was with smiled widely at Athena. "Only if you don't mind," she continued, nodding at the drinks. "They look so good."

"Ah, you can have this one. I made an extra for the lush here." She tilted her head at Lizzy with a half-smile. Athena had planned to drink the second one herself but didn't trust her hands not to shake if she made another. She couldn't believe Quinn was standing right in front of her, looking all casual and annoyingly sexy in dark jeans and a long-sleeved sweater shoved up to his elbows. Why did his forearms have to look so good?

"Ha, ha." Lizzy snagged her drink as Athena stepped out from behind the bar. "Athena, this is Quinn Brody and Dominique Castle. They both work for Red Stone but Dominique is almost as new as you."

Forcing a smile on her face, Athena nodded politely at both of them—and tried to ignore the way Quinn was staring at her. She'd had no freaking idea he worked for Red Stone. He looked a bit like a hungry wolf. Just like on their last date—two months ago. When he'd decided she was too much trouble, being a virgin and all. Jackass. "It's so nice to meet you both." She did a mental fist pump when her voice sounded normal. "I promised Belle I'd help out inside but I hope to see you both around tonight." *Liar, liar.*

"Me too. Thanks again for the drink," Dominique said cheerfully while Lizzy just gave Athena a strange look.

Athena wasn't sure what Quinn's expression was because she'd decided to do the mature thing—and studiously ignore him. When she looked at him it was just a reminder of all those intense kisses they'd shared. He'd lit her body on fire like no one ever had. They'd gone on half a dozen dates and she'd thought they were on the same page, had wanted the same thing. Obviously not, and she thought she'd been over it.

No, she *was* over him. She simply needed to get it together before she saw or talked to him again.

Lord, talk about totally unexpected.

Since she didn't know everyone at the party it was easy enough to make her way inside without having to make small talk. She hurried to Belle and Grant's bathroom, not bothering to use one of the guest ones. Not when she just wanted a couple minutes of privacy and she knew her cousin wouldn't mind.

As she shut the bathroom door behind her, she leaned against it and let out a stupid rush of breath she hadn't realized she'd been holding in. The man should not be able to affect her at all. Not two months after…the hottest dates of her life. She'd been so sure—

No. Just, no.

She would not think about those midnight dark eyes of his and the dirty things he'd whispered to her as he'd nibbled along her jaw, making his way to that sensitive spot on her neck.

When she suddenly wondered if he and Dominique had come here tonight together, as a couple, it was as if she'd been doused with that clichéd ice water. That certainly cooled Athena's thoughts down. Those two probably were together. Worse, they *looked* perfect together too. Both tall, sleek and too sexy for mere freaking mortals like herself.

Sure, Athena might be named for a goddess but she wasn't some siren. Ugh, and she'd worn a boat-neck cashmere sweater, jeans and ballet slipper type shoes. *Super sexy*, she thought sarcastically, wishing she'd opted for heels at least. Even if she did think heels were ridiculous. At five feet two, she could use a bit of height but she liked her feet too much to constantly subject them to torture. God, just seeing him here, with someone so seemingly perfect for him, made Athena feel like that chubby girl in high school again. The girl with the big personality. The girl everyone wanted to be friends with. But not date.

She tried to shake off the old insecurities. Gritting her teeth at herself, she took a deep breath and opened the door. She wasn't going to hide in her cousin's bathroom and berate herself. She'd had a few dates with the man. It hadn't worked out. No big deal.

She was going to get another glass of champagne, enjoy herself and get to know her new co-workers. The thought came to an abrupt halt as she opened the bedroom door and found Quinn leaning against the wall opposite her, almost casually. But she wasn't fooled by his stance.

Nothing about him was casual. Those muscular arms were crossed over his broad chest and there was an almost predatory gleam in those dark eyes. No, that look on his face couldn't be mistaken for anything but raw lust.

Which wasn't exactly a shock. Their attraction to each other hadn't been the issue.

CHAPTER TWO

Seeing Athena again in person had been like a punch to all of Quinn's senses. Everything about her was sensual and he knew she wasn't trying. She screamed sex appeal and it was all in her big blue eyes and sultry mouth. Her bottom lip was perpetually pouty and drove him just a little crazy. He couldn't believe she was working for Red Stone or that she was at Grant's place. He knew she came from a huge family and seeing her again, now the resemblance to Belle was clear.

Her lips pulled into a thin line for a moment, her expression one of annoyance before it quickly morphed into what he thought of as her fake, forced smile. He'd seen it once when a waiter had been rude to them.

Quinn didn't like being on the receiving end of it. "It's good to see you again," he murmured, the urge to reach out and…hell, touch her, was so damn strong. And insane. He had no right to touch her.

Fake smile in place, she nodded once. "Yeah, nice to see you too." Then her brow furrowed as she looked down the hall then back at him. "What are you doing here?"

"Waiting for you."

"Oh." That smile faded only to be replaced by a look of bewilderment.

He wanted to reach out and smooth the lines of confusion from her forehead before claiming her mouth. He was a fucking idiot for walking away from her. The past two months he'd hadn't been on any dates. Though he'd asked two women out, he'd cancelled for both dates, claiming work as an excuse. After Athena everyone else was too bland, too...*not* Athena. He didn't want anyone other than her and that was disturbing.

She'd left her long, espresso-colored hair down in big waves he wanted to run his hands through. The last time he'd seen her she'd looked the same except for a single braid she'd fashioned as a headband of sorts. She'd told him it was Bohemian.

"Ah, I didn't say we'd met because I thought it might be weird," she continued.

He'd figured as much and he'd been too stunned at seeing her to say *anything*. He forced his gaze from her delicious mouth to her eyes. "When did you get hired by Red Stone?"

She lifted her shoulders in a jerky, awkward shrug and flicked a glance down the hall, as if she was biding her time to escape. "A little while ago. My first official day's not until Monday. Is Red Stone the same company you've been with the last six years?"

He'd told her that he was in private security but hadn't mentioned the name of the company and she'd been understanding. His rule was not to tell women who he worked for unless things turned serious. Things had never actually turned serious enough with anyone for him to be open about who he worked for. "Yeah. Listen, I'm sorry about the way things, uh, the way I..." Damn it, he'd never been tongue-tied around a woman before. Not even as a teenager. Looking at Athena now, he couldn't believe he'd been dumb enough to walk away from her. When he'd realized how innocent she was it had freaked him out, to put it mildly. Had made him feel guilty for the dirty things he'd said to her, wanted to do to her. With her—

Her annoyed voice cut through his thoughts. "I really don't want to talk about it. It's not a big deal." But her stiff stance and almost neutral expression said the opposite.

In his limited experience with her, her expressions had always been so open and animated. Now it was clear she was putting a wall between them. Even if he deserved it, it still irked him.

"Okay." He didn't really want to talk about it either. Clearing his throat, he continued, "Dominique is my cousin." For just a moment out by the bar there'd been a flash of something in Athena's gaze.

Maybe he'd read into it, maybe not. Either way, he wanted it clear that he wasn't with anyone else. Not that he was sure it would matter to Athena one way or another.

For the briefest moment, relief flared in those Mediterranean blue eyes. God, those eyes. She wore a soft-looking pale blue sweater that made her eyes seem even brighter against the hue of her skin. Even though it was February it seemed she had a sun-kissed look all year. He wanted to run his hands over all her soft curves, pull her close and devour her mouth. Damn it, he needed to get his thoughts under control. He'd already fucked up with her before, he didn't need to sport a hard-on right now. That'd go over real well.

"She seems really nice," Athena murmured, taking a step into the hallway and away from him.

It took a second for it to register what she was saying as he was mentally ordering his dick to stay down. What. The. Hell. He'd always been in control of his body. Always. Being around Athena again reminded him of why he'd run. Well part of the reason. The virginity thing had been an excuse he'd used to convince himself to end things. Because he'd known that after her, he'd be turning in his bachelor card forever. There was something so sensual and raw about her that called to him on the most primal level he'd just known she could be *it* for him. Quinn hadn't thought he was ready for anything serious or to settle down.

Seeing her again, he couldn't believe he'd actually walked away. Over the past two months he'd tried to convince himself he'd built her up in his head. No such luck.

It was clear she wanted to head back to the party and he didn't want to make her uncomfortable so he tilted his head toward the end of the hallway. "Want to grab a drink?"

"That sounds good." A real smile touched her lips then, fleeting, but long enough for him to feel the effects of it through his entire body. "It was kind of a jolt to see you out there," she said softly as they headed down the hallway.

Something eased inside him at the slight shift in her tone. "Yeah, no kidding. You look like Belle, I can see the resemblance now." She was a little shorter than her cousin, but they were both knockouts.

She lifted her shoulders, no awkwardness there now. "Our fathers are brothers."

"On Monday I'd like to take you to lunch," he blurted. They'd reached the end of the hallway and he knew his time with her was limited. He didn't think she'd want to stand around talking with him much longer even if she did seem more relaxed. "Since it's your first day," he tacked on, even if it was a lie. He'd make it seem casual even if that was the last thing he felt.

A tactician by nature, he was going to play things right this time. Or give it his best shot.

"Ah..." She trailed off as they reached the end of the hallway.

It emptied into the oversized foyer where Grant, Belle and Carlito Duarte, a detective for the Miami PD, were talking.

Carlito—good-looking bastard—smiled at Athena with a familiarity that grated against Quinn's nerves. "Hey, Quinn. Athena, I didn't know you'd be here," he said, moving in to give Athena a hug like he had every right in the world to do so.

For all Quinn knew, the guy did. Athena didn't spare Quinn a glance as Carlito hustled her off toward the kitchen where the sounds of the loud partygoers filled the air.

"Who died?" Belle asked, drawing his attention to her.

Blinking, he looked at Belle and Grant to find her watching him curiously and Grant with an almost knowing expression on his face. "What...oh, I just need a drink."

There was a loud knock on the door, making Belle push out a laughing breath. "I'll get it," she said nudging Grant with her hip. "Go find a drink for Quinn and get me one too while you're at it."

Grant dropped a quick kiss on her mouth before clapping Quinn on the back. "I recognize that look," he said as they entered the half-full kitchen.

Quinn decided to play dumb as he made his way to an ice bucket filled with beers. He grabbed two, handed one to Grant. "What look is that?"

Grant just snorted as he took the beer then set it on the nearest counter. "She's my wife's cousin and a new employee. Tread carefully." There was an unexpected warning bite to his friend's statement as he pulled a half-empty champagne bottle from the same bucket and began to pour a glass, presumably for Belle.

Maybe the tone shouldn't be unexpected. Grant would consider Athena family. "I will."

"Good. Then we won't have a problem."

Quinn took a long swig of his beer, surveying his friends and co-workers talking, eating, laughing. It was good to see everyone having such a good time. Which was the whole point of this party. He'd heard that it had been Belle's idea even though she didn't work for Red Stone. She'd told Grant they needed to have another party to welcome some new employees and to let everyone get together away from work. Various people from work had barbeques often enough but this was different, more organized.

"Where's your dad?" Quinn was going to circle back to the topic of Athena—who must have gone outside with Carlito—but wanted to ease into it.

Grant snorted and leaned against the counter, picking his beer back up. "Watching his grandson—with his girlfriend."

Quinn joined him against the counter. "Keith's dating someone?" He'd known Grant's dad a lot longer than the last six years he'd been with Red Stone. He and Harrison went back all the way to their Marine Corps days and he'd met Keith during a leave.

Grant nodded, amusement on his scarred face. It was good to see him so happy and relaxed. "Lana Gonzalez."

"From the community center?" Keith would have about fifteen years on her but yeah, Quinn could see it.

"Yep. I think he's gonna propose."

That was definitely a surprise but it made Quinn smile. "She's good people."

"Hell yeah." Then Grant lifted his shoulders. "Besides, she makes him happy and he deserves it."

"Anyone who puts up with you and your brothers definitely deserves it."

Grant just laughed in agreement before taking a sip of his beer.

Screw it, Quinn needed to know what he was up against. "So, Athena and Carlito? They together?"

Grant glanced at him, beer halfway to his mouth, which split into a huge grin. "I was wondering how long it would take you to come back to that."

Quinn gritted his teeth. "So?"

"I should make you sweat it, but they're not together. I heard her tell Belle he's too pretty and too much of a player."

A bark of laughter escaped. "That sounds like something she'd say," he muttered. As soon as the words were out, he inwardly cringed.

Grant's eyes narrowed a fraction as he took another pull from his beer. "How would you know?"

Crap. "We went on a few dates a couple months back." Six dates to be exact and he'd been like a man possessed. Right about now, thinking of her outside talking and flirting with Carlito, he wanted to kick his own ass. Being tied to someone like Athena wasn't a bad thing. But some fears ran deep, especially after his only real relationship died a fiery, bitter death.

Now Grant's expression morphed to one of amusement and something else Quinn couldn't define. Shaking his head, a ghost of a smile flickering across Grant's mouth, he picked up the champagne glass and moved away from the counter. "Watch your junk, man."

Frowning, Quinn started to ask him what he meant but the back door opened and the sound of Athena's laughter filled the air, rolling over him and wrapping around him. Out of the corner of his eye he saw Grant headed toward Belle but all Quinn's focus was on Athena. Who was unfortunately still talking with Carlito.

That was okay. Quinn would bide his time. If he could get her to agree to go out with him again, he wouldn't make the same mistake twice. No way in hell.

Glenn White stared at the most recent email message then closed the program on his phone before tossing it onto his kitchen counter. Another fucking rejection letter. This one generic. At least the company had responded at all. Some never did.

Finding work was hard enough but with his prison record it was proving impossible. Any type of law enforcement or security was out because of the crime he'd been charged with. That thought brought up a wave of rage.

He was lucky he'd had family to watch his finances while he was in prison but his money wouldn't last forever. He needed a damn job.

And not something menial. Before he'd been put away he'd been respected. Now, most of his former friends wouldn't talk to him.

They just didn't understand. Almost no one did. If his slut of a wife hadn't pushed him, hadn't talked or looked at other men so often he wouldn't have had to punish her, keep her in line. It was her fault. She'd sometimes gone out of her way to provoke him. He knew it with utter certainty.

If it wasn't for her and Quinn Brody he'd never be in this situation.

Glenn's hands balled into fists as he jerked open the refrigerator door. A beer would take off the edge and after six long years of shitty prison food, he was going to eat and drink whatever the hell he wanted. The only good thing about being locked up was that he'd had a lot of time to work out. He was in better shape now than he'd ever been.

His wife—ex-wife if you wanted to get technical—would never cheat on him again. He'd make sure of it. If he could just find her. It was like she'd fallen off the face of the earth. He'd find her eventually though. He'd never stop searching. At least Quinn wasn't hiding.

That bastard was just living his life, not a care in the world despite what he'd done. Not for long though. Glenn was going to make Quinn suffer first.

It was Quinn's fault his wife had left him, pressed charges against him. She'd made him out to be a monster. Glenn knew deep down that she must have been sleeping with Quinn. That bastard had manipulated Suzanne, preyed on her weakness. That had to be the reason she'd turned on Glenn and their marriage vows. It was the only thing that made sense.

Sure he'd had to punish her sometimes but they'd had so many good times. The sex had been amazing. He knew she hadn't been faking with him, not in the bedroom. If he could just find her, remind her how good they'd been together. He could convince her to come back to him. Make things like the way they were before. He just needed to see her, talk to her. He'd never stopped loving her. And no one would ever love her as much as he did.

His fist clenched around the cold bottle and he realized he'd drank all of it. Blinking, he looked around the empty, sterile kitchen. This place was a hole, but it served its purpose. He just needed a place to rent, to sleep at night. His parole officer could stop by at any time but he wasn't worried about her.

Glenn wasn't worried about anyone but Quinn.

Decision made, he knew that the time had come. He needed to take care of Quinn before he could move on. He'd gotten out of prison a month ago and couldn't find a job, couldn't focus on anything. It was impossible to move on knowing that bastard was out there enjoying his life. He'd have to be careful about it though because no way in hell was he going back to prison.

And Quinn must know where Suzanne was.

She was too stupid to disappear without help. When Glenn started to think about her living without him for six long years, that red haze descended, making it hard to breathe. He chugged his next beer, enjoying the coolness as it went down. Suzanne hadn't respected their marriage vows when they'd been together so he was certain she hadn't respected them since he'd been gone.

It didn't matter that they were divorced—that she'd divorced him. She belonged to him. Always would.

He grabbed another beer and headed to his bedroom. He opened the bi-fold closet door and arousal swept through him at the sight of Suzanne. On the interior wall of the closet he'd put up a picture of her on their wedding day, looking off into the distance, surrounded by white flowers. She looked so perfect and they'd been so happy then.

Until she'd begun disobeying him, flirting with other men.

His head started to hurt as he tried to figure out where things had gone wrong; when she'd started to change, to provoke him. His gaze shifted to the right of her picture where another picture was positioned.

Of Quinn.

Seeing it reminded Glenn of what had to be done, who had to be destroyed. He refused to go back to prison but he didn't mind getting his hands dirty with Quinn. Not one bit.

CHAPTER THREE

A buzz of energy hummed through Athena as she stepped out of the elevator onto her floor at Red Stone Security. She hadn't expected the majority owner, Keith Caldwell, to be at her presentation this morning. People always said he was so intimidating but the truth was, he reminded her of one of her uncles so his presence hadn't fazed her. It was Harrison Caldwell, his son, who had a sort of edge. Nothing she could really put her finger on but the guy was a teeny bit scary. Or maybe intense was the right word.

Either way, the presentation had gone well. Some of the security stuff for her first event would need to be ironed out because that certainly wasn't her strong suit. Everything else though; it felt like she'd just fallen into the right position here. And being able to stay in one place—for the most part because she would still travel about fifteen percent of the time—was heaven.

As she neared the end of the short hallway she heard a familiar male voice, followed by the laugh of her assistant. Freaking Quinn. Of course he'd have to stop by on her first day. She'd chatted with him once more on Friday night but had gone out of her way to avoid the sexy man without seeming like she was. It had been easy enough considering how many people had been at the party.

At least she felt better prepared to see him today. She'd worn black pants with a skinny belt and a pale blue silk top under a tailored jacket that narrowed at her waist, making her look slimmer than she was. Even though she hated them, she'd worn four-inch heels. She'd kept her jewelry a little boring and business casual, at least for the first day. Athena had seen Lizzy this morning before her meeting and her friend had said Athena looked fierce. Right about now, she felt fierce. Perfect timing to be confronted with Mr. Sexy.

When Athena stepped out into the open assistant's area, her heart skipped a beat to see Quinn standing next to Raegan's desk.

And he was wearing a *suit*. She might have to check for drool in a second.

She'd never gone for corporate types before and the thing was, Quinn didn't *look* corporate. He looked like he'd be more comfortable wearing military fatigues and carrying around one of those big guns she didn't know the name for. He was wearing a suit because he had to. Which made him even sexier. There was no way to hide all those sleek predatory lines and muscles.

Sweet Lord the man looked divine. Best. Suit Porn. Ever.

That was when she realized Raegan and Quinn had stopped talking. Crap, how long had she been staring? Not too long if Raegan's casual expression was any indication.

"How did it go?" Raegan asked, her bright smile so big and welcoming it was hard not to adore the woman even though they'd only known each other a week. They'd spent time together before Athena's first day so today would go smoother. The fact that Raegan was Keith Caldwell's niece was a little weird but Athena had learned enough about their family dynamics that she knew Raegan wouldn't keep this job if she wasn't good at it.

"Ah, good I think. Really good."

"Was Uncle…uh, was Mr. Caldwell senior excited about it?"

Athena bit back a grin and nodded. Raegan was pretty much fresh off the farm—literally—and had moved to Miami only six months before from a tiny Midwest town and was trying so hard not to play on her relationship with the Caldwell's. But Athena didn't mind. "He was. Harrison was harder to read until the end and they've got some security concerns but I think it went well. How do you feel about going to the Vegas tradeshow with me next week?"

Raegan's eyes widened but the woman just nodded and seemed to struggle with not getting too excited. "That would be great. Thank you."

Smiling, she glanced at Quinn. "Hey, is everything okay?"

"Yeah, just wanted to see if you wanted to grab lunch." His expression was once again intense and even though those dark eyes didn't leave her face she felt as if he was undressing her with his eyes. She hated that he'd seen her partially naked. Sort of. They'd gotten so far as him taking her top off. Not her bra though.

Worse, she wanted to get naked with the man. Full-on, skin-to-skin. Gah. Stupid attraction. Athena cleared her throat, thankful she didn't actually have to lie. "I have an appointment but—"

"It was rescheduled when you were in with Harrison and the others," Raegan said oh-so-helpfully. "I moved some stuff around and sent the revised schedule to your email and synced all your accounts."

Though Athena was annoyed, Raegan was just doing her job, so she didn't show it. "Thanks." She looked at Quinn, keeping her expression as neutral as possible. "I'll meet you in the lobby in half an hour?"

He paused, his gaze sweeping to her mouth for just a moment before he nodded. "Looking forward to it," he murmured. Then he was gone.

How he managed to make that simple statement sound almost sexual was beyond her. Once he was gone and out in the hallway, she waited a moment, then peeked around the corner of the wall to see him disappearing into the elevators. His ass looked amazing in the suit too. Figured.

"Are you two together?" Raegan asked innocently as Athena turned back around.

"No. Just friends."

Raegan nodded once but it was clear she didn't believe Athena. "Oh, okay. I just met him for the first time today but he seems interested in you. A lot."

Athena didn't want to talk about her personal life at work. At least not on her first day and not until she knew Raegan better so she gave a non-committal shrug. "I'm going to check the schedule for the changes you sent me but after lunch do I have any free time?"

Raegan nodded. "About forty-five minutes before your first conference call."

"Good. Plan to meet with me in my office then. I want to go over some of the Vegas details and we can do some brainstorming."

Raegan blinked once in surprise but said, "That's great."

Athena hurried to her office and did a quick scan of her schedule for the rest of the day and the full week. It was jam-packed and for that she was grateful. She didn't like having spare time at work. Staying busy made her happy and feel useful. She knew she'd have to prove herself here, especially in the beginning, so she wanted to tackle everything full force. It was too soon to know for sure, but from what Athena had read from Raegan's resume and the woman's general attitude, Athena had a feeling she would be a big asset.

After she'd caught up on what she needed, Athena shelved thoughts of work and picked up her purse, coat and stood. She hoped they'd be walking somewhere since she wasn't taking a long lunch or even her full hour. Definitely not on her first day. There was simply too much to do.

Downstairs she found Quinn in the spacious, quiet lobby talking to a man with a Mohawk. The hairstyle seemed out of place but the guy was tall and ripped just like Quinn and had that same military air about him.

Quinn straightened slightly when he saw her, his look going all predator again and sending her mind into a tailspin. What was up with him? She didn't do hot and cold so during this little lunch she was going to make sure he understood they were just going to be friends. Not that she particularly wanted to be friends with him, even though she did genuinely like him. But she could do the mature thing since they were working together.

He was the one with the issue anyway and he'd had his chance with her. Since he'd lost it, anything else happening between them past friendship was a moot point.

She smiled at both men as she approached, shoving all those pesky thoughts aside. Time to put her game face on.

"Athena, this is Travis Sanchez," Quinn said, making quick introductions.

The big man nodded once, an easy smile on his face. "I've heard good things about you from Noel."

Athena blinked once before recognition slid into place. "You're Noel's husband?"

He nodded once, that smile still in place.

"Man she can make some serious hot chocolate." Athena had been at Lizzy's place when Noel had brought her own baby over for a 'play date' with Lizzy's boy. Since neither kid could walk or talk it wasn't much of a play date as far as Athena could tell. It had been more like a reason for the women to talk and relax—and she couldn't blame them.

His face flushed with pride. "Yeah, she makes everything from scratch. I was just telling Quinn that you two should head over to her coffee shop. They do Paninis, salads, soup and stuff like that. You can walk there and the service is fast."

She looked at Quinn, eyebrows raised. "Sounds good to me."

He nodded once.

After saying goodbye to Travis, who was heading back into work, she walked out with Quinn. A cool rush of air rolled over her as they stepped out into the bright day. It might be in the fifties, but she didn't bother with her coat. Not when there were no clouds in the sky and the sun felt so good against her face. "I can't wait until it's spring," she murmured, putting her sunglasses on.

"Summer's my favorite," Quinn said, doing the same with a pair of aviator-style shades that made him look too sexy for his own good.

The street was relatively quiet, with a few people strolling down the sidewalk all bundled up since Florida was actually having a winter. It wouldn't last though, she knew. She'd grown up here and in a couple weeks all those coats and scarves would be in storage for another nine or ten months.

She let out a light laugh at his comment and shot him a quick glance. "I'm guessing because it's bikini weather."

He snorted. "It's been a long time since I've worn one."

She nudged him with her elbow. "Ha, ha. You know what I mean."

He just lifted his shoulders in a casual gesture that shouldn't have affected her at all. But just being near him had her adrenaline pumping. Another good reason not to bother with her coat. It was as if being in his presence just heated her up from the inside out.

"So your meeting was good?" he asked as they reached the cute shop with outdoor seating. He held open the door for her and she couldn't help but notice the way he scanned their surroundings, as if it was second nature.

Athena had noticed that Grant and pretty much anyone who worked for Red Stone Security did the same thing. They were always on alert for any sort of danger. After traveling across the globe, she could appreciate that. "Yeah, I think so. Harrison's hard to read but I have a feeling he'd tell me straight out if he was unhappy with anything. Of course it's too early for him to be unhappy with me."

"Forgive my ignorance," he said as they got in the short line. "But what exactly is your position? I'm a little unclear on the details."

"Well, they've basically created a new position. Not for me specifically, but I'm a good fit." Or she really hoped she would be. "You obviously know how many different functions they provide security for?"

When he nodded she continued. "They're always expanding and now instead of just providing security, they're being asked to host or set up events taking place in Miami. I'm basically going to be an event coordinator for all local events—and an upcoming tradeshow in Vegas, but that's a little different." Something she didn't plan to get into now. "They want me—along with a team—to make sure the event isn't…"

"Boring, military, staid?" he asked, making her laugh as they reached the counter.

Smiling, she nodded because he was dead on. "Pretty much."

After they ordered, he paid for her food—much to her annoyance—telling her it was because it was her first day, but she wasn't so sure. It wasn't worth making an issue over, however.

Travis had been right because the service was quick. With her iced green tea and salad, she and Quinn managed to snag the last table

SWORN TO PROTECT | 141

outside. Considering the gorgeous weather it seemed everyone else had the same idea as they did.

Once they'd settled at their table, Quinn threw her for a loop when he asked, "So what's up with you and Carlito?"

Thankful she had her sunglasses back on to shield her eyes, she paused with her drink halfway to her mouth. "What do you mean?"

"Are you two dating?" Even though she was glad for her own sunglasses, she hated that Quinn had his on too.

All she could see was herself in the reflection. She shrugged, deciding not to give him a straight answer. It really wasn't any of his business. "Why do you care?"

"I want to know what kind of competition I'm up against." He took a bite of his Panini, his body language casual, as if he hadn't just shocked the hell out of her.

Okay then. If he was going to be blunt then she was too. "You ended things with me, Quinn."

His jaw tightened. She was glad for the little sign that he wasn't as calm as he wanted to put off. "I was a jackass."

"No arguments here." She let out a quick laugh and took a bite of her lunch.

"I'd like to take you out again. On a real date."

Well, hell. Of all people she appreciated honesty. She didn't like playing guessing games with people and in her job so many often couldn't be straight with her about what they wanted. Or they were simply indecisive. A serious pet peeve of hers.

"Nothing about me has changed, Quinn." Which, yeah, she could have tried to play coy about *that,* but screw him. She wasn't going to pretend to be something she wasn't. It had taken her years to get over her insecurities and okay, she actually hadn't gotten over them. Not completely. She needed to know where she stood with people. It made her feel grounded, she supposed, in control. And he'd just completely pulled the rug out from under her when she'd trusted him enough to be open with him. "Still a virgin."

He shifted in his chair and she couldn't tell if it was from embarrassment or something else. "I wasn't sure, but yeah, I figured."

"So what, it doesn't bother you now? Or you just got jealous when you saw me with Carlito and decided to act all caveman?" Now that he'd thrown down with the honesty, she was going for broke. She wanted to know what had changed for him in the last two months and the truth was, she felt like she deserved the truth. He'd hurt her more than she wanted to admit.

Sitting back in his chair, he rubbed a hand against the back of his neck. "Shit, not pulling your punches, huh?"

She shrugged.

"I haven't been able to get you out of my head the last two months. I screwed up, and seeing you made me realize how much." He leaned in closer now. "I... I've never been as attracted to someone as I am to you." His voice dropped an octave as he said the last part, the deep quality of it sending a shiver racing through her.

She refused to let him affect her. They had a serious physical attraction, something she had no problem admitting. She couldn't deny it anyway because it was like an electric thing, almost tangible. But he'd freaked out on her once, she wasn't going to deal with that again. "Look, I..." She struggled for the right words, not wanting to be too harsh. "Our attraction is intense, no denying it. But I'm not interested in pursuing anything with you other than friendship." And she wasn't going to give him a reason why either. She didn't have to and didn't feel like articulating why. He'd lost his chance, simple as that.

With his shades it was impossible to read his expression so when he nodded once and said, "Okay," she was a little taken off guard.

Maybe she'd expected more of an argument. She should be happy he was agreeing with her, not second guessing herself. But she wasn't going to sit here dwelling on it. Instead she asked him about his current job and how it was that he had a free lunch today. She knew most of the security people weren't in the office with much frequency, not with their erratic schedules.

As they fell into an easy rhythm of conversation she found herself oddly disappointed when their lunch break was over and they headed back to the office. If only she wasn't so attracted to him, maintaining a friends-only relationship would be a breeze.

———————————•••———————————

Athena shivered as she reached for another eggplant to put in her basket. The local grocery store was colder than outside. After today she was exhausted and ready to kick her feet up at home with a glass of wine. She might not cook well but there were a few staple meals her mom had taught her how to make—that Athena had actually bothered to learn—and eggplant parmesan was one of them. It was so stinking easy to make, too, and she really didn't feel like takeout. After years of living on the road, there was something to be said about cooking at home.

Tingles danced across the back of her neck, making her straighten. She glanced over her shoulder to see a blond-haired man staring hard at a bag of apples. As if he couldn't decide whether to buy them or not. She'd noticed him earlier when she'd been in the aisle with all the pasta and sauce options. And before that when she'd been looking at various cheeses.

The store was big enough that it wasn't odd they were in the same sections, but she could almost swear he'd been staring at her a couple times. As if he knew her or something.

It was unsettling.

That was when she realized he didn't have a cart or handbasket. Turning halfway to the side, she ignored him as she looked at cauliflower heads, but now she knew what had been bugging her all along. He'd just been going up and down the aisles without picking up anything.

Out of the corner of her eye she watched him put the apples back and look at her again. She wasn't imagining it this time either; he was tracking her. Maybe that was too strong of a description but she didn't care. She'd traveled enough to know when to pay attention to people.

Taking a steadying breath, she decided to go straight to the manager. The owner was friends with her parents so she'd just ask someone to walk her to her car after purchasing her items. Even if she hadn't known the owner she'd ask for help anyway. She'd read enough horrible stories to know what could happen to women alone in a parking lot—before or after dark. There was no way she was ignoring her instinct with this.

Ordering herself to remain calm, she moved to another section of fruit and picked up a small mesh bag of mandarins, her favorite snack food. When she glanced back over, the man was gone. Feeling a little silly, but not enough to disregard her feelings, she put the bag in her basket and headed for the front of the store. She'd seen a few employees idly talking by a cash register earlier because there didn't seem to be too many people here right now.

As she rounded the corner of the produce section she almost ran right into the tall, blond man. Her heart jumped in her throat but she reminded herself she was in a public place. All she had to do was scream if he did something.

Using her basket as a shield in front of her, she kept her gaze on his and took a step to the side. He moved with her, his look menacing.

"Move out of my way," she demanded. Loudly. Her mother had taught her and her three younger sisters that with people who could be potential threats, the only way to respond to them was with force—because it was usually the last thing they expected.

He blinked, as if she'd truly surprised him.

Well, good.

Then he regained his composure and a smile lit up his face. "Sorry, honey, didn't mean to get in your way."

"Yes you did." She took a small step back, needing to put some distance between them. She might be able to scream but that didn't mean she wanted this guy to hurt her before she drew attention. And something in his dark eyes said he'd take great joy in doing just that.

There was something wrong with him, a wild gleam in his eyes that made all the hair on her arms stand at attention. Physically, he was a really good looking man. Kind of like a Ken doll but with scary eyes. And a tattoo peeking out from beneath his sweater. Not that tattoos were bad—Quinn had a few himself—but she saw a snake head with red eyes that looked well, creepy. Just like the man in front of her.

She'd taken him off guard again, she saw, when he blinked in that same surprised manner. Then his jaw tightened a fraction, his gaze narrowing before he glanced around. Athena saw exactly what he did.

An elderly couple standing by the end of an aisle discussing whether to buy a higher priced box of organic pasta or their normal choice, and two teenage clerks flirting with each other instead of working. Not much of a protection, but it seemed to be enough of a barrier to make him take a step away from her.

But not completely and he didn't move enough out of her way so she could bypass him. He was definitely trying to use his size to intimidate her, she had no doubt. Asshat.

He leaned down, but didn't actually step closer, his dark eyes seeming to glitter ominously. She knew that was her own imagination because for a long moment, she was rooted to the spot. Her throat tightened and in that moment she hated herself. Hated that she was pretty much frozen.

"Tell that fucker Quinn that his time is coming. No one close to him is safe," he growled out before snapping his jaws at her like a wild animal.

She jerked back, both from the action and the stench of beer coming off him in waves. Before she could think about responding, he turned and strode away from her. By the time he was walking out the sliding glass doors, she could finally move again, her breath rushing out of her in a huge whoosh of air.

The man's words were terrifying enough, but his eyes would give her nightmares. She knew it without a doubt. And how the hell did he know Quinn?

She also knew there was no way she was walking to her car alone or even with a manager. Setting her basket right at her feet, she pulled her cell phone from her purse with a trembling hand and called Quinn.

No matter what was going on between them — or rather wasn't going on — she knew he would be here as soon as he could. That was just the type of man he was. She had no doubt the owner would let Quinn see the video footage too. Let him see exactly who that man was.

CHAPTER FOUR

Quinn's heart was beating overtime as he pulled into the parking lot of the grocery store where Athena had told him she was. At this point all he knew was that a man had approached her, said something about Quinn's 'time coming' and basically terrified Athena.

He'd heard it in her trembling voice.

He was glad she'd called him though. That said a lot. More than he wanted to analyze right now. What she'd said at today's lunch had been a setback to his plans but none of that mattered.

The only thing that mattered was making sure she was okay and that she stayed that way. He did a scan of the parking lot, looking for any threats before pulling out his cell phone and doing an actual scan with his video capabilities. Just because he didn't see something didn't mean there wasn't a threat lurking nearby. Later he'd review the video and blow up images of license plates if necessary. But he figured this was probably useless.

As he got out of his truck, he automatically reached back to make sure his weapon was holstered securely at his back. He preferred a shoulder holster for work but this was better for now. He immediately spotted Athena's cobalt blue Volkswagen beetle and a small thread of relief spiraled through him at the sight. She'd assured him she wouldn't go outside and would stay in sight of people at all times. Then she'd texted him to tell him she was sitting in the deli.

Once inside the grocery store he immediately located the deli, which was clearly closed given that all the display cases had been wiped down and there was no food in any of the trays. But as he approached the entrance to the seating area, he saw her sitting at a small black table with two men on either side of her. Both looked concerned, the older man with dark hair and a thick mustache, patting her hand in a paternal gesture. The other had on a white button-down shirt and black pants. Over the shirt was a red vest with a nametag that read Steven. His expression was pinched, his stress lines around his mouth were deep. The two men were clearly related, probably father and son.

Athena saw Quinn before the men did and the second their eyes met he felt it like a gut punch. Her expression lit up with pure relief. She and the men stood at once.

The older man moved in front of the table in a surprisingly fast move, his body language clear.

"Stephanos, this is Quinn, my friend."

The older man just made a 'hmm' sound and stepped back, but his wary expression didn't change.

For just a moment, Quinn tuned the two men out since it was clear they weren't threats. "You're not hurt?" he asked, sidestepping the younger man and moving around the table. Not caring what the strangers thought, Quinn rubbed his hands down her upper arms. She was wearing what she'd had on at work and her face was pale, but she looked otherwise okay.

"No, I'm fine. I keep thinking maybe I overreacted but my gut tells me I didn't." She shot a quick glance at the man named Stephanos, and whatever her look conveyed, the man just nodded once, then motioned to the manager.

"We'll be nearby if you need us." The man shot Quinn what could only be described as a don't-mess-with-her look before he and the manager strode away and out of earshot.

They only moved to the entrance of the deli where an unhooked chain 'separated' the small eating area and the rest of the grocery store. Looking back at Athena, Quinn took her hands and motioned for her to sit. He would have preferred to stand but she looked like she needed a break.

"Tell me what happened. From the beginning." He didn't drop

her hands as they sat across from each other. He wished they were dating or in an actual relationship so he could comfort her more. Because right now he wanted to pull her into his arms.

She gave him a shaky nod. "Okay, and thank you for coming." He just grunted, not wanting her thanks, not for something like this, and she continued. "I just stopped in here to grab a few things. I didn't want takeout tonight and wanted to make something for myself that would last for a couple days of leftovers... And I'm rambling."

He just squeezed her hands. "It's okay. Take all the time you need."

Taking another breath that seemed to steady her, she started again. "I felt like this guy, this man, was following me or at least watching me. And not in the kind of way where he was working up the courage to talk to me, you know?"

He nodded, understanding perfectly.

"He was just sort of watching and following me around. I didn't realize that at first but when I was in the produce section it hit home that he didn't have a buggy or a handbasket. He wasn't shopping at all and he was doing a poor job of pretending. So I made the decision to go find Steven... Ah, Stephanos is the owner and Steven—whose name is actually Stephanos, too—is his son and the manager. It was just luck Stephanos senior was here. Anyway, I was going to go find Steven but the man, the stranger, sort of came out of nowhere." She shook her head, as if clearing her mind and when she shivered, Quinn wanted to punch the unknown fucker in his face.

He hated that anyone had scared Athena.

"I told him to move out of my way and I was intentionally, well, bitchy about it. I wanted to stun him a little."

That was damn smart. Quinn didn't respond though, not wanting her to lose her steam.

"He didn't move and for about a second he tried to make it seem like he hadn't intentionally tried to block my way, but his charm—and I use that word lightly—faded pretty fast. He told me, and this is a direct quote, 'Tell that fucker Quinn that his time is coming. No one close to him is safe'. Then...he sort of chomped at me, like a shark or wild animal. It was seriously creepy. And the guy had like, a violent energy. I know that sounds weird, but I was scared of him. And I'm pretty sure hurting people makes him happy."

Iciness chilled Quinn down to his core. He didn't have enemies, not truly. There was only one potential man who Quinn could imagine doing this. And the guy had gotten out of jail less than two months ago so it was a definite possibility. Stupid of the man, but a possibility. "What did he look like?" Quinn asked, all his focus on Athena, who was breathing steadier now and had more color in her cheeks.

She brushed at stray strands of hair that had escaped the low twisty thing she'd done with her hair. "Tall, like you, uh, white guy, blond hair and dark eyes. This might sound weird but he was good looking in that classic American way I guess some people might describe, but his eyes..." She shuddered and glanced down, swallowing hard before meeting Quinn's gaze again. "He looked wild-eyed, it's the only way to describe him. His eyes were dark and hollow. And I know he'd been drinking. Or at least I smelled it on him. Oh, and he had a tattoo peeking out from his sweater sleeve. It was the head of a snake with red eyes."

Quinn frowned at the mention of the tattoo. Glenn hadn't had a tattoo back when he'd been in law enforcement, but things could have changed in prison. Quinn pulled out his cell phone and pulled up an old article about Glenn. It was a picture of him in his uniform—because the media had loved the idea of a bad cop, fucking vultures—next to the article about his trial. After zooming in on the face, Quinn handed his phone to her. "This him?"

Leaning closer as she took it, her eyes widened a fraction as she looked at the screen. "Oh my gosh, yeah, this is him. He's a little younger here, but yes, this is definitely him. Wait a minute, he's wearing... Is he a cop?" She whispered the last part, clearly horrified by the idea.

"Used to be. Not anymore. He just got out of prison a couple months ago."

Athena leaned back in her chair, her expression understanding. "You helped put him there, didn't you?"

Quinn nodded. He'd explain everything to her once they got out of here, but now wasn't the time for that story. He wanted her somewhere safer, where he could watch out for any potential threat. "Yeah. Listen, I'd feel a lot better if I could drive you home. I'll contact Grant and have him come get your car and—"

"Okay."

His eyes widened. "No arguments?"

She let out a shaky laugh. "Are you freaking kidding me? That guy scared the hell out of me. If you want to drive me home, I'm on board. What I don't get is, why would he have followed me here— and I'm assuming he must have. This obviously wasn't random."

Definitely not random. Which meant that fucker had been watching Quinn and had guessed that Athena meant something to him. Something he should have considered. But coming after Quinn was stupid. Beyond it in fact. It wasn't like he was the only one who'd had a hand in Glenn's arrest and prosecution. "He must have seen us at lunch today."

She shrugged. "So?"

"Honestly I don't know what his reasoning is. You're a beautiful woman and since he saw us together he might have thought you're important to me." Which she was.

"But...you said he got out of prison a couple months ago. Has he bothered any other women you've gone out with?"

Quinn snorted. "I haven't been out with anyone since you." Let her make of that what she wanted. Her lips parted in an adorably sexy way he'd seen her do a couple times when surprised but he didn't have time to dwell on that. Not now. "I need to talk to Stephanos about his security before we go and—"

"It's not working." She bit her bottom lip at his frown, but continued. "It's been on the fritz for about a week so they've got someone coming out Thursday to look at it. They've never had a problem here in the past since all the employees are either family or go to Steven and Stephanos' church so they didn't put a rush on it."

Quinn let out a growl of frustration.

"He's feels terrible," she whispered, leaning closer to him, moving so that their knees were touching. "And you're not going to make him feel worse."

A ghost of a grin tugged at his lips at her demanding tone. "Yes, ma'am," he murmured.

Her cheeks flushed pink. "Sorry, not trying to order you around."

"It's hot."

Now her cheeks went full-on crimson. But then she shook her head, as if dismissing his words. "Don't try to distract me."

He wasn't, but he didn't correct her, just stood. "Come on. I want to talk to the owner before we get out of here. Did you want to get your groceries?" She'd come here for a reason and he didn't want her leaving empty-handed.

"Steven already bagged them up for me. Said everything was on them, which is silly, but I think they just feel bad about the security situation. I tried to argue, but I know when I'm going to lose."

Quinn nodded his approval. He liked Stephanos and his son already. After talking to them and calling Grant to see if he could either pick up Athena's car or send someone else to get it, Quinn was getting Athena the hell out of here.

She might not realize it yet, but he was staying at her place tonight too. No way was he letting her out of his sight. She'd probably argue about that, but he'd face that when the time came. It was an argument Quinn wasn't losing.

Glenn White had regularly roughed up his wife, a woman he claimed to have loved. He wouldn't have a problem hurting a woman who meant nothing to him. And if Glenn thought it would hurt Quinn, yeah, he'd definitely come after Athena.

That thought was enough to send another frisson of raw fear punching through Quinn. Let White try. That fucker was going down if he came at Athena or anyone else in Quinn's life.

———————•◦•———————

From the parking lot next door to the grocery store, Glenn remained hidden in the shadows as he watched Quinn exit with that smart-mouthed bitch. She was pretty, but that mouth of hers, the disrespectful way she'd talked to him... Glenn had wanted to backhand her just to wipe that look off her face.

Approaching her like that had been a test. Hell, he hadn't been sure if he would talk to her at all tonight, but when she'd gotten up in his face he'd wanted to scare her. He'd wanted to see terror in her eyes.

Now Glenn was glad he had because she clearly mattered to Quinn. He hadn't been certain if she meant anything to that bastard. She could have just been a co-worker. Today Glenn had seen them having lunch together, but that could have been a work thing. Sure, they seemed to have chemistry but there hadn't been any hand-holding or any other little signs they'd been a couple.

So Glenn had planned to tail her for a few days, to see where she went and who she visited. Following her would be a lot easier than keeping up with Quinn. Quinn was trained and would see a tail a lot quicker. Not the dark-haired woman whose name he was going to find out very soon. She'd been completely oblivious that he'd followed her from work. She'd stopped a couple places before hitting the grocery store.

Soon he'd find out her name and where she lived. He still had some contacts he could use, one in particular. Because following her tonight would be stupid, especially when it appeared Quinn was taking her home. Either to her place or Quinn's, it didn't matter to Glenn.

Now that he'd made contact, had let Quinn know he wasn't safe, it was time to play. Glenn hadn't done anything illegal and it was his word against some woman's if she said anything to the police. He was well within following the rules of his parole requirements.

He'd keep doing so for a while. At least until it suited him. He needed to buy a new ID and papers just in case he had to run later. He wasn't going back to prison but he wasn't stupid enough to think that he might not get caught going after Quinn. The new ID would be his backup. Though he still needed to lay his exact plans out, figure out his best plan of attack. That meant he'd have to watch this bitch, learn more about who she was, her habits, everything.

So if he had to flee, he'd be ready this time. No matter what happened, Quinn was going to get exactly what was coming to him and Glenn wasn't going back to prison. Never again.

CHAPTER FIVE

Athena caught Quinn's look of surprise as she gave him her address. He'd been about to plug it into his GPS until he clearly recognized the name of the street.

"You live next door to Belle and Grant?" he asked, glancing in the rearview mirror before reversing.

"Yeah, moved in a few weeks ago. She still hasn't let go of her old place and it makes more sense to rent it than letting it sit empty."

"I'm surprised they haven't rented it before now."

Athena shrugged. Since marrying Grant, Belle had been trying to decide if she should rent or sell and Athena moving back had given her an excuse to prolong making the decision to sell. "You don't want to talk about my living situation any more than I do."

Quinn let out a short laugh. "Not really. I need to make some calls, then we're talking. Okay?"

She nodded, letting him do what he needed to. Being with Quinn after that strange confrontation soothed most of the jagged edges of her nerves. Not completely, because that guy, Glenn White, had seriously scared her. Now that she knew he was a former cop the whole thing was even more worrisome. She was so thankful that Quinn was taking her home too because she didn't trust herself to drive. She was too shaky and for all she knew, the guy could have tried to follow her. At that sudden thought, she turned around in her seat.

Quinn, who was on the phone, she'd surmised with Grant, shook his head and held the phone away from his mouth. "I'll know if we have a tail," he murmured.

Okay then. She sat back against the comfortable leather seat and didn't wonder why he was taking all sorts of random turns. If someone was following them, Quinn would figure it out soon enough. It relieved a bit of pressure in her chest to know that he was trained.

She didn't live far from the grocery store, roughly about ten minutes, but Quinn had made enough turns that it took double that. By the time they pulled into the driveway, Quinn was getting off the phone with Grant—and Grant and Belle were waiting in the driveway.

Belle practically had the passenger side door open before they'd parked or Athena had unstrapped her seatbelt.

"Athena!" Her cousin dragged her into a surprisingly tight hug.

"You're squeezing really tight," she rasped out.

Belle immediately loosened her grip and stepped back, but not by much. She grasped onto Athena's shoulders and looked her up and down, as if looking for injury.

"What exactly did Grant tell you happened? I'm fine." Jeez, Belle had been through a heck of a lot worse over a year ago, being kidnapped by a crazed maniac who turned out to be a serial killer. Athena getting approached by a jerk in a grocery store wasn't on the same scale.

"I know, I just worry about you."

Athena just smiled, knowing it was their family way. Belle was only a few years older, but older cousins and sisters or brothers always looked out for the younger relatives. It was just the way it was, and something Athena was grateful for. "Thank you, seriously. But I swear I'm fine." She turned to look at Grant and Quinn, who both stood there like formidable warriors near the closed garage door.

"I've already swept the house," Grant started. Of course he would have. They had the security code and an extra key. "And I called in one of our guys to pick up your car. He said he'd call me if Stephanos gave him an issue, but I doubt he will. Stephanos and Steven were worried, so they'll be happy to help."

Athena simply nodded. They'd left her car keys with Stephanos and Quinn had said he'd contact the man when they'd figured out what they planned to do about her vehicle. "Is your guy bringing it here?"

Grant shook his head. "No, he's taking it to Red Stone where it will remain in secure parking overnight. I'm going to have it swept for bugs or trackers."

"Wait...what?" She stepped closer to Quinn and Grant, staring at her cousin-in-law as if he'd lost his mind. "This guy just approached me in a grocery store. Don't get me wrong, it was creepy, but sweeping my car for bugs, seriously? That's overkill." She figured that if he wanted to find her, he could just use her license plate number and attempt to track her that way. Thankfully she hadn't updated her address yet.

But of course the man just shrugged as if what he was doing was no big deal. Worse, Quinn didn't seem fazed by it either.

"I don't care if it's overkill," Grant said, his tone resolute. "I almost lost my wife to a serial killer. You're family and we look out for our own. Deal with it."

Athena blinked, realizing that even if she argued it would be pointless. There were certainly worse things than an overprotective family. "Okay, thank you."

Grant's eyes narrowed a fraction, as if he didn't quite believe Athena's acquiescence. Belle slipped her arm through Athena's, tugging her closer. "We're just worried about you."

Athena nudged Belle with her hip. "I know, it's why I'm not going to argue. As long as you don't tell my mom. Or your mom," she rushed on. If her mother or pretty much anyone in the family found out about this, they'd rush over to her house like madwomen with covered dishes and desserts. As if someone had died. She'd just started a new job and had a stressful day; she couldn't handle her family descending upon her.

"Well, *we* won't," Grant said before Belle could respond. "But you know Stephanos—"

"Oh, hell, I wasn't thinking," she groaned, wondering which of her family members would now show up tomorrow morning before she had to leave for work. Because she knew it was happening. There would be a little army of them. Her mom for sure. Not her sisters because they'd all be in school. But her mom, likely two of her aunts, and—

"Grant." Quinn's voice cut off her train of thought and internal pity party.

Athena looked between the two men as they seemed to have a telepathic conversation. Which she knew was ridiculous, but *something* passed between them as they stared at each other. Finally Grant nodded and they both turned back to her and Belle.

"I'm going to grab my bag from the truck and I think it wouldn't hurt to park in your garage. If you have the room." Quinn's first words since they'd gotten out of his truck could have knocked her over.

She knew she wasn't misunderstanding either. "You want to stay with me?"

"Either he stays over—in your guest room—or you stay with Belle and me...or I call your mother. If you let Quinn stay I'll call Stephanos right now and tell him to hold off on contacting your family." Grant gave her an easy smile that she wanted to knock right off his smug face.

"That's blackmail," Athena muttered. "And it worked." She shot Quinn a grim look. "You can stay." Definitely not the way she'd once imagined him staying at her place, but it was late, she was hungry and she wasn't going to waste any time arguing. "I'll go inside and open the garage door."

Quinn's expression was too hard to decipher. She couldn't tell if he was pleased to be staying with her. Though she wasn't going to admit it, and even if she did think this whole thing was overkill when she wasn't even a clear target, she was glad he'd be at her place tonight. She'd certainly sleep better with him under the same roof. She'd just have to ignore her growing attraction to him.

Quinn looked up from the island in Athena's kitchen as she

stepped inside. He'd heard her on the stairs and knew she'd be here soon, but seeing her in the flesh still seemed to knock him back a few steps every single time. She'd already shown him to the guest room, where he'd left his duffel bag, and had told him she was changing out of her work clothes. While she'd been in her room he'd decided to put up her groceries and start on dinner for her.

Which clearly surprised her, given her raised eyebrows as she raked a gaze over him. "You're cooking?"

"Figured you could use the break." He'd already peeled the eggplants and was dipping the slices in egg yolk to roll in breading.

"I feel like I should tell you that you don't have to, but... I'm mentally exhausted and starving. So thank you." She gave him a tired smile and headed for her refrigerator. "I don't think I have beer or anything you'd like."

"Water's good for me." He motioned to the water bottle he'd grabbed earlier.

"You sure?"

He nodded, watching out of the corner of his eye as she moved to another counter and slid out a bottle of red wine before pulling down a glass from one of her cabinets. She was wearing a soft-looking gray and white striped sweater paired with gray lounge pants that fit snugly over her ass. He'd had a likely inappropriate amount of fantasies about what it would be like to run his hands over her ass — and entire body.

At that thought, his dick decided it had a mind of its own so he turned away and focused on the food. "How're you feeling?"

"Eh, okay. The whole thing is disturbing but you and Grant are right. I'd rather be smart about this while you figure out what to do — and I assume you're already doing something about White, right?" She pressed play on the small silver CD player on her counter and soft notes of jazz music filled the kitchen.

"Yeah. I've put in a call to an old buddy of mine from the local PD and he's going to find out who Glenn's parole officer is. What he did today wasn't illegal, and since no one else heard him, it's a case of he-said, she-said regardless. He won't be called in for questioning and there's nothing for you to do at this point other than just be aware, but I want someone official to know about this situation for the record." Quinn hated that they couldn't get Glenn on anything right now, but even drinking alcohol likely wasn't going to work against him unless Glenn's probation specifically stated he wasn't allowed to consume alcohol at all. And in Florida unless the crime was alcohol related, probationary terms usually outlined something along the lines of not drinking to excess. Which was too damn vague in Quinn's opinion.

"So," Athena said, taking a seat on the opposite side of the island across from him. "Who is this guy to you? Give me all the details."

He'd been ready for that question, and he owed her the truth. "Long story short, he was a wife-beater and I helped convince his wife to leave him." Quinn was thankful every day for how brave Suzanne had been. She'd been so terrified of her husband's position and looking back, Quinn realized what a leap of faith it had taken for her to come with him that day when he'd basically been a stranger to her.

"And he was a cop." Athena sounded disgusted, the words more of a statement than question.

"Yeah. He never should have been in the position he was, but he was smart. Suzanne, that was his wife, had been terrified to leave him. Things hadn't always been like that from what I eventually learned. Not that it would have mattered if it had been, but she married a different man than the one she ended up with." For the most part. The signs had been there, Suzanne just hadn't seen them. Most people wouldn't have because while Glenn was unstable, he was manipulative and smart.

For a moment, Quinn debated whether he should tell Athena everything, but decided for full honesty. There was no reason she shouldn't know, and to some extent she was involved with Glenn now too. "I was new to Glenn's squad, but during a chance run-in with Suzanne I realized she was being abused. Only later did I find out that two members of our squad knew, or at least had guessed, but did nothing." Quinn's fingers started to clench into a fist so he forced himself to ease up. It might all be in the past but he still got pissed when he thought about two men looking the other way when a woman had been in constant danger. After everything came out, they downplayed it, made it seem as if they weren't really sure, but screw that, Quinn didn't care. They should have said something to someone. When he glanced at Athena, her expression was soft and understanding.

She'd worn her dark hair down and washed her makeup off. She looked so damn innocent sitting there. Probably too innocent for him, but he wasn't walking away. Not again. "But *you* did something."

He nodded and ripped open a bag of shredded mozzarella cheese. He'd already done the first layer of eggplants, now it was time for the cheese and sauce layer. "Yeah, got her to a shelter and from there, the system did its job for once." Thank God. It didn't always work out that way. Of course Suzanne would have had to skirt the system in order to get a new, fake identity and he was glad she'd found those resources.

"So he went to jail for abusing his wife and what, blamed you for the fact that *he* beat his own wife?" Now Athena sounded incredulous and pissed. Her tone made him smile and when he looked at her again, her Mediterranean blue eyes were sparking with anger.

"That and..." He internally cringed. No way around telling her. "He tried to kill me. Came to my house to supposedly just talk but then attacked me with a pistol in full view of some neighbors. I disarmed him, but one of my neighbors got it on video, along with him clearly stating he was going to kill me." Quinn hadn't been sure if he should tell her, but hell, she needed all the facts, especially since Glenn had personally come in contact with her.

Athena let out a small gasp, her fingers clenching around the stem of her wine glass just a fraction harder. "How is he out of prison then?"

Quinn's jaw tightened again, but some things he had to let go. The justice system was broken and he could get angry about it, but it wouldn't change anything. "Him trying to kill me was actually a blessing. For Suzanne at least. He wouldn't have gone away for as long as he did for just spousal abuse."

"So how long did he get sent away for?"

"Six years."

She was silent a moment, watching him curiously. He swore he could actually hear her thinking. "That's how long you've been with Red Stone."

He nodded. "Yes, and to answer what you're not asking, that whole incident is why I left the police department. Well, part of the reason anyway." Quinn would tell her all the rest eventually, but it wasn't important now.

"Six years doesn't seem like a long time for murder."

"Attempted murder. He took a deal and accepted a lesser charge to avoid a trial. And the term was eight to ten years but he got out early for good behavior. That shit...ah, stuff happens all the time, unfortunately." He shook his head in disgust.

"So what happened to his wife, or ex-wife, I'm guessing now?" Athena took a small sip of her wine.

"I honestly don't know. She ghosted out of town, cut contact with anyone from her past. I think she probably got a new ID and settled somewhere far from here. Just a guess, of course, but I'm glad."

"You think he'll go after her?"

Quinn shrugged. "No. I think if he could find her, he absolutely would, but my gut says he won't." Because if Quinn couldn't locate Suzanne, then no way in hell would Glenn be able to. He didn't have the resources anymore. Suzanne had deserved a fresh start and the truth was, just moving wouldn't have saved her. Glenn would have come after her later and eventually killed her if he'd been able.

She shook her head. "That's terrifying."

"Yeah, but he fu...screwed up tonight with you. I'm on guard now, and he's not getting past me."

Athena was silent, contemplative for a long moment, but he saw the relief in her eyes. "What happened to the men who looked the other way, the ones who were with your squad?"

"They were eventually let go for unrelated issues. Technically anyway." Finished with the layering, he opened her oven and slid the glass casserole dish inside.

"Ah, so the powers that be couldn't fire them for looking the other way, but found another reason to get rid of them." Her tone was approving.

Another reason—not that he needed one—he wanted to kiss her. "Yep. They deserved it too." As he moved to the sink to wash his hands, she spoke again, and this time her voice was tentative.

"So...it's none of my business, but you opened the door earlier so I'm just going to ask. When you said you haven't gone out with anyone since me, does that mean you haven't slept with anyone else either?"

Because the two were very different things.

She didn't say the words, but he heard the silent question just the same. Grabbing a dishtowel, he dried his hands as he turned to face her. In that moment he was struck by how innocent she looked. He hadn't thought he wanted that in a woman, hadn't thought he wanted to settle down at all, but being in Athena's kitchen now...he could see getting used to this, being with a woman like her day in and day out. Hell, not like her, *only* her.

"I haven't slept with anyone else. Haven't wanted to." Confessing that took a lot more effort than he'd realized, but he was glad she knew. He wasn't done pursuing her, not by a long shot.

Her lips parted just the slightest fraction, as if he'd truly surprised her. Good. Taking a chance, he covered the short distance between them and moving slowly, reached out and tucked a few stray strands of her dark hair behind her ear.

She sucked in a shaky breath, her eyes flaring with an emotion he recognized well; lust. He wondered if she was remembering just how hot things had been between them. He hadn't been able to get her out of his head for two months. Hadn't been able to forget the way she'd looked as she straddled him in his truck, the little moans she'd made when he'd gently teased her nipples with his fingers—unfortunately over her lacy bra. She'd been so sensual, so reactive, and he couldn't get enough.

When she swallowed hard enough for him to hear, he let his hand drop.

Not because he thought she wouldn't be receptive if he kissed her. He could tell she was. Their attraction wasn't the issue. But he didn't want her to ever come back and say she'd made a decision under stress, that she regretted it. The next time they came together it wouldn't be because of a situation where they were forced together and she'd just been terrified by an asshole.

Because the next time, they weren't stopping at just kissing and he wasn't letting Athena go. Clearing his throat, he took a step back. "I'm going to grab a shower, but the timer should go off in an hour." He'd be back down before it did, but needed some distance or he was going to forget his good intentions.

CHAPTER SIX

One week later

Athena peeked through the peephole of her front door and let out a little sigh of relief to see Ivan Mitchell waiting for her. She was flying out on one of Red Stone's private jets today and he was her escort to the airport. Harrison wanted her in Vegas a day before the tradeshow started and that was fine with her.

The past week she'd practically lived at the office, mostly because of work, but she'd also been taking all her lunches in the lobby deli because of 'the incident' as she'd begun to think of it. She'd literally just gone from home to work and back again. Since the past week had consisted of a lot of conference calls and other types of planning that she could work on in-office, the schedule had been fine. But it wasn't a long-term option and she wasn't screwing up her new job because of this thing with Glenn White. If she needed to meet a potential client out for lunch—which she knew would happen often—she was doing it.

On top of everything else, she'd spent one night at her parent's house because her mom had freaked out when Stephanos—the traitor—had broken down and told her about what happened. Not something Athena wanted to repeat any time soon. Whenever she went home her parents treated her like she was twelve. To top it off, *all* her sisters were in high school now so it was constant World War III drama over there. Thankfully she, with Belle and Grant's help, had managed to convince her mom that she was fine to move back home. Athena would have left regardless, but it was nice that her cousin helped smooth the way.

Glenn White hadn't made any more contact with Athena and none at all with Quinn. Since White hadn't done anything illegal the police weren't involved. That didn't mean Quinn wasn't in a sort of protective overdrive mode. Which she understood, but she couldn't let her life revolve around something that may or may not happen. And he'd wanted to stay over too, but after that first night she'd had to say no. She had a security system—literally the best since it was from Red Stone's very small residential department—so no one was getting into her house. Plus Quinn and Grant made her check in with them every night and every morning. Overkill, but not the worst thing in the world to have people care about you.

Quinn had also been texting her and doing daily drop-ins to see her at work, but she'd been trying to keep things professional between them. It was so hard though, especially since he looked at her with a simmering lust that always got her flustered.

"I just need to set the alarm," she called out to Ivan.

"Okay."

She set it to away mode, then opened the door. Before she could think about protesting, the huge Viking-looking man picked up her suitcase and carry-on with a grunt. "You got freaking bricks in here?"

"Ha, ha." She shut the door behind her and locked it. "Something tells me Julieta packs a lot more than me." His adorable fiancée was a fashion plate. The woman owned a local shop that sold lingerie and sex toys and always looked so put together. Julieta was a few years older than her, but Athena had gone to high school with one of Julieta's younger cousins. Small freaking world.

"You wouldn't be wrong. She told me to tell you hi, by the way."

"Tell her hi back." Athena slipped her keys into her purse, feeling like she'd forgotten something even though she'd triple-checked everything. "You ready for Vegas?"

"There's been a change of plans..." He trailed off as his phone rang.

While he answered, she plucked her carry-on bag from where he'd set it down and slid it into the back of the open-hatch of the SUV.

He made a sound of annoyance, but she ignored him. She'd traveled on her own for two years and didn't expect anyone to carry her bags for her. He was faster than her with the bigger bag so she got into the back seat and pulled her tablet from her giant purse. She didn't recognize the driver but smiled at him before turning on her tablet. She could at least check her email before they took off.

At this point Athena had everything for tomorrow's event pretty much lined up but she was supposed to meet with Iris Christiansen early in the morning. Iris was head of The Serafina's hotel security — and was also the wife of billionaire Wyatt Christiansen. Athena knew the woman had once worked for Red Stone, and if she was being honest, she was a little intimidated to meet her. Whenever she'd heard any of the guys talk about Iris, it was with respect.

Ivan was still on the phone by the time they reached the private airport, going over what sounded like last-minute security additions to another job.

"Sorry about that. Didn't plan to be on the phone the whole drive," he said as they pulled up on the tarmac. "Blue's keeping me here this week, but Harrison wanted a familiar face to escort you to the airport."

It took Athena a moment to figure out who Ivan meant but then she remembered that Alexander Blue was Ivan's more-or-less direct boss. Blue ran one of the southeast divisions of Red Stone. There were so many names to remember but she thought she was doing a pretty good job so far. "No problem, work's work." Now real energy hummed through her at the prospect of handling her first real job for Red Stone. Raegan wouldn't be flying out until Tuesday, so tomorrow and most of Tuesday, Athena was on her own.

When the driver grabbed her bags, this time she didn't protest, just walked with Ivan to the waiting plane. She was surprised she didn't have any security with her since Harrison had made it sound like a team would be going, but maybe they were coming out Tuesday with Reagan.

Too excited about the job to be worried, she nearly stumbled when she stepped inside the plane to find Quinn standing next to a table where Travis sat looking at his laptop.

Concealing her surprise—and that burst of pleasure that detonated inside her at seeing him—she moved farther into the interior of the sleek plane. "Hey, I didn't realize you two were coming with me."

Travis spared her a quick smile and a nod, but didn't stop whatever it was he was doing. From his intense expression she guessed it was work related.

"Last minute change of plans," Quinn said smoothly, turning so he faced her fully.

There was something in his gaze she couldn't quite define, but it made her heart rate kick up just the same. After his revelation on Monday night about not having slept with or dated anyone since going out with her, she wasn't sure how to act around him. It was unnerving, reminding her of being in high school and feeling so damn unsure of herself. He'd really messed with her heart by ending things because of something that seemed so trivial, but she couldn't deny that the past week she'd started to fall for him again. Okay, maybe there was no 'again'. Just sort of a continual thing. "Oh."

"Don't sound too excited." His voice was wry now, those midnight dark eyes of his assessing.

Her lips curved into a smile. "I didn't mean it like that."

He started to respond when his gaze flicked over her shoulder. She turned to find the pilot and flight attendant—who looked like brothers—moving into the cabin with instructions about how they needed to sit for weight distribution and get ready for the flight.

Moments later Athena found herself seated next to Quinn—who smelled far too good—with Travis across the aisle from them. He'd closed his laptop and pulled out earbuds, and surprisingly, a sleep mask. Travis glanced at them and held up the mask. "Little man didn't sleep well last night so I'm going to catch a few Z's on the flight."

Athena could imagine—though didn't want to think about having kids for a long time—and nodded back. As the pilot's voice came over the speaker and the flight attendant moved past them to the back, she leaned back in her seat to the soft rumble of the engine starting. She'd been on so many flights over the past two years, including on private planes, and usually found take-offs almost cathartic.

Not today. Not sitting next to Quinn who was semi-casual in black slacks and a gray sweater that she was pretty certain was cashmere pushed up to his muscular forearms. Seriously, why did forearms have to be so sexy?

Why did *he* have to be so sexy? And why did she have the ridiculous urge to reach out and stroke his...sweater. She just wanted to see if it was as soft as it looked.

Right. She snorted at the thought then cringed as she saw Quinn glance at her out of the corner of her eye. She hadn't meant to do that out loud.

Half-smiling, she looked at him. "So Harrison gave you this last minute, huh?"

He paused for a moment, his dark eyes unreadable. "I requested the job."

Ah, okay then. She so absolutely did *not* know how to respond to that. She'd told him last week that there was no chance between them. But there had been that weird sexual tension between them in her kitchen the night he'd stayed over. She'd been so sure he would kiss her, but at the last minute he'd reversed course and left her pretty much panting for more. Because she certainly wouldn't have rejected him.

He wasn't pressuring her or anything, but he was just being so...honest about stuff. Why had he requested this job? Either he was worried about her because of White or he'd requested it because he wanted to work with her. Or maybe it was a combination of both.

She wasn't asking why though. Instead she decided to ignore the fluttery feeling in her stomach and stick to a safe topic. "Have you been to Vegas before?"

He shook his head. "Nah. Never wanted to, but I've heard The Serafina is amazing. You been?"

"I'm a first-timer too. And from the pictures I've seen, the hotel and casino really are amazing. Is there anything extra we need to go over for the tradeshow?"

"Once we get settled in we'll do a walkthrough of the tradeshow area and talk to all the onsite staff to get a feel for the layout, but I think we're good for now. I read over your files. Very detailed." A ghost of a smile teased those very kissable lips.

She had to resist the real—and again, ridiculous—urge to lean in and brush her lips over his. He was making her feel out of sorts and she couldn't deal with that. Not right now. "Good, that's my plan too. Did you ever work with Iris Christiansen before?"

"Yeah. She's the best. Very professional." Another smile touched his lips and this time she saw humor in his eyes.

"What is it?"

"Just thinking about the last job I worked with her. It was long before she married Christiansen and moved to Vegas. One of our clients—now an ex-client—thought he could get handsy with her. Before anyone on the team could move she had that guy flat on his stomach with one hand wrenched behind his back and was reaming him out with language that uh, could make a sailor blush. Working with her was always entertaining."

Feeling more at ease, Athena settled back against her seat as the flight attendant approached them, asking if they wanted anything to drink. After requesting a bottle of water—she'd learned to stay hydrated when traveling—she reclined her seat a bit more and decided to turn off her brain for the flight. Soon enough she'd be working her butt off and spending plenty of time with Quinn.

That thought excited her way more than it should have. She was the one who'd said no to more with him, but just being in such close quarters with Quinn was short-circuiting her brain. Despite that, he still made her feel safe, secure. Even though White hadn't reached out again she still liked knowing Quinn was nearby right now.

"I don't know how you made a tradeshow room about GPS and transportation not boring, but everything looks pretty great," Travis said as they got on the elevator to head up to the executive floor.

Their bags had been taken when they'd arrived at the hotel hours ago and they hadn't been to their rooms yet. And Athena didn't know that she was sharing a suite with Quinn. Something he knew was going to annoy her, but it was happening. He was still wired about Glenn. Didn't matter that they were across the country, Quinn took Athena's safety seriously. And yeah, he wanted to open up the opportunity for more to develop between them.

Since they'd have two separate bedrooms with an adjoining living room area, it was basically like they had separate rooms. He didn't think she'd see it that way since Travis would be across the hall, but she'd just have to deal with it.

"That wasn't me, it was a local design firm who set everything up," Athena said.

"You hired them and approved everything," Quinn said, pressing the button to their floor.

She shrugged. "I'm pretty sure this is going to be one of the more fun tradeshows I've done. Everything's set up ahead of time and there's no take down from day to day which will ease a lot of headaches—and how cool was that multi-tiered tire cake?"

Travis nodded, grinning as the elevator arrived on their floor. "I say we see if someone can save us some food tomorrow. The spread the catering staff already has set up is sick."

Quinn just shook his head. "We're in Vegas, and The Serafina has world famous restaurants."

"I want some of that cake."

"I'll make it happen," Athena murmured, laughter in her voice as they all stepped out.

Quinn had already pulled out his room key and handed Travis his as they approached the suite numbers. "Your bags should already be in your room," he said to Travis.

"Thanks. I want to Skype with Noel for a bit so I'm going to do room service. See you guys at six, right?"

Athena nodded as Quinn said, "Yep, meet you right out here."

"So where's my room?" she asked as the door shut behind Travis.

Quinn tilted his head at the door directly across the hall and slid the key card into it. He held the door open. "You and I are sharing a suite."

She stopped, eyebrows raised. "Excuse me?" Anger punched off her so sharply it was almost a tangible thing.

That probably shouldn't have gotten him so hot, but damn, she looked good angry. "Two separate rooms, two bathrooms, we just have a common living area." But there was only one exit. Which meant if someone wanted to enter the room, they had only one way to do it. "No one's getting past me."

She eyed him for a moment, her gaze narrowing. "Did you request this?"

"Yes."

For a moment, she looked as if she might snap at him, but just as quickly pushed out a sigh. "You are so maddening, but I'm too tired and too hungry to argue with you," she said as she strode past him. The sway of her ass was enough to make his entire body react.

He inhaled her subtle tropical scent as she moved. He wasn't sure what kind of perfume she wore, but whatever it was, or if it was just something that was intrinsically Athena, it drove him crazy.

She drove him crazy. Ever since their 'almost kiss' a week ago in her kitchen he'd been going out of his mind. Well, *more* out of his mind for her. Especially since he already knew what she tasted like, how she felt in his arms. "No argument at all?" he asked, trailing after her, but not before engaging the locks and security bar.

"If you really want an argument I might be able to build up some steam," she murmured, entering the huge living area. "Holy crap this place is huge. For past jobs I usually got the basic room. Nice, but boring. This..." She glanced over her shoulder at him as he moved to stand next to her. "This is beautiful."

He nodded in agreement, taking in the living area in one sweep. The silver and purple drapes had been pulled back to reveal the sparkling city below. A circular, ornate table sat in front of a huge half-circular shaped white couch. A gift basket with an assortment of food and champagne sat on the table. On another two tables by the window were huge vases of what he was certain were fresh flowers. Purple roses to go with the rest of the room.

"Give me a second to sweep the bedrooms," he said, though he was certain they were secure. This floor was one the owner reserved for business associates not necessarily in town to gamble, or for extra security personnel like him. It was more or less a private floor.

When he returned to the living area he found Athena had already opened a box of crackers from the gift basket and was cutting a block of cheese. "Want a snack?" she asked, smiling at him.

He wanted a snack all right. With the city lights illuminating her from behind, he thought she certainly lived up to her namesake. She'd taken off her fitted black jacket and high heels—which he knew she hated wearing anyway—and stood there in a slim-fitting black and red dress that hugged all her curves. He wanted to slowly peel off her clothes and feast on every inch of her delicious body. He'd only seen her partially unclothed when they'd been dating but he'd fantasized about what she'd look like completely bare to him.

Before he could respond there was a knock at the door.

Without thought he pulled out his weapon, ignoring her little gasp of surprise, and strode for the door. A glance through the peephole eased his tension though, and he pulled the door open for Iris as he sheathed his pistol.

The tall, darker skinned woman with clear Native American heritage gave him a small smile as she held out a hand for him. "Quinn, good to see you."

He nodded, shook her hand then stood back so she could enter. "You too. Everything okay? We were told you were off site today for something."

"Yeah, got back a little while ago and wanted to meet Miss Manikas in person. I like what she's done with the..." She trailed off as Athena strode into the tiled entryway, her heels clicking quickly as she approached.

Quinn wasn't surprised she'd put her shoes back on and though he knew she didn't like the heels, he'd had more than one fantasy involving her wearing them and nothing else. Something he did *not* need to be thinking about right now.

"Miss Manikas." Iris, who had a hard edge, gave her a surprisingly warm smile. "You look so much like Belle."

Athena blinked in surprise as she approached, took the hand Iris had offered, and returned the smile. "Call me Athena, please. I didn't realize you knew my cousin."

Iris nodded. "Yep. Did more than my share of jobs with Grant. And call me Iris. I just wanted to stop by and meet you in person before the madness of tomorrow — and this week."

Quinn was silent as the two women chatted, struck by the physical differences of them. Where Iris was tall, lean and had a fierceness to her he'd only ever seen in military or law enforcement individuals, Athena was petite, so open with her expressions and had a softness to her he found irresistible. For some reason he knew she'd hate that term, but there it was.

Once Iris left, Quinn locked and secured the door behind her to find Athena taking off her heels again.

"I'm going to grab a shower and probably crash," she said, heading back for the main area.

He barely bit back a groan. She was going to be naked soon with steam billowing around her hot little body, water rushing over her soft skin — fuck him, he needed to get his thoughts under control. He cleared his throat. "I was going to order room service. You sure you don't want anything?" It had been a long day.

"Nah, I'll just grab some fruit from the basket. But will you order breakfast tomorrow for us when you call for room service tonight? I know what I want."

"Sure." As he strode to the room's phone, his cell buzzed in his pocket, indicating a text. When he saw the message on screen from Grant, his chest tightened for an instant, but he kept his expression neutral.

White slipped our guard. Knew he had a tail. Could mean nothing, but he hasn't been back to his place all night. Also found something interesting. Can't text. Call when you're free.

"Everything okay?" Athena asked, barely glancing up from where she was picking through the fruit in the basket.

"Yeah." But he knew it wasn't. Grant wouldn't have texted otherwise.

Quinn knew that Grant had broken into White's apartment earlier today. Illegal as hell, but Athena was Grant's family. The truth was, if Grant hadn't done it, Quinn would have himself. There hadn't been a chance this week. So the text meant Grant had found something inside the apartment. Something he couldn't put in text form. No way in hell would Quinn ever tell Athena either. She didn't need to know what her cousin-in-law had done for multiple reasons. One being plausible deniability.

Quinn shot off a quick reply to Grant telling him that he'd call in a few minutes. As soon as he had privacy. It seemed a slim possibility that White would come after him while he was in Vegas, but with Athena here, Quinn wasn't taking any chances with her safety.

Whatever it took, he'd protect her.

CHAPTER SEVEN

Glenn vibrated with an urgency he hadn't felt in years as he handed the cab driver the cash. Once he got his change and tipped the guy the expected amount he slid out of the vehicle, duffel bag in hand. He kept the gratuity dead-on average. Not too cheap, but not too flashy either because he couldn't afford to stand out, for anyone to remember him. Bright neon lights glittered everywhere, people talking, laughing, stumbling along the sidewalk as they made their way to their destinations. The energy of the city was invigorating.

No longer was he just surviving day to day, keeping his head down and making sure he maintained his 'good behavior'. Now he finally had a chance to pay back the bastard who'd been the catalyst in his imprisonment. More than that, the one who'd taken Suzanne away from him.

The more Glenn thought about it, the more he realized that Quinn had to have helped Suzanne leave. It was the only thing that made sense. Since he'd helped her, he'd know where she was now. Under normal circumstance he didn't think Quinn would tell him where his unfaithful wife was, but now that Glenn had formulated a plan he knew Quinn would.

Glenn had called in every favor owed to him—mainly old CI's or criminals he'd let slip through the cracks—and through different sources he'd first discovered that the woman he'd seen Quinn with was named Athena Manikas. He thought he'd nailed down her address but it turned out to be old. Unless she had a sixty-year old black grandfather for a roommate, because that was the only person he'd seen coming in and out of her listed place of residence. That was okay though, he'd expected hurdles.

It didn't matter anyway because he'd just hit the jackpot with news that Quinn and the Manikas woman were both in Vegas. One of his contacts had tracked use of both their credit cards to the same hotel; The Serafina.

Coming to Vegas had been a huge risk, but he'd already checked in with his parole officer and she was just another malleable woman. She didn't care about him as long as he didn't cause any trouble. He had another five days before he needed to check in with her again and all he had to do was make a phone call. Didn't even need to visit her in person unless she requested it. And she never did. Wasn't like she tracked his phone—not that he'd brought his regular cell phone with him anyway. Lazy bitch.

February was cold in the desert and he liked the cool air rushing over him. Made him feel alive. Hell, he felt alive for the first time in six years, two months. Tugging his ball cap low on his forehead, he didn't feel out of place wearing sunglasses at night as he strode down the busy strip. Tons of other people had on sunglasses this late too.

No one was paying attention to him. No one cared that he was here. Soon Quinn was going to, though. That bastard was going to care a whole lot.

Once Glenn took Athena, threatened to hurt her—did hurt her—Quinn would tell him everything he wanted to know. It would probably only take a few slaps, punches, maybe he'd have to use a blade on her. Maybe not. It all depended on Quinn's willingness to talk. Glenn would still kill them both once he got Suzanne's location, but he wouldn't make the smart-mouthed bitch suffer if Quinn was straight with him. He'd give him that much. Glenn couldn't say the same for Quinn though.

He was going to hurt him before he died. They'd both worn a uniform, served together; Quinn shouldn't have ratted him out. It went against their unspoken code. Once Quinn was dead too, Glenn would bury him and his woman in the desert. If things got too hot for him he'd flee to Mexico, but if he did this right no one would even know he'd been here.

When The Serafina came into view, a sleek high-rise shimmering against the night sky, Glenn smiled. All the rage and anger that had been simmering inside him for years pushed at the surface, ready to break free.

Ready to make Quinn pay for what he'd done.

"You didn't eat enough today," Quinn murmured next to her.

Athena didn't open her eyes though. She had her head leaned back against the interior of the elevator and was close to passing out on her feet. The subtle vibration from the elevator was going to make her fall asleep faster if they didn't make it to their room soon. "Were you keeping tabs on me?"

He just made a grunting sound.

When the soft ding sounded, she opened her eyes and breathed out a sigh of relief. "I'm wearing lower heeled shoes tomorrow," she said as they stepped out into the hallway.

"And eating more."

She just shook her head. She'd been too nervous to put away much. Plus, and she knew it was her own issues, being around Quinn so much made her very aware of her weight and size. Around him she felt small and petite, but then an Amazon-beauty would make their way to Quinn, all smiles and big breasts right in his face, and those stupid insecurities flared back to life. She'd been busy today, but not so busy that she didn't notice all the women who'd gone out of their way to approach Quinn. It made her remember how chubby she'd once been and feel as if he was out of her league. She didn't like being that person, but there it was.

"I have a surprise for you." His voice dropped an octave as they reached their door.

Despite the shiver that rolled over her at his sensual tone, she shook her head. "Unless it involves a massage and a hot bath, not interested." As soon as the words were out, she wanted to snatch them back. Realizing what that had sounded like, her eyes widened as she glanced at him.

Wicked grin in place, he just slid the key in the lock and opened the door for her. "Unless you're inviting me to join you in the shower—and for the record I wouldn't say no—I hired someone from the hotel to give you an hour massage."

For once in her life she was stunned speechless. She was definitely going to go back to the part about him not saying no, but... "You hired someone to massage me?" Her heels clicked loudly against the tiled entryway.

"You looked like you could use the break after today." For a moment he looked impossibly insecure. "I...shit, was that too presumptuous? I just wanted to do something—"

"No! It's really nice. No one's ever done anything like that for me before. Thank you." She felt her cheeks heating up under his intense stare and tried to think of something halfway intelligent to say, but her brain had gone completely haywire. He'd hired someone to massage her? That was too sweet for words. Maybe it could have come off as too much, but she could tell Quinn had done it from a good place. And something told her he'd paid for it himself, not put it on the room.

"Athena?" A female voice made her turn. A tall, broad woman in scrub-like clothing and her hair pulled back in a tight bun smiled warmly at her. "I'm all set up if you're ready."

"Ah, yeah, just a second." She glanced back at Quinn, who was giving her what she thought of as his 'hungry look'. "Thanks," she murmured again. He was really making it impossible to even want to keep her distance.

He just nodded. "I'll order us room service."

She certainly wasn't going to argue about that. After the exhausting day she'd had, she was going to enjoy this gift and then dinner with him. And maybe...more. She did a mental head shake. She was way too twisted up over Quinn and right about now she was having a hard time remembering why she'd wanted to keep things professional between them. It wouldn't hurt to indulge just a little, right?

———————•••———————

Quinn stood by the oversized window looking out over the bright city, but he wasn't really seeing anything. All he could seem to focus on was that Athena was in her room right now, getting rubbed down by someone.

He wanted to be that someone. He's specifically asked for a female massage therapist because no way in hell was he actually hiring some guy to touch her. And yeah, he knew that made him a total caveman, but whatever. He just wished he was the one gliding his oiled hands over her smooth skin.

When someone knocked on the door, he automatically tensed and went to reach for his weapon, but stilled his hand. He'd ordered room service since he knew Athena was too tired to want to go anywhere. He'd seen the exhaustion clearly in her eyes and her body language as soon as they'd entered the elevator.

He couldn't help being tense though, not when according to Grant, White still hadn't returned to his apartment. Not to mention the freaking pictures Grant had found of Quinn and Suzanne in one of White's drawers. Just a couple and it wasn't illegal. But Grant said it appeared as if there'd been more pictures and newspaper clippings taped up in his closet. There were bits of tape and partially ripped photographs still remaining on the wall, but it didn't prove anything. And Grant had been in the guy's apartment illegally anyway so he couldn't report it.

If they decided to push with White's parole officer to check on him, they'd have to have a good reason and right now they had nothing solid. It was the waiting around for something to happen that had Quinn going nuts. Especially since White was unaccounted for. But Lizzy had done her magic and hadn't been able to find any recent credit card use or any travel records. That didn't mean anything other than White hadn't taken a commercial flight anywhere and was probably just using cash. So the fucker could be anywhere.

Keeping his weapon holstered, he checked to make sure it was room service before opening the door. As he was ushering in the server pushing a rolling cart, the massage therapist made her way out of Athena's room. Making casual small talk, he tipped both the therapist and server before seeing them to the door and securing it.

He knocked on Athena's door lightly and when she opened it a moment later wearing one of the thick white hotel robes loosely belted around her waist, he swallowed hard. Her hair was down and tousled and her eyes had a sated gleam to them. She looked relaxed and sexy and all he could think about was seducing her right there.

Wordlessly she took a small step toward him, that glint in her gaze flashing with lust. He wasn't sure if she was even aware of the tiny movement, but he wasn't backing down unless she told him to. He was already rock hard with wanting her. Hell, he seemed to stay in that perpetual state whenever he thought about her.

Tired of waiting, he closed the short distance between them. She stepped forward as he did, her intentions clear. Sliding his hand through her dark hair, he crushed his mouth over hers. She moaned as she arched into him, not even pausing in her reaction.

Hell yes.

Greedy for more, he fisted her hips and hoisted her up against him. Without pause she wrapped her legs around him, her robe easily splitting open.

His heart thundered in his chest as he grasped the back of her head. Her tongue danced against his in a fervent rhythm. It had been like this before with them, the need to taste her, to touch her, so overwhelming he felt practically possessed by it. The only difference this time was that he wasn't backing down or walking away.

He didn't move them far, just backed her up against the open door. It thumped slightly against the wall under their weight. Her fingers tightened on his shoulders, her short nails digging into him as she held on tight. He wished there wasn't a barrier between them, that he could feel those fingernails on his skin, that he could see and taste all of her.

His hand actually shook as he reached under the lapel of her robe, wanting to feel more of her. The second his hand cupped her full breast, she let out a little whimper and bit his bottom lip.

The unexpected sting of her teeth had him rolling his hips against her. His cock was heavy between his legs, pulsing with need and desperate to be inside Athena. He wanted to be her first... Her only. That thought sent a sudden jolt through him, but he accepted it. Nothing else to do. Athena had him all twisted up in knots and he wasn't going to fucking analyze it.

He lightly pinched her already hard nipple. She shuddered.

"More," she demanded, her voice ragged.

He slid her robe off her shoulders and she tensed as it pooled around her waist. Pulling back just a fraction so he could look down at her, he needed to see that she wanted this. Hell, he needed to hear the words.

"You want to stop?"

"No." Her answer was immediate, but he could sense hesitation there. Just a flicker of it in her blue eyes.

Not exactly surprising. Maybe it was the thought of being completely naked in front of him. He didn't know, he'd never been with a virgin before. And they'd never had a conversation outlining how much fucking experience she actually had. The farthest they'd gone was him taking her top off and caressing her over her bra. "Tell me if and when you want to stop." God, he wanted inside her though.

She nodded, her eyes a little wide, her chest rising and falling faster than normal. Okay, she was nervous, he could see it. So he left the robe pooled slightly around her waist, held up by the belt so that just her breasts were revealed.

They were perfection. *Compliment her*, his brain shouted at him. "I've been fantasizing about kissing these for two long months," he murmured. Pale brown nipples tipped pert, full breasts.

She let out a little gasp at his words, but he didn't give her a chance to respond. There was no need to and he was too damn greedy for the taste of her now anyway. Groaning, he dipped his head, sucking one bud into his mouth.

He heard more than saw her head fall back against the door. She arched up, pushing herself farther into his mouth. While he flicked his tongue over the bud, he cupped her other breast, teasing her nipple with his thumb in slow, lazy circles.

She squirmed against the door, her legs tightening around him in a harder grip. Continuing to flick his tongue over her in teasing strokes, he reached between their bodies, sliding the robe out of the way to cup her mound. He'd expected to have to push material out of the way but she wasn't wearing anything under her robe.

He felt the softest bit of hair on her mound as he slid a finger along her slit. Wet. So fucking wet.

Sucking in a breath, he drew his head back. "This for me?" The question was practically a growl. He knew the answer but wanted to hear it, was desperate to.

Her cheeks tinged pink but she gave him a small smile. "Yes. I thought about you while I was getting my massage too."

For a long moment his brain seemed to stutter before jerking back to life. "You wanted *my* hands on you instead?"

A quick nod, her breathing growing even harsher. The rise and fall of her chest was erratic now.

His throat tightened as he thought about her stretched out on the massage table, thought about smoothing his hands up and down her entire body, over her sweet curves, between her legs. He curled a finger inside her damp heat at that thought and her eyes went heavy-lidded again.

He loved seeing that expression on her, so relaxed and sensual. He shouldn't be surprised by how tight she was, but damn. Slowly, he moved his finger deeper, savoring the feel of her clenching around him.

His cock pressed painfully against the zipper of his pants but that was too damn bad for him. They wouldn't be doing everything he wanted tonight because it was too soon for her. He was going to learn more about her body, what she liked. Because he was going to feel her coming against his fingers or mouth tonight. Maybe both.

Keeping his hand right where it was, cupping her, he set her feet on the floor and knelt in front of her.

Her eyes widened slightly until he took his free hand and slid it up her ankle and calf in a caress. Her skin was smooth but he felt the goosebumps as he moved higher. That hint of nervousness was there again, but there was a heavy measure of trust in her eyes. One he wasn't going to betray.

He'd fucked up once, but if she trusted him with her body, he'd never betray that. Without much encouragement, she lifted her leg, seeming to know exactly what he wanted her to do. She propped her heel on his shoulder, opening herself up to him in the sexiest way. Part of him wondered if she'd ever done this before, if even this would be her first time too.

The scent of the tropical oils the masseuse must have used combined with Athena's sweet scent. It was damn near overwhelming. Just like everything else about her.

He looked up, seeing the mix of hunger and hesitancy in her expression. Soon, all she'd feel was pleasure. He'd make sure of it. Inhaling that sweet scent, he leaned forward and covered her clit with his mouth, lightly sucking on the nub without any buildup.

"Quinn," she gasped out, her hips rolling against his face.

He moaned, loving the sound of his name on her lips, especially under these circumstances. He hoped she felt the vibration of his moan, that it combined with the strokes of his tongue. If the way she was moving her hips against him was any indication, he'd hit a good rhythm.

Sliding his finger deeper inside her, his cock jerked as she tightened around his digit. The thought of thrusting inside her, filling her with more than a finger had all the muscles in his body pulling taut. He imagined how tight she'd be, the sounds she'd make —

"Quinn, oh hell, I'm coming." Athena's words were rasped out, the rolling of her hips growing faster and more unsteady against his face.

Yes.

He pushed his finger deeper into that slickness. She bucked against him again. He sucked on her clit with more pressure than he'd used so far.

Her inner walls clenched convulsively around his finger as she found her release, her orgasm seeming to go on forever as she let out gasping little moans and gripped his head with her fingers. As if she thought he might stop what he was doing or maybe just to support herself.

Eventually her climax ebbed, but he felt the little flutters of her pussy around his finger. And felt like a fucking caveman, all proud he'd made her climax. He didn't know if he was the first man to have pleasured her like this and a couple months ago he might have said he didn't care. But fuck that, he hoped he was. He planned on giving her a lot more orgasms. Next time he wanted to see her face though, wanted to see those blue eyes as pleasure pulsed through her. Wanted to see her expression as he pushed inside her.

Her fingers loosened their death grip on his head and she sagged against the door as he pulled back. Though he hated to, he withdrew his finger and stood. His heart beat was an erratic rhythm in his chest.

Her smile was slow, her expression completely satisfied as she looked at him. No regret there. Then to his surprise, she reached for his belt, tugging the buckle free as she kept her eyes pinned to his.

Unsure exactly what she planned, he placed his palms on the door on either side of her head and let her have her way. If he touched her now he was likely to hoist her up against the door and strip the rest of her robe completely off. But he didn't think that's what she wanted.

Slowly, she tugged his zipper down, then broke her gaze from his as she shoved his pants just a bit down his hips. He was dying with the need to feel her hand around him. Another grin teased her lips. "Boxer briefs. I've wondered," she murmured, hooking her fingers under the elastic and moving them down to join his pants.

His cock sprung free, heavy and thick. Before he had time to contemplate anything, she gripped him and stroked upward. Once, twice, and he groaned at the feel of her smooth fingers wrapped around him.

"Tighter." He watched her face, saw her lips quirk up a fraction as she did just that. But she wasn't looking into his eyes, she was watching herself stroke him, as if mesmerized.

It was fucking hot.

Her grip was harder now, faster, and he was so close he should probably try to hold off. But he didn't want to. When she cupped his balls, which were pulled tight, with her other hand and tugged gently, he gave up any sense of control.

Letting go, he crushed his mouth to hers as his climax slammed into him. She let out a yelp of surprise, his kiss taking her off guard. But she didn't stop stroking.

A growl erupted from him as he emptied himself over her hands and his stomach until what seemed like an eternity later, his brain cleared somewhat.

Breathing hard, he pulled back to see Athena's face. The hint of a Cheshire cat smile was in place, her eyes dancing with too many emotions for him to sift through. He didn't think she had any, but... "Regrets?"

Shaking her head, she nudged his stomach with her hand. "No, but we need a shower."

Laughing, he nodded. He was still stunned that she'd stroked him to climax, but glad there didn't seem to be any barriers between them anymore. "Agreed. We'll take it together." Without giving her a chance to protest, not that he thought she would, he tugged the belt on her robe completely free and let it fall to the ground. It had been mostly off by now, hanging low on her hips, but to see her standing completely bare in front of him did something ridiculously primal to him. He wanted to claim Athena, wanted to let pretty much every man with a pulse know that she was taken.

CHAPTER EIGHT

Athena curled up against Quinn's chest, pleased that he'd wanted to sleep in the same bed. She wasn't exactly sure what they were, if anything, relationship-wise, but she was glad he hadn't showered then headed back for his room. Not that she'd really thought he would.

The massage and orgasm had left her feeling almost lethargic. Add in the steaming shower with the beyond-sexy man stretched out on her bed and yeah, she was feeling good. He'd washed her hair and body in the shower, which had been a new, sensual experience. Even better than her massage because it had been Quinn's hands on her.

He was completely naked but she'd tossed a T-shirt on. She wasn't used to sleeping naked and still felt a little out of her depth with him regardless of what they'd just shared.

His finger traced up and down her spine almost idly. His heart rate was too fast, as was his breathing. And she could see the bulge beneath the covers. Though her knowledge was limited, he had a very impressive cock. Next time she wanted to taste him, but now wasn't the time. Of course she didn't think he'd stop her if she started going down on him, but this quiet holding was really nice and she wasn't ready to give it up.

"So, how is it that you're a virgin?" He asked the question quietly and she automatically stiffened before she realized his tone was just curious. He proved that by continuing. "I'm not saying it's a good, bad or abnormal thing, I'm just…curious. You're a smart, beautiful woman."

188 | KATIE REUS

Shifting against his chest, she looked up at him, wanting to see his face. Unlike the exterior room adjoining their suites, her bedroom had a jaguar print/jungle theme going on. The headboard was a fabric print with what she assumed was fake amber jewels lining the top. They glittered against the lights from the city through the sheer privacy drapes. Even though the bed was shadowed, Quinn was perfectly illuminated as well. "You first, when did you lose yours?" Not that she'd lost hers yet, but that would hopefully happen soon.

"Ah, the week I turned sixteen." He grinned almost sheepishly. "It was cliché too, with my girlfriend in the back of my car."

She let out a short laugh, relaxing at his honest answer. "Part of the reason is my family dynamics. I wasn't even allowed to date until I was sixteen and even then it was only in groups. Since I wasn't really rebellious and I went to a private school where I had male cousins in grades above and below me, even if I'd wanted to get involved with someone..." She shrugged, debating if she should tell him the real reason.

"Nothing can stop sixteen year old hormones," he murmured knowingly. When she snorted, he continued. "At least not in my experience."

She shifted again, this time rolling back over so that she was still tucked in the crook of his arm, but looking over his chest and out the window. "Okay, being completely honest, I was overweight in high school and the first two years of college. I didn't want anyone, especially a guy, to see me naked. Sex and dating just weren't a concern to me because of my own issues." She'd never told any of the guys she'd dated this truth and it was freeing.

"My third year of college I guess I semi-rebelled—according to my over-protective parents—and decided to move out of their house. I roomed with this girl who was a fitness nut. Built like a freaking goddess, no joke. Her name was Candy, also not a joke, and she was—is—awesome. She started dragging me with her to jog in the mornings using the excuse that she wanted a workout buddy. I think she just picked up on my insecurities and wanted to be a good friend. From there I started making little changes and..." Athena shrugged again, not needing to give him the breakdown of all the changes she'd made in her life. "I shed twenty pounds that year and started toning and watching what I ate."

Quinn kept stroking, his hand steady and strong. "That's impressive...though twenty pounds isn't..." He trailed off, as if maybe unsure he should continue.

She looked up at him. "It's not a lot, if that's what you're going to say, but when you're five feet, two inches, it kind of is."

"I bet you gain it in your tits and ass," he murmured, reaching down to squeeze her butt.

She blinked, taken off guard by the blunt statement. "Oh my God, you're such a guy!"

"I'm glad you noticed." The glint in his dark eyes was purely wicked. He turned his body now so that they were flush against each other, his erection pressing insistently against her abdomen.

She threw her leg over his hip, savoring the closeness. "Now that I've been honest... Why did you freak out when I told you I was a virgin?"

For a long moment, he was silent, his expression so neutral she hated it. Thankfully he answered. "It wasn't exactly that you were a virgin. But I used that as an excuse." Now he looked almost sheepish.

"Why?"

"The only real relationship I was in was back in my Marine Corps days. It didn't end well. And I take some of the blame, I'm certainly not perfect, but...she just got pissed at everything I did. Things I had no control of, like training or deployments. We fought more than anything else near the end and it was so damn tiring. Once we broke up it was like a weight had been lifted."

She nodded slightly. "Okay, I'm sort of following."

"I... I didn't think I wanted anything serious and since her I haven't looked or really even contemplated getting serious with any woman. Until you. It scared the hell out of me. And I know that sounds like bullshit, but when you told me you were a virgin, it was easy to make an excuse and end things."

"Okay. I can deal with that." When he half-smiled, she continued.

"Now you get to tell me something else real about yourself. Before you said that whole thing that happened with White is part of why you left the police department. What's the other reason?"

Sliding his hand up from where it rested on her hip, he cupped her cheek, his thumb gently stroking over her skin. She liked the feel of his faint calluses.

"I got out of the Corps after six years and going into law enforcement afterward seemed like the logical next step. I started working on my degree while I was in, but it was becoming clear that the job wasn't for me even before White. I respect the men and women who can do it, but the stuff you deal with day in and day out..." He shook his head, his expression dark. "It was starting to wear on me, so when Harrison offered me a job, I took it."

She thought there might be a little more to it than that, but wasn't going to push. "So you were in the Corps six years, with the police department for two and Red Stone for six... How old are you exactly?"

The corner of his mouth curved up, the grin so ridiculously sexy it made butterflies take flight in her stomach. "Thirty-two."

"Hmm, eight year difference. Not exactly robbing the cradle, but I think I might have to rethink this whole thing between us." She kept her voice light, teasing.

He snorted and pinched her butt, making her yelp. "Think all you want, I'm not going anywhere." Oh God, his voice dropped a few octaves when he said it, sending a shiver skittering down her spine.

She wasn't exactly sure what he meant by that and she didn't want to ask. Back in Miami he'd told her he wanted to take her out again, but that didn't mean they were dating or anything more serious. And yeah, she was too chickenshit to ask him. Her dating experience was limited and if this was just a fling she didn't need it spelled out for her now. She'd ask later, she told herself. Because right now she was feeling too relaxed to let anything ruin her mood.

When he suddenly rolled over, pinning her beneath him, she was glad she hadn't asked. The feel of him stretched out over her was...indescribable. She ran her fingers over the muscles of his upper arms, stopping at his shoulders. The man was so built it was hard not to get hot feeling all that power beneath her fingertips.

He nipped her bottom lip teasingly, his breath warm against her face, his spicy scent a total aphrodisiac. As he kissed a hot path along her jawline, she raked her fingers down his back. Whatever he had in mind, she was game.

"I don't think I got a good enough taste of you the first time," he said in a dark whisper that sent a shot of hunger straight to her core.

His words left her speechless and heating up to scorching levels in seconds. She'd never had a guy go down on her before, but her female cousins had been right. It *was* amazing. This time she planned to taste him too.

She pressed against his shoulder, making him raise his head, those midnight dark eyes seeming to gleam against the backdrop of the Vegas nightlife. "I want to taste you first," she said in a rush, sure her face was crimson. At least the room was dim enough to hide her reaction. She wasn't ready for full-on sex just yet, not when things were still so new between them, something he seemed to understand without her having to say anything, but she still wanted to make him as crazy with pleasure as he'd made her.

He stilled, almost like a statue for just a moment, before he swallowed hard and rolled off her. She was under the impression that it was unusual for him to give up control like this, which made the whole situation even hotter.

"On your back, hands behind your head." She attempted to make the statement as an order, but it came out more like a shaky whisper.

Which wasn't a bad thing considering his eyes went pure molten. "Take off your shirt and I'll do it," he said after a pause. That edge to his words sent a shiver streaking up her spine.

Pausing for just a second, she did as he instructed. He'd already seen her naked and tasted her, but he still sucked in a breath at the sight of her. It did something crazy to her insides that she affected him like this. "Flat on your back."

His eyebrows raised just a fraction, but he stretched out, showing off that gorgeous ripped body. Instead of straddling him right away she drank him in.

She should have gotten her fill in the shower, but her mouth was practically watering as she raked her gaze from the hard lines and striations of his chest and stomach down to his thick cock. His upper legs were like tree trunks, all built and...her nipples pebbled tight as her gaze swept back up to his impressive erection.

His breathing was unsteady now as he watched her, those eyes heated and hungry as she settled between his legs. Right about now she was incredibly thankful for her oversharing cousins because she was feeling pretty secure in what to do. One cousin in particular—with six kids so she was clearly doing something right—had been so blunt about it when Athena had asked. *Watch the teeth unless you're being playful, wrap your fingers around the base hard and stroke with your hand as you use your mouth, and don't neglect the balls.* She'd given Athena a freaking visual with fruit—something she'd tried to erase from her memory—and had been very explicit about a massage technique but Athena wasn't trying *that* her first time.

Feeling more powerful than she imagined to have this strong, sexy man at her mercy, she lightly gripped the base of his erection and inwardly smiled as he let out an unsteady, strangled moan. Oh yeah, she could do this. And she loved that he was letting her take the reins.

Instead of jumping into it, Athena leaned down and rubbed her cheek against the head of his cock. He rolled his hips and she realized his hands weren't behind his head anymore, but gripping the sheet beneath him. His breathing was ragged, but clearly he was okay with her doing what she wanted.

She inwardly grinned at his growing lack of control, liking this side to him. She flicked her tongue over the tip of his thick length, tasted pre-come. Tasting him like this made her damper between her legs. She was turned on, but this took things to a new level she hadn't expected.

Since she'd liked it when he'd feathered kisses all over her, she decided to do the same to him. Keeping her fingers wrapped firmly around his base, she stroked her tongue up the length of him, unable to fight the pleasure that ran through her as he shuddered again.

She wanted to tease him, but she really wanted to taste all of him. When she sucked him fully into her mouth he muttered a savage curse before groaning phrases like "So fucking good" and other variations of that.

She took him in her mouth as she stroked, in and out, sucking gently then harder, seeing what worked for him. It seemed clear he liked everything she did, but harder got more of a reaction so she took that advice she'd been given years ago and stroked and sucked until he fisted a hand in her hair. Not hard, but enough to get her attention.

"Shit, Athena. I'm going to come." The words came out a growl. A warning.

She knew he was telling her to pull back so he could come on his stomach, but she was having none of that.

He quickly realized it because his grip loosened, but he didn't let go. She swallowed as he climaxed against her tongue. His fingers threaded through her hair as she finished, taking all of him until he'd dropped his hand and his body had relaxed more or less boneless against the sheets.

Grinning, and okay, feeling proud of herself, Athena straddled him and shimmied up his body until she stretched out on top of him.

Moving like a fast predator, he took her off guard and had her pinned beneath him once again. She couldn't be sure but she figured he had a bit of a dominant streak. She'd thought that back when they'd been dating, and experiencing him in the bedroom now, yeah, she could see it. She liked that he'd let her explore his body all she wanted though.

"That was incredible," he murmured, dropping kisses onto her mouth, and along her jawline again.

The man seemed to already know the nuances of her body, seemed to know exactly what she liked and needed. So when he reached between her legs to cup her mound, she wasn't sure why he pulled back in surprise. Maybe because she was so freaking wet it should probably be embarrassing.

He slid a finger inside her, making her breath catch. She was tingling all over again, already wanting more. "This is all for me." There was a possessive note in his words that made her clench around his finger.

"Yes," she whispered.

And *that* made something dark flare in his gaze before he captured her mouth in a frenzied mating. One thing she was sure of, they wouldn't be getting to sleep for a while.

———————•◦•———————

"This looks great," Athena said, scanning the food list for tomorrow. "Just make sure you replace the cucumber canapés with the cheesy canapés — the ones with the roasted tomatoes — and veggie pinwheels. Those have both been a hit so just double up." The cucumber finger-foods had ended up getting soggy and looking all around disgusting by midday. It was almost five now and no one had touched them. No need to waste all that food or space.

The woman who worked for the outside catering company they'd hired nodded. "No problem. We're going to start breaking everything down now unless you think we should let the food sit?"

"Go ahead. If you or your boss need anything else just let me know. I've got my phone attached to me." Smiling, she patted her jacket pocket. "I'll be here for another hour at least." As the woman left, Athena turned, looking for Travis or Quinn.

Over half the vendors had already left and the other stragglers were either talking to potential clients or each other. No one had to break down anything today since the tradeshow was all week. The final day would be the crazy one, but for now things had run smoothly with only a few minor blips. Athena was running high on the adrenaline of the first day's success and everything that had happened between her and Quinn.

After fooling around last night and again this morning before their very early in-room breakfast, he'd been a little tense, almost distant, but she was ninety-nine percent sure that had nothing to do with her.

She'd heard him on the phone with who she guessed was Grant when she came out of her bedroom this morning, talking about Glenn White. But Quinn hadn't told her that she needed to be worried about anything and she knew he would if they were in imminent danger. So she was putting all that out of her head even though Quinn seemed to be worried about it. Not that she could blame him.

It took a few minutes of navigating through the display tables, but she found Quinn and Travis talking to an attractive woman with dark brown hair streaked with auburn highlights. She wore a fitted black suit similar to the one Athena had seen Iris in earlier. But as far as Athena could tell she wasn't carrying a gun, so she didn't think the woman was hotel security. She probably worked here though, given the style of dress.

Travis and Quinn both nodded when they saw her approaching, though Quinn's gaze softened just the tiniest bit. The woman looked at Athena, smiled briefly, then nodded at the two men.

She touched Quinn's forearm briefly. "I'll see you in a bit." Then she was gone, her heels clicking rapidly as she hurried toward one of the exits.

Athena wasn't sure what the woman meant and wasn't going to ask — even if curiosity clawed at her. "You guys tired after today?"

They both smiled, nodded. "And starving," Travis said.

Quinn shook his head. "You're always hungry."

She let out a brief laugh, tuning out the echoing sounds of the catering staff breaking down the food display tables. "How did everything go with security?" They'd only checked in with her a few times over the course of the day. Their job had been to coordinate with The Serafina's on-site security and she hadn't interfered because that wasn't her strong suit. She knew how to make an event run smoothly, but throw in the security aspect? She'd leave that up to the pros.

They did that dual head nod thing again, making her laugh as they said "Good" almost in sync.

"If there were any issues or anything I need to be aware of for future events, just send me a detailed report. I don't even want to talk about it until I get food. You guys want to grab dinner?"

"Absolutely," Travis said, running a hand over his Mohawk.

For the briefest moment, Quinn looked uncomfortable, but then his expression went carefully neutral in a way that made her stomach twist. "I can't."

Athena blinked, waiting for him to continue, to give a reason, something. When he didn't, she pushed back the disappointment that swelled inside her. "Ah, okay." She certainly wasn't going to ask him why he couldn't or what he was doing, not in front of Travis. She looked at Travis. "Want to grab a meal here or walk around and find something?"

The two men shared a look she couldn't quite decipher before Travis slid on another easy smile. "I've been wanting to try Cloud 9 and Iris said they'd fit us in anytime."

"Sounds good to me." She glanced at Quinn. "I'll see you later then?" Ugh, she felt so awkward. They hadn't defined their relationship and she didn't want to come off as needy by asking him when he'd be back to their room. Even though she really wanted to know.

He just nodded, his expression impossible to read. "I'll see you soon."

As she headed out with Travis she hated the uncomfortable feeling twisting in her gut. This morning she'd been so sure about them, that Quinn's mood and clear edginess hadn't been about her. But what if she was wrong and he'd changed his mind about them? What if he'd once again decided that the virgin thing wasn't something he wanted to deal with?

Those stupid insecurities flared up again but she told her inner voice to shut the hell up. She needed to trust him and stop over-analyzing everything. "So you've heard good things about Cloud 9?" she asked Travis, wanting to keep her mind off Quinn for now.

"Yeah, Noel told me she'd read an article about it and I had to try it. I'm surprised they didn't cater for the tradeshow."

"They're way too busy." Athena had wondered the same thing and that was the response she'd gotten. "So what's Quinn up to? Is there a security issue I need to know about?" So maybe she wasn't exactly keeping her mind off Quinn. *Freaking sue me,* she thought.

Luckily Travis didn't seem to have a clue about her and his friend because he shrugged. "He's meeting with Margot—that was the woman we were talking to before—for drinks."

His words were like a solid punch to Athena's gut. An unwanted iciness invaded her veins, but she pasted on a smile she didn't feel. "Should one of us pick up Raegan from the airport? I don't mind if you want to kick back after dinner." Her assistant's flight had been delayed but she was arriving in a couple hours.

Travis shook his head immediately. "I'll get her. You should stay at the hotel."

The noise level in the wide open lobby of the hotel as they crossed it was surprisingly minimal. Animated yes, but nothing too obnoxious. She glanced at him. "Why?"

He shrugged, but his shoulders seemed tense. "I know it's your first big job. Anything could happen with the tradeshow and you should be on site."

He wasn't wrong, but there was something off about his tone. She didn't know Travis remotely well though so she couldn't be sure.

"If for some reason you decide to leave, you need to tell Quinn or me." Now his tone was serious.

"Ah, okay." It seemed odd, but she'd known working for a security company would be different than her other jobs. And she wasn't just doing contract work anymore so this might be a companywide protocol. She started to ask Travis but they'd reached the entrance of Cloud 9. The restaurant was considered fine-dining but there was a man in front of them wearing a Tommy Bahama shirt, linen pants and flip-flops. Freaking Vegas, she supposed, the sight making her smile.

Not that it did anything to take away from the hurt and annoyance gnawing at her gut. So Quinn was having drinks with some woman? No big deal. Except it felt like it was. He could have told her. Unless his reason for having drinks with the woman was romantic.

Her mood darkened even more at that thought and when she caught Travis giving her a curious look, she pasted on another fake smile. She was good at that.

————————•◦•————————

Feeling smug, Glenn strolled across the lobby of The Serafina, disguise firmly in place. The beard he'd opted to use looked real and did the job of covering his facial features well. He doubted Quinn would ever imagine he was here in Vegas, but when Quinn and the Manikas woman went missing it was feasible that Glenn would be looked at as a suspect. So he'd taken all precautions. He'd left his cell phone in Miami so he didn't have to worry about his phone pinging off any towers here and being tracked. And on the very real chance that any of the cameras here at The Serafina were looked at, his face wouldn't show up on any of them because of the beard and hat. Any type of facial covering messed with the recognition software programs.

He'd even added padding to his middle so he looked as if he weighed about twenty-five to thirty pounds more. The pullover sweater he wore with jeans and sneakers was a simple attire and the sweater covered his tats so there were no visible identifying features. The ball cap and beard covered enough of his face so he'd never be identified. Yep, he'd covered all his bases.

The sight of Athena walking into a restaurant with one of Quinn's coworkers made Glenn smile, but he didn't look at them too long. He just kept making his way toward the entrance of the casino. All day he'd been in and out, coming and going as he pleased, keeping an eye out for either of his targets.

That alone sent the biggest rush of power through him. He'd seen that mouthy bitch working the tradeshow. Some kind of transportation thing going on. Tomorrow he'd go inside but today he'd wanted to get things in place.

So far he had a van that he'd bought in cash from a shady car dealer. It had been all under the table too. Glenn only needed the thing to transport Athena. After that he didn't care what happened to it. Though he'd probably burn it in the desert once he'd killed Quinn and Athena. Maybe with their bodies inside. He'd have to wipe it down first though to cover all bases. He wasn't taking any chances.

As those thoughts assailed him, he shook his head, focusing on his surroundings. He couldn't afford to get distracted now. The loud sounds of the various machines and people shouting in excitement at their wins accosted his senses as he stepped fully onto the main floor of the casino.

After the long day he'd had he was going to gamble a little then head back out and see if he could secure a place to hold Athena once he'd kidnapped her. He'd scouted a few abandoned places today, both residential and commercial, but he needed to see what they were like at night. That would make all the difference.

Tomorrow, using his new fake ID, he'd enter the tradeshow and get a feel for the layout, see what the woman did all day. He needed to look for security weak spots and when she went places alone. If he could get a handle on her schedule, getting Quinn to come to him would be easy.

Then the fun would begin.

CHAPTER NINE

Quinn was off balance, his need to get back to Athena overwhelming. But he kept his expression neutral as he stepped off the elevator with Margot onto the security floor. The fiftieth floor wasn't accessible to the general public or even most of the hotel and casino staff. Just select individuals.

"How long have you been with Red Stone?" Margot asked, placing her hand on the biometric scanner of the security area.

Glass doors whooshed open and they were immediately inundated by a steady hum of voices. Walls were covered with video screens and people in suits and headsets talked at rapid speeds. "About six years."

"That how long your guy was in jail?" she asked, motioning for him to follow her along a walkway that rounded the main security center.

"Yeah." Quinn wanted to send him right back there too.

"He'd be stupid to follow you here, but I'm glad you told us about the threat." Margot stopped in front of a closed door, rapped once.

It opened a second later. Iris smiled and stepped back. Once they moved into her sleek, not-surprisingly minimalist office, she pressed a button on a window that Quinn now saw overlooked the hub of the security area. It immediately frosted over, giving them complete privacy.

"We've got some possible matches," Iris started, stepping over to a panel of four wide screens. "But nothing more than thirty-eight percent probability, which you know as well as I do is useless. These matches might as well be Martians."

Though it punched through him abruptly, he didn't show his disappointment. "How many matches?"

She picked up a remote and flipped on the screens. "Twelve." Twelve shots of men flashed on screen, layered next to each other. He stared at all of them. The images were clear enough, but most had beards and all of them had ball caps or other style hats on—and their body types varied. Quinn couldn't tell if any of them were Glenn because he could have made changes to his appearance. No, not could have, if he was here, he definitely had. The man wasn't stupid.

She continued. "We used White's driver's license photo from six years ago and his more recent one. We've also plugged in other identifying factors like his new tattoo. But none of this does us any good if he's wearing a disguise. Anything that covers his face or eyes messes with our program. It's top of the line, but technology still has limitations. And we're not focusing on the body at all since that can be altered far too much with padding."

Jaw tight, Quinn nodded, scanning over the images again. He resisted the urge to pace. Damn it, he hated that no one with Red Stone could track White down yet. The guy had just ghosted. "I appreciate you doing this at all."

Iris nodded while Margot leaned against the front of Iris's desk. "We've checked commercial flights and car rentals and haven't found anything," she said. "So why are you certain he's here?"

"I don't know that he *is* here. But his cell phone is still at his place." And who the hell left their cell phone for long periods of time? *No one.* Not unless they had a good reason. "My guys haven't seen him return to his place for days and there's been no use of his credit cards. It's like he fell off the face of the earth."

Iris lifted a shoulder. "Maybe he just rabbited out of the country."

"If he had he would have cleaned out his bank accounts." At least that was what common sense told Quinn. Because White would have wanted to buy a new ID. He'd have the contacts, but it wouldn't be cheap. But Quinn didn't think White would just leave without wanting payback. "Bottom line, my gut tells me he's here. Or at least trying to find me and possibly Athena. White isn't just going to walk away, flee the country. He'd want to kill me first. He blames me for his wife leaving." Which was complete and utter bullshit, but there would be no reasoning with a wife-beater like White. A man who blamed everyone else for his problems. Weak and pathetic at his core.

Giving Quinn a hard stare, Iris tapped a long, elegant finger against her chin for a moment. "I'm going to put a two-man team on Athena this week when she's at the tradeshow. They won't be in her way but they're not going to blend in either. In your suite she'll be more than secure, but with the tradeshow I think we need people specifically looking out for her during the day. I've never known you to overreact to anything and I don't want to take any chances."

Quinn breathed out a sigh of relief. He'd planned to ask and was glad he didn't even need to. "Thanks, Iris."

She shrugged in that nonchalant way of hers. "From what you've told us, in White's mind you took from him so he'll want to take from you. Not gonna happen on my watch."

Quinn hadn't come out and said that he and Athena were together, but Iris was perceptive. "Thanks. You mind sending the pictures to Travis and me? I'm going to go over everything with Athena tonight, let her know to be on guard. Even if none of these guys are White..." He glanced at the screen again, frowned. It was too damn hard to tell. "I still want her aware."

"No problem. I'm flagging my top three candidates—none of whom are staying at the casino and all paid in cash, unfortunately—because of their ears."

Quinn blinked once as understanding set in. He narrowed his gaze at Iris while Margot just shifted uncomfortably against the desk. "Are you saying what I think you're saying?" he asked.

Iris just grinned, the action a little feral. "Ears are the new fingerprints."

Yeah, he knew what kind of technology was available.

Margot snorted and pushed up from the desk. "Maybe one day they will be."

Iris sighed. "Okay, there are experts that disagree, but the Feds are using it to track people...and so are we if necessary. And that's off the record. We'll find your guy one way or another."

So she was saying exactly what he thought. "I know what the Feds have. You guys have the same technology?"

Iris patted his arm, as if amused, then turned back to the screens. "Ours is better. And since we have very good photographs of White for the program to compare, it's going to make tracking him, if he comes into our casino, much easier." She pressed a few buttons on her remote control and all but three photographs disappeared.

She zoomed in on them, placing one on each screen, leaving the fourth screen dark. The top half of the men's ears were covered with hair sticking out from their ball caps, making it impossible to get a full scan. "The other nine are pretty much a no-go if you use the ear technology alone, but I don't want to narrow your results too much since the technology is still controversial in some circles. In my opinion, and because of our experiences here using it, it freaking *works*. But..." She shrugged. "You need to have all the facts."

He knew about the technology too, how effective it was. "Send all the pictures to me. Were you able to track the three men offsite?" He figured it was almost impossible and definitely illegal, but wanted to ask anyway.

Iris shook her head. "No, but now that we're aware there could be a problem, no one's going to get past my guys. I'll let you know who I pick for tomorrow and have them attached to Athena. Unless you and Travis want to be her shadows?"

His instinct was to say yes, but he paused. Part of the reason he and Travis were here was to help Athena figure out potential security issues for any future tradeshows, get her used to thinking about both sides of the coin with events. She might not want him and Travis to guard her. "Let me ask her first." If Athena preferred Iris's guys— and Quinn trusted her to have hired only the best—then he'd deal with it. Of course he still wouldn't let Athena out of the tradeshow room without him.

That she'd just have to deal with. Because he could compromise but only within limits.

To his surprise, Iris's lips curved up a fraction. "Smart man," she murmured.

He figured he understood her meaning, but didn't comment directly. "I'm going to meet up with Travis and Athena now, go over everything, but I've got my phone on me and we'll be meeting again tomorrow morning at six to head to the tradeshow."

"Just let me know if you want my guys to shadow her or replace you on the ground. Either way they'll join you at six sharp. And, I'll send you their resumes," she added, clearly reading the expression on his face.

"Thanks." Now that he'd gotten this out of the way, it was time to come clean with Athena and tell her what Grant had found in Miami and that Glenn White was potentially in Vegas. Maybe he should have told her sooner, but he hadn't wanted to needlessly worry her.

Not when she already had so much on her plate. This was her first job with Red Stone and he knew she needed to be focused. But her safety came first and if White thought he could hurt Quinn through Athena, Quinn had no doubt the bastard would try.

When he reached his floor he immediately went to Travis's door, knocked.

A few seconds later Travis opened the door in jeans, a T-shirt and his cell phone held loosely in his hand. "Hey, I was about to do a video call with Noel, everything cool?"

"I wanted to do a run down with both you and Athena at the same time so I don't have to do it twice. Want to wait?"

Travis shook his head as he stepped out into the hall. "Nah. I felt bad lying to Athena about where you were. I hadn't planned to say anything but she asked." The door shut with a soft click behind him.

Frowning, Quinn slid his key card into his suite's door. "What did you tell her?" He moved inside, Travis right behind him.

"That you were having drinks with Margot. Figured it was better than—"

His gut tightened. "Shit." He bit back the more savage curse that sprang to mind. He'd been unsure how to act around Athena in front of Travis. He hadn't wanted to embarrass her if she wasn't ready to let people know they were together. He sure as hell wanted the whole fucking world to know but it was pretty much her first week on the job so he'd wanted to move with caution. She probably thought the worst of him now.

"What is it?" Travis asked, his voice tense as Quinn headed straight for Athena's room.

"Nothing, I'll tell you in a sec." He knocked once sharply on her door. When he didn't get an answer he glanced over his shoulder at Travis. "Move back." Because he didn't want anyone to see Athena naked or in any state of undress, not even his happily married friend.

Travis looked at him as if he'd lost his mind. "Dude, you can't barge into her room. She's probably in the shower or something."

"We're...together."

Travis blinked in true surprise. Quinn figured under other circumstances Travis would have picked up on it, but he'd been asleep on the flight over and they'd been so damn busy today. "Oh...oh, hell, she's gonna be pissed at you. Sorry man, I wouldn't have said..." He trailed off at Quinn's glare, stepped back as Quinn turned back to the door.

"Athena, it's Quinn. We need to talk." He knocked again and when there was still no response, he opened the door. Something akin to fear jumped in his throat as he immediately took in the room. Untouched, the bed was still made from the daily cleaning. The bathroom door was ajar but the lights were off. Even so, he did a complete sweep of the room. She wasn't there and her purse and phone weren't anywhere visible.

He pulled out his cell as he headed toward his room. When she didn't answer his call, he texted her. No response. And she wasn't in his room either, not that he'd thought that was a real possibility. Travis gave him a concerned look but Quinn ignored him as he called Iris.

Iris answered her phone on the first ring. "Yeah?"

"Athena isn't in her room. Can you do a security check of the place?" He knew it would be easy for Iris to do a facial search and pinpoint her in less than a minute.

"On it. Where'd she go?"

"No idea." He held the phone away from his mouth as he listened to Iris give someone orders, and spoke to Travis. "She mention anything about leaving, even casually?"

"No. I told her not to leave the hotel without one of us though." He ran a hand over his Mohawk, the worry in his dark eyes clear as they headed out of the suite, made their way to the elevators.

"Got her," Iris said, the relief in her voice clear. "She's in the Cloud 9 bar area with... She's at the bar."

Instantaneous relief surged through him as they entered the plush elevator, but... "Who the hell is she with?"

"Ah, business acquaintance of Wyatt's. Pseudo-friend I guess. I'll text him now, tell him not to let Athena leave his sight. Your girl's not going anywhere."

"Who's his friend?" Quinn demanded, something in Iris's tone making him even tenser. She was holding back information.

She let out a sigh. "Name's Rhys Martin Maxwell IV. Same monetary league as Wyatt and uh, he's into BDSM. Owns a few clubs in London." She snickered before ending the call.

"Fuck!" Quinn wanted to smash his phone against the elevator wall but shoved it into his pocket.

"What is it?" Travis was in battle mode now. "Is she here?"

"Yeah. She's fine." That was all Quinn could squeeze out. Luckily Travis didn't push him, but wisely remained silent.

Quinn was aware of his surroundings at all times, but his focus was on getting to Athena. As he reached the entrance to Cloud 9 it hit him square in the chest that he was...irrationally jealous. Or maybe not exactly that, but he was what, worried that Athena was going to be swept off her feet by some fucking billionaire in the next minute? He couldn't ever remember feeling this edgy and worried. It was unsettling.

After Travis spoke to the hostess—thankfully because Quinn didn't trust himself not to snarl at the woman—they made their way to one of the bars. It was three people deep but he didn't spot Athena anywhere.

"There she is. Oh, she's with Raegan," Travis said. "She must have taken a cab from the airport. Can't believe she didn't call," he muttered.

Quinn followed the direction his friend was looking and spotted Raegan, some dick and Athena. Okay, the guy probably wasn't a dick, but Quinn was fucking revved right now. Yeah, he knew he was being beyond irrational but his brain didn't want to listen to logic at the moment. For all his woman knew, he'd been out having drinks with someone else, right after he'd told Athena he couldn't make dinner. And Quinn hadn't given her a reason for his absence, he'd just said he couldn't make it. He knew what she was thinking right now — that he was an untrustworthy ass.

"Will you make sure Raegan gets to her room safely? Make sure she knows to meet at six tomorrow?" Quinn murmured to Travis as they made their way through a cluster of high-top tables to the roped off section of modular chairs and soft lighting. He asked because he didn't plan to stay long with Athena and he wanted to make sure Raegan was taken care of. He was pretty sure the woman was even more innocent than Athena.

"Of course. You need to wipe that rabid look off your face though."

Fuck, Travis was right. He needed to get his shit under control. He'd never been like this. Never. The Corps had trained him well. But this wasn't some mission or another job.

This was Athena, and she mattered to him more than any other woman ever had.

Raegan spotted them first and smiled brightly as she stood. "Hey, guys!" Her eyes were bright, excited. He knew she hadn't been much of anywhere in the world, much less Vegas.

Quinn smiled briefly at Raegan because hell, he just couldn't be rude to the woman, ever. Ignoring the man in the no doubt custom-made suit, he pinned his gaze on Athena.

Those Mediterranean blue eyes he could drown in watched him with a complete neutrality that sliced him to the bone. There wasn't an ounce of the sensual woman who'd come against his mouth and fingers multiple times in the early morning hours. Right now that almost seemed like a lifetime ago. He should have made things clearer this morning, should have spelled out exactly how he felt about her. What he wanted and hoped she wanted too.

"I need to talk to you about a security issue now. It's important." He kept his tone professional.

Her expression immediately morphed into concern. She stood, glancing at Raegan and Travis, then back to Quinn. "Is it the tradeshow? Should we all—"

He shook his head. "It's not the show, but we need privacy. Travis will make sure Raegan gets to her room."

"Oh, ah, okay." Athena smiled warmly at the man Quinn knew was named Rhys, then made apologies to him and Raegan before telling Raegan she'd see her in the morning but to call if she needed anything.

Quinn barely resisted the urge to bare his teeth at Rhys before possessively placing his hand on the small of Athena's back and steering her out of the restaurant. It would have been impossible to miss the way she stiffened against his touch. Maybe it shouldn't have, but it pissed him off.

"Are you sure we shouldn't have included Raegan and Travis in this?" Athena asked as they reached a set of elevators. Her voice was tight, her expression pinched.

Quinn just shook his head, not trusting his voice. He wanted to tell her right then that he hadn't been out with another woman but they were surrounded by a dozen people and no one else was hearing this conversation. Because as soon as he said what he needed to, he was staking his claim on Athena.

CHAPTER TEN

A thena could feel Quinn buzzing with energy. She was beyond annoyed with him, but if there was a security issue she wanted to know about it. Now she felt just a twinge of guilt at ignoring his call and text.

She would have worried about Raegan, but Travis would be with her. Still, she couldn't imagine what kind of security situation warranted Quinn dragging her upstairs. Especially when he'd been off having drinks with another woman.

"So what's the deal?" she asked as they stepped onto their floor. They had to wait until everyone else got off on their floors before the elevator took them to this exclusive one. She had to admit it was nice to be staying in an executive area. It was so quiet compared to the rest of the hotel and casino.

Quinn placed his hand on the small of her back again, as if he had every right to touch her. As if he hadn't been out with someone else. And yeah, she knew that it might have been work related, but then why not just tell her? His behavior had been too weird and now she figured she knew exactly why. She was just glad she hadn't slept with him.

She stiffened at the touch and the man just slid his hand farther around her waist, pulling her close. When she looked up at him, he had an odd look in his eyes. Challenging almost. "Well?" she asked, since he still hadn't answered her.

"Why did you meet Raegan downstairs?"

She blinked, surprised by his question. "Why wouldn't I meet her? She got here early and is so excited to be in Vegas. She's like a freaking kid on Christmas." Despite Athena's annoyance with Quinn, she couldn't help but smile thinking about Raegan.

Even Quinn's expression softened. "Yeah, she is. Who was the man you were talking to?"

"Who was the woman you were off having drinks with?" Athena smoothly slid out of his hold as they reached the suite door. She turned her back to him, opened the door. "And why don't you tell me what this emergency is so I can get back downstairs?" She heard him let out what sounded like a growl. An actual *growl*. It shouldn't have heated her up from the inside out, but it did.

"I wasn't having drinks with Margot."

Athena nearly snorted. "So Travis is a liar?" Her voice dripped with just a bit of saccharine sweet sarcasm. As the door shut behind them, she turned to find Quinn with a dark expression on his face. She resisted the urge to take a step back.

Growling in that annoyingly sexy way, he raked a hand over his dark, cropped hair. "No, yes, I mean, no, he's not a liar but he didn't tell you the truth."

Not stepping any farther into their suite, she faced him, hands on her hips. "And why is that?"

"He didn't know you and I were — are — together."

Were they together? Her temper flared, a bright blaze inside her. "Because if he had, he wouldn't have told me you were having drinks with another woman?"

"Yes...damn it, Athena. I didn't tell Travis we were together, because I wasn't sure what you wanted. I should have brought it up to you last night or this morning, but hell, I didn't want to screw things up between us. It's been a long time since I've been in a relationship and I know this job is important to you. It's not like I'm your boss or there's a conflict, but I wasn't sure what you wanted people to know."

Some of the steam that had been building inside her faded, but... "Okay. I appreciate that. And I don't want to keep us — if there is an us — a secret."

At that, his eyes seemed to darken even more. "If?"

There was something in that one word that sent a thrill down her spine and had her nipples pebbling against her bra cups. She didn't respond because she couldn't find her voice.

He advanced on her with two strides until she found herself pressed up against the wall of the entryway. The light was dim, casting shadows over the hard, handsome lines of his face. He didn't touch her though, but laid his hands on either side of his head as he looked down at her. His breathing was slightly erratic and there was no mistaking the gleam of lust in his gaze. It was tempered with something else she couldn't quite define though.

Her heart rate kicked up about a thousand notches so that all she could hear was the blood rushing in her ears. "Where were you earlier?" Athena hated that her question came out as a whisper.

"Meeting on the security floor with Iris and Margot—she's part of their web security team. White's unaccounted for in Miami and I'm concerned he might be in Vegas. I needed all the facts before I came to you because I didn't want to worry you unnecessarily."

Athena felt a rush of relief that he hadn't been out having drinks with another woman. She knew she should be more concerned about what Quinn said regarding White, but her initial response was one of such pure relief. She'd go back to the White situation later. "Oh."

"Oh?" Still not actually touching her with his hands, he leaned down, nipped her earlobe between his teeth. "You were mad at me," he murmured.

Feeling the freedom to touch him now, she slid her hands up his chest. "Maybe a little annoyed."

He pressed down a little harder on her earlobe before oh-so-gently raking his teeth against her neck. God, the sensation of him teasing her like that made her instantly wet. She dug her fingers into his shoulders, shuddered when he started kissing along her jaw.

"I should have told you about the potential threat," he murmured, his mouth just above hers now, his breath warm as it feathered over her. "I should have told you that I'm not going to be seeing anyone else, that I don't want you to either. This thing between us is rare. I want to give us a shot."

She melted at his words and arched a little, instinctively. She wanted to jump the man, wrap her arms and legs around him and feel him push into her right against the wall. She wanted his mouth and hands on her, everywhere. "I want to be exclusive too. I felt so…" Athena almost said annoyed again, but decided to go with the truth. "Mad at you. And really hurt." Because Quinn hadn't seemed like a liar, thankfully wasn't.

For a moment, Quinn looked as if he'd say something more but then his eyes got that heavy-lidded lustful look and she knew they'd be talking much later.

"I'm on the Pill," she blurted the instant before his mouth would have descended on hers.

His big body went impossibly still, his nostrils flaring ever so slightly as he looked at her. They were so close now she could swear she heard his heartbeat — though she knew that was just the thump of hers pounding erratically. "Have you been on it long enough to go without a condom?"

"Couple months." She'd gone on it the first week they'd gone on a date because deep down she'd known that she planned to sleep with him. Because the thought of not doing so felt almost criminal.

"I'm clean." The two words were said so matter-of-factly she knew he'd been tested.

If it had been anyone else she wouldn't have taken him at face value but this was Quinn. She trusted him. She simply nodded.

He crushed his mouth to hers. Which was just as well because there was nothing left to say. His kisses were hard, demanding. She savored the commanding way he dominated her mouth, leaving her breathless and wanting more.

Clutching onto his shoulders, she arched into him. She wanted to wrap her legs around him but her knee-length dress was too fitted. As if he read her mind he tugged the zipper down the back. Instead of letting it pool around her waist, he shoved it all the way off.

Cool air rushed over her as she stepped out of her dress wearing a black matching bra and panty set and heels. She knew that was supposed to be a man's fantasy. If the hungry look on Quinn's face was any indication then yep, it definitely was.

Taking her by surprise, he fell to his knees, his intent clear. She'd thought—well, she'd thought since she'd made it obvious she wanted to have sex that he'd have gone straight for that. She didn't mind skipping a little foreplay, she desperately wanted to experience all of him and she was already wet. So wet she trembled for him.

"Gotta taste you." The words seemed to be torn from him as he tugged her underwear off.

Those words made her melt just a little more. The need and hunger that emanated from him mirrored what she was feeling. When she stepped out of the panties, he grasped her ankle, kissed her inner calf as he lifted her foot over his shoulder. Familiar with this position by now, her inner walls tightened in anticipation of what was to come. Even the feel of his lips feathering over her leg made her shudder.

"You make me fucking crazy," he murmured, glancing up at her.

The look in his eyes was electric, scorching. She was thankful for the wall holding her up.

With his gaze on hers, he slid a hand up her leg, stopping only when he reached her inner thigh. Gently, he trailed a finger along the crease of her skin where her thigh and pussy met. He was barely touching her, but it was as if she could feel his hands on her everywhere.

She wanted to tell him to hurry up, to ease the ache between her legs, but couldn't make her throat work.

When he finally teased a finger along her slick opening, he closed his eyes for a long moment. He didn't stop what he was doing though, but pushed his finger fully inside her.

She tightened around him, automatically rolling her hips, wanting way more than just this. She couldn't ever remember being so turned on, wanting something so much.

He groaned, the sound so tortured and sensual before he leaned forward and placed his mouth on her clit. There had been moments last night when she'd felt a little insecure, especially when he'd joined her under the bright lights of the shower and could see all her flaws, but right now all of that fell away.

Quinn liked and wanted all of her. When he slid another finger inside her, she sucked in a breath and tightened her grip on his shoulders.

He groaned against her clit as he teased her, flicking and massaging her mercilessly with his tongue. When he started moving his fingers in and out of her, curving them at just the right angle, she let go completely, her orgasm punching through her fast and sharp.

It should have been a shock how fast she climaxed, but she'd been aching for him since…well, when wasn't she aching for him? It seemed that when they were in the same room, her body just flared to life.

Even when she'd been angry at him, when he'd placed his hand on her back down in Cloud 9, then again when they'd stepped out of the elevator, she'd felt that light touch all the way to her toes. And had wanted more of it.

Now she felt his touch deep inside her, craved more than just his fingers as she came apart against his mouth. She'd fallen hard for him all those months ago and when he'd pretty much run from her, it had sliced her deep. But now she knew she hadn't made a mistake wanting, needing this man so much. "Quinn," she rasped out, unable to say anything else. It was difficult to think much less speak.

He made a satisfied rumbling sound against her clit. The vibration against her sensitive bundle of nerves nearly made her collapse. When he withdrew his fingers, another shudder of pleasure spooled through her, the after effects of her orgasm lingering.

Moving with the speed of a lethal predator, he was on his feet in seconds, his mouth over hers once again.

Not for the first time had she thought it was a sensual experience to taste herself on his lips. She held onto him, hooked her legs around his waist. She knew exactly what she wanted, knew he did too. She wondered if maybe she should be more nervous about her first time but all she felt was excitement.

In seconds he had her bra off, tossed somewhere behind them. His big palms smoothed down her ass, clutched her hard as he started walking them somewhere. Her room or his, she didn't care. Hell, she didn't care if they went right down to the floor as long as he was inside her soon.

Moments later she was aware they'd entered her room as she found herself flat on her back, the glittering lights of Vegas in the background. The bed was soft, cool under her skin. The heat surging through her now was a direct contrast.

When he paused over her, his gorgeous body covering hers—and covered by too many clothes, she practically ripped his shirt off. Luckily he seemed to be more in control than her, just barely, and managed to get it off in seconds. After he did, he pushed off her, removing all that warmth and strength.

She must have made a protesting sound because he let out a low chuckle as he slid off the edge of the bed.

"I'm not going anywhere, sweetheart." There was a dark promise in those words as he started stripping off the rest of his clothes with economic movements.

When he was naked at the foot of the bed, he looked like a perfectly sculpted statue, all defined lines and striations. And he was hers. That thought sent another one of those waves of heat through her.

She started to push up so that she was on her knees, but he moved atop her with a speed that continued to surprise her given his size. She spread her thighs for him, loved the feel of him settling between her legs with no barrier. His cock pressed against her abdomen. Just the feel of it on her skin made her smile.

She slid one hand to the back of his neck, held onto him as he looked down at her. The man was absolute perfection. She was so glad he was going to be her first, was glad now that she'd waited. No matter how things played out between them, she trusted Quinn with her body and her heart.

Lazily he cupped one of her breasts and slowly, torturously rubbed his thumb over her aching nipple in little circles. This was different from the frantic energy she'd been feeling out in the hall. She still wanted him with a wildness that terrified her a little, but she was pretty certain he'd slowed things down just a bit. For her benefit or his, she wasn't certain. But she knew that he'd given her an orgasm to get her ready for him.

"This might hurt a little," he murmured, the regret in his dark eyes warming her from the inside out. She loved how much he cared.

"I know." And she *didn't* care. Not when this was Quinn. The pain, if there was any, wouldn't last. And she was so physically active she doubted it would hurt much. At least that's what her cousins had told her.

Leaning down, he took her mouth in a tender kiss as his hand moved from her breast to her mound. She arched into his hold, her hands going around his back as he tested her slickness.

In and out, he stroked her inner walls with a sweet slowness now. She let out a groan of frustration, wanting so much more. She was tired of waiting. Trailing her fingers down his back, she grasped onto his ass.

He understood what she wanted and when he withdrew his fingers, her entire body trembled with so much pent up need she felt as if she might go into sensory overload.

She wanted to see him entering her but was too shy to ask him to shift positions. It didn't matter though, the feel of his tongue dancing with hers, his hard body covering her, was heaven. His thick cock nudged her entrance and she let her head fall back from his mouth, sucked in a breath as he pushed inside her.

He didn't pump hard, but he also didn't pause, just slid into her with one smooth thrust. She met his gaze as he filled her completely. There was a moment of discomfort that she should have expected, but it was over so quickly. All she could focus on was this beautiful man inside her, on top of her. She felt so full, so possessed by him.

She dug her fingers into his backside. "More." It was all she could manage to get out, but he knew what she wanted.

He held himself up on his forearms so that she was caged in and his gaze was pinned to hers. The look in his eyes was territorial and possessive. The sight took her breath away. He pulled his hips back and began thrusting in a slow, steady rhythm.

Her hips met his, stroke for stroke, the sensation of being filled by him too incredible for words. She could feel another release building even as she wanted this to go on and on.

His breathing grew more erratic as he pumped into her, his eyes blazing with a raw heat. Part of her wanted to look away, but there was no way she could.

"Touch your clit. Come around my cock." The words were a growl. A demand. And his expression was primal.

She didn't even pause, didn't want to. Reaching between their bodies, she began rubbing herself in that very familiar way. She knew how to get herself off. It never took long, but to have someone as sexy as Quinn thrusting into her while she stroked herself put things on a whole other level.

Her inner walls began clenching around him tighter and tighter. "Faster." The word came out as a plea. She hadn't expected to come again, but felt a climax building the faster he moved. Each stroke inside her stoked that greedy fire.

She couldn't keep her eyes open any longer, let her head fall back as the sensations of another orgasm rushed through her. Pleasure poured out to all her nerve endings as she savored the sensation of him moving inside her, filling her. She'd never felt so connected to anyone. And not just anyone, but this was Quinn. She arched into him, wanting to rub her breasts against his chest, to experience more stimulation.

Suddenly she felt his mouth clamp over the tip of her breast, suck her nipple hard. The action was so unexpected, so erotic, it pushed her over the edge.

"Quinn!" His name sounded like another plea as it tore from her throat. She slid her fingers through his short hair, clasped his head with her free hand. He flicked and teased her nipple as her orgasm continued to punch through her. The sensations of his wicked mouth seemed to prolong it.

Finally she pulled her hand free from her clit, the stimulation almost too much. As she did, Quinn seemed to let go of whatever had been restraining him.

Shouting her name, his thrusts became unsteady, rough and when he buried his face against her neck, she felt him come inside her in hot strokes. The muscles in his arms and shoulders were corded tight, his back damp with sweat. It seemed to go on forever and at the same time, not long enough.

She trailed her fingers down his back in lazy strokes. His muscles tightened under her soft touch, twitched slightly as he relaxed.

"I'm too heavy," he murmured against her neck a few moments later.

She grinned though he couldn't see her. "I like the feel of you on top of me."

He pulled back, his dark eyes gentle as he looked down at her. "You okay?"

"That was amazing."

Relief immediately bled into his eyes before he dropped a sweet, almost chaste kiss on her lips. "Give me a sec." He pulled out of her and she immediately felt a difference.

Just a slight soreness she hadn't been aware of. When he'd been inside her it had been all pleasure, but yep, she was going to feel this tomorrow. Totally worth it though.

He slid off the bed and strode into the bathroom. Seconds later she heard water running. For a moment she wondered if he was just taking a shower without her, but that seemed weird.

He popped his head through the doorframe. "I'm running you a bath. Do you like it warm, hot or scorching?"

She was touched by his thoughtfulness, but didn't feel much like moving. "I don't need a bath."

Quinn stepped fully into the doorframe now and gave her one sharp headshake. "You're getting one."

She blinked in surprise at his authoritative tone. "What?"

"This was your first time, I'm not fucking this up for you." Now he strode toward her with purpose.

An unexpected laugh broke free. The man was too sweet. "Such poetry."

He froze in place and tensed. He rubbed a hand over the back of his neck—and showed off delicious muscles she wanted to trace with her tongue. "Shit, Athena—"

"I'm messing with you. And thank you. I think a soak probably wouldn't hurt." She liked that he was actually cursing in front of her now. Which was maybe a little weird, but she liked that he was being himself. It had been sweet how he'd held back before, but this thing between them felt so real. She wanted to keep it that way, didn't want any barriers between them.

"Good." He strode to the bed then scooped her up in his arms. He brushed his lips over hers, and this time his kiss was a bit more heated than the last. She clutched onto him, deepening it until he pulled back.

He groaned, simmering heat in his gaze. "Let's get you in the bath before I lose my head."

"Maybe after the bath you can lose it." She grinned at him, loved seeing the easy relaxation on his face. They still needed to talk about the potential threat but for right now she didn't want to think about anything else but this.

CHAPTER ELEVEN

Three days later

Quinn stood by the huge window of the suite, staring out at the city below. The lights twinkled like jewels under the breaking dawn sky. It was the last official day of the tradeshow, but he'd asked Athena if she wanted to stay on an extra day so they could enjoy themselves afterward. After the call he'd just received he felt a thousand times lighter. He and Athena could actually have a good time without worrying about that fuckhead White.

At a soft rustling sound he turned. Athena stepped out of her room—their room now—dressed in fitted black pants and a red wraparound top. When he realized she wore the gold necklace he'd given to her yesterday, that possessive flare he was getting used to jumped inside him. She'd protested when he'd given it to her, but he liked seeing her wear something from him. It made him feel like he was staking a claim.

"Necklace looks good," he murmured, stepping away from the window, eyeing the three tiered chains looped around her delicate neck.

She flushed pink and gently touched one of the links. "I still think it's too much," she muttered.

They'd managed to sneak away last night for a dinner outside the casino and had gotten to walk, see some of the city. He'd seen her admiring it at one of the shops so he'd gone back later and bought it. He didn't care that they hadn't been together long, he already knew he was in this for the long haul. Seeing the pleasure on her face when she'd opened the box had made him feel a hundred feet tall. Not just the pleasure though, the pure surprise. She'd admitted that no one outside her family had ever given her jewelry before and that knowledge made the caveman inside him irrationally pleased.

Not commenting, he just wrapped his hands around her hips as he reached her and pulled her close. The slightly tropical scent rolling off her wrapped around him. He couldn't keep his hands off the woman. Just being in the same room and he wanted to hold her, kiss her. "I've got good news."

"Yeah?" She slid her arms around his waist. Since she hadn't put her heels on yet she had to look up at him.

"Just talked to Grant. One of his guys saw Glenn entering his apartment."

Athena sucked in a sharp breath. "When? Is he positive?"

A smile tugged at Quinn's mouth. "I asked the same thing. About an hour ago and Grant said unless he's got a twin—and I know he's an only child—then his guy is convinced it's him. Still, Grant's going to head down there and try to get a look." There had also been recent activity on White's credit card and cell phone, all in the Miami area. Whatever he'd been off doing the past few days, he was home now—and far away from Quinn and Athena. That didn't mean Quinn was letting the guy off his radar but for now it was a relief not to worry about White for the next couple days.

She squeezed him tighter and laid her head against his chest. "I know we'll have to be careful when we get home but at least now we can relax the rest of the today. Well, relax being a relative word because it's going to be insane today. Maybe..." She pulled back to look up at him, her blue eyes just a little wicked. "Maybe we can stay Sunday too and get home early on Monday. I don't mind going straight from the airport to work."

As that familiar hunger surged through him, he leaned down and brushed his lips over hers. She'd been insatiable the past three days. They both had. He wasn't ashamed to admit he'd quickly become addicted to her. "I bet we don't even leave the room," he murmured against her mouth.

"What do you think room service is for?" She nipped his bottom lip playfully.

Hell yeah, he thought, deepening their kiss. The next two days were going to be amazing.

———————— ••• ————————

Today was the day, Glenn thought as he parked his stolen van a few houses down from his first destination. He'd been covertly watching Athena and Quinn the past few days, mostly keeping his focus on the woman. He hadn't wanted to tip his hand and if Quinn sensed eyes on him, it would make him even more vigilant. What he'd first noticed was that the woman had two guards from the hotel pretty much at all times when she was at the tradeshow.

The first day Glenn hadn't been positive they were shadowing her, but the second it had been clear. Which meant Quinn somehow knew Glenn wasn't in Miami. Not hard to figure out how. Bastard had probably cased his apartment, maybe even tracked his credit cards or phone. Quinn wouldn't mind breaking the law for his own gain. So Glenn had done the last thing he wanted to and asked his cousin for a big favor. It might come back to haunt him later, but for now it was helping him cover his tracks.

He and Henry looked like brothers, the only real difference between them was about two inches in height. But they had the same build, coloring, hair, everything. People always commented that they looked like brothers so today he'd taken advantage of it.

His cousin had agreed to go to his place to check on it and get his mail. Glenn had also asked him to buy a few things for him — with Glenn's credit card — so that when he got back home he would have groceries. Easily explainable to his cousin. Getting his cousin to use his phone was a bit trickier so he'd told him he was calling it because he couldn't remember where he'd left it. Henry answered it, telling him it was in the master bathroom on the countertop.

Which gave him an alibi in Miami for today. If he was a betting man, he'd guess that whoever Quinn had sitting on his place would report that he was in Miami. Getting back to Florida after what he planned to do would be tricky, but luck had been with him so far. He was banking on it lasting, refusing to settle for anything less. Quinn deserved to pay for what he'd done.

The neighborhood he was in was quiet enough, but it connected with a busy street. Glenn slipped from the van, thankful for the cooler February weather. His gloves, knit cap and jacket weren't out of place. His fake beard was still on, but he'd dropped the padding for this job. He needed full range of movement.

He felt a little guilty for what he had to do, since the guy he was about to kill wasn't involved in this, but getting access to the tradeshow was paramount. The security had been good but today was the last day so he knew he'd have an opening to get Athena out and away from Quinn. Or he would have one if he played this right. He'd paid a shitload of money for the right equipment to jam one of the hotel's video feeds but it wouldn't last long.

His soft-soled boots were silent as he hurried down the sidewalk. He checked his watch. Almost time.

Yesterday he'd followed the van of catering staff back to their headquarters. From there he'd waited, watched, then followed a man home who'd been at the tradeshow. Glenn had picked a guy with the crappiest car, reasoning he'd have lax security at home. It wasn't a guarantee, but he went with the odds. Once he'd seen the guy's place, he'd sat on it for a few hours last night, just watching. No one else had come or gone so unless the guy had gotten a really late night booty call, he should be alone right now.

If not, Glenn would deal with anyone else that got in his way.

Walking briskly, he held his head high and tried to appear as if he had every right to be here. Using shadows to hide his movements, he made his way to the guy's carport. He used a moldy plastic kid's pool as cover. Glenn couldn't figure why the guy had one propped up in his carport, but he didn't really care. The guy also had dirty car parts, a fax machine that looked decades old and a rusted bicycle without wheels.

Now, he just had to wait for the man to exit. Then he'd take his uniform, force him to call in sick and…likely kill the man.

It wasn't that Glenn wanted to, but this guy was in the way of Glenn getting to his wife. Because in the end, that was all that truly mattered. He needed to make Quinn not only suffer, but to spill his guts as well. Glenn needed to see Suzanne, and Quinn was the only one who would be able to tell him where she was. That bastard had been the one to convince her to leave him, to press charges. He must have been complicit in helping her hide.

When he heard the rattle of the doorknob turning, Glenn set aside thoughts of what had to be done and took a quiet, steadying breath as he withdrew his pistol. He'd kill the guy with a knife, but for now he would use the gun as a threat. His heart rate and hand were steady.

Time to take care of business.

———————•••———————

Athena's feet were killing her, but she didn't even care. They were in the last stages of breaking down the tradeshow and the week had been a huge success. She'd just gotten off the phone with Harrison and he informed her that he'd been hearing positive things so far. There'd been a few blips but overall, it had run smoothly.

Better than all that, that psycho Glenn White wasn't in Vegas. It made it easier to move around today without feeling as if a dark cloud was hanging over her. Quinn had been more relaxed too.

As she strode down one of the aisles of displays being broken down, her cell phone buzzed. "Yeah?" she answered, immediately recognizing the number of the owner of the catering company.

"Athena, it's Jodi. I've got a bit of a situation. There's a van that's not supposed to be parked by the kitchen exits and it's blocking one of our vans. I can't figure out who it belongs to but I need it moved because we're almost loaded up."

"Where are you now?"

"Kitchen."

"I'll be there in a sec." She ended the call then held up a hand to signal Raegan, who was talking to one of the vendors.

Smiling brightly, as seemed to be the norm for Raegan, she strode over, her heels clicking quickly with her movements. She wasn't that much taller than Athena, maybe five feet five or six, but she was a lean woman and it made her appear taller. Today she'd pulled her dark hair back into a twist at her nape. "Hey, boss."

Athena snorted. "Stop calling me that." She was only two years older and it felt weird.

"Only if you stop snorting when I do it." Raegan's grin just grew wider as she fell into step. "So what are we doing now?"

"Tiny emergency in the kitchen."

"Today's been pretty smooth though, or at least it seems like it, right?" she asked as they sidestepped a vendor breaking down a display of GPS systems.

"Exceptionally so."

"Can I ask you something totally non-work related?"

Athena shot her a glance. "Ah, sure."

"Have you ever dated more than one guy at once?"

She had to think about it. Quinn might be her first lover, but she'd dated in college. Well, a little, the last two years of it. Once she'd been more comfortable in her skin dating had been somewhat more enjoyable. "Not really. I mean, I went on dates in college, sometimes with a different guy week to week, but I was never exclusive with any of them and now that I think about it, I guess there wasn't any overlap." Because deep down, she was a one man kind of woman.

"Okay." Raegan's pretty mouth pulled into a frown as they reached the kitchen.

The volume level instantly raised as they stepped inside, the voices seeming to echo in the smaller space. "Uh uh, you can't leave me hanging like that. Why are you asking?"

Athena wasn't exactly surprised when Raegan's cheeks flushed. "I had a couple dinner dates with one of the security guys from the hotel this week. We've only kissed, but today, oh, you remember the man we met Tuesday?" When Athena nodded, Raegan continued. "Well, he called to let me know he'd be in Miami next week and wanted to know if I wanted to have dinner with him."

She nodded approvingly. "Nice." Rhys Maxwell was a handsome man by any standard. Blond hair, blue eyes, he looked more like a tan surfer than a billionaire with holdings in…well, whatever. Lots and lots of stuff.

"I don't know why I was getting hung up. I mean, I only went on a couple dates and it's not like we talked about the future—I *leave* tomorrow. I don't know why I feel so guilty saying yes." The frown was back.

She didn't respond because it sounded like Raegan was having an internal battle more than looking for real advice. Athena called out to one of the servers from the show. "Where's Jodi?"

Though he was in the middle of packing up serving trays, he nodded to one of the exit doors. "Out back."

"Thanks." As she and Raegan maneuvered their way through the expansive kitchen, she frowned when she realized the exit door was propped open and there was no security guard standing there. She'd been very specific with the entire staff about this, both in-house and outside hires. If any doors remained open there *had* to be a guard.

"That's not supposed to be open, is it?" Raegan asked, concern in her voice.

"No, it's not." And Jodi was going to get an earful when Athena found her.

Outside a chilly breeze rolled over them. A van with the catering company's logo was backed right up to the exit door but there was more than enough room to maneuver around it. The interior was half-packed but she didn't spot a driver or any other employees around.

When she stepped around to the side of the van she realized what Jodi had been talking about. This section of the hotel was for employees only and was more or less a loading area, with a row of ramps for vans or delivery trucks to come and go.

Another van with a florist logo on the side was parked directly in front of the caterer's. Sighing, she pulled out her cell and called Jodi.

When she heard a phone ringing, she continued down the side of the ramp, looking for Jodi. As Athena reached the front of the other van, an icy fist clenched around her chest. Raegan sucked in a breath behind her.

A man was crouched down in front of the vehicle, holding Jodi's phone—and a gun.

"Drop your phone," he said quietly. With a thick beard that had to be fake, a ball cap and sunglasses, Glenn White wasn't easily recognizable but she knew his voice immediately. It sent chills scratching down her spine.

Athena wanted to run, but there was nowhere to go. The drop off the ramp was too high up and if she tried to backtrack she'd just slam into Raegan.

"Both of you. Do it or I shoot. I'll start with your knees." His voice was dead calm as he lowered the weapon, aiming right for her knees. The calmness scared her more than anything. Like he'd have absolutely no problem just pumping her full of bullets.

Heart thudding, Athena did as he said, praying that someone from the kitchen saw them and alerted security. Or that someone in actual security saw them. There were plenty of surveillance cameras out here. Seconds ticked by, but felt like eons as she stared at the gun.

Next to her Raegan let her phone fall too. It clattered to the ramp.

Gun out, he pointed it at them menacingly. "Move to the back of the van."

With no choice but to do as he said, they both started backtracking along the side of the van. Athena couldn't stop the fear filtering through her or the thoughts of Quinn. The thing developing between them was intense and amazing. The thought of losing it all because of a lunatic was too surreal.

"Stop," White ordered as they reached it.

Athena knew he was going to put them in there and she refused to go. He would kill her anyway. She'd rather die here than her family never knowing what happened to her. "You can fucking shoot me but I'm not getting in there." Her voice came out surprisingly strong. Inside, however, she was trembling with terror. He hadn't actually ordered them in the van but she knew it was coming.

"Fine, how about I shoot her?" White grabbed Raegan by the arm and held the gun to her temple.

Oh, God. Athena's stomach roiled. Raegan's eyes were huge, her skin pale and…her smart watch caught the light. A tiny glimmer of hope flickered through Athena, but her terror pushed most of it back. She couldn't let Glenn see it anyway. She held up her hands. "I'll get in but please leave her here. She's not part of this."

He just snorted and shoved Raegan at her before opening the back door to the van. Then he tossed them zip ties. "Tie your wrists together tight. Use your teeth to pull it closed. Make it quick." He glanced down the side of the other van, his agitation clear.

They did as he said, then climbed into the back of the empty van, urged on by his gun. There was nothing but two metal poles running along the ceiling. She'd seen dry-cleaning vans before that delivered and they'd had the same layout.

Smiling, he pulled out two sets of cuffs. "Glad I came prepared with two."

He jumped in the back with them and slammed the rear doors shut, using his gun as a barrier. As he started to hook Raegan's wrists to the pole, Athena rolled back from her kneeling position and kicked at his chest. It was hard with her odd position and secured wrists, but she clipped him in the thigh with her heel.

Grunting in what sounded more like annoyance than anything else, he moved lightning quick, slamming his fist into her jaw before she could defend herself. Pain shot through her face.

"Fucking bitch," she heard him mutter as her head lolled back. She didn't pass out, but everything around her was hazy.

"Oh my God! Athena, are you okay?" Raegan's voice sounded far away.

It hurt too much to answer, but she was aware of her wrists being raised, then heard the distinctive click of the handcuffs around the pole.

As if from the far end of a tunnel she heard him moving from the cargo area to the driver's seat. The van rumbled to life and she jerked backward, sliding against the cold metal floor until she thumped against the door.

"Athena, talk to me," Raegan whispered.

"I'm okay," she managed to push out. She was pretty certain he hadn't broken her jaw since she could talk. She wanted to tell Raegan that Quinn and Travis would find them, that the smart watch Raegan had on might save them if the guys remembered she was wearing it. But she was afraid White would hear her so she kept her mouth shut and prayed.

CHAPTER TWELVE

Quinn was about to slip his cell phone back into his pocket when it rang in his hand. When he saw Iris's name he answered immediately. "Yeah?"

"We've got a problem with the video surveillance in the west sector…directly outside the kitchen the tradeshow staff are using." He was already moving before she'd finished. He'd seen Athena heading to the kitchen and Iris wouldn't be calling him unless this was important. Quinn grabbed Travis by the arm, but didn't say anything as he started moving through the vendors packing up their displays. He didn't need to. They'd worked together enough to operate as a unit.

Iris continued. "I've got guys on the way to check it out but previous feeds show a woman who owns the catering company heading outside, then Athena and Raegan not long after. Now we don't have a visual… It's coming back on. Something's not right." She cursed.

His heart stuttered in his chest. It was just a computer glitch, he told himself. "I'm on my way there now." Quinn and Travis moved through the kitchen, ignoring the shouts of protest as they barreled through two men carrying a stack of glasses.

"The fucking door is propped open," he growled, barely registering the sound of glass shattering behind him. They burst outside. He motioned to Travis to move around the right side of the catering van while he went around the left side.

"I see you guys," Iris said.

Withdrawing his weapon, he continued down the side of the van.

If there was a threat Iris would have seen it on her end, but he wasn't taking a chance. Where the hell was Athena? If she'd come out here, there was nowhere else to go except out to one of the roads that ran through the hotel and casino's property.

As he rounded the front of the van, Travis did the same on the opposite side. Quinn's heart felt as if it stopped dead in his chest when he saw Athena and Raegan's phones on the ground. He recognized the cases to both. Fear surged up, raw and cold in his chest. "Call the cops now. They've been taken," he said to Iris, not needing to specify who. His gut told him who was behind the kidnapping too. "Check your exterior cams—"

"Wait," Travis said, snagging his own phone out of his pocket. His fingers moved across the screen at a rapid speed.

Quinn could hear Iris in the background shouting out orders, but he tuned her out as Travis spoke. "Remember the vendor that gave us all the smart watches?" He twisted his wrist once to show he was wearing his. Quinn didn't respond, but Travis didn't seem to expect him to. "Raegan and I have been going to the gym here every morning and using them. There's a GPS on them and I know she's got hers activated because we created free accounts. I've got full access to hers...there!" He held out his phone. A red dot was moving along a marked road on a virtual map. "She's moving at forty-five miles per hour right now."

Heart pounding an erratic thump against his chest, Quinn scooped up the phones on the ground. "You hear that Iris?" he asked as he jerked open the door to the catering van. He didn't have to tell Travis to shut the back doors, he was already doing it by the time Quinn slid into the front seat. Luckily he didn't have to hotwire the vehicle or waste time trying to hunt down someone with keys. They were sitting in the ignition.

"Yeah," she said as he started the engine. "I'm calling the police regardless. Stay on the line."

He set his phone down on the center console and started the ignition. Travis jumped in and Quinn jerked the van into drive. Years of training kept his movements calm and precise as Travis indicated which direction he should go. But inside, he felt as if his entire world was splitting apart at the seams.

Someone had taken Athena and Raegan and Quinn's gut told him it was White. He was supposed to be in Miami, far away from them. She was supposed to have been safe. Quinn was going with his gut though, this wasn't some random coincidence. White must have figured out a way to fool the Red Stone guys. It terrified Quinn that Athena was likely with him right now. The guy was a bastard who hadn't cared about hurting his own wife. Athena would just be a tool to him. Quinn could only hope White wanted to keep her alive to lure Quinn to him. Fuck it, Quinn should have been with her. He decided to berate himself later when she was safe and in his arms.

"Looks like they're slowing down, hmm, hold on." Travis rattled off an address.

"That's a rundown shopping strip," Iris said immediately, clearly recognizing the location. "Wyatt bought it recently. He's going to renovate it. There's a pawn shop, tattoo parlor, and ah, an old barber shop there I think. Couple other empty shops. Nothing's been open for about five months but even before that the places were pretty bad."

"She's stopped completely." Travis held out his phone for Quinn to see.

"Don't tell the cops where we're going," Quinn said as Travis used a map app on his phone to plug in the address where Raegan— *and please God, let Athena be with her* —was.

"Hell, Quinn." Iris sighed.

"If they show up sirens blazing we lose the element of surprise. Travis and I are both trained. We get in to where he's holding them, save them. If the cops show up you know as well as I do that it could turn into a hostage situation." If that happened, it was anyone's bet what would happen. Especially if White was the one who'd taken them. He'd been a cop and understood hostage negotiations and tactics. And he was also unpredictable as hell.

"All right. You want backup?"

"No."

She was silent for a long moment. "Too fucking bad. I'm on my way."

"We're not waiting."

"I know. Be careful, Devil Dog."

If he hadn't been so terrified for Athena he might have smiled. "Ooh Rah." He disconnected and glanced at Travis. "I don't want to wait for backup. You're free to wait though." Quinn knew Travis wouldn't but wanted to put the offer out there. He was going in no matter what. According to the map they'd be there in less than five minutes considering all the traffic laws he was breaking.

Travis just snorted in derision. "From the grid of Raegan's GPS map, I can't be sure, but it looks like the driver parked behind the shopping strip. And it appears as if she entered through the pawn shop rear door."

"Do a search, see if there's somewhere nearby we can park and enter through the back." Because if this was White, he was likely working alone. While he might want to, the bastard couldn't cover every exit. He sure as hell hadn't realized Raegan had on a smart watch. Maybe he didn't even know what the thing was.

Unfortunately he wouldn't have to cover every angle, all it would take was one bullet from White to take away the woman who'd come to mean everything to Quinn.

Glancing briefly in the side mirror he swerved into the next lane of traffic, cutting someone off. He ignored the blast of the horn as he took a sharp turn. He had to get to Athena.

Hang on, sweetheart.

"This guy is out of his mind," Raegan whispered.

Athena nodded, her throat tight with fear. White had brought them to an abandoned shop of some kind and shoved them in a matchbox-sized windowless office. She could hear him outside it, pacing, and knew he'd hear them if they attempted an escape. There was nowhere to go anyway unless they wanted to 1) attempt kicking through a wall or 2) climb through the ceiling tiles. He would hear them if they tried to do either of those things and there was nothing in the tiny room they could use as a weapon either.

She desperately wanted to say something to Raegan about the smart watch, but didn't want to draw any attention to it. Athena was terrified that the guys hadn't thought of it. They'd all been given one, but still. She'd remembered but Quinn and Travis might not.

Suddenly the door swung open. White had ditched the ball cap and sunglasses. She had no problem recognizing him now even with the beard. He flicked a glance at Athena, but focused on Raegan, something almost apologetic in his dark eyes.

"You weren't supposed to be with her," he said, just a hint of regret in his voice.

Athena realized he intended to kill Raegan when he took a menacing step forward. She popped up from the rickety chair she'd been sitting on and blurted, "You want to know where your wife is. Suzanne, right?"

His gaze snapped to hers, laser sharp and bright with a kind of wild madness that made her shudder. "What do you know about Suzanne?" His breathing increased, the madness intensifying.

Cold sweat trickled down Athena's spine. "I just know that she left, disappeared. And Quinn knows where she is." A total lie but she needed to keep this madman talking. "If you kill Raegan or me you'll never find out where she is. We're you're only bargaining chips. You *need* us alive if you ever want to see your wife again." Athena was rambling now but desperately wanted to stall him.

"I only need one of you to negotiate," he snapped.

She swallowed hard. "If you kill her now you lose a bargaining chip. And…" Athena decided to play the only card she had. The only thing she could really think of since the mention of White's ex-wife wasn't working as well as she'd hoped. "Raegan is Keith Caldwell's niece. His *only* niece." That part wasn't true but whatever.

White's hand shook, his gaze jerking over to Raegan.

Athena needed his focus on her though. "You know who he is then. And you know what will happen if you kill her. He and his sons will hunt you to the ends of the earth. I'm just a Red Stone employee, a new one at that. Killing Raegan guarantees you die."

"Fuck, fuck, *fuck*." He glanced away from them for a moment and she could practically see the wheels of the crazy-train in his head turning.

At a soft thudding sound from somewhere nearby, Athena's heart jumped in her throat. She prayed it was Quinn. Or the police. *Someone.*

White stiffened and immediately reached for her. He yanked her upper arm and tugged her to him. She cried out in pain until he shoved the gun right to her temple. "Shut the fuck up."

Swallowing hard, she nodded once, afraid to move more than that. Her entire body was numb as he nudged her forward. The only pain she was really aware of was her throbbing jaw from when he'd punched her. But she could deal with a little pain.

"Stay in front of me and don't try anything stupid." His breath was hot against her ear, making bile rise in her throat.

She could smell alcohol too, beer maybe. He moved the gun away from her head and for a moment she allowed a shred of relief to slide through her — until he pressed it against her ribs.

He pushed her forward, but never lost his grip on her upper arm as they moved through a doorway. There was no door, just a frame.

Slivers of light filtered through windows that had been boarded up. There were a couple dozen display cases but they all appeared empty. There was a musty scent in here that hadn't been in the back. Flickers of dust floated through the beams of light, as if something had just been disturbed.

"Show yourself or I blow her fucking head off." White's voice was quiet, deadly.

She didn't see anyone else and she couldn't hear anything, but maybe he'd seen something. Or maybe he was just guessing Quinn had come after her. Oh God, what if there was no one here and he shot her because —

Travis rose quietly from behind one of the cases, his expression practically feral. She'd never seen him look like that, like...a killer.

His weapon was pointed at them but it made her feel better. At least if White shot her, Travis would take him out. Quinn had to be here somewhere too. Fear for both Quinn and Travis surged through her, battling with hope that they were here to save her and Raegan.

"Step out from behind that case and drop your weapon. Now!" White barked.

Travis moved slowly from behind the display case. As he did, White moved too, using Athena as a shield. Travis hadn't dropped his weapon though. Athena could barely move, was so numb with terror. Everything was surreal, as if she was watching all this happen to someone else.

"Drop it!" White pointed his gun at Travis, his hand steady.

In that moment Travis dove to the side. She had a millisecond to question it. Something wet sprayed over the back of her neck as White's gun fired.

The blast made her jump. She screamed as one of the boarded up front windows exploded, glass and wood splintering. Before she could register what had happen, White wasn't gripping her anymore. His gun fell to the floor.

She started to turn when two strong hands gripped her arms tight from behind and swiveled her around. It took a moment for everything to fall into place.

"You're okay, sweetheart," Quinn said, his voice unsteady. Worry bled into his eyes as he ran his hands up and down her arms, looking for wounds. He cut her zip-tie free in a second.

She felt weird, numb as she looked down at White. He was dead, his throat slit, blood pouring onto the floor. Quinn must have done it while Travis distracted him. She shivered, thinking that anything could have gone wrong. But it hadn't.

"Tell me you're okay!" Quinn shook her a little.

The command in his voice snapped her out of her thoughts. Focusing on him, she saw a huge, skilled man with raw fear in his dark eyes. The sight clawed at her. "I'm fine. Are you...hurt?" Another dose of panic punched through her. Now she started to scan him, but he just tugged her into his arms in a bear hug. The feel of him holding her close was too much to handle. She finally felt safe.

She wrapped her arms around him, burying her face against his neck and let the tears come. "You guys found us," she sobbed out, unable to stop the tears.

"You're wearing a smart watch from now on too," he murmured, his voice right next to her ear.

She wanted to get away from White's body and out of this disgusting place but more than anything, she just wanted to hold on to Quinn. She needed to reassure herself that he was really here and she was safe.

"I fucking love you," Quinn murmured against her ear. "I don't care if it's too soon to say it. I love you."

She pulled back and grabbed his face between her hands. "You're not telling me that with a dead body a few feet away!"

To her surprise he let out a loud, harsh laugh and scooped her up in his arms. "Let's get the hell out of here then and let the cops deal with this garbage." Undeniable rage threaded the last couple words as he strode through the building toward the back.

When he stepped through the back door with her in his arms, she sucked in a breath of fresh air and wanted to start crying all over again. Out of the corner of her eye she saw Travis and Raegan by one of the vans but all her focus was on Quinn. "You can put me down now."

He resisted for a moment but did as she said. She cupped his cheeks, gentler this time, as her heels touched the ground. "I love you too."

EPILOGUE

Four months later

"**W**hat are you grumbling about under your breath?" Quinn pressed the elevator button and glanced at Athena, humor in his voice.

"Nothing, I'm just annoyed. Like this couldn't wait until Monday?" Harrison had asked her to check the rooftop dining area of a new, exclusive hotel that would be opening in about a month. She'd been planning to check it out anyway, but he'd asked her ten minutes before she was supposed to leave for work. And he'd been insistent she see it tonight—even though he knew she had birthday plans.

"It's okay if we miss the reservation. This is your work." Quinn wrapped an arm around her and tugged her close as they stepped inside.

She wanted to press her nose against his neck and inhale. The man had a spicy, masculine scent that drove her crazy. Ever since that insanity in Vegas they'd been pretty much inseparable during their off-work hours. She couldn't get enough of him. It still scared her what could have happened to them. To all of them. She and Raegan had enrolled in self-defense classes since returning to Miami and it gave Athena a sense of control. Thankfully Quinn had been cleared quickly in White's death and the caterer White had knocked out had been found unconscious but alive. Unfortunately he'd killed someone else who worked for the catering company. White had been careful and smart jamming the security feed at the casino. Not to mention using his cousin to make it appear as if he was still in Miami. Athena wondered if he'd have gotten away with kidnapping her and Raegan—in addition to his other crimes and planned crimes—if it hadn't been for Raegan's smart watch and Quinn and Travis's training. Fighting off a shudder, she shelved that thought. She couldn't worry about 'what-if's' anymore.

"I know, but I realize how hard it was to get that reservation. I don't want to be late." She squeezed him back. Her birthday was tomorrow and Quinn had gone to a lot of trouble to get a reservation for them at one of her favorite places. He seemed more excited than her about her birthday. She knew it was a little nerdy, but she'd never celebrated a birthday with a boyfriend before and she wanted to enjoy this one.

He kissed the top of her head as the elevator came to a soft halt and dinged. A sensual, husky female voice announced that they had 'reached their destination and to have a pleasant day'.

She snickered as they stepped out into the tiled space of the dim dining area. "What do you want to bet it was a man's idea to have that audio program installed?"

Before Quinn could respond, lights snapped on and too many people to count shouted "Surprise!".

She nearly jumped out of her skin. A happy birthday sign had been hung above a bar and her parents and too many friends to count all stood there wearing silly birthday hats and grins on their faces. She couldn't find her voice and fought the tears that pricked her eyes. She squeezed Quinn's side. "You did this?" she asked, looking up at him.

"Happy birthday," Quinn murmured, kissing the top of her head.

She pulled him into a tight hug, unable to find her voice. Her throat clogged with tears at the sweet gesture.

Nearly two hours later, after a few too many glasses of champagne, cake, and mingling with her family and friends, she found herself blessedly alone with Quinn on one of the open balconies.

"You're very sneaky." She let him take her glass, watched in pleasure as he set it on one of the high top tables. She just loved to watch him move. He had a gracefulness that seemed incongruous with his size.

When he turned back to her and sank down on one knee, it took a moment for her champagne-addled brain to realize what he was doing. His hands shook, something that surprised her, as he pulled out a small box and popped it open. "Marry me?"

She stared at his face, not even glancing at the ring, then threw herself into his arms. "Yes!" Since he was still crouching she nearly toppled him over.

Laughing, he slid the ring on her finger and stood, gathering her into his arms.

"You're going to have a hard time topping this birthday next year—or ever." Talk about the best gift. She'd known they were heading in this direction but hadn't expected it anytime soon.

"I love you, Athena." His eyes glinted in that wicked way as he crushed his mouth over hers.

As their tongues danced together, she briefly wondered if they could find a private place to sneak off to before the night ended. The balcony was private from prying ears but anyone could see them from inside. And she wasn't an exhibitionist by any stretch.

When he pulled her even tighter, she melted into him, thankful to have found such an incredible man. She'd never expected to fall in love so hard or so fiercely, but now that she had, she was never letting him go.

SECRET
OBSESSION

CHAPTER ONE

R aegan was practically vibrating with energy as she shut down her computer. She couldn't remember the last Friday she'd actually gotten to leave at five o'clock. She loved her new job at Red Stone Security, but working with Athena in the new marketing/PR division kept them incredibly busy. Late nights and weekends were standard — the benefits and money were freaking worth the crazy hours. And she took full advantage when she was off, enjoying everything Miami had to offer.

"What are your plans for tonight?" Athena asked, stepping out of her office, a big smile on her face.

Raegan knew exactly why she was so happy too. She got to go home to her sexy fiancé. Even though Athena was only two years older than her, she seemed to have her shit together in a way Raegan could admit she envied a teeny bit. She'd traveled the world as an event planner for two years after getting a job at Red Stone and was so put together.

Raegan felt like an imposter most of the time. She'd grown up on a farm, hadn't seen much of the world, and she knew people thought she'd gotten this job because she was Keith Caldwell's niece. Which was sorta true. Of course, she wouldn't have kept her job if she wasn't good at it. "Going dancing with your cousin-in-law-to-be. Or whatever Dominique will be to you soon."

"Let me guess, Ruby and Julieta are going too?"

Raegan snorted as she pulled out the small gift bag she'd tucked into her desk drawer, and stood. "Yes, which means Ivan will be there as a brooding bodyguard." It was actually nice that Ivan went out with them. He was such a huge, scary-looking guy he kept pretty much all jerks away from them.

Raegan loved dancing but that didn't mean she wanted to grind with every guy on the dance floor, and it seemed most guys couldn't take a hint. It was like they thought that simply because she was dancing with her friends she needed a dance partner, and then said dance partner got to rub all over her. No thank you.

"Good. Remember the buddy system," Athena said, falling in step with her as they headed toward the elevators. "And watch your drink at all times. And—"

"Oh my God, I'm going to start calling you Mom if you don't stop." Raegan pressed both the up and down buttons on the elevator keypad. "I'm going to see Porter," she said when Athena raised an eyebrow.

"Okay, well, I'm allowed to worry. I can't help it. You're the best assistant I've ever had and I don't like change, so if something happened to you I'd have to train someone else," she grumbled.

"You're such a liar." Raegan knew Athena felt guilty over the kidnapping. She'd been extra protective since Vegas. As if she could have prevented what happened. Raegan had simply been in the wrong place at the wrong time when Athena had been targeted by a nut job and had gotten kidnapped along with her.

Athena just shrugged. "Oh, Harrison wanted to know if we could both attend the Celebration of Chefs event tomorrow night. I know it's last minute so I told him yes for me but maybe for you. Absolutely no pressure. This is just something fun for us but he wanted us—"

"I'm actually going already."

Athena raised an eyebrow as her elevator arrived. She held her hand in between the doors so they wouldn't close on her, but didn't get in. "As in, with a date?"

"No, just as friends."

Now her boss and friend's eyes narrowed. "Is this with a certain billionaire who your cousins hate?"

Raegan resisted the urge to roll her eyes. "They don't hate him and I'm not having this conversation again. Just tell Harrison I'll be there." When her elevator dinged she ducked into it and called out, "Have fun with your sexy man tonight!"

Athena grumbled something but Raegan missed most of it as the elevator door whooshed closed. She adored her older cousins but they were ridiculously overprotective. Because of their age differences and because she'd never left the Midwest until almost a year ago, she'd never been close to them. But now that she lived in Miami and worked for their company it was like she had three older brothers who thought every man was an enemy. And they'd apparently recruited Athena into their way of thinking.

Raegan might not have much world experience, but she'd been fending off the opposite sex since she was fourteen. She could take care of herself.

Besides, there was only one man she was interested in and he seemed to have absolutely zero attraction to her. She'd never even seen a flicker of awareness from him, which, perversely, made her want the sexy cop even more.

So there was no reason she shouldn't do whatever she wanted with whoever she wanted. But she hadn't been lying to Athena — tomorrow she was just going to the Celebrity Chef event with a friend.

The soft elevator music flowed into another bland song as the car arrived on the floor for one of her adorable, overprotective cousins: Porter Caldwell.

When she reached the plush office of his assistant, she was surprised to find it empty. The door to Porter's office was cracked open and she heard male voices. Normally she wouldn't interrupt, but she heard both Porter and Grant talking and knew they wouldn't mind.

After a light knock she started to step into the office, but felt all the air rush out of her lungs when she saw that it wasn't just Porter and Grant, but Ford Burke as well.

The sexy man made her feel like that naïve little farm girl she'd been trying to shed. Just looking at him turned her knees to mush. He was tall, with ridiculously broad shoulders she wanted to run her fingers over. He kept his dark hair closely cropped and had a neatly trimmed beard that on most guys she wouldn't have liked. She'd never been a fan of facial hair until Ford. But she'd had a fantasy or two of what it would feel like to have his face buried between her—

She blinked when she realized they were all staring at her. She felt her cheeks heat up and wanted to kick her own butt. Raegan wasn't sure if they'd said anything to her directly so, holding up the little gift bag, she said, "I brought this for Maddox."

Just like that, Porter's normally hard expression softened. "You spoil him," he murmured, moving away from the desk, a grin on his face.

"Of course I do. I'm going to hold onto the title of favorite older cousin forever and I have no shame buying his love." During her lunch break today she'd found a cute little boutique downtown and snagged an adorable Darth Vader pajama set. On the front of the shirt it said 'Not Afraid of the Dark Side.'

Laughing, Porter kissed her forehead and pulled her into a light embrace. "You coming by for dinner tonight?"

"I can't. Plans with the girls. It's why I wanted to bring this to you now. But I'll stop by tomorrow to see my little man." She didn't want kids of her own for years yet, but little Maddox had completely stolen her heart. He'd just turned one last month and was walking and babbling like a little maniac. And she loved spoiling him.

She was vaguely aware of Ford watching her, but of course he was—she'd interrupted them. She wished his focus was on her for other reasons.

"Where are you guys going tonight?" Grant asked and before she turned to face him she could hear the frown in his voice.

"None of your business," she said cheekily, giving him a frown of her own when she saw the plethora of weapons on Porter's desk. "What the heck is this? Are you guys starting your own army?"

To her surprise, Grant's cheeks flushed the faintest shade of pink. "Maybe don't say anything to Belle about this?"

Now that surprised Raegan. As far as she knew her cousins didn't keep anything from their wives. "Um, about what? Your new arsenal?" She eyed the guns again. They all looked really old.

He nodded at Ford. "They're antiques and Ford's helping me refurbish them."

Raegan smiled at Ford, murmured "Hi," and he just nodded, his expression the same as it always was. Brooding.

Grant just continued. "Once they're in good shape they'll be worth a lot but..."

"Belle gets annoyed with too many guns around the house?" Raegan guessed. She'd grown up on a farm so she was no stranger to guns, especially not rifles, but she'd seen how some of the guys at Red Stone acted around their guns. They might as well stroke them and start calling them 'my precious.'

"Well, we're...pregnant and—"

"Belle's pregnant?"

"Yeah and she's really emotional right now and wanted me to get rid of all my guns so I'm waiting to tell her about this..." He trailed off, shrugging.

Raegan pulled him into a big hug. "Congrats! How far along is she?" she asked, stepping back.

"About four months. We wanted to wait until she was a little past the first trimester, but we were going to announce it next week."

"That's great. I'm so happy for you guys."

"Thanks." He grinned in a way she'd never seen. A mix of pride and a little bit of terror. Which was just way too adorable.

She heard her phone buzz in her purse, knew it would be Dominique telling her to hurry up. A relief, since it would get her out of here and away from Ford's penetrating gaze. "I've gotta run, but can I call Belle and congratulate her?"

"Yeah, of course. Why don't you come over for dinner Sunday? Her mom gave us a couple casseroles," he tacked on when she would have automatically asked if he was cooking or Belle was.

"I'll be there." After giving her two cousins another quick hug, she nodded once at Ford, who'd been quiet as usual. "Nice to see you again, Ford."

He just watched her with that brooding stare he seemed to have down pat, and made a sort of grunting sound that could have meant any number of things. And damn it, she kinda liked it. Which was ridiculous. She was no one to him. Just Grant, Porter and Harrison's younger cousin.

Just as she reached the door, Porter said, "Hey, are you going to the Celebration of Chefs event tomorrow night? Harrison said something about you and Athena maybe going. If you are, you can catch a ride with me and Lizzy."

Thanks to Porter's generosity she was renting a one-bedroom condo in the same high rise he lived in with his wife. Many, many floors below them, and her place was a lot smaller, but it was a great home. She knew they'd bought it as an investment and had been planning to rent it out, and when they'd offered to let her rent it, it had been impossible to say no. Partially because of the way they'd guilt-tripped her into it but also because it was a safe place and they'd given her such a great deal.

"I won't need a ride, but thanks. I'm going with someone." When her phone started ringing she used it as an excuse to race out of there before they could question her about her 'date' that wasn't actually a date. They wouldn't see it that way though.

She actually had gone on one date with him back in Vegas but since then she'd made it clear she just wanted to be friends and he was okay with it.

She'd dated other guys in Miami since, but nothing ever went past the first date. And she knew it was because she was so incredibly attracted to Ford "too sexy for his own good" Burke.

———————◆◆◆———————

"What's that look?" Ford asked as Grant and Porter exchanged an annoyed glance between them. Now that Raegan was out of the room he could finally breathe again. The woman made him crazy. She was a combination of sweetness and jaw-dropping sexiness. Impossible to resist.

"Nothing," Grant muttered, turning back to the desk. But he looked at his brother again. "You see the way she ran out of here?"

Porter went back to his standard stoic mode now that Raegan was gone, and nodded once. "I bet she's going out with that dick again and didn't want to tell us."

Ford didn't like the sound of that. At all. Sweet Raegan had had him twisted up for damn near eleven months. He'd met her at a few of the Caldwell family functions and each time it was like he forgot to act like a human. He couldn't even talk to her, and he'd never been nervous around women. Hell, he'd done undercover work for a year back when he'd been on the drug task force. He was comfortable around people as a rule.

But around Raegan? He was a moron.

She was a decade younger than him, or at least close to it. He didn't think she was older than twenty-three. And that made him feel ancient and a little bit like a perv. But he couldn't help it.

She had that girl-next-door thing going on and it pushed all his buttons. If she'd been anyone but Grant and Porter's cousin he'd have asked her out by now. Or at least tried to. Because God knew talking didn't come easy when she was around.

He cleared his throat. "What dick?"

Grant crossed his arms over his chest as he leaned against the front of the desk, looking every bit the intimidating detective he'd once been. He'd nearly died in an explosion almost two years ago, and half his face and upper body had been burned, scarred because of it. Right now he looked ready to take someone's head off. "Some British guy she met in Vegas. They're just friends, supposedly, but…why would a guy keep taking her out when he's in town if they're just friends?"

"Especially one like that," Porter muttered, starting to put one of the rifles back into its case.

"Like what?" He'd never asked about Raegan, had basically forced himself not to ask Grant about her, but screw that if this British guy was bad news.

"Some rich prick," Grant practically snarled.

"Harrison said he was inquiring about using our services," Porter tacked on, using a terrible British accent.

It was like the two men had devolved to adolescents, but he understood the sentiment. Raegan was beautiful, no doubt, but she was sweet and way too kind for her own good from what he'd seen. The kind of woman assholes would like to prey on.

Ford rubbed the back of his neck, forcing himself not to ask any more questions. No good would come of it. He didn't need to know who she was or wasn't dating. Even if he hadn't been able to fuck anyone else since meeting her. His dick knew what it wanted: Raegan. He had good taste, that was for sure.

When she'd walked into Porter's office wearing that slim pencil skirt, pretty pink top and high heels, all his naughty librarian fantasies had flared to life. She was lean, with a runner's build, and had long, thick dark hair he'd fantasized about running his hands through as he claimed her mouth.

Then her body.

He always had the urge to mess up her perfect hair, to get a rise out of her just to see her cheeks flush pink. And he always froze like a teenager around her.

As the two brothers continued to talk about the merits of Raegan's date and how they'd like to kick his ass, Ford started packing up the rest of the rifles. Grant had found them at a yard sale, of all places, and snatched them up for a steal. Now he wanted Ford's help to restore them. Some wouldn't be worth much more than the money they put into refurbishing them, but a couple Grant would be able to sell to collectors if he didn't keep them himself. It was a solid investment.

"...and BDSM. What the hell?"

Ford snapped back to reality at the last few words snarled by Grant. "BDSM?" They couldn't still be talking about Raegan. Could they?

Grant slid the last rusted rifle into the long, padded case. His expression was disgusted. "I ran the guy Raegan's 'not dating' and yeah, turns out he's into that shit. Owns a couple clubs. But she's a grown woman. We can't tell her what to do."

"She's really not dating him. At least that's what Lizzy says." Porter lifted a shoulder but Ford could see the tension humming in the man's body.

Ford gritted his teeth and turned away from them, making himself look busy. He wanted to ask what the guy's name was, do a run on the guy himself. Only that was insane behavior. He rolled his shoulders once. He had no claim on Raegan. She barely looked at him.

"You guys mind if I head out? I promised a buddy I'd do some light recon tonight. We're trying to track down some guy they suspect of a bunch of jewelry store burglaries." At some downtown club that wasn't remotely his style, but it was overtime and he owed the detective a favor.

"I'll walk down with you," Grant said. "You want to take these now?"

He nodded, picking up two of the cases. Anything to get his mind off Raegan and why he could never have her.

CHAPTER TWO

He kept his hood pulled up over his head as he watched Raegan on the dance floor of the loud, obnoxious club. In a place like this the hood didn't stand out and it kept his face blocked from any security cameras. He'd seen enough guys wearing hoodies, sunglasses and ridiculous bling that he wasn't even a blip on anyone's radar tonight. Just another club-goer.

He wasn't even sure if he'd make a move tonight, but he liked to think two steps ahead of everyone. So if an opportunity presented itself, he'd take it.

It was how he'd come to be where he was.

She was such a fucking tease. It would be easy to write her off as another Miami whore, but he knew she wasn't like that. But she constantly teased him, made him crazy. She was so nice to him, always smiling at him, asking him how his day was, what his weekend plans were. He wondered if she knew what she was doing, if that big-eyed farm-girl thing was all an act designed to make him sweat.

Right now she sure as hell didn't appear as if she'd stepped off any farm. The dance floor was outside and looked out over the white sand beach. Strings of colored lights were the only roof for everyone out there.

But he stayed back at the main bar, his seat giving him the perfect view of her and her friends. Unfortunately she'd come with three other girls and three men. He'd seen them before too. Well, all except one of the men. A guy with a messed-up face who looked like he might be related to the other Hispanic man.

The big blond guy with them looked like a damn Viking and he rarely left the table where the women's drinks were. The guy with the ugly face didn't leave often either, but he was watching one of the blonde women who was friends with Raegan on the dance floor. He never seemed to take his eyes off the curvy woman.

Raegan was a lot leaner than her friends. Slim, but with enough curves that she was smoking hot. As the music shifted to a slower, more sensual song, he watched as the Hispanic guy at the table stood, moved closer to the dance floor. As if he couldn't keep away from the blonde.

The Viking stayed at the table, unfortunately. Still...he might be able to make this work. If he could get her loose, pliant, he could get her the hell out of here. Then she'd be his to do what he wanted with. He tossed a bill on the bar and stood, drink in hand. As soon as he'd taken three steps his seat was already occupied, no surprise.

The Latin beat of the music vibrated through him, pumped up his adrenaline as he reached into the pocket of his pants. Just having the small container was a schedule-one felony but it was easily disposable. He was going to use it now anyway.

Always be prepared. His motto.

Tonight he'd just planned to follow Raegan like usual, but given this opportunity, he had to take advantage. He was always ready for an opening because he knew one day, he'd get one. Normally she was surrounded by people, even at work. And her condo building was difficult to get into. Not impossible, but they had more security than a place like this did.

It would be easier to lead her away once he got this drug in her system. He'd have to break her away from her pack of friends. That would be the difficult part. Getting her dosed was also difficult, but he was up for the challenge. And if he failed, no harm, no foul. She'd never know he'd done a damn thing. That was the most important part. She couldn't know he'd been here, what he'd done.

He was going to spend time with Raegan alone. Naked. With no other distractions. Then she'd see how good they could be together. She was always so nice to him, but...she didn't seem to see the real him. That was all he wanted. He wanted her to see him, to touch him, to tell him how much she wanted him.

Winding his way through the throng of half-dressed people, he felt secure enough that he blended in with everyone else. Standing out was the one thing he couldn't do.

As he passed the table where the blond giant was sitting, watching the cadre of women he'd come with, he didn't bother trying to move up behind him out of his line of sight. Instead, he acted as if he'd go around him, then tripped, spilling his drink on the guy's pants.

He grabbed onto the man's shoulder as he weaved on his feet. "Shit, man, I'm sorry." He intentionally slurred, using sleight of hand to dump the liquid into Raegan's glass on the table.

The guy shrugged off his hold, his expression hard as he stared at him. "It's fine. Move along."

"Yeah, yeah, really sorry." Keeping his head low, he held up his hands as he hurried off, blending into the crowd of people and high top tables behind him. He didn't turn around even though he wanted to. He wouldn't look to see if the Viking had noticed what he'd done. Maybe the guy would remember his face, maybe not. It wouldn't matter. No one could pin anything on him anyway.

Adrenaline humming through him, he kept his pace steady. He needed to find another spot so he could watch Raegan unobtrusively. If his move had worked, he'd get Raegan alone a lot sooner than he'd planned.

And then he'd do all the things he'd been fantasizing about.

Raegan pressed a hand to her stomach as a wave of nausea swept through her. Blinking, she shook herself. She'd only had two drinks, but it had started to get hot. Even with the huge fans and chilly breeze kicking up from the Atlantic it was getting sticky. Summer in Miami wasn't remotely cold anyway, but the place kept huge misting fans blowing to cool everyone off. That wasn't working right now.

She'd worn a brightly colored halter wraparound dress but that didn't seem to matter now. She needed fresher air, ASAP. There was a live DJ tonight and he'd been playing mostly Latin dance. The beat of the music seemed suddenly too loud, pounding in her head, everything too stifling. There were too many people. She felt suffocated.

She started to tell Ruby she needed some water, but she noticed that Montez had finally worked up the courage to do more than just stare at the blonde bombshell. They weren't exactly dancing, but they were talking near the dance floor. That was progress. Sandro and Dominique were still tearing it up. Though Sandro didn't have a chance with Dominique, that much Raegan knew. And Julieta and Ivan might be at the same table as her, but they were in their own world.

She started to tell them that she was going to grab a bottle of water, but slid off her chair instead when Ivan leaned down to his fiancée's ear and started whispering something that made Julieta laugh and blush.

"I'm gonna grab a water," she murmured, not sure if they'd heard her, and at this point she didn't really care.

The huge bar was half inside and half outside the building. But she knew there was also a small tiki bar on the other side of the expansive dance floor overlooking the beach and ocean.

It seemed to take forever to get to the edge of the dance floor where larger seating like couches and plush lounge chairs were set up. She knew this place was popular for beachgoers and transitioned to more of a club at night. According to Julieta it was one of the top-rated clubs in Miami because of the fun atmosphere and celebrity sightings.

Not that Raegan had seen anyone famous. Or she didn't think she had. And right now, she didn't care. She just needed water and a cool blast of air.

As she continued on through a throng of people, another wave of nausea combined with dizziness assaulted her.

She blinked, clutching on to a high top table. The occupants, three college-age-looking guys grinned at her.

"Buy you a drink?" one of them asked.

She couldn't even shake her head, couldn't say much of anything. Instead she dropped her hand and continued walking. Her body felt numb, and the floor was beginning to tilt, but she knew she didn't want to sit there with a bunch of frat boys.

Something was wrong with her, she wasn't sure what, but it was getting worse and she was getting worried. Instead of continuing toward the tiki bar she turned back around.

She needed to find her friends. And go home.

"You okay?" A man wearing a hoodie and jeans sidled up to her, put his arm around her waist to steady her.

She tried to answer but struggled to find her voice. The scent of his cologne turned her stomach even more. She shook her head. Or tried to.

"Let's get you some fresh air," he said, guiding her back through the thick mass of people.

The bright lights above suddenly seemed like a manic kaleidoscope of colors, flashing and hurting her eyes. She was barely aware of moving, but when he shoved open a big door that opened up onto a short set of stairs that led to the sandy beach, she tried to pull back.

She didn't want to go to the beach or anywhere with this stranger. "Leave me alone," she said. Or tried to. Her words came out slurred.

His grip on her upper arm tightened as he shoved her through the door.

She cried out and tried to turn back around but he slammed the door shut.

Iciness invaded her veins as she tripped and fell into the sand. This was not good. She needed to call her friends. Get help. Waves crashed in the distance and she could hear the thrum of laughter, voices and music through the big wall behind her, but she knew that no one could help her now. Even if she screamed. And she couldn't find her voice. Everything was all screwed up. God, what was wrong with her?

Before she could push up, strong arms yanked her to her feet.

"Don't know why you're wearing these stupid heels," the guy muttered, tugging her close. As if he had a right to touch her at all. He wrapped an arm around her waist but she shoved at him.

Or, again, tried. Panic punched through her, but her fingers wouldn't obey as he dragged her across the sand. She lost one of her shoes in her struggle. "Let...me go." Her words didn't come out as strong as she'd intended.

"Hey!" A deep, vaguely familiar male voice from behind seemed as if it was coming from a long way away. "What the fuck are you doing?" He was angry.

"No, no, no," the guy holding her muttered.

Suddenly she was falling, her knees and hands hitting the soft sand. The grains rolled across her knees and palms. She tried to push up, but another wave of dizziness swelled through her.

She was aware of someone calling her name. Someone...familiar. She couldn't place the voice, could barely remember her own name, as callused, strong hands gripped her upper arms and pulled her to her feet.

CHAPTER THREE

Ford pulled Raegan to her feet as gently as he could. "Are you okay, sweetheart?" The term of endearment just slipped out, but she didn't seem to notice.

She blinked at him with big, blue eyes. "Ford?"

He held onto her upper arms. "Did you know that guy?" Right about now he wanted to race after the asshole who'd shoved her and run, but no way was he leaving Raegan to fend for herself. Not when she could barely stand.

"What guy?" She blinked again, swaying in his arms now.

Cursing, he glanced over his shoulder as the side door to the beach club opened. A giggling group of three women stumbled out. Instead of heading their way, they turned and started for what he knew was the parking lot. He turned back to Raegan, who was beginning to fade fast.

He cupped her cheek, shook her a little. Her eyes were glazed. "How much have you had to drink?"

"What...you doing here?"

Damn it, she was drunk. Or...worse. "Who did you come with?" Because it sure as hell hadn't been that guy.

Instead of answering, she wrapped her arms around him, pressing her very full breasts against his chest as she practically nuzzled his neck. "You smell good," she murmured.

He groaned at the feel of her pressed up against him, felt like a dick for liking it so much. "Listen, sweetheart, we need to get you out of here." Without pause, he lifted her into his arms, holding her close. She had one of those slim wallet-sized purses with the strap securely around her wrist. He scooped up her fallen shoe as they passed it, tried not to notice the soft swell of her breasts peeking out of her halter dress as she cuddled against him. Or the way she was rubbing his chest and nuzzling his neck.

"Who did you come with, Raegan?" he asked as he carried her along the exterior of the club. It was just chance he'd seen her stumbling out the side door with some shady-looking guy. He'd come here tonight because a detective friend had needed a favor. A suspect they were trying to bring in was known to frequent this place and half a dozen others. This was the club he'd been chosen to stake out.

"Friends. Who'd you come with? Your...girlfriend?" Her words were still slurred, uneven.

"Don't have one," he muttered. Because the only woman he wanted was currently in his arms. And she wouldn't be acting like this if she were sober. That much he knew.

The music faded as he made his way past the door they'd come out of. As he rounded the building, he noticed two security guys talking and smoking. They didn't even give him a second glance as he carried a practically unconscious woman into the parking lot. Not doing their damn job. He knew who the owner of this place was and he'd be making a call to him very soon.

But Raegan was his priority. When they reached his truck, he got her into the passenger-side seat.

"You smell good," she said again, this time nipping his earlobe. Her voice was sensual, her eyes heavy-lidded as she looked at him.

Inches separated them as he stared into blue, blue eyes. Eyes he could drown in. Looking at her now, however, he wondered if she'd been drugged. "So do you," he said quietly. "I need you to focus for a second. I'm going to take you to see a friend of mine." Because Ford was pretty sure she'd been drugged, and that guy who'd ditched her had clearly had something bad planned. "He's a doctor—"

She listed forward suddenly but when he went to steady her, she grabbed onto his shirt and tugged him down to her. Her mouth skated over his, her lips soft and pliable.

He needed to pull back. To stop this. Right now. She wasn't herself, wasn't thinking.

But when she moaned against him and bit his bottom lip, he lost the ability to think. Almost.

"Raegan, no." He withdrew from her, strapped her in, slid back and shut the door as she made a protesting sound.

Cursing, he leaned against the side of the door, scrubbed a hand over his face. Raegan was not for him and she wouldn't even remember the kiss anyway. He shouldn't have let it go that far. Continuing to curse himself, he rounded the truck and slid into the front seat.

"Do you remember how much you had to drink?" he asked, starting the ignition.

"Um...two. Maybe one and a half. I started to feel...dizzy though. Why are you here again?" She closed her eyes, let her head fall back.

Damn it. Drugs. He decided then and there that he would make it his personal mission to find out who the hell had drugged her. Because this clearly wasn't a case of her drinking too much. "Open your eyes," he said sharply, rolling down her window to get a burst of air rolling over her.

Her phone started to ring in her purse and he guessed it might be one of her friends wondering where she was. "You want to check who that is?"

"Um...hold on." It took her a few tries to get her small purse unzipped and when she did she squinted at the screen. "It's Jules."

"Is that who you came with?"

"Yesh," she slurred out, her eyes starting to droop again.

He plucked it from her hand, not bothering to ask for permission as he swiped his thumb across the screen. "This is Ford Burke. I'm with the Miami PD and I'm taking Raegan to a doctor."

"Oh my God! Is she okay?" the woman named Jules shouted. He could hear music and other voices in the background.

"She's fine." Or she would be. He wouldn't let anything happen to her.

"What's going on, then? Why are you taking her to a doctor?" Her voice was bordering on panic.

"I found some guy trying to take her out of the club and realized it's likely she's been drugged. I'm friends with her cousins, Grant, Porter and Harrison. I used to work with Grant. Please call him and confirm."

"What hospital are you taking her to? We'll meet you there."

"Not taking her to a hospital." Because the ER on a Friday night was a nightmare. Didn't matter that he was a cop. That would only get him so far in the favor department. She'd still have to wait hours to be looked at. They'd check her vitals, stick her in a room with three other people and come back and check on her when they could — and that was only after they finally got her to a damn room. No way was he going to put her through that when he could get her looked at immediately.

"I'm taking her to a local clinic. Friend of mine runs it. Call Grant and confirm who I am. You know his number?"

"Uh, yeah. Well, my fiancé does. He's with me. He works with Grant."

"Good. She's fine. I've got her phone and she doesn't need to deal with a bunch of people down at the clinic."

"I don't know how this happened. We were all together, then when I turned around she was just gone. I thought maybe she'd gone to the bathroom or to grab another drink, but then none of us could find her. Is she really okay?"

"Yeah. I think…someone slipped her Rohypnol." He didn't want her friend to freak out even more, but decided to be honest. It was also known as a date rape drug, something he guessed her friend knew by her worried gasp.

"There's no way!"

He turned on his blinker as he neared the turnoff to his friend's clinic. The neighborhood bordered a sketchy area of town, but that was sorta the point of the clinic's location. People who needed medical care the most often couldn't get it. His friend tried to combat that problem by providing affordable medical care. In some cases, free. And he was better equipped to give Raegan his complete attention as opposed to the harried, Friday night ER staff at a hospital. If Ford had been worried she'd overdosed he'd have taken her straight there.

"Well it happened. Look, I gotta go. Gotta get her inside now. Call Grant, confirm to make yourself feel better. I'm sure she'll call you in the morning. She's safe, I swear." He cut her off before she could respond. He didn't care if it was rude. Being polite wasn't a concern right now. Raegan was his only concern.

"I've never heard you talk so much at once." Raegan giggled a little as she watched him.

He was glad she was awake, but having all her focus on him was jarring. "How're you feeling?"

"Funny. You think I was drugged?" She giggled again, softer this time.

"Maybe."

"I've never done drugs. And I'm not saying that because you're a cop. A very sexy cop." She laughed at that, seeming to think it was hilarious.

"We're going inside here," he said, nodding at the darkened clinic. It was late but he knew his friend was still here in the back. He always stayed until midnight even though he locked the doors—to keep out would-be thieves and junkies looking for a fix.

"You sure it's open?"

"Yeah." He was out and to her side in seconds. He hated that someone had done this to her, but he'd worry about finding the guilty party later. Right now he just needed to make sure she was safe.

Montez frowned, listening to Ivan talking to Grant Caldwell on the phone. They'd all left the club after his sister Julieta had talked to some guy on Raegan's phone. Some guy who claimed he was a cop and was allegedly taking her to a clinic.

Now they were in the parking lot, waiting while Ivan talked to Grant, confirming whether this was true. He hated the thought of anything happening to Raegan. Hell, any woman. But Raegan was a sweet girl and a little naïve in general. It was hard not to like her.

After a lot of one-word answers and short questions, Ivan finally hung up the phone. "She's okay as far as Grant knows. He said he'll keep me updated."

"That's so scary," Dominique said, wrapping her arms around herself.

Next to her, Ruby looked as worried as he'd ever seen her. And he'd seen the beauty in a hospital room after nearly being hit by a car. She'd only sprained her ankle and suffered from a few cuts and bruises but he'd never forget seeing her there, injured. It had shaved years off his life, knowing that day could have been much worse. The maniac driving the car could have killed her and wouldn't have cared.

When she looked at him, he automatically looked away. Because yeah, he was a coward where she was concerned.

As everyone started talking about heading home, Ruby sidled up to him. It surprised him. "Give me a ride tonight?" she asked quietly.

For the briefest moment, his mind went where he swore to never let it. He'd love to give her a ride. Over and over. But he'd never have a shot with a woman like Ruby. Not with his jacked-up face. She was friends with his sister, had worked with Jules for years. He'd only ever met her a year ago for the first time though. Since then she'd consumed his fantasies. Which was just plain stupid. "Sure," he said instead, surprising himself.

She gave him a sweet smile, but there was a glimmer of...something in her eyes. Something he couldn't get a handle on because it looked a lot like sexual attraction. He'd seen her shoot down pretty much every guy who hit on her, including his younger brother. Jules always joked that Ruby made grown men cry. And Montez believed it.

Ruby looked like Marilyn Monroe. Blonde, curvy and walking sex. And damn she had a mouth on her. He loved the smart-ass stuff she was always saying to people. Tonight she had on one of those pinup-style dresses his sister sold at the shop Ruby ran with her. She looked like one of those women painted on World War II bomber planes. He wanted to peel the black and white thing off her, to slowly reveal every inch of her luscious body before he kissed all of her smooth skin. But that was a stupid, stupid thing to wish for.

They weren't even in the same league, and not just because he was fucked-up looking. Though that was a big part of it.

After everyone said goodbye to each other and his younger brother gave him a not-so-subtle thumbs up about taking Ruby home, they headed out. He wasn't sure what the hell Sandro thought would happen, but this was just a ride, plain and simple.

"Are you working tomorrow?" Ruby asked as he steered out of the parking lot. She crossed her legs so that she was turned toward him.

He got hard at just that flash of leg. Who was he kidding? He'd been hard practically all damn night watching her. Because simply watching her was addicting. The thought of actually touching her…nope, not going there.

"Yeah. Saturday nights are always busy." He owned and ran La Playa Grill. Had pretty much since he'd gotten out of the Marines. He might not have come back from his last combat tour whole, but he could cook and he knew numbers. Not to mention he'd grown up in his parents' restaurant. He knew what it took to make a restaurant successful. The right employees, enough startup capital and a lot of hard work. Mainly hard work.

"I'm surprised you were even out tonight."

He hadn't planned on coming at all. And he probably wouldn't have if he'd known she'd be there. Being around her hurt too damn much. Seeing what he could never have. But his brother had asked him, so he'd come. "Sandro begged me."

She snorted, laughing. "As a wingman for his fruitless quest to land Dominique, right?"

He shot her a quick glance, saw the laughter dancing in her eyes. "You would be right."

"He needs a woman to take care of him, but D isn't it."

"Why do you say that?"

"Which part?"

"Both."

"Well, your brother is the type of man who needs a woman to take care of him. Period. I blame your sweet mother for that."

Now he snorted because it was the truth. "*Dios*, my mama spoiled him."

"And he's not D's type. She wants a man to take charge of her."

Montez cleared his throat. This was the first time he and Ruby had ever been alone together and this was veering toward...interesting territory. He wondered if she wanted a man to take charge of her. It was hard to imagine, knowing what he did of her. "Yeah?"

"Not, like, financially, but you know..." She trailed off, her grin wicked. "In the bedroom."

"What type of woman are you?" The question was out before he could stop himself. He didn't want to know. Except even he couldn't make himself believe his own lie.

"I want a man who knows what he's doing in the bedroom. And..." For the first time since he'd known Ruby she actually looked vulnerable. She paused a little longer than was normal before continuing. "I want someone who can take charge. To dominate me." She said the last three words in a rush before looking out the window, away from him.

Shock threaded through him. Yep. His dick was never going to go down at this rate. Different responses were on the tip of his tongue, but he couldn't voice any of them. His throat was too tight. All he could imagine was tying Ruby down, pleasuring her with his mouth as she came on his tongue, as he tasted her pleasure. He'd never pictured her as the type of woman to let herself lose control.

He shifted uncomfortably as he drove through the bright streets of Miami. Even this late, the city was alive, pulsing with energy. Some places would be quiet, especially the older, more established neighborhoods, but Ruby had a townhome in one of the newest parts of the city.

They weren't that far from the club, about twenty minutes. Her townhome was in an area that neighbored a shopping center complete with a Target and locally owned boutiques. It also wasn't far from where she worked with Jules.

"My car is in the garage but you can park in the driveway..." She blinked suddenly, her eyes narrowing at him as he put his truck in park. "How the hell do you know where I live?" she demanded, shifting away from him until she was practically against the door.

The flash of fear he saw in her eyes stunned him. "I brought you food before, when you hurt your ankle. Jules gave me the address. I swear." The streak of terror rolling off her slashed at him even as it surprised him. He wanted to reach out, to comfort her, but sensed it wouldn't be welcome.

She pushed out a harsh breath, raked a shaky hand through her hair. "Of course, I'm...jeez, I'm sorry. I just, I was stalked by this guy once. It freaked me out. Wait...you're the one who brought me all that food?"

"Yeah." He slid out of his seat as he answered. He didn't want to talk about that. And even if they weren't dating, he was still walking her to the door. And he was going to go back to that stalking thing.

"Why didn't you ever say anything?" she asked as he opened her door for her.

Of course she wouldn't let it drop. He shrugged.

She smacked his shoulder as they walked to her front door. "That's not a good enough answer. I'm going to need some actual words here."

"I don't know, I figured you knew it was me." Which was a lie. He'd just wanted to do something nice for her but he hadn't wanted her thanks or anything. She'd been injured and...he couldn't even think about what might have happened to her. He knew she'd assumed it was his parents or one of his siblings and he'd never felt the need to correct her.

"Well I didn't. I would have said something." She dug out her keys and slid one into the lock. "Want to come in for a drink? I'm still kinda wired after tonight. I won't sleep until I hear from Jules that Raegan is really okay."

Montez knew he should say no. But... "Yeah, okay." He already had a feeling he'd regret staying, but he couldn't leave her now. He hadn't had any alcohol tonight so a beer or whatever would be fine. Once they were inside he looked away as she turned off her alarm system. "You had a stalker?" That better be past tense too, because if someone was bothering Ruby, they wouldn't be for long.

"Yeah. It was years ago." Sighing, she motioned that he should follow her down a short hallway. Her place was bright and colorful and even smelled like her. A sort of vanilla and something, maybe cinnamon, that always reminded him of Ruby surrounded him here.

It was hard not to stare at her ass as she walked. And it was really hard not to wonder what she'd meant about being dominated. He wasn't into kink, but the thought of having Ruby all to himself... He rolled his shoulders once. He needed to stop thinking about something that wasn't going to happen.

"He killed himself," she continued. "Not that I'm happy about it, but that's a former part of my life."

He could tell by her tone she didn't want to talk about it so he didn't push. When they reached the kitchen she flipped on the lights and slipped her heels off by the kitchen entryway. Oh, hell, he should have done the same earlier. "You want me to take my shoes off?"

Laughing, she shook her head and made a beeline for the refrigerator. "Don't worry about it. Tomorrow's my cleaning day. I don't care about the floors right now. That's crazy about Raegan," she said, pulling out a beer and a bottle of water.

When she handed the beer to him, he realized her hand was shaking.

Well hell, she was really shaken up still. Of course. He hadn't even thought about that. In Afghanistan he'd seen more than his share of death. Had killed men and seen his own friends killed. Tonight sucked for Raegan but it didn't even register on his scale of screwed-up shit. Going against his self-preservation instinct, he took both drinks, put them on the nearest counter and pulled her into a hug. Seeing her shaken like this made all his protectiveness kick into high gear.

To his surprise she practically lunged at him, wrapping her arms around him tight. "I had a friend in high school who was roofied at a party. She wasn't as lucky as Raegan." Her whole body shook so he wrapped his arms tighter around her.

Tried not to notice how good she smelled. Or how amazing she felt pressed up against him. Her breasts were full, more than a handful. And he felt like a total dick for noticing. "I'm sorry."

She shook her head, her face tucked against his chest. "Tonight was just a reminder how careful we've always gotta be." Her voice was a little muffled.

"People suck," he muttered. He couldn't comprehend the need that some people had to hurt others, to violate them. But it permeated the world. That entitled, bullshit behavior.

"Yeah, no kidding." Her voice was soft as she pulled back, but only enough so that she could look up at him. Her eyes were wide as she watched him, and there was more than a hint of lust there.

The sight made something shift inside him. She'd had a few drinks tonight and she was clearly feeling vulnerable. He didn't want to take advantage of her but he'd give his left arm for a kiss. Just a taste.

"We got some new naughty nurse costumes at the store," Ruby murmured, her gaze dropping to his mouth.

He swallowed hard. How the hell was he supposed to respond to that? She shifted slightly against him and yep, came right in contact with his erection. He barely bit back a groan. It was impossible to hide. Now that he was holding her, touching her? No way it was going down anytime soon. Thinking about baseball or anything else wouldn't matter because Ruby was in his arms. That meant he was going to stay hard.

"They come in two different styles," she continued, her eyes locked onto his mouth, clear hunger there.

All he could do was stare at her beautiful face.

Now her gaze snapped up to meet his. "I was thinking I could model them for you, see which one you like better." Her voice was low, sultry and a mix of emotions bled into her gaze.

He couldn't get a read on any of them. He just knew that whatever this thing was, it wouldn't last. After getting burned before, literally and figuratively, he knew what his limits were. He could only offer her one thing. "Ruby..."

"Don't give me some song and dance about how you're Jules's brother and this can't happen. I know you want me." But she didn't sound sure. If anything, the confident woman he'd known the past year looked almost vulnerable.

That had to be bullshit though. She was perfect. "Of course I want you," he growled. "But I don't have anything to offer you other than sex. Just straight fucking and no promises of anything else. It'll be good, that I can promise, but nothing else will ever happen between us." He knew the words were crude, harsh, but this gave her an out.

Maybe she wanted to sleep with him, but he knew she wouldn't be proud to have him on her arm out in public. His ex-girlfriend had made that clear when he came back with a screwed-up face. He was good enough to sleep with but not to take out in public. Things between him and Ruby would only ever be physical. He hated it, but he was a realist. He could lay things out early so that he didn't get hurt, so that—

She stepped away from him, hurt etched into every line of her face. "Lock the door on your way out." Her voice was soft, too soft, as she walked out of the kitchen. He wished she'd have slapped him or...something else instead.

Fuck him. He gritted his teeth, rubbed a hand over his face. The feel of his damaged skin, the way he looked, was the only thing that kept him from going after her.

He shouldn't even be alive. He shouldn't have been the one to come home. Not when so many of his friends had been husbands, fathers. He didn't deserve Ruby. He didn't deserve anyone. Some days he thought the scarring on his face was his punishment for returning home alive. A constant reminder that he should have died in that desert.

So he left the way he'd come, locking the bottom handle of the front door before he pulled it shut behind him.

CHAPTER FOUR

Raegan felt as if she was coming out of a haze or a fuzzy dream in which nothing made sense. She could remember parts of it, but everything was cloudy.

"You sure she's gonna be okay?"

She blinked at the sound of male voices…Ford's voice. He was talking to someone in scrubs. A man. A doctor. They were at a clinic, not a hospital.

Why was he with her… She remembered now. The doctor — Dr. Hernandez — put this oxygen mask on her in case she had respiratory distress. He'd also taken her blood, given her something called activated charcoal and had kept her talking. She vaguely remembered Ford talking to her and sitting next to her, holding her hand. He'd been constantly by her side, she was pretty sure. She thought he'd told her she was drugged, maybe roofied? She couldn't remember though. She actually couldn't remember much of what she'd said at all. Or what he'd said. It was like there was a block in place, preventing her from remembering anything.

Which was scary.

"I'm sure. According to her blood work, the dosage was very low. You'll need to stay with her tonight." The doctor glanced at his watch, frowned. "Well, this morning. But she's showing no signs of respiratory distress, no convulsions and she hasn't been nauseous except when she first arrived. You'll need to watch her to make sure she doesn't get sick when she sleeps, but at this point there's nothing else I can do. It's been five hours and her symptoms are improving. She's okay to go home."

She pulled her oxygen mask down. "I've been here five hours?" An iciness slid through her. She couldn't believe she'd lost that much time.

Ford swiveled to her and hurried across the small room. He sat on a short, round stool next to her, his expression pure concern. "How are you feeling?"

"Okay. I think. What...happened again?" She was glad to have him by her side. Everything about him was solid, comforting.

His brow furrowed. "You don't remember anything?"

"A little. I remember leaving for a club with my friends and...I remember you and Doctor Hernandez asking me a lot of questions and keeping me talking." Even if she couldn't remember what she'd said. She could feel her cheeks warming up as she worried about what she might have inadvertently confessed. She'd never done drugs so she wasn't sure if she would have blurted out stuff. Oh no— what if she'd admitted how much she wanted him?

"That's normal." The doctor came to stand on the other side of the bed, his expression gentle. He sat on a rickety-looking plastic chair. "You were given a very small dose of...the street term is GHB. You were very lucky."

Feeling sluggish, she turned to Ford. "You thought it was Rohypnol though, right?" Or maybe she'd imagined that conversation.

He nodded. "Yeah. GHB is pretty much the same thing though. Someone likely put it in your drink. In liquid form it's odorless and a little salty. So your drink likely covered up the salt taste."

"My drink... Are my friends okay?" She hated that she couldn't remember much about the night. There was music, laughter, dancing...bright lights. Somewhere near the beach.

"They're okay and they're worried about you. I've been in contact with a woman named Jules and with Grant."

"Julieta's so sweet," she murmured. "Wait, Grant came out with us?" That didn't sound right.

"No, but he knows what's going on."

"Oh, good, I guess. Why are you here?" Because she couldn't

imagine what would have made him come out with her and her friends. It didn't even make sense.

"I was at the same club you were. Work thing. Purely by chance, saw some guy dragging you outside. He ran off and I couldn't leave you by yourself."

As the reality of his words set in, she shivered, wrapped her arms around herself. She was glad she was still in her own clothes and not scrubs. If Ford hadn't been there she could be in a hospital right now for a very different reason. A tremble racked her body and she couldn't stop it.

Ford took one of her hands, pulled it against his chest. His hold was steady, comforting. "You're okay. Something could have happened, but it didn't. And this isn't your fault. In the next few days and weeks you're going to second-guess yourself, berate yourself over 'letting' someone put something in your drink. Don't. You did everything right. You were with friends and shit just happened. An asshole drugged you and it wasn't your fault. And...I know it doesn't feel like it. But you're lucky." There was an understanding in his gaze, as if he knew what could have happened to her. Considering he was a cop, he'd probably seen the worst of humanity.

His expression and kind words broke something free inside her and to her horror, tears started rolling down her cheeks. Oh, God. This was pretty much the exact opposite of how she imagined spending time alone with Ford. It wasn't even in the same galaxy as her fantasies. He'd had to save her from being drugged and probably assaulted, maybe worse. At the very least, robbed. Now his Friday night had been spent at a clinic with her. This definitely wouldn't make him see her in a different light. Okay, that wasn't true. He probably thought she was a complete mess.

"Don't cry, sweetheart." His voice was deep, soothing as he pulled her into a hug and rubbed a big, steady hand down her spine.

She hitched in a breath at the word sweetheart, her tears drying up. That wasn't the first time he'd called her that, was it? She vaguely remembered... *Oh no!* She pulled back from him, wiping at her wet cheeks. "Did I kiss you?"

His neck flushed red and he did a weird shake then nod of his head. As if he couldn't decide whether to tell her the truth. But it was so obvious.

Ohmygodohmygodohmygod. That had been real. She remembered basically attacking him. Then him easing her back. She covered her face with her hand. It was official. Tonight couldn't get any worse. "Can I go soon?" she mumbled.

"Yes," Dr. Hernandez said, his voice sympathetic. Which made her feel even crappier. "And Ford is right. None of this is your fault. I've started a file for you and I'm keeping a record of your blood work, but...you weren't assaulted. Someone dosing you with an illegal substance against your knowledge is a felony but unless the police catch who did this I don't know that my records will matter."

She'd rather have everything documented, regardless. "I...have insurance. I don't think I have my card with me though. Do I even have my purse?" Now panic punched through her. Her credit cards, her driver's license—

"I've got it. And your phone," Ford said.

"Don't worry about paying me. Make a donation to the clinic later," the doctor said in a tone that made it clear this wasn't up for discussion.

"Okay. Thank you." She laid her head back against the flat pillow typical of medical places. She waited while Ford and the doctor talked quietly again, out of earshot, then she waited more as the doctor came back and talked to her again, going over everything one more time.

When it was time to leave, she wasn't surprised that Ford wrapped an arm around her shoulders, steadying her, but having the huge, sexy guy so close was jarring to her senses nonetheless. "I've already talked to your cousins. Porter wants me to bring you to his and Lizzy's place. They want—"

"No. I'm just going to go home. They have a one-year-old. They don't need me there interrupting them in the middle of the night." And she was embarrassed. Right now she wanted to be alone.

The humid, salt-tinged air rushed over her as they stepped out into the dimly lit parking lot. They must not be far from the beach if she could still smell it.

He didn't respond, just frowned at her. She turned away. She wasn't going to bother her cousin and his wife, and she didn't care what Ford said. There were two vehicles in the parking lot. One was a truck she was fairly certain belonged to him.

Sure enough, he led her to the truck, opened the passenger-side door for her. The action was so sweet, reminding her of where she'd grown up. Aaaand she remembered kissing him the last time she was sitting in here. Her cheeks burned with embarrassment but she shoved the thought away and got inside. Once she was alone she'd wallow in mortification at the way she'd attacked him.

Once he slid into the driver's seat he turned the ignition on but didn't make an attempt to leave. "Look. You shouldn't be alone right now."

"I'm not going to Porter's." *Ugh.* She knew she was being stubborn, but she'd worked hard to get her independence. The thought of heading over there now at almost three in the morning? Just no. She didn't want to do it.

"I was going to say you could stay with me for the next few hours, get some sleep. In the morning, or later this morning, I can take you home. So either my place or Porter's — or your place. But if you go home, you know Porter will just drag you up to his condo, probably using guilt. So your choice." There was no give in his voice.

"Your place." She should have just said Porter's, because putting Ford out like this was probably taking advantage of him. But something told her he wouldn't make the offer if he didn't mean it. And okay, she wanted to be with him right now. She felt like a total mess and this man made her feel safe. She didn't care what that said about her. And he was right. If she went home, Porter or Lizzy — or probably both — would insist she come upstairs to their condo or just plant themselves in her place. "Only if you don't mind."

His eyes dipped to her mouth for a long, heated moment. "I don't mind," he rasped out, looking away from her before kicking the truck into drive.

She blinked in surprise. What the heck had that just been? Did Ford...*want* her? Raegan was still a little fuzzy on some things but she was pretty sure that had been a healthy dose of lust she'd just seen.

Well that was...interesting. And very, very welcome.

Damn it, damn it, damn it.

He slammed his fist into the punching bag in one of his extra bedrooms. He'd set it up as a personal gym instead of a bedroom. He had to stay fit.

In middle school he'd been picked on, bullied. Nothing he could ever tell his father about because he had to be tough. He'd gotten tough, all right. By high school he'd been in track and ripped. No one picked on him again.

Now he still worked out, kept his body perfect. He wasn't bulked up though. No, he was all lean muscle. Something Raegan would appreciate when he finally got her alone.

He'd hinted that he might want to take her out, but she'd laughed it off. As if the very idea was hilarious. It wasn't as if he wanted for pussy. He got pretty much whoever he wanted when he went out.

But he wanted Raegan. He would have her.

Tonight she'd been so out of it, hadn't even seemed to recognize him. She was his. He'd do whatever he wanted. He hadn't wanted to hurt her though. Just make sure she understood she belonged to him. Then that guy had shown up. He'd seen him before...somewhere.

Frowning, he stopped, stilled the swinging punching bag. He had seen that guy. But where?

Grabbing a towel, he wiped the sweat off his face and neck before heading to his office. One wall had a display of pictures of Raegan. She had no idea he took them. No one did.

He scanned the pictures, didn't see anyone in the background who looked like the guy from the club.

But these were of her anyway. He'd made sure to only put up

images of her or mostly her, cutting out anyone who might be in the background.

He pulled out a box of extra photos, the ones that didn't make it to the Wall of Raegan. After twenty minutes of flipping through pictures, he found one with the guy in it. The picture had been taken outside Grant Caldwell's house.

He'd followed Raegan there once, hadn't realized who the home belonged to until later. He'd taken pictures of everyone coming and going from some party. A barbeque-type thing. He tapped his finger against the guy's face. He might not know his name, but this guy knew Grant or at least worked for Red Stone.

Though...he didn't remember seeing the guy at Red Stone. Maybe he was just friends with Raegan's cousin.

Or maybe he was fucking Raegan.

Rage surged through him at that thought but he quickly shoved it back down. No.

He refused to believe that. She wasn't seeing anyone. He'd know. And she hadn't shown up with that guy tonight. And no man, not if he was Raegan's boyfriend, would let her go out with a bunch of friends. Especially not dressed like she'd been.

Her dress had been bright, revealing. As if she wanted attention.

She'd certainly gotten his.

He didn't want anyone else to look at her though. Once she was his, he'd make sure she understood that she couldn't dress like a whore.

He closed the box and slid it back into a drawer, but he kept out the picture of the man who'd interrupted him.

"I'm going to find out exactly who you are," he said, tracing an X over the guy's face.

Tonight would have been perfect if not for this bastard. He'd gotten in his and Raegan's way. That was unacceptable.

CHAPTER FIVE

For a long moment Raegan looked around the unfamiliar, masculine bedroom. Panic spread through her until she remembered where she was.

Ford Burke's house.

In his bed.

Wearing one of his T-shirts.

After a very terrifying night. *Ugh.* It tasted like something had died in her mouth and she had a wicked headache.

Everything was still pretty fuzzy but she remembered Ford bringing her back to his place. She'd tried to insist on sleeping on the couch but he'd pretty much run over her arguments in a few seconds flat. She'd have never agreed to come to his place if she'd known he didn't have another bed. He had another room, but it was an office. She couldn't worry about that now.

After washing her face and brushing her teeth in his bathroom, she found him in the kitchen.

Cooking.

It was probably one of the sexiest things she'd ever seen. He had on a pair of jeans and nothing else. His broad back practically begged for her to run her fingers over all those carved lines. Something was sizzling at the stove and whatever it was, it smelled delicious.

"How're you feeling?" he asked without turning around.

Feeling guilty at being caught staring — and how had he even known she was there? — she nearly jumped. "Um, good, thanks. I used your toothbrush," she blurted. She felt bad about doing it, but she couldn't face the idea of seeing him this morning with breath like a garbage can. "I'll buy you a new one."

Laughing in clear surprise, he glanced over his shoulder to pin her with a sensual look. "That's okay. I've got extras."

She didn't know what to do about that look, was feeling way too out of sorts after last night. She knew what he'd told her had happened, but she didn't even remember being taken out of the club by some guy and she barely remembered the five hours at the clinic. Only after was clearer. "Thanks. I just...I felt really gross. Thanks again for letting me stay over. I know what a big inconvenience this is."

He just snorted, which could have meant any number of things.

"I, uh, I was just going to call a taxi and get a ride back to my place but I'm not sure where my phone is." And she hated the thought of heading home in her club dress and heels.

Flipping off the stove, he slid the pan off the burner before turning to her. "First, you're going to eat." He nodded at the rectangular table next to a window that overlooked a neat backyard with an S-shaped pool. It glistened under the bright morning sunlight. "Then I'll take you wherever you want to go."

She wasn't sure how she felt about taking orders, but there was no reason to argue when he was just looking out for her and was possibly one of the sweetest men she'd ever met. And food sounded really good. Wishing she'd put on sweatpants or something other than the long T-shirt that came to mid-thigh, she sat at the table. "Do you need help with anything?"

"Nope." He moved around the kitchen like a pro, which, again, was ridiculously sexy.

"Have you talked to Grant or Porter this morning?" *Please say no,* she thought.

"I talked to all of your cousins. Keith too."

She cringed. Crap. Her uncle was even more protective than his sons. "I'm a little surprised they're not here. They can be total cavemen." Because she could actually see them storming over to Ford's place like lunatics. They were normally sane, well-trained security guys who ran a multi-million dollar company—or maybe billion, she wasn't sure. But they could act like big kids sometimes. She just hoped Belle had a son, for Grant's sake. And their future child's sake. She couldn't even imagine how nuts they'd all be if Belle had a little girl.

"They wanted to come over." There was something in his voice, an edge almost, that did something strange to her insides.

Not many people could tell her relatives to back off—and actually have them listen. Another point on the Ford sexiness scale. The guy was pretty much off the charts by now. She wondered what he looked like in uniform. She figured that was the last thing she should be thinking about but it was hard not to be curious—and fantasize. "I've never seen you in your uniform," she murmured as he brought her a plate of eggs, bacon and toast. She wasn't sure why she'd said it out loud. Apparently she didn't have a filter this morning. She'd blame it on the drugs.

He lifted a big shoulder. She tracked it with her gaze, suddenly feeling just a bit warmer. "I don't wear it often. Mainly for funerals or a mandatory event. Coffee?"

She nodded. "Cream and sugar. And, seriously, thanks again. You don't have to do all this." She felt bad just sitting there while he waited on her. It was disconcerting.

"I want to." The words came out pointed.

And she didn't know what to do with that. She was still feeling out of sorts simply by being in his kitchen, his house, alone with him. This was one of those surreal situations she'd never planned on being in. Of course, no one planned on getting drugged and almost assaulted.

Against her will a shudder streaked down her spine. If she let herself think about what could have happened last night she was pretty sure she'd have a breakdown. A blank space in her memory was terrifying. She couldn't remember the face of the man who'd tried to take her away from her friends. She could have woken up this morning somewhere else and... Her stomach roiled as her mind filled in a dozen different scenarios. Before she realized it, Ford was crouched in front of her.

"You okay?" God, he watched her with such concern in those beautiful green eyes.

For the first time, she saw that he had little gold flecks in his eyes. She cleared her throat. "I'm just feeling really stupid right now," she whispered, a chill overtaking her despite the even temperature in the room and the sunlight streaming through the windows, bathing her and the table.

His frown deepened. "Stupid?"

She nodded once, her throat tight. "From the time I was fourteen I've pretty much known the things I have to do to watch out for myself. Watch my drinks, don't go to parties with boys or men you don't know. Always have a buddy no matter what, especially if you're at a club. Meet up for dates in public places, don't let anyone pick you up from your house unless you really know him. Stuff like that. I just, God, I want to kick myself—"

His mouth was suddenly on hers, soft and sweet and, okay, a little bit demanding.

Even though she was surprised, she didn't question it, just leaned into him. Because of the way he was crouched, they were practically at eye level. She dug her fingers into his shoulders, moaned into his mouth. It was hard to believe she was kissing Ford but if last night was the crappiest night she'd ever had, this was the best morning because holy hell, the man could kiss.

He let out a low, almost growling sound as he slid one hand through her hair and cupped the back of her head. Now she was really glad she'd brushed her teeth. His hold was dominating, sexy and she felt it all the way to her toes.

He tasted like coffee and cinnamon. Maybe his flavored creamer. Whatever it was, she wanted to bottle it up because he tasted like heaven. The subtle scent of his cologne or body wash teased her, wrapped around her and she knew the smell was permanently imprinted in her brain. Everything about Ford was absolutely delicious.

When he flicked his tongue against hers, teasing, taking, she started to slide off her chair, wanting to get closer to him.

Wanting to get totally naked with him.

Yeah, she knew it was way too soon, but it was hard to care. The attraction she felt for Ford was off the charts crazy. The first time she'd met him it had been a punch to all her senses. She'd wondered if maybe it was because she'd been relatively sheltered growing up, but nope — since moving to Miami she'd met plenty of men.

No one got her turned on the way Ford did. She could hardly believe he was kissing her, clearly wanted her. He'd been so standoffish in the past.

When he pulled back, she made a little protesting sound. She didn't want to stop. Not now. Things were just getting good.

His big palms spanned her thighs as he clutched onto her. He laid his forehead against hers, his breathing erratic. "You need to eat."

She ran her fingers along his bare shoulders. He should never, ever wear shirts. "I need to kiss you again."

He half grinned, closed his eyes as if in pain, then stepped back. "Eat. You had a rough night. I don't...you just need to eat."

She wanted to tell him that food could wait, but he turned away from her and started making his own plate. Way too many emotions pummeled through her, but if he didn't want to kiss anymore she wouldn't beg him. Her stomach growled, as if on cue. Okay, maybe she *should* eat.

She wanted way more of what sexy Ford had to offer. He was impossible to read though. She wondered if he'd kissed her just to shut her up. No...she could see that she very much physically affected him. No way for him to hide his erection.

Not that he seemed to be trying.

So why did he stop? Under different circumstances she might have questioned him, but she needed food, a shower and her own clothes. And to call her friends, let them know she was okay. Not to mention her family. It didn't matter that Ford had already talked to them — she needed to let her cousins and her uncle know she was totally unharmed.

But she knew he wouldn't have kissed her unless he was interested. She'd ask him about it. Eventually.

Ford wasn't sure what had come over him, kissing Raegan like that. Okay, he knew exactly what had come over him. She was under his skin.

And he knew that wasn't going to change anytime soon.

"Thanks again for taking me home," she murmured as they pulled into the private parking garage at her building.

He knew Porter was renting one of his condos to her, was glad she lived somewhere so safe. "You don't have to keep thanking me." It made him uncomfortable. He'd helped her the way he'd have helped any woman. Okay, he'd gone a little beyond what he normally would have done by letting her stay over.

"Fine, I'll try not to." Her voice was light, a little teasing. "Did you tell Porter we were coming here?" she asked.

"No." He'd decided not to for purely selfish reasons. He wanted to spend more time with Raegan. And if her cousin knew she was in the building, he'd take the elevator down to see her.

She let out a sigh of pure relief. "Thank God. He seemed fine when I talked to him earlier but I have a feeling he's going to go into lockdown mode and try to keep me close to home."

That wasn't a bad idea, but Ford didn't say anything. It was common enough in clubs for assholes to drug random women. Sometimes men just drugged whoever they could, with no intention of assaulting any particular woman. Of course that didn't mean the woman wasn't hurt by some other asshole taking advantage of a situation. He'd seen enough of that shit when he'd been on patrol. Just because it was likely Raegan had been a target of pure convenience didn't mean he wasn't going to follow up. He'd already put in a call to the club's owner and apparently so had Keith Caldwell.

Considering Keith was respected—and feared—in pretty much every circle, Ford had a feeling getting the security feeds from that place was going to be easy. "What are your plans for today?" He hated that he couldn't insist she take it easy and stay home. But he had no right. She wasn't his.

Even though he wanted her to be.

"I want to stop by Julieta's—that's the friend you talked to. She owns a little boutique and runs it with another friend, Ruby, who was there last night too. I just want to see them in person. Jules sounded pretty torn up when I talked to her. I think she feels guilty."

"Sometimes shit just happens," he said, parking when she pointed to a numbered spot.

"No kidding."

He had a feeling she'd have to keep reminding herself of that over the next couple weeks. A scare like this would make her question herself and everyone around her, at least for a little while. He wished he could be around to protect her from…everything.

"This must be what it's like to do the walk of shame," she muttered, looking down at her clothes. Raegan had on a T-shirt and sweatpants she'd borrowed from him.

They were too big, but he liked the sight of her in his clothes. Something he didn't plan to analyze too closely. He laughed at her words. "I wouldn't know."

Her hand on the door, she half smiled. "Me neither. I just hope no one from my floor sees me like this."

"You're a grownup. They'll get over it if they do."

She grinned at his words and slid from his truck at the same time he did. "I didn't notice it before, but seriously, you're driving a Ford truck?"

"I can't drive a Chevy or anything else, not with my name," he said, rounding the hood to meet her.

She motioned toward the east side of the parking garage. "Elevators are at the end of this aisle, around the corner. How did your parents come up with the name Ford anyway?"

He shot her a sideways glance as they headed across the quiet garage. He knew the security here was good, but he automatically scanned for any threats. After what had happened to her, he was feeling particularly vigilant. "Guess," he said.

"Don't tell me it's because you were conceived in one?" Her eyes widened slightly.

He wished he could say no. "Yep. I'm just glad my name's not Mustang."

She snorted as they reached the elevators. "That's pretty awesome. Is it just you?"

"I have a brother." Who he didn't want to talk about. Or think about. He rolled his shoulders once as she swiped her access card against the security pad.

"What's with the tone?" She glanced up at him, her expression curious.

"There's no tone." She was just good at reading him, apparently. It surprised him a little, but it was easy to let his guard down around her.

Her very pretty lips quirked up as the elevator dinged softly, the doors whooshing open. "You're definitely lying but since I'm wearing your clothes and you saved me last night, I'll let it slide."

He loved the way she was with him, with people in general. In their past interactions he'd noticed that she had a way about her that put people at ease. Everything about her was so real, and in a sometimes plastic city, it was refreshing. "So if I hadn't saved you, you wouldn't let me off the hook?"

"Pretty much." She gave him a full-on smile and his heart rate kicked up to epic proportions. "You're from here, right?"

"Yeah, born and raised in Homestead, then later I moved to Miami when I got a job with the PD." He'd also been in the Corps in between those years but didn't bring it up.

"I heard from a little birdie that Grant keeps trying to get you to work for Red Stone," she said as the elevator doors opened onto her floor.

"Ever since he went to the dark side he's been trying to bring me with him." Grant had been a detective before going to work with his family at Red Stone Security.

She nudged him with her hip. "Hey, I work for said dark side. And the benefits are great in private security."

Grinning, he shook his head. "I like my job."

"Good. This is me," she said as they came to stand in front of a door halfway down the plush hall. "You...want to come in for a coffee? You don't have to," she rushed out.

He'd just planned to make sure she got to her door safely, but there was something in her expression that looked a little like fear. Which made sense. After last night, of course she was probably feeling scared. He nodded. "Yeah."

Blushing prettily, she opened the door and he followed after her.

When he didn't hear the telltale beeping sound of an alarm, he frowned. "Don't you have a security system?"

"Yes, but I was running late yesterday and forgot to set it. The building is ridiculously secure though, so it's fine—what's that look?"

He lifted a shoulder, trying to remain casual. Every protective instinct inside him was pretty much ordering him to do a full sweep of her place. Just in case. He knew it was crazy because she was right—the building was one of the most secure in the city. But logic didn't play into his need to protect Raegan.

"You totally want to check out my place right now, don't you? To make sure it's secure."

"Maybe."

She gave him a slightly wondering look. "You really are cut from the same cloth as my cousins." Surprising him, she motioned down the hallway with her hand, a grin tugging at her lips. "Go for it."

Not caring that he'd ventured into complete overprotective mode, he did just that, quickly sweeping her one-bedroom place. He found her in the kitchen, pulling two bottles of water from the stainless steel refrigerator. "Is my home free of burglars?" she asked, handing him a bottle.

"You're good to go." Of course, now that he'd seen her bedroom, a place he'd fantasized about, all he could think about was her lying in it. Naked. Under him or on top of him, it didn't matter.

"Good. And I know you said to stop thanking you, but whatever, I'm doing it again. Thank you for this. I...was a little scared to come home by myself, which feels stupid, but..." Trailing off, she shrugged.

"It's not stupid," he murmured, his gaze dipping to her mouth even as he told himself not to. After that kiss in his kitchen, the memory of her taste and the sweet way she'd moaned into his mouth had been replaying over and over in his mind.

She cleared her throat, almost nervously. "So…after running up to Julieta's shop this morning I was going to head to the beach for a couple hours. Do you want to come with me? No pressure if you can't, I—"

"I'd love to." The words were out before he could stop himself. He hadn't been to the beach for relaxation in as long as he could remember. But getting to spend more time with Raegan, and seeing her in a bathing suit? Yeah. Even if he knew he was playing with fire, he couldn't seem to make himself walk away from her. For once, he made himself ignore the voice in his head that told him things would end badly, that he'd just end up getting burned again.

CHAPTER SIX

"**A**re you trying to destroy my new shipment?"

Ruby looked up to find Julieta frowning at her. With a box cutter in one hand and pieces of a destroyed cardboard box on the ground around her, Ruby figured she probably looked a little nuts. "I already took the clothes out."

"So you just decided to attack a poor, defenseless box?" Julieta lifted an eyebrow, her lips curving up into an amused grin as she looked at the tattered remains littering the otherwise clean floor.

"I'm in a bitchy mood today, sorry." She figured she might as well be honest. Well, as honest as she could be. She certainly wasn't going to tell Julieta that her oldest brother was a big jerk who she wanted to punch in the face right now.

Immediately Julieta's expression morphed to one of concern. "I'm feeling weird about last night too. Raegan's on her way over though. She just called. That cop who helped her is with her."

Ruby's mood lifted a fraction. She set the box cutter down on the table they used for unloading. "Is this the same guy she's had a thing for since moving to Miami?"

"I don't know. She was cagey on the phone."

"Well if he's coming with her..." For months, Raegan had had a crush on some guy who her cousin Grant was friends with, but she'd never told them the guy's name. She'd been really private about it. Not that Ruby could exactly blame her. Ruby hadn't admitted to anyone she was half in love with Montez—because he was Julieta's brother. After last night though, she realized she needed to move on from him. It was clear nothing could ever happen between them.

"Yeah, I thought so too. And he knows Grant so I think it must be the same guy, because she told me Grant and Mystery Man used to work together."

At the buzzing sound, letting them know a customer had just entered the store, Ruby smoothed a hand down her red, scoop collar vintage-style dress. This was one of her go-to dresses when she was feeling crappy. "Do whatever it is you came back here to do. I've got the front."

"I'm hiding this box cutter and all knives," she called out as Ruby disappeared through the door to the front.

The laughter died on her lips when she saw Montez standing in the middle of the store. He looked out of place among all the displays of lingerie. Thankfully the sex toys were at the front of the shop in a discreet display case, but she didn't want to see him right now.

Not when she was still so hurt after last night. That's what she got for putting herself out there. She'd thought Montez was different. They'd been friends for months and…whatever. It didn't matter now. "I'll get your sister," she said, already turning back to the storeroom door.

"I came to see you."

She should have known, but nerves still skittered through her. Montez had been in here maybe once since Ruby had been working here. Sandro came in all the time, but that was because he was a huge flirt and liked to hit on all of Julieta's friends. Pasting on a fake but friendly smile she turned back around. She didn't want Julieta to know anything was wrong so she could pretend if she had to.

"Need help finding something? A dildo perhaps?" Her heels clicked against the smooth wood floor as she rounded the cash register to greet him. She might not want to talk to him, but she wasn't going to hide from him.

He rubbed a hand over the back of his neck, turned the injured side of his face away as he so often did. As if she gave a crap about his scars. Yeah, they were hard to miss since they covered half his face, but they didn't take away from who he was, how he'd gotten them. She knew he'd nearly died saving his friends and even though he hadn't saved all of them, he was the bravest man she'd ever known.

"I was a dick last night," he said.

At least he admitted it. "Yep. A big one." She was glad he seemed nervous. Served him right.

"I'm sorry. I shouldn't have talked to you like that. I...there's no excuse. I'm just sorry."

She looked into his dark eyes and realized he truly was sorry. But that didn't ease any of the pain in her chest. She'd had it bad for him for a year. Pretty much ever since she'd met him. He could be so sweet and kind, especially to his family. But he could also be a surly jerk. He'd just never been that way to her before. Until last night. He'd talked to her like she was nothing and it cut deep. "Fine. Apology accepted."

"Damn it, Ruby." Expression pained, he stepped closer, until only a foot separated them.

She could see the tension in every line of his incredible body. She knew he ran every day. Some mornings when she opened up the shop she'd see him jogging in the area, as if demons were chasing him. For all she knew, maybe they were. He worked, spent time with his family, and worked out. As far as she knew that was pretty much all he'd done the past couple years since getting out of the Marines.

But she'd seen the way he looked at her and had kept waiting for him to make a move. After she'd almost been hit by that car and avoided what could have been a much worse fate from a lunatic, she'd thought he'd finally make a move. She was an old-fashioned kind of girl and she'd wanted him to. But when it was clear he wouldn't, enough was enough. She'd decided to go for it. After last night, however, she just wanted to smack him. "I said, apology accepted."

His jaw tightened, pulling his scars tighter. "You're pissed at me."

"Of course I'm pissed!" She winced, glanced over her shoulder. The storeroom door was still closed and they didn't have any customers, but still, this was where she worked and she didn't want Julieta overhearing any of this. She turned back to face him. "You talked to me like I was a whore," she said quietly, rage surging through her. Last night she'd been too shocked to respond other than to tell him to leave. But now that he was standing in front of her she couldn't hold back.

He moved lightning fast until he was right in front of her. He reached out, grabbed one of her hips with his hand.

She blinked at the possessive grip, but also didn't step back. She hated that she liked the feel of him holding her.

"You're not a whore," he bit out, looking as pissed as she felt. "I was crude because I was... It doesn't matter. Fuck. I was wrong and I'm sorry. I didn't mean to talk to you like that or make you feel like that. Let me make it up to you, please."

"There's nothing you can do. I want more than sex, more than fucking." She whispered the last part, still angry at the way he'd spoken to her. "I won't settle for something less than I deserve, even if I am into you. I thought you were different, but last night—"

His fingers tightened. "Ruby—"

"No. You're just another asshole." She pushed at his chest as she heard the storeroom door opening. Almost at the same time the front door to the store opened and two women, sisters if she had to guess, came in laughing to each other.

Perfect timing.

Completely ignoring Montez, she sidestepped him and went to greet the customers. She hoped he'd leave because she had nothing left to say to him. Work was exactly what she needed when all she wanted to do was cry.

"What's that look?" Raegan asked, her beach bag hooked on her shoulder as Ford pulled out a towel and beach umbrella from the back seat of his truck. He was glad she'd asked him to come with her.

Ford's lips curved up at her question. His aviators hid his eyes but apparently she was learning to read him. Which was...interesting.

She was more perceptive than some cops. "Nothing. Just thinking that it's been a long time since I've done this."

"Done what?"

"Gone to the beach."

She pushed her own sunglasses down, gave him a pointed look as he shut the door. "You live in Miami. That's wrong on so many levels."

He just snorted as they headed for the boardwalk. "Sand just reminds me of the desert." And he hadn't had a lot of fun there. Not to mention he always felt like a sitting duck on the beach. Which he knew was ridiculous. But there was literally no cover from an attack. Not that he expected to be attacked on South Beach, but some things had been ingrained in him long ago.

"Oh, right. Grant mentioned you were in the Marines too." She glanced at him. "Was it hard to transition back?"

He lifted a shoulder. That was a complicated answer and not one for a beach day. "I had it harder than some, easier than others."

She nudged him with her hip. "That's a very evasive answer."

He just grinned. Being around Raegan was a breath of fresh air. "Maybe I'll tell you more one day." The thought of opening up to anyone was hard enough, but especially a woman who he was starting to have real feelings for.

"I'm glad you came with me today."

"I am too." After their kiss this morning he'd been feeling unsettled. She hadn't brought it up and he wasn't going to either. Not yet anyway. "Your friends were nice."

"Thanks. I think Jules feels a lot better now after seeing me. Or she seemed to."

He nodded. It was clear both her friends had been experiencing a lot of guilt over last night.

"Ford?" A familiar male voice made him stop dead in his tracks. All the muscles in his body pulled taut at the sound of his brother calling his name. *Seriously? What the fuck?*

Raegan stopped with him and they both turned to watch Dallas, wearing board shorts and a T-shirt, heading toward them. His dark hair was a little longer than Ford's, but there was no mistaking they were related. Even though this was the last person he wanted to see, he forced himself to be civil even as annoyance surged through him. He was past anger, but that didn't mean he needed or wanted to see his brother. "Hey, Dallas."

"What are you doing here?" his brother asked, an iced coffee in hand.

"Public beach." He shrugged, not caring if he sounded like a dick.

"Oh yeah, I mean, I just...I'm surprised, is all. It's good to see you." He looked at Raegan, gave a nervous smile. "I'm Dallas, Ford's brother."

Raegan was all smiles as she shook his hand. "Raegan, Ford's friend."

He wanted to be more than friends, but right now, he just wanted Dallas gone. Being around his older brother brought up too much bullshit he didn't want to deal with. Especially when he was with Raegan. He just wanted today to be about her.

"You guys here for the windsurfing thing?" Dallas continued when all Ford wanted to do was leave.

Ford had no idea what his brother was talking about. "No."

"Oh, well...I'm here with my new girlfriend." He motioned over to a blonde-haired woman in her thirties. The woman smiled at them. "She works for the firm. Another lawyer like me," he said, looking at Raegan, his smile polite. "If you guys want to join us—"

"We've got plans, but thanks for the offer." Yeah, Ford knew he was being an ass but he couldn't just stand around and pretend with Dallas.

"Right. Well...maybe I'll see you at Mom and Dad's next weekend?"

"Yeah, maybe." He avoided Sunday dinners when he knew Dallas would be there. Something his brother had to know.

"It was nice to meet you," Raegan murmured, hitching her bag slightly against her side.

"You too. Ford, I, uh, I'll see you around."

He didn't say anything as his brother left. "You want to grab a drink before we hit the sand?" he asked, turning back to Raegan.

"Um, no." She linked her arm through his as they continued down the boardwalk. He savored the unexpected closeness, even as he braced himself for the inevitable questions. "Is your brother a puppy murderer or something?"

He snorted. "No."

"Then what was that about? I know it's a super nosy question but I've never imagined you being so cold with someone."

"But you have imagined me in other scenarios?"

Now she snorted. "You're such a guy."

"That's not an answer." And he wanted to know if she had thought about him, fantasized about him. He might have been burned before but sweet Jesus he needed to let that shit go. If he wanted to move on, he knew he needed to deal with the past. He'd just never wanted someone enough to move on from that. And he sure as hell didn't want to think or talk about his brother anymore.

Even through his shades he could see her cheeks flushing red as they reached the sand. "You're deflecting from my question, but...fine, maybe I've thought about you in certain scenarios."

He bit back a groan. Maybe was good. "You feel like expanding on that?" he murmured, taking his shoes off as they started across the white sand beach.

"Nope. Two can play your game."

He sighed. "What do you want me to say?"

"I want to know what happened between you two. And also, was your brother conceived in Dallas?"

A laugh escaped before he could stop himself. "Sadly, yes."

"That's pretty awesome."

"Apparently he was conceived when they were there on a trip and my mom didn't want to name him after the hotel so she settled on the city instead."

"Your mom sounds fun."

A real smile lifted his lips. "Yeah, she is. Is this spot good?" He motioned to one of the only free strips of space on the packed beach. People with towels, coolers, radios and umbrellas were scattered out in every direction. That was another thing he didn't like about beaches—how crowded they were.

But when Raegan dropped her bag and stripped off her sundress he realized what a fool he was. Beaches were the best place on earth.

He swallowed hard, was glad for his sunglasses as he drank in the sight of her. Her bikini was plain black and showed off every inch of her body. From her full breasts to her slender waist and the soft flare of hips—he wanted to cover her up so no one else could see her. Which, she would say, was completely caveman of him.

She was of average height but because of her lean build and sexy-as-sin legs she seemed taller. Her legs were toned, slightly muscular, and he could imagine her wrapping them around his waist or shoulders as he buried his face between them.

Tearing his gaze away from her, he made himself busy with the umbrella. Anything was better than staring at her because he was having a difficult time keeping his reaction to her locked down.

Once the umbrella was in place he looked back at her to see that she was spraying on sunscreen and smoothing it over her arms and chest.

Scratch that, impossible.

He stripped off his shirt. "I'm gonna head to the water," he rasped out, unable to hide his erection.

Not only had he endured some of the toughest training in the world, he was now in his thirties. Not some randy teenager. But around Raegan none of that mattered.

It didn't matter that she was one of his best friend's cousins, or that she was a decade younger than him, or that he knew he'd likely get burned by her. He wanted to taste her again and this time he wasn't going to stop at kissing. Not unless she told him to.

CHAPTER SEVEN

R aegan didn't miss the looks a few women on the beach gave Ford as he practically stalked from her to the water. She wasn't sure what was going on with him but she also didn't blame people for looking at him. Heads popped up and swiveled, watching those long legs stride with purpose toward the ocean.

The man was a work of art. His physical appeal was part of it. There was no denying the man simply looked good enough to eat. He was all hard lines and raw sex appeal. But it was more than that. The way he carried himself was confident, clearly secure in who he was. That alone was damn sexy.

Earlier when he'd run into his brother he'd been different though. Not the secure man she knew. It had been so obvious his brother was trying to be nice and drag a conversation out of Ford. That had been a little strange and she couldn't deny that she was curious. But if he didn't want to talk about it, she wouldn't push.

After making sure her phone was tucked away in her bag, she zipped it up and headed to the water. The sand was warm against the soles of her feet, the sensation soothing. What had happened last night now felt a little surreal, almost like it had happened to someone else.

She just felt lucky that things hadn't been worse. And now here she was, hanging out with Ford. That was the best kind of silver lining she could imagine. When she stepped into the cool water, a sense of peace invaded her. Since moving to Miami she didn't think she would ever want to leave. For the first time in pretty much ever, she felt at home, like she belonged. She loved her parents and where she came from, but Miami was where she was supposed to be. She knew that bone deep.

"I have a confession to make," she said as she reached Ford. The water splashed around her waist as she moved farther out.

"Oh yeah?" His voice seemed a little deeper than normal and way more sensual.

Shivers skittered over her skin. "You're not the only one named after something." Or in her case, someone. "My mom had a crush on Ronald Reagan and named me after him. She apparently spelled my name wrong at the hospital and that's how I ended up with the 'e' and 'a' reversed."

His mouth curved up, sending another bout of butterflies off in her stomach. "Your name fits you."

"Thanks. Can I ask you something?" When he tensed she figured he thought she'd ask about his brother. But that was the last thing on her mind.

"Sure."

"Are we ever going to talk about that kiss?" Because she really, really wanted to. If she didn't remember how he'd tasted, how his lips felt against hers, that little groaning sound he'd made, she might have questioned whether it happened at all.

It was clear she surprised him. He scrubbed the back of his neck. Water rolled down from his arm, making soft splashing sounds. "I was worried that maybe I took advantage of you this morning."

Laughing lightly, she cut through the water so that only a foot separated them. She slid her sunglasses on top of her head so she could look at him and was glad when he did the same. She didn't want any barriers between them. "I liked it. A lot." Maybe that wasn't polished of her, to come out and say it, but she didn't care.

"I did too." His gaze dropped to her mouth, his eyes going heavy-lidded as he moved even closer. The water was clear enough today that she could see his hand moving toward her. When he loosely gripped one of her hips, she completely closed the distance between them.

And came right in contact with his erection as her body drew flush against his. She wasn't sure why she was surprised, but it shocked her a little. In the best way possible. There were a dozen or so people around them in the near vicinity but no one closer than thirty feet so they had plenty of privacy.

"I'd like to take you out. On a date," he added, as if to make it clear.

She had to squint a little because of the bright sunlight glinting off the Atlantic. "I'd like that too." Excitement danced out to all her nerve endings. She'd dated since moving to Miami, but she hadn't slept with anyone since...ugh, her sophomore year of college. Sex had just seemed overrated. Or more likely, she'd been with the wrong guys. Being this close to Ford, close enough to kiss him again, she had a strong feeling that sex with him would be incredible.

"Tonight?" he murmured, rolling his hips once against her.

Heat flooded between her legs. That sounded perfect. "Y—oh, I can't. I've got a stupid thing to go to. With a *friend*." And she hated that she'd agreed to be her friend's date. Part of her wanted to cancel, but that was a crappy thing to do to a friend. Plus, she'd promised.

For a moment his jaw tightened and she remembered that he'd been in her cousin's office when she'd told them she had that thing tonight. She wondered if they'd mentioned who she was going with.

Gah. "Tomorrow instead?" Because she didn't want to wait to go out with him.

His eyes were on her mouth again as he nodded and she felt that heated look all the way to her toes. "I'll pick you up around six?"

"Sounds good to me." Did it ever.

To her surprise, he leaned down, slowly, giving her time to back away if she wanted, but she had no intention of pulling back from sexy Ford.

For a brief moment, his lips skated over hers before he completely took control. He pulled her closer to him until their bodies collided while he slid his free hand through her hair, holding onto the back of her head.

Just like before she felt overwhelmed by him in the best way possible. Her palms settled against his chest as she leaned into him.

She flicked her tongue against his, moaning into his mouth as his hand moved up, up, up, his big callused palm sliding up her waist and ribcage until he stopped just below her breast.

Her nipples ached and her entire body felt as if she was one giant exposed nerve. He didn't move any higher, but she could feel the tension humming through him, knew he wanted to touch her elsewhere.

Probably just as much as she wanted to touch him. But this was the beach and getting naked was definitely frowned upon.

Groaning softly, he pulled back, his breathing harsh, uneven. "I want to do more than kiss you right now." The words seemed to be torn from him as he watched her intently.

"Right back at you." She wanted to touch the man everywhere, get him worked up, see him lose total control.

But she'd heard anticipation was a good thing. It sure didn't feel like it though.

———————•••———————

The beach was crowded today which wasn't a surprise. It was a beautiful, sunny Saturday in Miami. The perfect cover for what he needed to do.

He'd tracked Raegan here using her phone—which he'd cloned, since she'd been stupid enough to leave it lying out at work. It was like she wanted him in her life, watching her.

So far he'd just been intercepting her incoming messages and learning her schedule. He wanted to know everything about her. Where she went, who she hung out with. Copying her SIM card had been easy. But it wasn't enough.

He needed to be inside where she lived, to see where she slept at night. He'd tried to snag her keys a few times, but she always kept them locked up in her desk with her purse. But not her phone. She carried that everywhere. Cloning it had given him the perfect insight into her life, into who she really was. That was when he'd realized that they truly were perfect for each other.

That she was his. He started getting hard thinking about everything he wanted to do to her, so he shut off that train of thought.

When he saw her bag he knew she had to be nearby. Scanning the throng of beach chairs, people on towels, the bright rainbow of umbrellas fanning out along the white sand, he frowned. She had to be somewhere close. Stepping around a trio of umbrellas he continued looking—his throat constricted when he saw her in the water, kissing someone. Or he thought it was her. It was far away, maybe a hundred yards. But yeah, it was her. Raegan's long dark hair fell down her back as she pressed up against someone.

The man from the other night.

Stupid whore.

The man appeared to be holding onto her as if he owned her. No! She was his. None of her texts that he'd read had made it sound like she was with anyone. So this guy must be new.

He'd take care of the fucker soon enough.

Forcing himself to turn away, he moved back behind the umbrellas, using them as cover. He had on blue and white striped beach shorts, a T-shirt, a ball cap and jeans. Standard gear for the beach. This morning, when he'd intercepted one of her texts to someone named Dominique, she'd told her friend that she was headed out to 'soak up some rays.'

He wanted to get a full view of her in a bathing suit, but she was too far out in the water. Which was just as well. She couldn't sneak up on him.

Acting as if he had every right to be digging in her bag, he quickly unzipped it and pilfered through it. *Damn it.* Other than extra clothes and a towel, he found only her phone, her ID and some cash in a zippered pouch. No keys.

Maybe the guy had her keys or maybe they were in the guy's vehicle. He couldn't be sure if she'd driven herself or come with the man.

Feeling as if someone was watching him, he looked up, scanned the surrounding area. A woman in a teal one-piece bathing suit had sunglasses on and was turned around in her beach chair, watching.

Or it looked as if she was watching him. It was impossible to tell with those sunglasses.

Even so, he'd already pushed his luck too much.

Standing unhurriedly, he moved away from the umbrella, bag and towels and headed back the way he'd come. Part of him wanted to stay, to watch, but he couldn't afford to be noticed.

Especially not after last night. For all he knew the man with her would remember him, would be able to identify him.

Not gonna happen. He'd been careful, had gotten to where he was in life because he was smart. He wouldn't start getting sloppy now.

Not when he was so close to claiming the prize.

CHAPTER EIGHT

"This is basically a glorified food and wine festival, isn't it?" Raegan asked her date, Rhys Martin Maxwell IV. She'd met him in Vegas during her first job with Red Stone—before her first and hopefully last kidnapping. They'd gone on a date and she'd quickly realized she had no attraction to him. He'd been okay with it after she'd told him she didn't want to go on another date with him.

But he'd wanted to stay friends so here they were, just friends. And he was always fun company.

"Yes. If I'm in town, I never miss it." He laughed lightly, his British accent faint and oh so proper sounding.

She didn't blame him, though she wished she was here with Ford—and felt guilty for even thinking that. Looking around the expansive outdoor setup, it was impressive. Twelve celebrity chefs were all manning various stations, cooking and talking to the guests, and gorgeous displays of food, wine and other cocktails were at various tables. Low-key music filtered in from speakers she couldn't see and there were always servers walking around with trays of drinks even with all the displays available. No one could possibly leave tonight hungry or thirsty.

Next to an owner/head chef of a local beach restaurant who was there for the celebration, a huge piece of driftwood had been hollowed out down the middle, filled with ice and bottles of blue champagne lining the entire thing. She was just glad the event wasn't formal. Most of the men were in slacks and button-down shirts and the women in cocktail dresses. Even with the misting fans and hidden coolers placed strategically around the space, it was still

Florida in the summer. Getting overdressed would have made this miserable.

"Are you taking notes?" Rhys murmured, leaning down just a fraction. His cologne was crisp and masculine.

She turned to look at him, smiling. "Is it that obvious?" She was part of the new event planning department at Red Stone and couldn't help but be impressed by whoever they'd used for the setup tonight.

He gave her a half smile and briefly touched her bare shoulder. She'd worn a strapless black cocktail dress and heels. "You're looking sun-kissed."

"I went to the beach today." She stepped back just a fraction so that his hand dropped. She'd made it clear she just wanted to be friends and his touch wasn't unfriendly or creepy, but she just…wished it was Ford touching her. The man had gotten under her skin.

Rhys started to say something when Dominique appeared out of crowd, looking like a tall goddess. She'd left her long blonde hair down and had on a bright yellow dress that should have looked wrong with her hair color, but against her bronze skin and killer curves, she had most men and some women in the near vicinity turning to look at her. Which was pretty much standard for wherever Dominique went.

She smiled brightly when she spotted them, and to give Rhys credit, he didn't stare. Too hard. Not that Raegan cared if he did. Dominique was a beautiful woman, and Raegan and Rhys were just friends anyway.

"Athena said you were here," she said, swooping in with a hug and cheek kisses. She was five foot ten, but in her heels she was over six feet tonight and stunning.

"I'm still trying to decide where to start. All this food looks amazing." She motioned to Rhys, who was almost as tall as her friend. "Dominique, this is Rhys Maxwell."

After making introductions and brief small talk, Rhys said, "Champagne for you both?"

"Yes, thank you," Raegan said as Dominique nodded.

"Nice," her friend murmured once he was out of earshot. Just as quickly her expression morphed to one of concern. "I didn't want to say anything in front of him in case you hadn't told him, but...you're sure you're okay? I kinda can't believe you're here tonight."

She grasped Dominique's hand once before dropping it. "Thank you for not saying anything. And I'm fine, I swear. I've been fine since this morning. Just...weirded out." Raegan had already told her all this earlier in the day but she was glad her friend was concerned enough to ask again.

"Okay, well, you look fantastic."

"So do you. You're like a beach goddess."

Dominique just snorted. "So you're here with a sexy Brit but I heard from a reliable source that you were out this morning with a sexy cop. Spill everything."

"There's nothing to tell." *Not yet anyway.* "He's friends with Grant and...I don't know. We kissed and have a date tomorrow night." She felt her cheeks heat up even as she thought about the feel of Ford's lips against hers. For the tenth time tonight she wished she was out with him instead of here.

"That must have been some kiss. So you're really just friends with this one?" she asked, glancing over in the direction of Rhys, who was talking to a man Raegan had never seen before. Before she could respond, Dominique turned back to her, her jaw set tight. "I hate that man," she practically snarled, her cheeks flushing red.

The change in Dominique's composure was jarring. Raegan blinked. "The guy with Rhys?" Dominique simply nodded, as if talking was too much for her. She'd never seen her friend upset before. "Who is he?"

"Viktor Ivanov. He's a monster."

Concern punched through her. "Did he hurt you?"

She just snorted. "Please. He's the owner of the club we were at last night. I didn't find that out until today or I never would have gone there."

"Well don't look now but he's headed this way with Rhys."

Dominique's expression darkened, but she didn't turn around.

"Sorry to do this, but I can't even be around him. If he was on fire I'd throw accelerant on him. I'll see you later." Just like that she was gone, hurrying in the other direction before Rhys and the apparent monster reached them.

The man frowned, his gaze following Dominique. "Who is your friend?" He had a slight Russian accent and was a freaking giant. The guy had to be at least six foot five and looked more like a thug with his shaved head and tattooed knuckles.

Raegan frowned at Rhys as he gave her a glass of champagne. She wasn't going to tell this stranger anything about her friend. Her date cleared his throat. "Ah, Viktor, this is Raegan. She works for Red Stone Security. I believe you have some acquaintances in common."

Blinking, the man turned back to look at her, as if seeing her for the first time, which obviously wasn't true since he'd asked her about Dominique.

"It's nice to meet you." He smiled politely, held out a hand that was surprisingly gentle when she took it.

"It's nice to meet you too." She turned to Rhys. "Will you give me a few minutes?" She didn't want to tell him in front of this stranger that she was concerned about Dominique so she motioned toward the back where the bathrooms were.

He smiled warmly. "Of course."

After ten minutes of searching she couldn't find Dominique anywhere. The event was pretty huge, but her friend stood out so Raegan wondered if she'd left. She'd already seen all three of her cousins, their wives, her uncle and his new fiancée, and Athena and her fiancé so it was a little off that she couldn't find Dominique. Unless…maybe she really was in one of the bathrooms.

She started to head to one of the closest ones when she saw a flash of yellow through the glass doors to the building connected to the event. The Celebration of Chefs was in an outdoor park-type area with lights and a gauzy canopy strung high in the air above them, creating a fairytale effect. It was nestled in between two buildings: an art center and a convention center. She knew from Athena that the catering company was using the facilities of the latter.

As she opened one of the glass doors a woman wearing black pants and a white button-down shirt—definitely one of the servers—smiled at her as she carried a tray of champagne flutes. "Would you like one?"

"Ah, no, but thanks." She'd already put down her drink earlier when searching and after last night she was feeling a little strange about drinking anything she hadn't seen poured. "Are there bathrooms back there?" She pointed in the direction she'd seen Dominique go. Because why else would Dominique be here?

"Yeah. You're not really supposed to use them, but other guests have been sneaking in. I won't tell." She winked conspiratorially before heading outside.

Raegan felt a little bad leaving Rhys, but she was worried about her friend. Dominique was one of the nicest people she'd met since moving to Miami and it was clear that man had upset her, even if he didn't seem to know who she was.

She passed a handful of caterers and partygoers as she headed across a big lobby. When she turned down the nearest hallway she spotted a woman in a pink and black cocktail dress coming out of the ladies room. She smiled at her before heading inside.

There were eight stalls including the handicapped one. She started at the end, gently pushing the doors open. Compared to outside it was freezing in here. A chill raked over her as she reached the fourth door. As she pushed it open, she heard the creaking of the main door opening right before the room was plunged into blackness.

"Someone's in here!" she called out. "Damn it." Blinking, she tried to adjust to the darkness but it was impossible. She took a step toward the door, but stopped as she heard a squeak.

Like a shoe against the tile.

A healthy dose of fear and paranoia slid through her veins. "Hello?"

When no one answered, she moved into the stall and locked the door. Stepping out of her heels, she picked one up to use as a weapon if need be. Maybe she was being paranoid but she didn't care. Not after last night.

With trembling hands, she pulled her phone from her clutch

306 | KATIE REUS

purse. Her heart hammered against her chest mercilessly as she heard another squeak. Then another.

Someone was definitely in here. And they'd turned the lights off intentionally.

"Think you can hide from me, whore?" a raspy male voice asked. It was like he was trying to hide his identity. Or maybe that was what he normally sounded like, but she didn't think so.

Pure panic punched through her as she stepped back. Her feet were cold against the floor and there was nowhere to go. She stepped up onto the seat of the toilet to give herself more distance as she covered her screen and dialed Grant. The phone started ringing as her fear skyrocketed.

"I've been watching you, know everything about you." The voice was closer now, somewhere outside the door. "You're a fucking tease." The door rattled once.

Oh, God. She held up her heeled shoe, prepared to use it as a weapon. It was the only thing she had. Damn it, she wished she'd thought to bring pepper spray, but her purse was small and she'd planned on being surrounded by people tonight.

Grant picked up on the second ring. "Hey, Raegan." His voice seemed loud in the enclosed space.

There was no way to hide what she was doing. "I'm trapped in the bathroom of the convention building with a man trying to hurt me! The first hallway off the right. I don't know if he's armed." The words fell out of her like machine gun fire. She wasn't sure how much time she'd have.

Grant cursed and she heard a crash, then, "I'm coming."

"You bitch!" The door rattled violently. "This isn't over," he snarled before the squeaks of his shoes hurried away.

She heard the door open but she wasn't sure if he'd truly left, could barely hear anything over the blood rushing in her ears.

Shaking, she stayed where she was, heel and phone in hand. She was aware of Grant saying something to her, but fear gripped her throat tight. She couldn't talk, couldn't do anything. And she hated herself for it. It was like fear rooted her in place.

Suddenly the lights were on, blinding her as the door slammed open. "Raegan!"

"I'm here." Oh God, he'd found her. As if she'd been released by an invisible string, she jumped down from the toilet and yanked the stall door open to find Grant racing toward her, his expression dark and a weapon in his hand.

She dropped her shoe as Porter, Harrison, her uncle and even Mara followed after him — all carrying guns like a civilian SWAT team. And she burst into tears.

———————

Raegan knew she shouldn't be embarrassed. It wasn't as if any of this was her fault. But the level of humiliation she felt that the cops had been called to such a huge event, that all her cousins and their polished wives were witnessing all this, that her own date had been dragged away from the party because of this — it was embarrassing.

She felt like she'd ruined everyone's night, even if it wasn't her fault.

Someone had opened up a private room called 'Banquet Hall Two' at the center, and it was filled with her relatives, police and some other people she didn't know.

She sat at a round table drinking hot tea that Lizzy had brought her while Grant was talking to his former partner, Detective Carlito Duarte. Her own date had disappeared to get her a plate of food even though she'd told him not to bother. But it had seemed as if he wanted something to do after she'd subtly tried to brush off his concern. She knew he meant well but she didn't want him fussing over her. Thankfully Belle had gone with him as well.

And Lizzy was on the phone with her babysitter. Now her cousins and uncle were all huddled together by one of the exit doors, talking quietly, and they kept looking over at her. Even though it was the first time in the last hour that she'd been relatively alone, it made her feel like a bug under a microscope.

As she sat, Mara Caldwell, her cousin Harrison's wife, slid onto one of the cushioned chairs next to her, moving ghost quiet. Raegan was still a little stunned that Mara had burst in with the others earlier, a gun in her hand. And clearly she'd known how to handle it. She wasn't sure what Mara had done before moving to Miami but she guessed it was law enforcement.

"So, you look as if you want to run out of here," Mara said quietly.

She swallowed hard, wrapping her hands around the warm mug. "I'm really grateful everyone's here and the police responded so quickly."

Mara lightly squeezed Raegan's arm. "You still look overwhelmed. Tell me what to do and I'll do it for you."

The gesture from the normally hard-to-read woman made tears rush to the surface.

"Oh, hell, don't cry," Mara muttered, looking horrified.

Raegan sniffled, felt even more pathetic. "I can't help it," she muttered. "After last night and now this, I just want to go home and hide out for a week." Because what the hell was going on? Had she pissed off karma? First someone drugged her and now this?

Mara frowned, squeezed her hand once, before standing. "Sit tight."

Raegan watched in awe as Mara singlehandedly kicked almost everyone out of the room, including Uncle Keith, until it was just Grant, Detective Duarte and Raegan. Well, and a uniformed officer by the door, but she was pretty sure he was there to keep people out. Mara gave her a thumbs up as she ushered the last person out of the room and left herself.

"Did they find anything on the security cameras?" she asked as the detective and Grant pulled up chairs and sat in front of her.

"There's nothing set up in this hallway—or most of them. Their security is focused around the exits more than anything. Cheaper for them," Carlito said, lifting a shoulder. But she saw the annoyance in his expression. He glanced once at Grant before looking back at her. "Have you been having any problems with anyone? A man who can't take no for an answer, who keeps asking you out? Anything unusual?"

She blinked, surprised by the questions. "No. I mean, yeah, I get asked out by men and sometimes I say no, sometimes yes. It's been a while since I've been on a date though. And I've never had any weirdos who kept asking once I said no."

"What about the man you're here with tonight?"

"Rhys? We're just friends."

Grant's mouth flattened, but he didn't say anything.

"You're sure he doesn't want more?" Carlito continued.

"I...I don't know but nothing's ever happened between us. Besides, didn't you," she looked at Grant, "say he was outside when I called you for help?"

Almost grudgingly, her cousin nodded. "Yeah."

"Tell me more about last night."

"Last night?" More surprise ricocheted through her, but it was hard not to make the connection of why he was asking. "You think the two things are linked?"

"I didn't say that. But I've got to be thorough—"

They all turned at the sound of raised voices.

She stood when Ford stormed in, looking a lot different than she'd ever seen him. He looked almost afraid, but totally in battle mode. Wearing cargo pants, a T-shirt and his weapon and badge, he looked ready to charge into a war zone. She wasn't sure why he was even there, but she didn't care. She was just relieved to see him.

She was moving before she'd fully processed the sight of him. He was faster than her, covering the distance across the largely empty banquet room in long strides.

"Are you okay?" he asked, his gaze roaming over her even as he pulled her into a close, very proprietary hug.

"I'm fine, I swear. Just shaken up." She held him back just as tightly, pressing her face against his chest. He felt good. Solid. She didn't want to let go but at the sound of a throat being cleared she stepped back to find Grant watching them.

Not with anger exactly, but his expression was as hard as his voice. "You didn't need to come down here. I just called you because you helped her last night."

So that was how he'd known. "Well 'her' is right here and I'm glad you called him." She turned in Ford's arms. "Grant's right though, you really didn't have to come—"

"Yeah, I did." Now he looked almost offended as he wrapped an arm around her shoulders.

Something that did not go unnoticed by Grant. She figured he'd want to have 'a talk' with her later but she was a grown woman and she really liked Ford. And she was grateful for his presence. Just having him here made everything seem bearable. She wrapped her arm around his waist and leaned into him, making her feelings clear to them all.

The detective cleared his throat. "I still need to finish interviewing Raegan. We can do it here or down at the station but I know she wants to get out of here."

Raegan guessed he was letting her make a statement here instead of taking her down to the police department because of his friendship and former partnership with Grant. "Here is fine with me."

Carlito nodded once before giving Grant an almost apologetic look. "I need you to wait in the hall with everyone else."

Next to her Ford tensed, as if waiting for the detective to say the same thing to him.

It was clear Grant wanted to argue, but after kissing her on the cheek and giving Ford a look of warning, he stalked out.

"I'm not going anywhere," Ford snapped.

Carlito just sighed. "I figured that. Come on. Let's sit down."

Once they were back at the table, Carlito cleared his throat. "Why didn't you report what happened last night?" Carlito asked Ford point-blank. "Grant filled me in on everything."

"Is this on the record?"

He sighed, leaned back in his chair. "Not if you don't want it to be."

"I don't. We both know how seriously her report would have been taken." He snorted at that, disgust in the sound. "There's nothing anyone could have done for her last night that I'm not already doing."

The detective raised an eyebrow. "What's that supposed to mean?"

"That tomorrow morning one of her cousins is meeting with the owner of the club she was at. He's bringing the security feeds. No warrant needed, no red tape. And you know what his reaction would have been if the cops had asked for the feeds. If possible, we'll get the identity of the guy who drugged her."

Well that was news to her. She shouldn't be surprised that none of her cousins had said anything, but she was annoyed Ford hadn't at least told her. Carlito's expression darkened and it was clear he didn't like that. She was sure there were a multitude of reasons he didn't.

The detective's jaw tightened once before he pushed out a sigh. "I get it, but I want you to make a report now," he said, focusing on her again. "I don't know that what happened tonight is connected to last night, but I don't believe in coincidence. I want this on the record so later, if this goes to court, there's a pattern of escalating behavior."

As his words sank in, chills spread through her like slow-moving ice. "You think...that's possible?" That the same person really wanted to hurt her enough to drug her then come after her so blatantly at a public venue a second time? She couldn't imagine anyone that angry at her. That this might end up in court someday made a wave of nausea sweep through her. "The guy in the bathroom, the things he called me...I don't know why."

"What did he call you?" Ford demanded.

"Ah, a whore and a tease." She winced as his expression darkened. The detective already knew, had put everything in his report.

Ford picked up one of her hands, linked his fingers through hers.

The detective gave her a hard look. "I think it's better to be prepared for the worst-case scenario."

"Okay, I'll make the report on that too. Do you mind if I tell my friend that he should just go ahead and leave?" Because she didn't want Rhys waiting around here any longer. It was unnecessary and she felt bad. For that matter, she was going to tell her cousins to leave too. Even if she knew it wouldn't do any good, she still had to try to get them out of here. There was no need to ruin everyone's night.

Ford's fingers tightened in hers slightly at the mention of her friend, but he didn't say anything otherwise. Just let her hand go when Carlito nodded that she could take a quick break.

When he stood, she shook her head. "My cousins are in the hall and so is my uncle. And all their significant others. I'll be fine, I promise." She actually wanted him with her, but she didn't want to throw it in Rhys's face that another man was taking her home, even if they were just friends. It felt mean somehow.

As she hurried across the room she felt Ford's heated stare on her back. As worried as she was right now, she was still inordinately pleased that Ford had shown up tonight.

CHAPTER NINE

Tension knotted Ford's shoulders as he waited for Raegan to finish saying goodbye to Lizzy, Mara and Belle.

Keith, Harrison and Porter were all giving him what equaled death stares from across the room, but he didn't give a shit. They were pissed he was taking Raegan home—and probably that he was clearly interested in her—but they could get over it.

She brought out all his protective, possessive instincts and they could just deal with the fact that he was the one taking care of her. He would keep her safe.

Grant stepped back into the room and made a beeline for him. He'd been out in the hallway wrapping up with Duarte, a man Ford actually liked and had worked with on multiple occasions. He was a damn good detective, cared about finding justice and protecting the people of his city.

"So, you and my cousin?" Grant asked as he reached him, his voice low.

"I was going to tell you, and...we have our first date tomorrow night." He didn't know what else would happen, but he was into her. More into her than he could ever remember being with anyone. He knew he didn't want casual. Not even close. That little voice in his head still fucked with him, told him that she was too good to be true, but he ignored it.

Grant gave him a hard, assessing look. "We've all noticed the way you avoided looking at her at parties. And the way you'd sneak glances when you thought no one was paying attention. Which tells me all I need to know. So this isn't exactly a surprise, but..." He scrubbed a hand over his face. "Treat her right."

Or Grant—and likely his brothers—would kick his ass, was the implied threat.

That was a given. "I like her. A lot," he murmured, not wanting to say more. Guys didn't talk about shit like this and he wasn't going to start talking about his feelings now. It was time for a subject change. "Who's getting the security feeds, you or Porter?" He'd briefly talked to Grant about it when he'd called earlier but didn't know all the details.

"Ivanov is coming by tomorrow. He's personally picking up the recording from the offsite company the feeds go to. He's...not happy with his security team."

"Good." Though they both knew shit like this happened, even with the best security. From what Ford had seen, however, Viktor Ivanov needed to get a new team at his club. "Is he here tonight?"

"Yeah. Or he was earlier. I think he actually met Raegan but he probably doesn't know who she is."

"Is her friend gone?"

Grant's lips curved up. "Yeah. Can't believe you were okay with her coming here tonight with that fucker."

"She's a grown woman." He hadn't liked it, but it wasn't like he and Raegan were together. Not yet anyway. But that was coming. "You think he's got anything to do with this?" For all Ford knew the guy didn't like being stuck in the friend zone. Maybe it was too much for him.

"Nah. And we ran the guy hard too."

Ford didn't doubt it, but nodded as Raegan broke away from her cousins-in-law and made her way to him and Grant. She looked beautiful and utterly exhausted.

"Can we go?" she sighed, moving to him like a magnet, wrapping her arm around his waist like it was the most natural thing in the world.

His slid his arm around her shoulders and pulled her close. He was glad she didn't want to hide their...relationship. Or whatever they had. That had been a fear, lurking in his subconscious. That she wouldn't want to let her cousins know about them. "If you're ready, we can leave."

"I'll follow you guys to your truck," Grant said, no room for argument in his voice.

Not that Ford planned to. He didn't care if Grant came along. More security was always better. He just cared about getting her home. Keeping her safe.

———————•◦•———————

He wiped his damp palms against his pants as he steered into his garage. Tonight had been stupid.

He had been stupid.

What the hell had he been thinking?

He hadn't, that was the problem.

He'd seen Raegan in that hot-as-fuck dress and lost his mind. It was her fault for setting him off. She hadn't even noticed him. At work she always said hi and was friendly. Way more friendly than she needed to be. But tonight she'd looked right through him, as if she had no idea who he was.

She'd been out with that guy he'd seen her with in the past. The rich one. After she'd been off with some other asshole this afternoon. Making out with that one like a whore for everyone to see.

From her texts and phone calls he didn't think she was fucking the one she'd been with tonight.

But he could be wrong.

God, he'd certainly been wrong tonight.

He was still shaking as he pressed the button to close his garage door. The trembles didn't stop when he was inside his house.

Shudders racked him.

He'd been careless, could have been caught. That was not on his agenda. Not like so many losers who 'wanted to get caught.' Fuck that.

He'd wanted to frighten her, to wrap his hand around her throat, to show her that he was in charge. He'd been so stupid though. Tonight had been too risky. Getting caught wasn't something he ever wanted. It was why he didn't send her threatening messages, contact her. It would leave a way to be traced back to him. Instead, he just watched. Waiting for the right time. He did actually write her letters, he just never sent them. Once he had her in his possession, he'd let her read them then.

She was his secret obsession. He loved watching, but he was tired of women teasing him, tired of being invisible.

He ran a hand over his erection as he shut the mudroom door behind him. He shouldn't even want her, but he couldn't help it. She called to him.

He still wondered if he'd worked her up in his mind, made her out to be something she wasn't. When he'd first met her he'd thought she was sweet, innocent. Now she seemed like every other woman. Just another whore.

He didn't bother changing, just went straight into his workout room and slammed his fist against his punching bag.

The impact against his knuckles loosened some of the rage building inside him, let him focus and channel his energy.

He had to get back under control. After his slipup tonight, he had to be back in command. He'd likely see her next week, get his temporary fix. He'd only gone to the event tonight to see her. After reading her texts he'd known she'd be there. One look at her was all he'd wanted. When she'd separated herself from her date, the opportunity to scare her had been too much. If she hadn't had her stupid phone—something he would have thought of if he'd been thinking clearly—he'd have been able to do more than scare her. He could have touched her, shown her that she was his.

He slammed his fist into the punching bag again and again, imagined pummeling the man she'd been with tonight. Or the other one from the beach. Both. It didn't matter.

They were both obstacles.

Maybe... Maybe Raegan wanted him to fight for her, to show her that he could eliminate any competition. That he was the right man for her. Women liked that shit, when guys were all alpha.

His arms were sore and sweat was pouring down his face and neck by the time he forced himself to stop punching the bag.

He was finally back under control, his head clear. And he wouldn't be making a mistake like tonight again. He was done waiting and writing letters he never sent. Next time he went after her, he was taking her. Simple as that.

CHAPTER TEN

R aegan wanted to tell Ford that he didn't need to check her condo, not since she'd had her security system armed. But it would have been a fruitless effort. He was totally geared up, the energy rolling off him a little intense.

He'd point-blank told her uncle that he'd be the one taking her home and looking after her. And nobody ever told Keith Caldwell anything.

She certainly hadn't disagreed, even if she didn't need someone to look after her. Not in her own home.

Tonight had scared the hell out of her but she felt safe in her home. And while she didn't necessarily feel like an obligation to him, she also didn't want this to be a defining thing in their potential relationship.

He was older than her and likely way more experienced. She liked that. But she also didn't want him to feel like she needed taking care of. It made things feel too unequal between them.

While he did a full-scale sweep of her place, she headed to the kitchen and pulled out a bottle of Tylenol. She took two with a glass of red wine instead of water because yeah, it was one of those nights.

"Ugh," she muttered to herself, hating the whole situation.

"What's wrong?" Ford was suddenly there in her small kitchen, his expression worried.

Half smiling, she shook her head. "Nothing. Just annoyed in general." Even thinking that the person who'd tried to attack her tonight was the same one from last night was beyond scary. She always thought stalkers left creepy messages and made heavy breathing phone calls. If someone had been harassing her, she'd have gone to the police. And her cousins. It was like this insanity had come out of the blue.

"Do you want to rest?" Ford looked unsure what to do as he stood there. As if he wished he had a specific target to fight.

"No. Look, thank you for driving me home and for coming to the event when Grant called you. That was so sweet. But don't feel like you need to stay or anything. Or to take care of me." She wanted that out there, wanted him to understand she didn't want to be —

"Oh, I'm staying."

She blinked at his matter-of-fact tone. "Excuse me?"

"On the couch, but I'm staying. Or I'll walk you up to Porter and Lizzy's place. You're not going to be alone tonight."

His bossy tone rankled her. Setting her wine glass down, she pushed away from the counter and stalked toward him. "I'm grateful for what you've done, but you don't get to tell me what to do."

"Pretty sure I just did," he answered, his gaze dropping to her mouth.

She was torn between being offended and turned on. Raegan didn't like men to tell her what to do. She didn't like *anyone* to tell her what to do. 'A problem with authority,' her mother had always said.

But heat pooled between her thighs at that take-charge tone of Ford's. She certainly wasn't going to tell him that—it would just encourage him. She placed a hand on his chest. "Ford—"

He covered her hand with his bigger, callused one and lifted it. Taking her completely by surprise, he skated his lips over her knuckles. As he did, he let out a shuddering breath. "When I got that call I was terrified for you."

Immediately she softened, stepping even closer to him. He was such a solid presence. "I'm okay."

"I'm still staying over." Once again his tone was all domineering.

"You can't do that," she muttered.

"Do what?" He stepped closer, moving until he had her back against the counter and there was nowhere for her to go.

Even as his bossiness annoyed her, she wanted to arch into him, to rub up against him like a feline in heat. Everything about the man was sexy, and this need he seemed to have to take charge was insanely hot even if it was maddening. Clearly she should have her head examined. This type of behavior had never turned her on before. Once a guy tried to tell her what to do, she was out the door. Now, however... "Drive me crazy being all caveman."

"I think you like it." There was a hint of a question in his statement. His green eyes seemed darker tonight, as he looked down at her with blatant heat and hunger.

"You would think that." Even if it was true she wasn't going to tell him.

"If I slid my hand up your dress and cupped that pretty pussy, would I find you wet?" His voice was raspy, unsteady and there was no mistaking he was turned on, given his thick erection pressing against her.

Her mouth fell open at his words. She'd never had a man talk to her like that. The rawness, the dirtiness of the words got her even wetter. She swallowed hard. "Why don't you find out?"

He blinked once, as if she'd surprised him, but just as quickly, he moved into action. One hand slid behind her, gripped the counter tight as he leaned into her.

The only sound was their breathing, and that seemed over-pronounced as his other hand reached between them and slowly began pushing her cocktail dress up. The rustling of her dress seemed just as loud as their breathing. She was surprised she could hear anything anyway with her heart beating in her ears.

Nerves danced in her belly when his fingers grazed her inner thighs, barely touching her. Another rush of heat pooled between her legs at the teasing.

He had her pinned in place with his gaze when he slid her panties to the side, stroked a finger through her slick folds.

"This for me, baby?" he murmured, his eyes still trained on her mouth.

Her nipples tightened at the feel of him touching her so intimately. "Yes," she whispered, loving how he called her baby or sweetheart. Oh, how she wanted him to push inside her. Her inner walls clenched, needing to be filled, but he just slowly stroked against her folds, barely penetrating her.

She rolled her hips against his hand and he shuddered. "You're killing my good intentions."

She clutched onto his shoulders, needing him for support. "What intentions?" she rasped out.

"You need rest," he murmured, even as he slid a finger over her clit, gently massaging.

No, what she needed was more of this. But she couldn't find her voice when he increased the pressure.

She started to close her eyes when his lips covered hers. Unlike their kiss at the beach, this one was slow, sensual, as if he didn't mind taking his time. The pacing was just as easy as his gentle strokes against her clit.

She had no idea what Ford wanted, or whether this was just casual for him.

He nipped her bottom lip. "I want to taste you." His words came out guttural.

She moaned into his mouth, pretty much the only response she was capable of when he was touching her so intimately. But he was already tasting her— *Oh.* It took a few seconds for her brain to catch up to his meaning. She felt her cheeks flush as he grasped the edge of her panties and tugged them down.

Gravity did its job and when they reached her ankles she stepped out of them.

"I want to taste your come, to feel you climaxing against my mouth." He lifted her onto the counter and she couldn't find any words as he kneeled between her legs.

The sight of his dark head between her spread thighs under the bright light of her kitchen was one of the most erotic things she'd ever seen.

He looked even bigger like that, his shoulders broader than she'd realized. And talk about exposed. She'd never felt so vulnerable and turned on before.

It was clear that Ford had a lot of experience and liked talking dirty. She'd never been a big talker during sex and wondered if he wanted that. She wasn't going to start now because she figured anything she said would sound stupid.

He didn't seem to mind her quietness though. Not when he inhaled deeply before burying his face between her legs.

And that's when she lost the ability to talk or really think about anything other than the pleasure he was giving her.

He swiped his tongue up the length of her folds, practically growling against her. She felt the subtle vibration trickle out to her nerve endings. And the way his facial hair teased her inner thighs made her just as crazy.

Sliding her fingers through his short hair, she held on for dear life.

"Feet on my shoulders, spread wider," he demanded against her body.

She did what he said, feeling even more exposed. He shoved his tongue deeper inside her after she shifted position.

"Ford," she groaned, shudders racking her as he continued teasing her with his wicked, talented tongue. His beard rubbed against her folds now too, not just her inner thighs. The sensation was different…stimulating.

When he reached up and began massaging her clit with his thumb at the same time, she lost it. She hadn't even realized how close she was to climax, but the pressure was intense, perfect.

"Right there. Don't stop. Please." The last word came out as a plea, but she didn't care. She *didn't* want him to stop.

He increased the pressure against her sensitive bundle of nerves even as he increased the stroke of his tongue. It was all too much.

Her orgasm slammed into her, sending a shock of pleasure out to all her nerve endings in a harsh, pulsing wave that had all her muscles tightening. Oh God, it had been so long since she'd felt anything remotely close to this. And her vibrator had nothing on Ford's talented tongue.

She was a quivering mass of nerves when Ford finally stopped, the teasing too much for her sensitive flesh.

When he stood, the hunger in his gaze was scorching as he watched her. And when he crushed his mouth to hers, the only thing she knew was that she needed him inside her right now.

He said something against her mouth, but she couldn't make it out. Something about her taste. Buzzing with adrenaline, she reached between their bodies, grasped at his belt buckle and pants even as she felt him unzip the back of her dress. Next he stripped off his shirt.

The material of her dress slid to her waist, cool air rushing over her already hard nipples as she shoved his pants down.

His tongue teased hers as he slid a finger inside her, and groaned again. Scooting to the edge of the counter, she grasped his cock, stroked once. Twice.

He pulled back, his neck muscles corded tight as he seemed to struggle to breathe. "Fuck, Raegan."

Feeling insanely powerful, she stroked him again, watched the way his whole body reacted. He rolled his hips once into her hold, but just as quickly he moved her hand aside and positioned himself between her thighs. Apparently he liked to be in control.

She stared down at his thick length and grew even wetter. The man was big all over. Feeling it and seeing it were two different things. She rolled her hips against him as he thrust inside her.

He cupped the back of her head and held firm as he buried himself deep. "You're so fucking tight." His words were harsh.

She couldn't talk at all, and couldn't believe he could. Not when he felt so damn good inside her. As he began thrusting, she let her head fall back and closed her eyes. Pleasure rolled through her with each push inside her.

He kissed a path up her neck, nibbling at her earlobe as he continued those long, steady strokes. She arched into him, sliding her hands up his broad chest, digging her fingers into him as her inner walls started to tighten quicker and quicker around him. She hadn't thought she'd be able to come again, but her body said otherwise.

When his head dipped suddenly and he sucked on one of her nipples, her eyes flew open and she jerked from the sharp pleasure pervading her body once again. As a second orgasm crested inside her, he groaned against her breast, his whole body trembling.

He drew back as his thrusts grew faster, wilder, until all his muscles pulled taut. The lines and striations in his arms were more defined as he emptied himself inside her, his shout of pleasure raw and harsh.

As his thrusts slowed and he grew soft inside her, she buried her face against his chest, inhaled his scent. She loved the way he smelled, a spicy musk.

His big hands settled on her hips, his breathing steadying as his chin rested on her head. Suddenly he stiffened and muttered a short curse.

She couldn't imagine what was wrong until he said the word, "Condom."

That was when she realized they hadn't used one. *Crap, crap, crap.* It had been so long since she'd been with anyone that she hadn't thought about it. Okay, the truth was, she hadn't been thinking, period. Which wasn't a good excuse, just the way it was.

Cringing, she pulled back to look up at him. "I'm on the pill." She had been since she was fifteen, thanks to an erratic menstrual cycle and horrible cramps.

He let out a sigh of relief and she didn't blame him. She wanted kids—eventually. But not anytime soon.

"I'm sorry, Raegan. That was fucked up of me. I should have—"

"There are two of us right here. I forgot too. God, I wasn't even thinking." She didn't like him shouldering all the blame.

He shook his head, his expression annoyed, clearly at himself. "I've never had sex without a condom. And I'm clean. I was tested six months ago and it's been about a year since I've been with anyone. I'll get tested again though if you want."

"I haven't been with anyone since..." Ugh, she didn't want to say it out loud. But she couldn't hold back, not when he was being honest, not when they were talking about something serious. And not when she was wet with his come between her thighs. "Since my college boyfriend. Almost three years ago," she rushed out, just wanting to get it out of the way. "I'm clean."

He looked surprised, maybe at how long it had been for her, then he simply crushed his mouth over hers with one of those sexy growls she felt all the way to her toes. She wrapped her legs around his waist as he lifted her off the counter. He was already growing hard again, which was a big surprise, but a welcome one.

She lost her dress completely and he lost the rest of his pants on the way to her...living room. Yeah, they weren't making it to the bed tonight. Not this second time anyway. Her back hit the couch and then they toppled to the floor.

He lifted up on his arms so he wouldn't squish her, caging her in beneath him. He let out a short laugh. "Shit, sorry."

"Don't be." She grinned, happier than she'd been in a long time. Even with all the insanity of the last couple days, she was still glad that it had inadvertently brought her and Ford together.

She just hoped that this meant something more to him too. That this wasn't a one-time thing. He'd seemed okay with her going to the event tonight with another man, even if she had told him that they were friends. Her own cousins had been annoyed with her — because they apparently didn't want her to even talk to the opposite sex — but not Ford. She should be glad he hadn't been all stupid caveman about that, but still, she wished she knew if he did care. If this was more than just physical for him. She wouldn't focus on that now, didn't want to bring herself down from the high of being with him.

In the morning she'd deal with reality.

Ford frowned at the sound of Raegan's front doorbell going off. She was in the shower and it was too damn early for anyone to be here. Anyone other than her relatives. Which didn't create a problem, but he didn't like throwing it in Grant's face that he was sleeping with Raegan.

Sighing, he pulled on his clothes from yesterday, sans his work belt, but he still kept his weapon in hand. Right now he wasn't going to let his guard down when it came to Raegan.

After looking through the peephole he grimaced. It was Grant and Porter. Tucking his pistol away, he disarmed her security system and opened the door.

Both men stared at him, Porter more in surprise than Grant. Just as quickly that surprise turned to annoyance and something a little more heated. Ford didn't have a sister, and it was clear the Caldwell brothers thought of Raegan more like a sister than a cousin, so he could understand their annoyance at finding him here.

"Look, before we go any further," he said, not bothering to ask them why they were on Raegan's doorstep at seven in the morning, "you need to know that this isn't casual for me." He kept his focus on Porter since he was the one who seemed annoyed about it and he'd already told Grant this. "I like Raegan a lot and unless she tells me otherwise, I'm not going anywhere."

Porter seemed to relax at his words, and gave a sharp nod. "Good. You hurt her, I hurt you." He said it so matter-of-fact, not waiting for a response as he continued. "We got the security feed from the convention center. The cops are still waiting on a warrant to get a copy, but my dad called in a favor."

Ford stepped back and let them in as Porter pulled out a USB drive. "Got a ton of footage on here and for all we know, there's nothing useful. We just thought Raegan might recognize someone from last night and be able to place him at the club too. Which is nothing the cops can use unless she can pick out the guy who tried to take her Friday."

"She says her memory's a blank from that night," Ford muttered. Fucking GHB did that to people, wiped out blocks of time. And he hadn't gotten a good-enough look at the guy that night, not with that fucking hoodie and sunglasses, to give a description or even pick someone out of a lineup.

"I know. Still, if she recognizes someone not even from Friday but somewhere else, someone she's seen around and didn't realize until now, maybe it'll trigger something in her memory and hopefully we'll be able to narrow down who's after her."

"So you think the two nights are related?" He'd had a bad feeling about that.

Both Grant and Porter shrugged and Porter said, "We're not ruling anything out."

"Good." Because he wasn't either. It just seemed like too much coincidence that she'd been drugged, some guy had tried to take her out of the club and then someone had come after her when she was alone last night.

If last night hadn't happened he would have written off Friday night as bad fucking luck. Now…he was going to be on guard 24/7 until they caught this asshole.

CHAPTER ELEVEN

When he looked into Raegan's office, his breathing automatically grew ragged, his heart rate ratcheting up. She wasn't here—probably in a meeting because it was too early for lunch—but this was her space. It even smelled like her. When he started to get aroused, he stepped away from her office door.

Glancing down the hallway, he saw that there was a normal amount of activity on this floor. Plenty of armed men and women going about their business. Raegan wasn't armed of course, but he'd never be stupid enough to try to take her or hurt her in the Red Stone building. He'd never get out alive.

But he liked being around her things, liked imagining her touching her things, talking on the phone.

Since he had no business being in her and her boss's office, he continued down the hallway. It wouldn't do to get caught being inside her space. He'd be able to talk his way out of it if he was caught, he had no doubt. He could just pretend he'd gotten mixed up with office numbers.

But if he did that, someone might remember he'd been somewhere he wasn't supposed to be. Then later, once he had Raegan, someone could remember and report it to her family. It wasn't the police he was worried about, but the Caldwell family.

He didn't know much about Keith Caldwell, but he'd heard the rumors that he was a dangerous man. No, he wouldn't risk getting on anyone's radar. After he took Raegan, he wouldn't even change up his routine. At least not for a month or so.

He had it all planned out. Once he got her to his place, she'd be his. He had a room specifically set up for her. It had plenty of insulation so no one would be able to hear her scream. Not that he wanted to hurt her. He just wanted her to be his. Once he convinced her they were meant to be together everything would be okay.

Just taking her was the biggest problem. She was always surrounded by people. Pushing his cart down the hall, he smiled and nodded at people he saw almost every day.

Keeping up his façade was becoming more difficult, but for Raegan he could do it. To have her, he could do anything.

———————◆◆◆———————

Ford loved his job, especially now that he was at the range full time training officers. He'd briefly been on patrol, had done undercover work and been part of the drug task force for a while in addition to being part of SWAT, but the training was where he really excelled.

It had surprised him, but not his superiors when they'd promoted him. He'd thought he would miss being on the streets, but this was a different kind of fulfilling.

Except today, when all he wanted to do was get the hell out of here. He'd been looking at his watch every ten minutes, practically counting down until he could leave. Because all he wanted to do was see Raegan. She'd asked him if he wanted to come over tonight and he planned to cook for her.

At least to start the night. Then he planned to have her naked and under him for hours.

Stopping in front of his locker, he rolled his shoulders as he slid off his shoulder holster. Today had been long and tiring, and right about now he wanted a hot shower and Raegan on a platter. As he started to strip off his T-shirt his phone buzzed in his pocket. He always kept it on silent out at the range, and sometimes he didn't bring it at all.

Today he'd wanted to be available if Raegan needed him. When he saw her name on his caller ID his heart rate jacked up triple time.

He couldn't remember the last time a woman had gotten him this worked up.

Try never.

"Hey," he said, answering on the second buzz.

"Hey yourself."

He smiled at the sound of her voice, pressure easing inside his chest. Even though he knew her cousins had had an undercover guard with her all day, hearing her on the other end of the phone made him feel sane again. "How was work?"

"Long, tiring," she said, laughter in her voice. "And unfortunately I'm not done." Now there was regret.

Disappointment swelled inside him as he realized she was going to cancel their plans, but he understood she had to work. He leaned one shoulder against the neighboring locker. The room was mostly empty, almost everyone except another trainer gone for the day. "You have to stay late?"

"Yeah. It's... I'll fill you in later. I still want to do dinner tonight though, if you're game?"

"Yes." He didn't care what time, he just wanted to see her, to hold her in his arms again. He loved the way she blushed so very prettily when he talked dirty. Every time they'd been naked together over the weekend, she'd seemed to get even wetter the more he said, which had taken him by surprise. "What time were you thinking?"

"Seven thirty, eight, which I know is kinda late for dinner. If you want to cancel, I understand."

He snorted. "I'll be there. Still want me to cook?"

"That sounds like heaven." He could hear the fatigue in her voice, wished he was there to hold her.

Yesterday she'd looked over the feeds her cousins had brought over, to the point of exhaustion. Unfortunately she hadn't seen anyone she recognized leaving the conference center. "Did Porter get those other security feeds today?" The owner of the club was supposed to have brought them over.

"Yeah. He texted me about it, but I've got too much to do. I'd planned to look at them on my lunch break but Athena and I ended up having a work meeting I didn't want to miss."

"I'm sure Athena wouldn't mind if you skipped one." Especially for something like this.

"I know, but..." She trailed off, sighing. "I know it's stupid, but I almost don't want to see the video. I don't want to see myself when I can't remember most of that night. It's scary." She whispered the last part.

He wanted to pummel whoever had drugged her—and likely gone after her at the event Saturday—right then and there. "Want me to watch it with you tonight?"

"If you don't mind."

There was a hint of hesitation in her voice that surprised him. "Of course I don't."

"Then yeah, I'd really appreciate it. Listen...I'm not going to be dating anyone else. I don't even know what we are or where we're headed, and I know we're just starting whatever this thing is. But I've never dated more than one guy at a time. Okay, that's not true. I tried but it's just not me." The words came out in a rush, as if she'd been practicing. "Considering we had sex this weekend, a lot of sex, without a condom, I'd appreciate it if you'd tell me if you—"

He shoved up from the locker. "Raegan, I'm not dating anyone else and I don't plan to. I don't want anyone else but you." Which he probably shouldn't admit either, but fuck it. He'd never been one to play relationship games. He wanted her to know where they stood, and while he wouldn't push her for exclusivity or a commitment—yet—he liked knowing she wouldn't be dating anyone else right now.

She let out a short breath of air. "Okay, then."

He bit back a laugh at the way she said it, as if she'd been expecting a different response or something. "So I'll see you tonight?"

"Yes. I've already let security know to expect you so they'll buzz you up whenever you get there."

"Good. Listen, you, uh..." He knew he didn't have a right to ask, but he couldn't help but be worried about her. "You gonna have a guard with you the rest of the evening?"

She snorted softly. "Grant told you about that?"

"Yeah."

"Why am I not surprised? And yes, his name's Travis. He's been a shadow to both me and Athena all day. He's coming with me this evening as well."

"Good." That eased most of the tension in his chest, but until he was with her, nothing would completely do that. "See you soon."

After they disconnected he realized he was grinning like a fool. He probably looked like a jackass but he didn't care. Raegan, one of the sweetest—and yeah, sexiest—women he'd ever known, would be crying out his name later tonight as he made her come against his mouth. She'd been so damn sexy Saturday night, coming apart against him like that the first time.

"I recognize that look," Kip Rawlings, another trainer, muttered as he stepped up to his own locker and yanked it open.

Ford pulled his bag out of his locker, ignoring his normally laid-back friend. The past couple weeks Kip had been a giant asshole and nothing was going to ruin Ford's mood today.

"You seeing someone?" Kip asked as he started stripping.

Ford sat on the long bench, took off his boots. "Yeah." He wasn't going to give more details than that. Normally he would have, but fuck. Whatever had crawled up Kip's ass had made the guy piss on everything lately.

Kip muttered something about women being bitches as he sat on the bench next to him.

Ford couldn't rein it in anymore. "Dude, what the fuck is your problem lately?"

Kip let his shoes drop but didn't turn to look at Ford. Just sat there staring at his locker. "Robin's leaving me. She's been cheating on me for months. I found out, confronted her and she didn't deny it. Said she's been unhappy for a long time. That she's just glad we didn't have kids together because it can be a clean break between us. Easy for everyone," he muttered, bitterness lacing each word. "Easy for her, maybe."

Oh, hell. Ford had never liked Robin, but that wasn't the kind of thing you said to a friend. And he'd been there, understood what the guy was going through. "Sorry, man."

His friend lifted a shoulder.

"That why you've been such a dick the last couple weeks?"

Kip snorted and half laughed, which was what Ford had been going for. "Sorry, man. Yeah." He scrubbed a hand over his face. "I'm not handling it well. Clearly."

"I've been there." And it had been a dark time in his life. "Want to grab a couple drinks?"

Kip finally looked at him, dark circles under his eyes. "Yeah. Maybe dinner too? I don't want to go home, man."

Ford nodded. He had time before Raegan was off work. "Of course. Let me grab a shower and we'll head out."

Kip nodded and didn't make a move from his seat so Ford grabbed his bag and headed for the showers.

Turned out it was a good thing Raegan had to work late. He hated that his friend was going through this, but Robin had never been a good partner in Ford's opinion anyway. Not that he was going to say any of that to his friend. And not that he was much of an expert anyway.

Nah, he'd just take Kip out, let him blow off some steam and probably be the designated driver if Kip wanted to put back a few. After Ford's ex had cheated on him things had been crappy for a while. He'd never imagined wanting to get serious with anyone again. Until Raegan. Deep down he hated that he worried the same thing would happen with her. He didn't like being that guy, worried the woman he was with would cheat.

"So who's this mystery woman you're dating?" Kip leaned back in his seat, seeming more relaxed than he'd been in weeks. He brought his bottled beer to his mouth, took a long drag.

Ford shrugged. He didn't want to talk about Raegan. He knew it was bullshit, but cops were superstitious as a rule. He didn't want to jinx what had just started to develop between them. Plus he didn't want to rub it in Kip's face, regardless. "Just someone I met."

Kip snorted and waved their server over. "That's an evasive answer if I ever heard one." As the woman approached he ordered another basket of wings and a beer for him.

Ford had decided to make it a one-beer night and it looked like he'd be driving Kip home anyway. They'd chosen a local hangout on Bayside that had good beer, cheap eats and a bunch of big screen televisions with various games on. "You got a lawyer yet, or what?"

"I've talked to a few. I keep hoping she'll change her mind."

Which meant he was waiting for Robin to make the first move. Ford wanted to tell him he should make a move and take control now, but knew that wasn't what his friend wanted to hear. He just hated that Kip was holding out hope. "I can give you my brother's info if you want. He doesn't do divorces but he'll know someone good."

Kip nodded, glanced at the TV above the bar. They were at a booth next to a huge window that overlooked the street and half a dozen shops. Ford didn't like feeling so exposed, but he liked having a visual of the street.

"Wait, your brother?" Kip seemed to jerk to life as he turned back to face him. "Fuck that guy."

Ford gave him a wry smile. Kip knew about everything that had gone down between them. "It's water under the bridge." Even if it *wasn't*, Dallas was still a damn good attorney. "He'll be able to give you a good recommendation. It's better than going into this blind."

"Yeah, maybe." He frowned though, clearly not liking the idea. "I'll be back in a sec. Gotta hit the head."

Ford nodded, turning to look out the window, scanning the people out of habit. He was always looking for a threat, it seemed. Unfortunately this had been the only free booth when they'd arrived. For a Monday night it was pretty busy, but people were getting off work and this place was close to one of the hospitals, the police department and even Red Stone. He'd almost texted Raegan to let her know he'd be nearby in case she got finished with her work thing early, but he didn't want to bug her.

After getting burned badly before, he could admit he was gun-shy when it came to relationships. Raegan had him letting his guard down though. Everything about her seemed real, sweet and honest. Still...he kept waiting for the shit to hit the fan, to find out she wasn't as perfect as he'd made her out to be.

He laughed to himself when he saw her get out of an SUV across the street. Shouldn't be a surprise, not when her work was so close. A man he vaguely recognized, wearing a dark suit, got out after her.

Ford could immediately tell the guy had training as he scanned the surrounding area, his posture stiff, alert. Just watching her, his heart rate increased.

Her long dark hair was down in soft waves and she had on a vivid blue wraparound dress with heels. She was too far away for him to truly appreciate her, but the way the dress hugged her body had him primed to peel it from her later tonight. He'd tell her to leave the shoes on as he went down on her. Seven thirty couldn't come soon enough.

When her 'friend' from Saturday night got out of the vehicle next, his good mood darkened. The guy set his hand on the small of Raegan's back as they stepped up onto the sidewalk, his body language completely territorial.

"Just friends, my ass," he muttered. Even if Raegan thought so, clearly her 'friend' didn't. Ford had only gotten a glance at him the other night and he didn't like him. He wanted more than friendship with Raegan. And what the hell was he doing with her anyway? She'd said she had a work thing.

Feeling like he was spying, Ford started to look away when the guy leaned in and kissed her on the mouth. The sight was like a punch to Ford's gut. He stared for what felt like forever until Kip's voice jerked his attention away.

"They haven't brought the wings out yet? I'm freaking starving," his friend muttered, sliding into the booth across from him.

Just like that his surroundings came back into focus again. The laughter of patrons, some people shouting at the TVs, the general buzz of energy in the place. It all rushed back, rolling over him even as iciness invaded his veins.

He tried to tell himself it was a misunderstanding, but...what the fuck. And she'd said she had a work thing. That did *not* look like work.

Their relationship might be new, but after earlier he believed her when she said she wouldn't be seeing anyone else. Or he had believed her. He should have learned his lesson before.

He rolled his shoulders once, and against his better judgment looked out the window again. He couldn't see any of them anymore, just the big SUV they'd arrived in. Which was just as well. He didn't need another visual of Raegan with that asshole.

He wanted to give her the benefit of the doubt but the past punched its way to the surface, that little voice in his head telling him that of course she was too good to be true. That guy was wealthy and had everything to offer her. God, he was such an idiot.

CHAPTER TWELVE

Raegan shoved at Rhys's chest, her heart racing, but not in a good way, as he stepped back. "What the hell was that?" Her palm itched to smack him right across the face.

To give him credit, he looked like he felt awful. "I...read your signals wrong. Really wrong," he muttered. "I'm sorry."

"Guys, either move back into the SUV or let's head inside." Travis Sanchez, a man from the office—and a friend—had been her official shadow today. Right now he looked a little like he wanted to deck Rhys, though he was curbing his impulse. He'd been with her when she'd been in Vegas and in the aftermath of the kidnapping and had been a little overly protective since. This was a man she trusted and genuinely liked.

She glanced up and down the sidewalk, annoyed that this jackass had kissed her without her permission, and embarrassed that Travis had seen it all. People were walking by in twos and threes, some talking on their cell phones and some carrying way too many shopping bags. No one was paying any attention to them at all, but he was right. "We'll get in the SUV. I'm sorry—"

"Don't be sorry, Raegan," Travis murmured, holding the door open. "I'll give you a couple minutes alone but I'm right here if you need me." He patted his jacket pocket too and she realized he was making sure he still had the vehicle keys. Probably so Rhys couldn't run off with her. Not that she was actually worried about *that*, but she'd come to realize that the security personnel of Red Stone didn't think like civilians. To them, anyone was a threat.

She slid into the back seat of the SUV, moving over so Rhys could follow suit.

"I'm very sorry, Raegan. I thought...well, it doesn't matter what I thought."

Part of her wanted to let it go. The 'polite' girl she'd been taught to be would have let this go a couple years ago. But after moving to Miami, after being freaking kidnapped, she'd learned a lot about herself in the last year. "You're right. It doesn't matter what you thought. I told you we could be friends and I thought you were okay with that. I've never given you any indication I wanted more. If you thought you read my signals wrong, I don't know what signals you're talking about. *You* contacted Red Stone today, wanting to work with us on an event. And I know that you requested you work with me. Athena told me. I haven't been pursuing you or sending any fucking signals." She snapped out the last part, taking both of them off guard.

She rarely cursed and especially not in work mode. But after Friday and Saturday night she was feeling more than out of sorts and she was shaking with anger the longer she thought about the way he'd just kissed her without her permission. It was making her second-guess herself. Maybe she'd been 'too' friendly with him before, but...she didn't think so. And it didn't matter if she had been friendly. That was part of her damn job and, you know, just being a decent person. She shouldn't have to worry about some guy kissing her because he thought she'd given some imaginary signal.

"You're right. I'm incredibly sorry." His accent was thicker now, the distress punching off him seemingly sincere. "I've...never had to chase after a woman. Ever. We've been spending time together and I obviously read things wrong. I'm embarrassed by the way I've acted. There's no excuse for what I did."

She softened a little, but not much. Nodding stiffly, she said, "Apology accepted, but I won't be working with you on this project. You can work with Athena or someone else." They'd hired two more full-time staff in the last five months in the event coordination department, so he could take his pick.

He looked as if he wanted to protest, but nodded. "Of course."

Awkwardness settled in the interior until Travis opened the driver's seat door. He slid behind the wheel, and looked at Raegan, not Rhys, something she really appreciated. "We staying or going, Raegan?"

"Let's head back to the office." She was pretty much at her limit for yearly bullshit and it was only the summer. Right now she wanted to put as much distance between her and Mr. Jackass sitting next to her.

She needed to tell Athena, of course. And unfortunately she'd have to tell Porter, otherwise he'd find out and just get annoyed with her for keeping him in the dark. And he was her first choice to tell because he had the most level head of all her cousins and uncle. She simply didn't want to deal with anything else right now. It was like karma had decided to crap on her this week.

At least she'd get to see Ford soon. At that thought, she looked out the window and smiled to herself. Despite the insanity of the last few days, Ford was the silver lining in everything.

<hr />

Once she was safe and alone in her condo, Raegan slipped off her high heels and stripped off her clothes as she made her way to her bedroom. She had enough time for a hot shower before Ford got here and she needed it. Though the idea of inviting him in to join her was more than appealing, she needed some downtime to herself.

When she heard her phone ding in her purse, she practically scrambled for it, hopeful that it was Ford telling her he was on his way. She saw his name on the screen before she swiped her code in.

Got caught up, won't be able to make it tonight. Sorry.

She blinked at the shortness of his text. It was abrupt and unlike him, but it was hard to read tone in a text. Still, she frowned. *You can still come over*, she typed back. *I don't care how late.*

There was a pause, then, *Don't think I'll be able to.*

She fought the disappointment that swelled inside her, but it was a fruitless effort. Her fingers swiped across the screen. *How about you cook for me tomorrow, then? I want to see if you're as good as you say.*

A longer pause this time before, *Not sure what my schedule looks like. I'll let you know.*

Oooookay. She sat on the edge of her bed, not sure what to make of this conversation at all. Heck, she wasn't even sure how to respond so she went with something generic. *Hope you have a good rest of the night, talk to you later.*

His response was just as generic and depressing. *Sure.*

Tossing her phone onto the bed, she headed for her shower. "Screw you, Monday," she muttered to herself.

"Would you mind grabbing takeout for us at the restaurant?" Jules asked Ruby as she stepped out from the back storeroom. "I've already called up there but I want to unload a couple of the new shipments."

Ruby glanced up from the cash register where she was running reports. They would be closing in about fifteen minutes and her aching feet were grateful. "Sure, no problem. Want me to lock the door on the way out?"

"Yeah, since I'll be in the storeroom."

"Sweet. I'll grab the food and be back in a bit." They had a ton of new shipments in and she knew Jules wanted to unload at least half of them tonight so they could start stocking tomorrow. As soon as she was back with the food, she was taking off her heels and slipping into her comfy slippers.

The walk to Julieta's parents' restaurant was short, only a block away. The street was quiet tonight, with most of the shoppers long gone or already settled in at one of the restaurants in the area. In an older, established residential Miami neighborhood, their street was the only one with shops and places to eat. They saw some tourists, but it was mainly local foot traffic.

Ruby's heart skipped a beat when she saw the sign for Montez's Grill. It was named after Montez Sr., not the Montez she was trying to put out of her mind. She hadn't seen him since Saturday morning, but that didn't matter.

He'd been on her mind ever since their confrontation at the shop.

She felt a little bad about calling him an asshole, but she certainly wasn't going to reach out to him. Things were already awkward. They'd both said what they needed to say and she planned to do the mature thing — and just avoid him for the next couple months.

When she pushed the door open she was inundated with laughter, murmured voices, the sound of clinking plates and glasses and subtle Cuban music.

Jaidyn, one of Julieta's cousins, smiled at her as she stepped out from behind the hostess stand. She had on the standard black pants and black T-shirt uniform of the restaurant. "Hey, Ruby."

"Hey, Jules said she called in an order."

"Ah…kitchen's backed up but I've got an empty booth you can wait at."

"Oh, that's okay, I'll just wait up here." She didn't want to take up any seating. Not when it was clear they were busy and could probably use all the space they could get tonight.

A big hand settled on the small of her back, making her jump until she realized it was Montez moving in next to her. He gave her a heated look that made her insides melt just a teeny bit. "I actually asked Julieta to send you down here. There's no takeout waiting and she's going to be headed home soon. Said she'd bring your purse down here once she closed up. Have dinner with me? I'd like to talk to you."

Ruby blinked as she digested his words. "You set this up so we could talk?"

"I figured you'd probably ignore my calls and I wanted to make sure you came."

There was something about the way he said the word 'came' that brought up an altogether *different* mental image. Just like that, her cheeks heated.

He didn't miss the reaction either, if the low, muted groan he gave was any indication. "Say you'll stay," he murmured, his gaze dipping to her mouth.

Unable to find her voice, she simply nodded.

She was barely aware of their surroundings as he guided her to a

342 | KATIE REUS

corner booth with a decent amount of privacy. When she saw a bottle of red wine and two glasses already waiting she nearly stumbled. This was definitely unexpected and incredibly sweet, but she didn't want to get her hopes up too much. She was pretty sure Montez would break her heart if this ended up being some sort of let-Ruby-down-easy type of thing where he told her again he just wanted sex and only sex. But...despite being a cynic, she was pretty sure that wasn't what this was. Even if she was too afraid to hope it was what she'd been wishing for, for a year.

After she sat, he slid in across from her, his dark gaze full of way too many emotions for her to figure out. Lust was a definite one, but...he looked almost nervous too. "I know I apologized Saturday but I'm doing it again."

"You don't have to." Nervously, she traced her finger up and down the stem of the delicate glass.

"I do. I never should have said those things to you. I'm not making excuses, but I want to explain...why I did."

She nodded once, wanting him to continue. "Okay."

"Adjusting to the civilian world was harder than I expected. Way harder. Probably because of this," he said, motioning to the side of his face. She noticed he sat with the scarred side facing the wall. "But even dealing with people I know love and care about me and don't give a crap about my face is still sometimes an adjustment. Cooking and my restaurant and even my crazy family have kept me sane. Then...I met you."

There was a note in his voice she couldn't read. "And that's bad?"

He gave her a wry smile. "Hell no. I wanted you, still want you. But I thought there was never a chance between us. When I got back from Afghanistan..." He scrubbed a hand over his face, looked away for a long moment.

She wanted to reach out and touch him, to comfort him. "You don't have to go on."

"No, it's not..." He pushed out a sigh. "My ex made it clear that I was good enough to fuck but not good enough to be on her arm in public. Ever. She ended things the first night I got home. So when you said all those things to me I wanted to give you an out—and to protect myself from getting burned by you."

His words were raw, real, and broke her heart. And she wanted to punch his ex-girlfriend in the face for ever making him feel inferior. "Montez—"

He cut her off with a sharp shake of his head. "I just need to know if this is some weird...savior complex you have. Like, fuck the scarred guy out of pity. Even saying it out loud I know it sounds fucking stupid," he muttered. "Trust me, I absolutely know it. I just... I don't know why you want me. You're the most beautiful woman I've ever met. I've literally seen men trip over themselves trying to get a better look at you."

She watched him for a long moment, digested everything he'd said and chose her words carefully. "You're one of the nicest, most sincere men I've ever met. Ever. I see the way you treat your mom and sister and yes, even your brothers. God, they're enough to drive anyone crazy. Your brothers, I mean. You're like this solid pillar, the one everyone goes to for advice. And I know how much volunteer work you do down at the VA. Jesus, Montez, how could I not want you?"

For the first time since she'd met him, his cheeks turned crimson. He cleared his throat, embarrassed, but she didn't care. He was such a good man and he needed to know it.

"Since I was fourteen, I looked like this." She motioned down at herself. Yeah, she knew what she looked like. She had a freaking mirror and it would be stupid to deny it. "I had to learn early how to figure out who the assholes of the world are. And despite what I said Saturday, you're not just another asshole. You just hurt me. You're the sweetest man I know—and I wasn't kidding about trying on those naughty nurse costumes." She whispered the last part.

Pleasure hummed through her when his cheeks flushed again, but this time for a very different reason.

Before he could respond, his mother, a slightly older version of Julieta, appeared out of nowhere wearing a wraparound leopard print dress and subtle gold jewelry. She smiled at the two of them. "My favorite oldest son," she murmured. She briefly cupped Ruby's cheeks lightly. "And *mi futura nuera*." Her gold bangles jangled as her hands dropped. "Don't worry about a thing. Your appetizer and salads will be out soon."

"Thanks, Mama," Montez murmured as Ruby did the same.

Seleste Mederos simply patted his cheek and winked at Ruby before moving on to another table.

Ruby had seen the woman at work before and she always came out and greeted customers at least once a night. The restaurant was a staple in the neighborhood and it was clear that she and her husband thought of their regulars like family.

Once Seleste was out of earshot, Ruby leaned a little across the table. "What does *nuera* mean?" She'd learned a lot of Spanish since she'd started working with Jules, but some words she couldn't even begin to guess. Not unless Jules used it in everyday conversation.

Montez just lifted a shoulder, his expression unreadable. "I'll tell you later," he said, after a long moment. "But first I want to get back to that nurse costume you brought up."

She laughed, the weight that had been on her chest for days finally lifting. She wasn't sure what kind of future she and Montez had but she sure wanted the chance to find out.

After dinner Montez walked her back to her car, which was parked across the street from the shop. Thankfully Julieta had dropped off her purse so she hadn't had to go back to the shop to get her stuff. Even though it was summer, a cool breeze kicked up as they headed down the sidewalk.

When Montez picked up her hand and slid his fingers through hers, she was pretty sure her heart was about to beat through her chest. She'd never been so excited about a man before. She could admit she was cynical when it came to the opposite sex, but he pretty much blew away all of that.

"I want to take you out again," he murmured as they reached her car.

"I would like that." She turned to face him, glad he was still holding her hand. The hum of excitement punching through her, wondering if he'd kiss her or not, was unbearable.

"I've got to work tomorrow night, but how about Wednesday?"

"Sounds good." Did it ever.

"Pick you up from work?" he murmured, his gaze dropping to her mouth, hunger simmering in his dark eyes.

Ruby nodded, unable to find her voice.

They both leaned in at the same time and when his lips brushed against hers, she saw those clichéd fireworks. A wild energy buzzed through her as he grasped the back of her head and held tight as his tongue teased against hers.

She could totally fall for this man. She'd seen her mother go through loser after loser, had been so adamant that she'd never let a guy close enough to hurt her. Then she'd met Montez and he'd shoved his way right into her heart without even trying.

She nipped his bottom lip, moving closer into his embrace. His erection was thick against her stomach and the feel of it made her groan into his mouth. As she clutched onto his shoulders, he pulled back, his breathing erratic.

"Gotta stop now," he rasped out.

She nodded even if she didn't want him to. But they were in public and yeah, they didn't need to have a crazy make-out session on the side of the street—across from where she worked.

"Call me when you get home," he said. "So I know you made it safe."

"I will. Or I can just text."

"Call. I want to hear your voice."

Pleasure slid through her veins, warming her from the inside out. She wanted to hear his voice too and it touched her that he wanted to know she'd made it home safe. "I will."

He waited until she was in her car and had pulled away before heading back to the restaurant. As soon as she was on the road she slid her Bluetooth earpiece in and called Raegan. She'd thought about calling Jules but wasn't sure how weird it would be to talk to her about Jules's older brother.

"Hey, Ruby," Raegan said, picking up on the second ring.

She couldn't hold back her excitement. "Guess who I just kissed?"

CHAPTER THIRTEEN

F ord covered his surprise at seeing Grant leaning against his truck in the parking lot outside the range. One of the officers on security must have let him through because civilians weren't supposed to be here. His surprise immediately morphed to concern as he realized there was only one reason Grant would be here.

He shoved his sunglasses up on his head, broke into a jog. "What's wrong?" he demanded, coming to stand in front of the former detective. Had something happened to Raegan? He hadn't talked to her in three days, hadn't known what the hell to say to her after seeing her kissing that guy.

Grant pushed up from the truck, and despite wearing a suit, he looked nothing like a typical businessman. He looked a little like a caged animal—and like he wanted to deck Ford right across the face. "I just wanted to make sure you weren't fucking dead." The words were spoken quietly, but there was no mistaking the undercurrent of anger. "Since you apparently cut things off with my cousin like a total douche, without a word. What the hell is the matter with you? If you don't want to be with her, fine, end things like a man. I never expected you to sleep with her and then just stop calling. It's a dick move."

Tension ratcheted up inside him, all his muscles going taut. "Raegan and I are none of your business."

Grant's jaw tightened. "You're right. But you and I are friends. And my very emotional, pregnant wife is upset for Raegan. I overheard them talking. That's the only fucking reason I'm here right now. I really don't want to be having this conversation but...what the hell, dude? I've seen you practically panting after her for a year."

Ford had mistakenly thought he'd done a good job of hiding his feelings for Raegan, but that was beside the point. He rubbed a hand over his face, feeling awkward talking about any of this. "Look, whatever you overheard is wrong. It was casual for Raegan but it wasn't for me. I can't...be with her if she's with someone else."

Some of the anger seemed to subside from Grant as he frowned. "I can't believe I'm having this fucking conversation," he muttered. "But what the hell are you talking about?"

Yeah, Ford couldn't believe it either. "I was out with one of the guys Monday and saw her kissing some guy. I wasn't following her," he tacked on, as if that even needed to be explained. "It was dumb luck I saw and...I'm just not wired that way." Not to mention she'd told him she wouldn't be dating anyone else. He felt like such an idiot. He should have known she was too good to be true.

Grant blinked, as if Ford had truly surprised him. Then his expression hardened. "Monday night she had a business thing and the guy kissed her out of the blue. She was so pissed about it she passed the job off to Athena — but we decided not to do business with him anyway. And not just because it's Raegan. The women who work for Red Stone need to feel safe at work. Need to *be* safe."

At Grant's words, a sinking sensation filled his gut. He'd jumped to the wrong conclusion. He knew why he'd done it. He'd let his past cloud his judgment. "Fuck." Ford wanted to kick his own ass. Repeatedly.

"I've known you a long time, man, so I know your baggage. I get it, especially after what happened with your brother. But..." He shrugged and pulled out his car keys. "Raegan's not like your ex. Not even close. You're a dumbass if you think that." He didn't say anything else, just tapped his key fob and stalked across the parking lot.

Feeling like the biggest dick on the planet, he pulled out his cell phone and called her. It went to her voicemail after two rings, making him think she'd rejected his call. Not that he blamed her. It had been three days since he'd contacted her. He wondered if she'd even listen to him. He had to come clean about his issues, to make her understand why he'd jumped to the wrong conclusion—and apologize because he'd been so wrong to make an assumption like that.

Grant was right; he did have baggage. He *thought* he'd dealt with it, but seeing her kissing someone else had brought up all those feelings of betrayal and inadequacy. And instead of phoning her and confronting her about what he'd seen, he'd walked away without giving her a chance to explain herself.

Instead of calling again, he texted her. *I'm sorry I've been a ghost the past few days. I'd like to see you in person and apologize.* He also wanted to explain everything to her, but texting wasn't the way to do it.

He doubted she'd text him right back or maybe even at all, so he got into his truck and headed home. He'd screwed up because of his own bullshit. Now he might have lost the best thing that had ever happened to him. He'd convinced himself that something would go wrong, then, when he'd thought it had, he hadn't even fought for her.

Losing Raegan because of his own issues was something he knew he'd regret forever. Now he had to make it right.

"I'm surprised Dominique isn't here tonight," Raegan said to Ruby and Julieta. A group of her girlfriends had come out tonight but Dominique had said she couldn't. In fact, she'd been surprisingly MIA since Saturday's event. She'd been at work, but she'd been acting a little off and hadn't wanted to hang out with anyone.

Before either of them could respond, Lizzy, Porter's wife, snorted from across the big round table. "She's busy with a certain Russian, from what I hear."

Everyone at the table quieted and stared at her.

"Who? What?" Raegan asked. Dominique hadn't dated a man in...well, since Raegan had known her. She was always so quiet about that part of her life. She wondered if it was that Russian from

Saturday's event, the one who'd dropped off the security feed of the club to Porter. But Dominique had seemed to hate the guy. That being an understatement.

Lizzy stared at all of them in clear surprise. "Seriously, I'm the only one who knows about this?"

"Apparently," Athena said. "Come on, spill. She's been cagey all week and I need some good gossip."

"No way." Lizzy shook her head. "Dominique is Porter's assistant. If I make her mad she might screw up his schedule or…I can't think of anything else right now, but she can be scary. So nope, no spilling of secrets will be happening." She made a zipping motion across her lips and mimed throwing away the key.

"We'll get it out of you," Julieta said, picking up her own wine glass.

Julieta had known Lizzy since they were kids, but Raegan knew her cousin-in-law well enough that if Lizzy didn't want to talk about something, she wouldn't.

Everyone quieted for a moment as their server dropped off three appetizers and placed them around the big table. Raegan had been working like crazy and going straight home every day this week, thanks to the unknown threat looming over her head. Unfortunately she'd been going home alone because a certain jerk had decided to cut all contact with her. It hurt way more than she'd imagined. She'd thought they had something good, that they were moving in a positive direction. Then he'd just cut all contact.

She mentally shook herself, not even wanting to go there right now. She'd reviewed the video feed from the club and from the event but hadn't seen anyone she recognized or that stood out to her as a threat. And she hadn't received any creepy messages or anything. Still, she was being smart, and the only reason she was even out tonight was because Jules' and Lizzy's significant others were at the bar keeping watch over them while they had a girls' night. She hated that she was the reason for the 'security' but she was glad to get out with her friends. Especially since Ford had pulled the rug out from under her. She hadn't decided whether to text him back or not yet.

"If you want gossip," she said to Athena as everyone started reaching for the appetizers, "guess who just called and texted me after days of radio silence?"

"Ooh, sexy cop is back on the scene?" Ruby asked. The beautiful blonde was happier than Raegan had ever seen her since she'd started dating Montez a few days ago.

"Uh, no." And she didn't know if she even wanted to contact him. She didn't play games, and he'd really hurt her. She started to reach for the crab-stuffed mushrooms when she saw the almost guilty look on Lizzy's face. "What's that look?"

"Nothing."

"You're such a liar. Do you know something about Ford?"

Lizzy shrugged as she scooped a few of the coconut fried shrimp onto her plate. "I know a lot about him. He's been friends with Grant for years."

"Don't be a smart-ass."

"I'm not supposed to say." She picked up a shrimp, nibbled on it as everyone watched her.

"If you don't tell her, I'm going to make you wear the ugliest bridesmaid dress possible. With ruffles and bows and everything you hate. In pink. It'll be a special dress, reserved just for you." Julieta's expression was deadpan as she lifted her glass of wine, her eyebrows raised challengingly.

"Fine..." Lizzy turned back to Raegan, her expression apologetic. "I might have overheard Grant telling Porter that he was going to see Ford today."

Mortification swelled inside Raegan as Lizzy's words settled in. "Oh, my God," she breathed out. She did not need her cousins 'defending her honor' or whatever misguided idea they might have. A little overprotectiveness was fine, but this was nuts.

"I *know*. I told Porter it was a bad idea but apparently Belle is super emotional right now—and I understand. I was crazy emotional when I was pregnant too. But she was really upset for you, was talking about going to see Ford and punching him," Lizzy sighed, "and I quote, 'in his big dumb face.' So...I think Grant might have gone to see him today to make her happy."

Raegan felt her cheeks flush with embarrassment. She'd been ranting to Belle yesterday about Ford's disappearing act but that had just been to release her frustration to a friend. She was a grown woman. She didn't need or want her family getting involved with her fizzled relationship. Hell, it had barely been a relationship. Just sex. At least to Ford. And yeah, that stung pretty deeply because she'd really been into him. "I think I need another glass of wine," she muttered.

"It's probably not as bad as you think," Ruby said, giving her a hopeful expression.

"Yeah, sure." At least now she had her answer as to why Ford had called and texted after days of the silent treatment. She'd really thought they were on the same page. She'd started to think they might have something real together. At least this had happened before she'd really fallen for him.

Who was she kidding—it hurt no matter what. She had absolutely nothing to say to him, especially not since he was only calling because of her cousin.

CHAPTER FOURTEEN

F ord pushed away from the wall when he saw Raegan round the corner from where the elevators were.

She paused when she saw him, her lips pulling into a thin line before she continued toward him.

"How'd you get in the building?" she asked, pulling her key out of her purse. She had on one of those wraparound dresses he'd noticed that she favored. This one was solid black. It highlighted all her curves—not that he should be focusing on that right now. Not when he owed her an apology. Just seeing her made him ache inside, only reminded him how much he'd missed her.

"I was still on your guest list." Which yeah, showing up uninvited was a shitty thing to do, but he wanted to see her, to do this in person. Even if he was pretty sure she never wanted to see him again. But he had to try and make this right. He missed her and wanted another shot.

She crossed her arms over her chest, her expression neutral. "Look, Lizzy told me that Grant might have visited you today so if that's the case, know that I had nothing to do with that. You shouldn't be here because you think you have to apologize for...whatever."

"I do need to apologize..." He trailed off as a couple a few doors down stepped from their condo. They both waved at Raegan, who smiled and waved back.

Sighing, she opened her door. "Let's do this inside," she murmured.

Feeling more nervous than he could ever remember, he trailed after her. He'd screwed up and he knew he'd get one chance to make this right. That meant laying it on the line for Raegan, being totally honest. Even if he didn't want to talk about his past, he knew he needed to.

She didn't go far, just into the entryway. The door shut behind them, but she didn't bother locking it. Just leaned against it, eyeing him warily. "Why are you here?"

"I owe you an apology. I saw you out early Monday evening—completely by chance—kissing the guy from Saturday's event." Her eyes widened and she started to protest but he shook his head. "I now know that you weren't kissing him, that he kissed you. Not that it's an excuse for me just falling off the face of the earth like I did. I'm sorry for the radio silence." He shoved his hands in his pockets, trying to get a read on her, but for once he couldn't tell what she was thinking.

He hated that there was now a wall between them—and that it was his fault. He hated that he'd hurt her. That he'd misjudged her.

"So you saw me kissing some guy, or what you thought was me kissing some guy, and decided to just...not ask me about it?" Hurt filled her blue eyes, making him feel worse.

"I should have asked you about it. Hell, I shouldn't have jumped to conclusions." From where he'd sat, it had looked like a pretty intense kiss, but he hadn't looked that long. Hadn't wanted to. He'd let his past get in the way, blur his judgment. He knew that now and was afraid he'd screwed up the best thing that had happened to him.

"Why didn't you?"

He drew a deep breath and came clean. "I was scared of your answer."

She made a scoffing sound, which he figured he deserved. "You were scared?"

"I..." He cleared his throat. "Years ago I was with a woman who was cheating on me. A lot, I found out later. I ignored my instinct because I was hung up on her. I thought I loved her. So when she said she was working late or told me I was paranoid, I believed her. I've never been the jealous type and she made me feel fucking nuts for questioning her. For questioning what my instinct was telling me."

He took another deep breath, hated admitting this at all. He still couldn't believe how stupid he'd been.

"Turns out she was sleeping with my brother. Things got really messy for a while, especially after Dallas proposed to her. She left him a month before their wedding. He'd been on a fast track to a partnership with one of the biggest firms in Miami, but when that didn't happen, she split." Ford had thought he'd feel some sort of vindication or happiness, but instead he'd felt bad for his brother. Dallas had lost his job and the woman he'd loved, no matter how horrible she was, in the span of days.

Raegan's defensive pose dissipated and she dropped her arms from around herself. Sighing, she hung her purse on the hook by the front door, slipped off her heels and locked the door. "Come on, let's finish this conversation in the kitchen. It sounds like you need a beer."

Even though he was surprised, he didn't question her as he followed after her. Since she lived in a condo, her kitchen was relatively small, but there was a built-in bar top with stools on the outside of her actual kitchen. She pointed over the bar top for him to sit as she went to the refrigerator.

"So, you decided to lump me in with your ex?" she asked as she pulled out two beers. She handed him one as she popped the top of her own.

He fought the urge to squirm. "Yeah."

"That's pretty stupid."

He scrubbed a hand over his face. "I know."

She leaned against the bar top opposite him, watching him carefully. "You just fell off the face of the earth. It was...hurtful. We shared some pretty intense sex, and then nothing from you. And I'll admit, it was more than just sex for me. I missed you." She looked so damn vulnerable as she said it. "Even if you thought I'd been kissing someone else — and I can understand you being annoyed after we'd had that talk about not seeing other people — you could have *asked* me about it."

"I know. I should have. And I know words are bullshit, but I really am sorry. You deserve better than the way I acted. For the record, I've missed you too."

She continued to watch him carefully, as if debating something. "I should be a lot madder at you right now, but okay."

His heart rate kicked up. "Okay?"

"Okay, I forgive you. Only because I know you've been checking in with Porter about my whole 'stalker' situation—or whatever's going on—and I can tell you're being sincere. And okay, that story…" Her eyes widened a little. "Seriously, your brother? Then she got engaged to him? Holy awkward Thanksgiving dinners."

He let out a wry laugh, the tension in his chest easing. "Yeah, it's why things are still strained between us."

"How long ago was this?"

"About two years."

"No wonder you have trust issues." He snorted at that, but she just continued. "I can't be with someone who cuts all contact like that, so if you do it again, we're done. I don't play relationship games, and I like you, Ford. I…I'm going to let this go, but I just can't deal with something like this again. If you have a problem with anything, talk to me. Okay?"

He was surprised she was giving him a second chance at all, realized how lucky he was, but he nodded. "I will."

"And…I'm just going to say it so we're on the same page. I like a little possessiveness but I need to be with someone who trusts me. I'll trust you unless you give me a reason not to."

"That's fair. But I can only show you that going forward." And he planned to.

She nodded once. "Okay. So…want to pop a pizza in the oven and watch a movie? I was out with friends earlier but only munched on some appetizers and I'm still starving."

Warmth glowed in his chest, a huge weight lifting off him. Being able to spend the evening with her was a gift he could hardly believe he deserved after what he'd done. "Yeah. I'll put the pizza in if you want to pick a movie."

"Oh, I think I get to pick the next five movies." Her grin was just a little wicked as she said it.

He couldn't help but grin back. "Is that right?"

"Yep. Call it part of your apology."

His gaze fell to her mouth and hunger surged through him. Everything about her got him hot. He'd been trying not to think about her the last three days, but had failed. She shouldn't be letting him off the hook so easily, but he wasn't going to question his luck. "I can think of some other ways to make it up to you." He dropped his voice, the intent in his words clear. But he didn't want to simply jump back into sex, not after he'd screwed up so bad.

Her cheeks tinged pink. "If these ways involve you naked with your head between my legs, I'll allow it."

He groaned at the description. She'd been pretty quiet during their many bouts of sex, definitely not a dirty talker like him, but this…was fucking hot. He cleared his throat as his cock hardened, and just nodded. For once, he couldn't find his voice. All he wanted to do right now was just what she'd said.

But he also wanted to show her that this thing between them was more than just physical. Because he was playing for keeps with Raegan.

CHAPTER FIFTEEN

As he reached Raegan's office, his heart rate increased as it always did. His hands shook as he approached her desk. She wasn't there but he could see her crossed legs where she was sitting in her boss's office and could hear them talking.

They'd ordered lunch in today, something they only did about once a week. He took their boxed lunches off his cart and set them both on Raegan's desk. "Lunch," he called out, excitement humming through him as he waited to see her.

But the other woman, Athena, stepped out instead and smiled at him. "Hey, Teo. How much do we owe you?"

He was momentarily disappointed that it was just Athena, that Raegan wouldn't be coming out as well. Normally it was Raegan — she was the assistant, after all. But maybe she was working on something. It couldn't be that she didn't want to see him. Could it?

He curbed the anger that sliced through him, forced a smile for Athena. "Ah, sixteen ninety-five."

Smiling, she handed him a twenty. "Keep the change."

He nodded, murmuring thanks as she picked up the boxes and headed back into her office. Because of the angle he could only see Raegan's legs but he could hear typing. Maybe on her laptop. The must be why she hadn't come out. It had nothing to do with him.

Still…he wanted to see her. Was desperate to get a glimpse. He kept wondering if she'd remembered him from Friday night. But if she had, the police would have already come to see him.

He pretended to readjust the other boxed lunches for this floor in the hopes he'd get a glimpse of her.

"You can put that down for a few minutes," Athena said.

He watched as a laptop slid into his view, moving to the edge of the desk. So she had been working. It didn't ease his tension any. Some days he kept his food truck open longer just to get a peek of her leaving work, but the last week he hadn't seen her coming or going. He'd still been reading all her texts but they didn't tell him much other than she'd been in some argument with one of the guys she was screwing. Which was good.

He took a deep breath. He wouldn't think about her being with anyone else right now. It would just upset him. Soon enough she'd see that she was meant for him, no one else. He could forgive her if she was sorry enough.

"…dress fitting tomorrow. Supposed to be over by two."

"You'll have to tell me what La Boutique Bellissima is like. I've got an appointment scheduled there in two weeks to talk with the owner."

Teo knew he'd been lingering long enough as it was and pushed his three-tiered cart out into the hall. He'd gotten so much more than he imagined today. He knew that bridal boutique, had set up his food truck in the area on multiple occasions.

Red Stone Security was one of the only places he did actual deliveries to. Until a few months ago he hadn't even done the deliveries himself. One of his part-time employees hadn't been feeling well so he'd let him take over the food truck while he'd finished the deliveries personally. It was how he'd met Raegan for the first time.

Beautiful, vibrant Raegan.

Now that he knew where she was going to be tomorrow he'd be able to get there before her. He wouldn't even have to track her using her phone. He'd still check it, of course, but it was better for him to set up early and check out potential spots to take her from if the opportunity should arise.

He'd head down to the area later tonight, look for any security cameras in the vicinity. He could disable some and break others.

For once, it seemed fate was on his side. He had an advantage over her this time. It would give him the element of surprise. Grabbing her in broad daylight was a risk, but if he could get her alone he'd do it.

Soon she'd be all his. Once he made her understand that he was in charge, that she belonged to him, things would be good again. The burning anger inside him would be manageable again. At this point he almost didn't care about someone seeing him. He just needed to be with her, to have her. If he couldn't have her, no one could.

CHAPTER SIXTEEN

"**I**s it normal for guys to come to these fittings?" Ford asked Montez and Ivan, who were sitting on the bench next to him.

They were outside the bridal shop after Julieta had kicked Ivan out "for inappropriate suggestions," as she put it.

Ford understood why Ivan was there, even if he wouldn't be allowed to see Julieta try on her wedding dress. And Montez was Julieta's brother—though he was clearly only there because Ruby was. But Ford had never thought guys came to these kinds of things. He'd have been shadowing Raegan regardless, but she'd asked him before he could suggest it. He hadn't wanted to ask her if it was normal for significant others to be here and reveal how truly relationship-challenged he was. He'd grown up with a brother and most of his friends were either cops or retired Marines. And his ex hadn't had many girlfriends so this was new territory.

Ivan just shrugged as Montez nodded. "Yeah, things are different now, man. Women want their men involved in *all* of the wedding stuff. They've even got couples showers."

Wait…couples showers? He blinked, trying to figure out what Montez meant. Was that like a swingers thing? It seemed too weird for Montez to be talking about casually. God, he really felt old.

Montez burst out laughing, shaking his head. "Oh my God, not like that. I see where your mind just went. Showers, like for babies and weddings and stuff. Not all guys go and not all of them are joint, but yeah, it's a thing now. Trust me, I've got a lot of female cousins. You're gonna be expected to go to all sorts of stuff like this now."

Ford didn't think that sounded like a bad thing, not if he got to hang out with Raegan more. Just maybe not all the time. Baby showers didn't sound like fun. "Those drinks inside were fucking awesome," he said, referring to whatever the hell they'd given them in the shop earlier. It was bubbly and had fruit in it and he wouldn't be caught dead drinking it anywhere else, but damn.

"We'd still be drinking them if someone hadn't got us kicked out," Montez muttered.

Ford nodded, looking at Ivan. "I think you horrified the sales clerk, talking about making sure her wedding dress had an easy access—"

"Dude, I do not need to hear that again." Montez stood, shooting Ivan a pointed look. "She's still my sister. Keep some shit to yourself."

Ivan just grinned and shrugged again, which seemed pretty standard for the guy's communication style.

Montez rolled his eyes before nodding at the café next door. "I'm gonna grab a drink. You guys want something?"

Ford stood as Ivan said, "Iced coffee."

"I'll go with you." He wanted to stretch his legs and he needed to use the restroom. And Raegan had said it would take at least another hour for them to finish getting fitted. "You gonna go anywhere?" he asked Ivan, needing to know that someone would stay put in front of the store.

"Nope."

He nodded once. The guy was a former Ranger and he worked for Red Stone. Not to mention he'd been there the other night at the club and knew the deal with Raegan right now. Nothing had happened in the last week—no threats, no phone calls, no weird messages or attempted attacks.

But...his gut told him it wasn't random. Not after the things the unknown guy had said to her in that bathroom. It was just too personal. He knew the detective who'd been assigned her case, but the truth was, she wasn't a priority to the department.

Even with some of the guys at Red Stone working on finding out who'd tried to hurt her, they hadn't found much. They hadn't been

362 | KATIE REUS

able to get a matchup of faces from both the club and the event. When people wore hats or hoodies or anything that obscured their faces, it messed with the facial recognition software, making it virtually useless.

It wasn't like she was receiving strange messages they could track either. Which was good and bad. Maybe she didn't really have a stalker. Or maybe the guy who drugged her was just very patient.

That scared Ford more than anything. Someone who was patient was a bigger threat. They'd be less likely to make a mistake.

He rolled his shoulders once and glanced up and down the street as they reached the door to the café. There was a tingling sensation between his shoulder blades.

It put him even more on edge, made him wonder if he was being paranoid, but he'd seen enough combat to never ignore his instinct. Right then he needed to see Raegan, needed to know that she was okay.

"Hey, I'm gonna go talk to Raegan. I'll meet you back outside," he said to Montez. "Get me a bottled water?" he asked, pulling out his wallet.

Montez nodded and waved away his money.

A cool breeze rushed over him, making the wind chimes outside the boutique next door jingle as he reached the glass door to the bridal shop. He smiled at the sight of Raegan on the other side, already starting to push it open.

"Hey," he said, opening it for her.

"Hey, you," she murmured, lifting up on her toes to brush her lips over his. He covered a groan as she stepped back.

She gave him a wide smile and he could tell she was a little tipsy. The women had been drinking mimosas during the fitting and he knew she hadn't eaten much for breakfast that morning.

"Are you done?"

She nodded then glanced around him. "Jules said you can come back in if you're good."

Ivan just laughed but gave Ford a pointed look. One that clearly asked if he wanted backup right now.

Ford shook his head and held the door open again as Ivan stepped past them. He was armed and he'd been well trained.

"Can we grab something to eat really quick? I have a small buzz going and I'm starving," Raegan said. "I was the first done so we've got some time."

He wrapped his arm around her shoulders. After the second chance she'd given him, he wasn't letting her go. He knew he'd let his past cloud his judgment, but the way she'd truly let everything go told him everything he needed to know about her. "Sure, let's head next door."

"Can we head to the food truck instead? I've been to that one before and they've got amazing veggie empanadas."

"Sounds good. I'll snag one too." Out of habit he scanned their surroundings as they waited to cross the street.

There were half a dozen people in line across the street, waiting. He could see them looped down the sidewalk from their angle. A female couple walking a small dog was approaching from the right, but he couldn't see to the left of the food truck. He didn't like it, but he knew that Raegan couldn't live in a bubble.

Besides, he was with her. He'd do anything to keep her safe. As they reached the other side, he was relieved to see nothing out of the ordinary on the other side of the truck. A few benches occupied by people eating food from the truck. It was a typical, sunny Florida day. Everything seemed normal.

Raegan half nuzzled her face against his chest as they got in line. "What's going on in that sexy head of yours?" she murmured.

He laughed lightly, kissing the top of her head. "You are definitely tipsy right now."

"Mmm hmm," she agreed. "And I think we need to head straight back to your place after the fitting."

"Is that right?" he asked quietly. The two college-aged guys in front of them were talking to each other — loudly — about how drunk they'd gotten the night before, and how they needed hangover food. Definitely not a threat.

"Yep. I only got to see it that once. God, that feels like a lifetime ago." She seemed to sober at the comment.

"Yeah." It really did. "I hate what happened, but for the record, I'm glad it brought you into my life."

She looked up at him, eyebrows raised. "I was sorta already in your life."

He grinned. "Yeah. But I was still figuring out how to ask you out."

"Afraid of my cousins?"

He snorted. "More like afraid of you."

She blinked in true surprise, then that slightly wicked smile he loved spread across her face. "I've been told I'm quite scary."

He snorted again. "I'm sure." That word was pretty much the opposite of her. He'd just been a coward. Never again though. He'd let his past hold him back for too long. And deep down...he knew Raegan was it for him. It was that gut instinct. She'd knocked him on his ass and he was never letting her go. Yeah, it was too soon to make any declarations or be completely positive about their future, but he saw the writing on the wall. He knew where this was going. The fact that he was actually looking forward to going to couples showers with her was a pretty big indicator that she was damn special.

Only a couple more people to go now, he realized. When he made eye contact with the man behind the flipped down metal counter, he gave a polite smile, nodded. The guy didn't smile back, barely acknowledged him.

Ford kept his expression neutral, slid his sunglasses over his eyes as he scanned their surroundings again. "You said you've been to this food truck before?" he murmured.

She shifted slightly against him. "Oh, yeah. It's parked right on our street outside work. I bet the owner does crazy-good business, considering the area. Red Stone even opened it up to him to do deliveries a couple months ago."

"So you know the owner, personally?" Ford kept his voice low.

She shrugged against him. "Not really. I mean, we say hi, you know, the normal polite stuff. He delivers to Athena and me once a week along with our whole floor. I don't know of any food trucks that add that type of extra service. It's pretty great."

Ford's radar was going nuts as the guy continued to shoot looks at him and Raegan. The guy's body language was all wrong. All his muscles were pulled tight as he continued taking orders and preparing food. Ford was surprised no one was in there with him. He also wondered about the location of the truck. He knew that food trucks moved around a city, but he didn't like that this was the same one that parked outside Red Stone, and just happened to be at this location at the same time Raegan had a dress fitting here. Or that the owner had access to Raegan's office, to her at work. No, it was time to get her the hell out of here.

He didn't care if he was being paranoid, he was going with his gut. "You trust me?"

Raegan straightened next to him. "Uh, yeah. Of course."

"We're going to head back across the street to the bridal boutique. Stay to the left of me."

"Okay." There was a note of concern in her voice, but she didn't say anything else as they broke away from the line.

A sense of relief had already started pulsing through him as they headed back toward the street and away from the food truck. He didn't want to pull his weapon out in full view of everyone but as soon as they stepped down onto the curb, rounding the back of food truck, he reached behind his back for his pistol.

Just as the back door to the truck flew open.

A muscular man about five feet, ten inches tall was holding a pistol directly at Ford, his dark eyes glittering with hatred. Barely four feet separated them. He'd never survive a direct shot this close. It didn't matter how much training and experience he had, he couldn't draw fast enough to shoot someone who had a weapon pointed directly at him only feet away. Maybe on television that shit worked.

Everything slowed down in that instant as he stared down the barrel of the weapon. He wanted to shove Raegan behind him, but she'd clutched onto him tighter and he didn't want to make any sudden moves.

"Get your hands off her," the man snarled. "Raegan, get in the back of the truck."

There were gasps coming from people on the sidewalk and someone said "Gun," before running away. Ford could see other people scattering in his periphery but all his focus was on this threat.

"I'm going to take my arm from around her," Ford said slowly, moving just as slowly. Adrenaline surged through him, but he forced himself to remain calm. No sudden movements, nothing to spook the guy into shooting her. There was no way in hell he was letting her get in that truck, however, but one step at a time. "You don't really want to shoot anyone. You haven't done anything you can't take back yet."

The man's hand shook, his eyes just a little wild. "I'll shoot you right fucking here! I know you were going to take her away from me! You think I'm stupid?"

"Please don't shoot." Raegan's voice trembled but her words were clear.

The man's focus lasered in on her even though he didn't move his weapon in her direction. Thank God. "Didn't I tell you to get in the truck?" he snarled. "Why'd you come over here today? Just to show off that you're with him? I know what you want and I'm going to give it to you. Get in the fucking truck!"

A siren wailed in the distance, cutting through the air and making Raegan jump. The man turned at the sound, as if on instinct. His weapon hand wavered to the side. Not by much, but it was enough.

Ford knew this might be the only chance he ever got. He had to take it.

Years of training had prepared him for this moment. It would take too many steps to draw his weapon, bring it around his body and fire at the threat. No, he had to go with the only other option.

Adrenaline punching through him, he shoved Raegan to the side as he lunged at the man. Since the guy was raised up on the back of the truck, Ford rammed into the guy's upper legs and lower torso with a full-on tackle.

A shot boomed through the air as Ford slammed him to the floor. He heard the clatter of the weapon but couldn't see where it had gone as the guy screamed.

The man punched at Ford's head. He ducked to the side, the blow glancing his temple.

He struck out with his fist, slamming it against the guy's nose. Bone crunched under the force of his punch as the man's head slammed back against the metal floor.

Ford needed to take complete control of the situation, disable the threat. Everything else around him funneled out as that thought took over. He wasn't even sure if Raegan had been hit by that bullet and he couldn't risk looking out the door, couldn't take his focus off this man.

Fear and rage surged through him that she might have been injured, or worse. He slammed his elbow across the guy's face, breaking more bones.

The man cried out in pain, blood gushing out his nose as he punched at Ford's middle. Either he had training or he was just jacked up on adrenaline — or drugs — to keep fighting with broken bones.

His fist landed against Ford's ribcage, once, twice — *Slam*! Ford landed another face shot. When the guy's head thumped back against the floor again, his entire body went limp.

Not taking a chance that the guy wasn't out, Ford rolled him onto his stomach and yanked his wrists together behind his back. At a shuffling sound, he went to reach for his weapon but stilled when he saw Montez coming in through the front of the truck, his expression fierce and a weapon in his hand. He briefly wondered if Montez had a concealed permit, then dismissed the thought. He didn't give a shit right now.

"Raegan?" Ford rasped out.

"Okay," Montez answered.

Relief nearly overwhelmed him, but he shoved it back down. "I need something to secure him," he said as Montez moved into action, rummaging around the small kitchen.

Spicy scents teased the air as he suddenly realized the sirens were growing even louder in the distance. "Anyone get shot?"

"No." Montez hurried over with a type of bungee cord. "I saw what was happening as I came out of the café across the street. Ivan must have seen it from inside the shop."

Ford nodded, securing the man's wrists as Montez continued to talk.

"Ivan had to carry Raegan across the street. She didn't want to leave you. But she's fine, man. Completely unharmed. Someone saved us the trouble of calling the cops too. They should be here soon."

If those sirens were any indication, Ford guessed fewer than sixty seconds. "Got something for his feet?" he asked as the man started to groan softly. Ford kept his knee firmly against the asshole's back. He resisted the urge to hurt the guy more as the words the man had thrown at Raegan replayed in his mind. 'I know what you want and I'm going to give it to you.' He could just imagine what the fucker had planned for her. A shudder racked him, but he tightened his control.

Seconds later Montez was back with white zip ties. "We use these at my place for chill bags."

Ford just grunted, grabbed a handful of the ties. He secured the man's feet, then his hands again for good measure, making sure they were double-tied. Heart racing, he looked up at Montez. "Will you—"

"Go. I got this."

Ford was glad he didn't have to waste time with words, that Montez understood he needed to see for himself that Raegan was unharmed.

He jumped down from the food truck, immediately saw a giant hole in the back of a silver car. Bullet hole.

The relief that surged through him was almost too much when he saw Raegan on the other side of the street behind the glass doors of the bridal shop. Her eyes were wide as she stared at him, one hand pressed to the glass. Ivan was next to her, his hand on her shoulder. More people lined the windows, staring out in horror, but he only had eyes for her.

After looking for oncoming vehicles, he raced across the street, his heart thundering in his chest. He just needed to hold her. He'd made it halfway across when she shoved Ivan's hand off and pushed the door open.

As he reached the sidewalk edge she threw herself at him, a sob escaping. "Ford! I thought..." Her words were garbled as she buried her face in his neck.

He was unable to say anything as he held her tight. Probably too tight, but she didn't complain. "You need to wait inside," he finally managed to rasp out, still holding onto her. The subtle vanilla scent of her shampoo wrapped around him, grounded him. She was okay, he repeated to himself. She was unharmed and in his arms. She wasn't going anywhere.

And the threat to her was down. That was what was important. Ford was going to find out everything there was to know about that bastard and make sure he never got the chance to hurt anyone again.

She shook her head against his neck. "Not leaving you."

At the sound of the sirens screaming down the street he turned, saw a line of police cars coming. But he still didn't let her go.

They'd face this together. The way he intended to face everything life had to throw at them from now on.

CHAPTER SEVENTEEN

Raegan was exhausted, but at least she wasn't still shaking out of control. She'd thought she'd never feel normal again. Still didn't. Not really.

Everything about earlier today was too surreal. The way Ford had taken on that guy with a gun like a real-life superhero, the way he'd just tackled him.

It was…God, she didn't even know. The only thing she did know was that she'd never get that image out of her head as long as she lived. She'd been terrified for him. Then Ivan had appeared out of nowhere and carried her away like a linebacker. He'd moved with such precision and speed, clearly just as trained as Ford.

Ford squeezed her hand and she realized she'd zoned out. "What?"

"Detective Duarte asked if there was anything else you wanted to add," he murmured.

They were sitting in the detective's office in front of his desk. "No, I'm just glad this is all over. I can't believe he cloned my phone. It's so…" There were too many words. *Invasive, horrifying…* She shuddered. "Are you sure he won't be getting out?"

The detective gave her a sharp, satisfied grin. "Yes. And I don't get to say that nearly as often as I'd like, but he won't even be eligible for bail. Not after what we've found at his house."

She shuddered again, was so grateful for the Miami PD—and Ford. Once Teo King had been arrested, they'd searched his house and discovered an insulated, padded room with a bed and hundreds of pictures of her covering all the walls. Not only that, but boxes of pictures of her by herself and with friends, taken over the last couple months. Right about the time he'd started delivering to Red Stone Security.

But that wasn't the reason he'd be going away. The police had discovered a body buried in his backyard, and considering the social security checks coming in for his mother — who hadn't been seen by any neighbors in months — they were pretty sure it was her. No doubt it was a murder, not with the bullet holes in her skull. Something Raegan didn't want to think about.

"Can I go home, then?"

The detective nodded. "Yes. For what it's worth, you were lucky. This guy...he's been flying under the radar but now that we know who he is, we're going to rip his life apart, see if there have been more victims. Anything we can charge him with, we will. No matter what, he's already going down for his crimes. And we're taking another look at that club's security feed from the night you were drugged."

"Thank you. For everything." She kept questioning herself, wondering if there had been signs. But the guy had never asked for her phone number, never shown any interest. Not that she'd been aware of. She hated that she was questioning herself, but was just glad this nightmare was over and everyone had come out unscathed. She tried to banish the image of Ford tackling that lunatic but it kept replaying in her mind.

As they stood, Ford looked at the detective. "Give us a few minutes before we head out?"

The detective nodded and quietly exited his own office.

Raegan guessed the reason he'd asked for privacy was because all her family and friends were waiting for them in the lobby of the PD. They hadn't cared that it would take hours to make a statement and deal with answering a hundred questions. They'd all descended on the police department, and according to Lizzy, the only person she'd talked to as of yet, no one was leaving until they saw her.

"This is a stupid question, but how're you feeling?" Ford asked, his big hands settled protectively on her hips.

She placed her hands on his chest, glad she had him to lean on.

"Tired and hungry. And I'm pretty sure I should be asking you that question."

He blinked as if she'd surprised him. "I'm okay."

"I was so scared for you. You just...went at him like a battering ram. It all happened so fast." Trembles racked her body and she hated that she seemed more affected than him and he was the one who'd taken on a guy with a gun. "How are you so okay about this?" Maybe he wasn't. Maybe he was just putting on a good show.

"I hate that you had to witness that violence, that an asshole could have killed you, but that's not the first time I've faced down a loaded weapon."

Her fingers clutched his shirt. "That's not making me feel any better."

His smile was wry. "I just mean I've had training — the best in the world — and experience. First in the Corps, then with the PD. If you want to talk to someone about what happened, I know some people."

She shrugged, not sure she needed or wanted to talk to anyone other than him. But she said, "Thanks. You ready to face my family?"

He let out a short laugh. "Yeah, but after they see you're okay, we're heading back to my place and not leaving for a couple days. I took off Monday already and I've told Porter you're not coming in either."

She blinked. "Seriously?"

He nodded. "Yep. Porter wants you to take off all of next week, but I figured you'd shoot him down pretty fast."

"You really do know me," she murmured. "Taking Monday off seems like a good plan though." Definitely not something she'd say no to. Especially not since it would mean nonstop sex with Ford. At least if she had anything to say about it.

After brushing his lips over hers, he slung an arm around her shoulders. "Let's get out of here."

Leaning into him, she knew without a doubt that this was a man she could depend on for anything. When she'd thought she might lose him she'd realized that her feelings for him were way more than 'like.' "Ford, I'm falling for you. Pretty hard." Saying the words was terrifying. She'd never been in love before and she was pretty sure she was fast on her way to being just that if she wasn't already.

"I'm falling for you too. And I'm pretty sure I'm not letting you go." His words were raspy and his voice steady.

Her heart flipped over in her chest. "I'm not letting you go either."

"Thank you for waiting at the police station," Ruby said as Montez pulled into her driveway.

He snorted. "Like I'd have left." After making an official statement, he'd waited along with the whole crowd of people for Ford and Raegan to wrap everything up. It had been a madhouse down there. He hated crowds for the most part, but not staying hadn't been an option. "That was some crazy shit," he muttered, turning the ignition off.

"No kidding." Ruby unstrapped her seatbelt, but didn't make a move to get out. Instead she turned to him. "Will you stay the night? I don't...want to be alone tonight."

They'd been exclusive for a week, but hadn't slept together. He wanted to, obviously, but he was going to do things right with Ruby. Because he was pretty sure she was the one for him. Had been sure for a long damn time. He just hadn't wanted to admit it. He and Ruby had had the 'safe sex' talk a couple days ago. He knew she was on the pill and hadn't been with anyone in over a year. And they'd both been tested since their last lovers.

But he'd noticed she hadn't said anything about sex tonight, just asked him to stay. He wasn't surprised she was shaken up. It didn't matter that they read about or saw shootings on the news all the time. Being in close proximity to one—that her friend was involved in—was terrifying for anyone. He'd seen his share of combat but she certainly hadn't, so if he could make her feel safe by staying, he would. "Of course."

Her whole body relaxed at that, the relief rolling off her almost palpable.

"You hungry? I'll whip us up something."

374 | KATIE REUS

She grinned as she opened her door. "Having a chef boyfriend definitely has some perks."

"Only some?" He got out with her, shutting his door behind him. He liked the sound of the word boyfriend.

"You need your ego stroked?" she murmured, meeting him halfway around the vehicle.

He bit his tongue, grunted a non-response, even though he wanted to suggest she could stroke something else. *Dios*, even the thought of her hands on his cock had him getting hard. But that wasn't what tonight was about. He knew she just didn't want to be alone. Because if she wanted more, he knew Ruby would flat-out tell him. He adored that about her.

She gave him a cheeky grin as they reached her front door and he couldn't believe how nervous he was. Which was stupid. He was a grown man, but since getting out of the Corps he hadn't been with anyone since his bitch of an ex. He'd had a few offers, but…those had felt more like pity fucks. So his hand had done well enough.

"You mind if I change out of this? My feet are killing me." She didn't turn around as she disabled the alarm then reset it.

"No problem. I'll see what you've got in your fridge."

She laughed, giving him a brief kiss before heading to the stairs. "I'm embarrassed to say there's not much. We might have to do takeout."

"I'll be able to work with whatever you've got," he said, watching the fine sway of her ass as she headed up the stairs. He tried not to imagine her stripping off her sexy summer dress and heels but failed.

Slow, he reminded himself. Tonight wasn't about him. She was just scared to be alone.

When he opened her refrigerator he frowned. She hadn't been kidding. A carton of eggs, some funky-colored stuff in a container that he was definitely not opening, yogurt, and bottles of water. After looking at the yogurt he realized the little cartons were expired.

"Takeout it is," he murmured, rummaging around in her drawers until he found a thick pile of takeout menus. He laughed at the stack. She must never cook.

"Find anything you like?"

Montez turned at the sound of Ruby's voice — and dropped all of the takeout menus to the floor.

His brain short-circuited as he saw her standing there in what was most definitely one of the 'naughty nurse' costumes she'd talked about. This wasn't a Halloween type of thing though. No way in hell could she ever go out in public wearing it.

The low-cut minidress was sheer white with red trim and a red and white cross over each nipple. Not that the crosses did anything to cover her up. He could see every delicious inch of her through the dress, including the tight buds of her nipples. Her high heels were ruby red and her little nurse hat had a red and white cross on it as well.

Her grin was wicked when his gaze finally landed on her face. "So? What do you think?"

He made a strangled sound since he couldn't find his voice. *Fuck me.* The reality of her eclipsed any fantasy he'd ever had. The two things were in different stratospheres.

She placed her hands on her hips. "I've got another one upstairs. Want me to try that one on for comparison?"

Her question jerked him back to reality. It would require her leaving and he didn't want that.

Wordlessly he strode across the kitchen, cupped the back of her head in a hard grip and crushed his mouth down on hers. He wasn't letting her get away.

Ever.

She arched against him, moaning into his mouth as she clutched his shoulders. It took him a second to realize what she planned as she hoisted herself up, wrapping her legs around his waist.

He grabbed her ass and hurried out of the kitchen. Bed. He needed to find a bed. Or a flat surface other than the floor.

She bit his bottom lip before nuzzling along his jaw, her little kisses and nips making him even harder. Something he hadn't thought possible.

But Ruby, the sweetest, sexiest woman he knew, was half-naked in his arms. And he was pretty damn sure he loved her. Had known for a while.

When they reached the top of the stairs she slid her hand between their bodies, cupped his erection. He tried to keep his balance but his brain short-circuited yet again. He started to trip, half turned so that she ended up splayed on top of him on the landing.

Her blonde hair fell loose around her face in waves, the little nurse hat askew as she looked down at him. Her hand was still cupping him and he could see the wicked glint in her gaze, knew that she liked making him crazy.

He also knew she wanted him to take control, if one of their previous conversations and his interactions with her were anything to go by.

He grasped her wrist, pulled it away as he shifted so she was under him. Cupping her cheek, he devoured her mouth. He wanted to go slow, ordered himself to, but when his lips touched hers this time it was as if he lost all ability to reason.

But he forced himself to pull back, to slow down. He wanted to make this good for her, make it as sexy and hot as whatever fantasies she'd spun about him in her head. "Put your hands above your head," he rasped out. He didn't have anything to restrain her hands with — this time. But from what he knew of the little minx, that would be coming soon enough.

Stretched out on the landing, she did as he said without hesitation. The action pushed her breasts out more. They strained against the sheer material. He wanted to rip it away, but he was going to savor this. Savor her.

His cock pulsed once. *Dios*, this woman was going to be the death of him, he was sure. Sitting back on his knees, he drank in the sight of her splayed out for him.

Reaching back, he lifted one of her ankles, brought her leg up and gently kissed her soft skin. She jerked slightly at that brief contact.

Sensitive.

He slid her heel off, heard it clatter behind him in the foyer. Did the same to her other shoe. Keeping his gaze pinned to hers, he moved her feet so they slid over his shoulders. Her breathing grew erratic as he leaned down closer, closer, spreading her thighs for him.

He'd been able to see she wasn't wearing anything under the little minidress earlier, but when he tore his gaze from her face, lasered in on her sweet pussy, he saw just how wet she was for him. "Open wider for me," he ordered.

Groaning, she spread her legs farther. She had just a bit of fine, soft blonde hair covering her mound. The smell of her arousal killed most of his control.

He buried his face between her legs, stroking his tongue up her slick folds.

"Montez." His name came out a choked moan.

And it sounded like pure heaven.

She slid her fingers through his hair, gripped his head tight as he flicked his tongue over her clit. "Oh...yeah." She rolled her hips against his face, the hottest thing he'd ever experienced, as she completely lost herself to pleasure. Her heels dug into his back, made him glad he'd taken the shoes off as she arched up against his mouth, going wild as he increased the pressure.

She was damn reactive.

His cock kicked against his pants as she dug her fingers tighter against his head.

"I'm close." Her words were strangled, unsteady.

He teased her slick entrance, slid two fingers inside her—and she started coming. Her inner walls clenched around him so he added a third finger, never letting up on her clit.

He continued stroking as she came against his tongue, her words garbled nonsense. Which, yeah, made him feel ten fucking feet tall. He loved that she'd come apart for him so easily, wanted to make her do it again.

And again. It would never be enough. Not with Ruby.

When she finally said something that sounded a lot like "Stop," he lifted his head to see her looking at him with a dazed expression. Even so, she reached for his pants.

He let her unbuckle him as he slid the straps of her dress down.

His hands actually shook as he bared her to him. The breasts he'd been fantasizing about for too damn long were utter perfection, her tight little nipples a pale pink.

He sucked one into his mouth as she completely freed him. He'd gone commando today, like usual, and was glad for it as she stroked his cock once, twice, three times.

He bit down gently on her nipple, causing her to cry out with what he knew was pleasure. He wished he had more hands because he wanted to touch her everywhere, kiss her all over. And never stop.

"In me, now," she demanded, the words more pleading than anything.

He couldn't force his voice to work, but he lifted his head, positioned himself at her entrance. He was glad they'd already had the talk, that he could slide into her bare this first time. Every time. He didn't want any barriers between them. Ever.

He kept his eyes pinned to hers, grasped her hips as he thrust inside her.

He wanted to kiss her, for her to taste herself on him, but this first time, he wanted to watch her as she came again. And she damn sure would.

Then he wanted her to watch him, to be completely vulnerable to her. He'd never wanted that with anyone, but he trusted this woman. She saw through all his bullshit and baggage and wanted him anyway. And she didn't make him feel like she was doing him a favor by being with him.

She wanted him with a desperation he could see clearly in her eyes. They were both completely gone for each other and he was glad he wasn't alone in this all-consuming hunger.

The tingling at the base of his spine built and crested, his balls pulled up tight as he felt his own orgasm coming up fast and hard. He wanted to slow down but there was no stopping it. Not this first time. Not after a year of lusting after her.

She dug her fingers into his back, her breathing out of control.

He reached between their bodies again, tweaked her clit. Her head fell back against the stairs, her mouth parting on a silent cry as she started clenching around him again, her inner walls milking him harder and harder.

When her back bowed tight and she cried out again, he let go of his control, thrusting hard inside her, taking everything she had to offer. He emptied himself inside her until he practically collapsed.

Instead of doing just that, he rolled to the side, half dragging her with him. The stairs were uncomfortable as shit, but he didn't care. Not when Ruby laid her head against his chest, sighed contentedly.

"That was..." She didn't finish, just let out another happy sigh as she slid her hand over his stomach.

"*Mi futura nuera* means my future daughter-in-law, by the way," he murmured after a few moments, his breathing returning to normal. He wondered if she remembered what his mom had said to her on Monday.

Ruby lifted her head, blinked at him once, her blue eyes wide. "Wh...I don't even know what to say to that."

"Don't say anything. I'm just telling you. And I'm also telling you she's probably right." He threw the 'probably' in in an attempt not to freak her out completely. Putting himself out there for her like this, especially when he'd just come to terms with the fact that she wanted him as much as he wanted her, made him feel vulnerable in a way he'd never experienced.

"God, I love you." Her voice was low as she leaned in, brushed her lips over his.

He jerked in surprise at the words, hadn't expected her to say them so soon, or at all. Something he hadn't realized had been missing filled his chest with happiness. "Ruby—"

"You don't have to say it back," she said simply. She was telling the truth. It was clear in her bright blue eyes.

He shook his head. "I do love you and I don't care if it's too soon. I know what I feel." Because he'd never felt anything like it. Not even close. It had to be love and he wasn't questioning it.

She gave him one of her brilliant smiles that lit up her whole face, and kissed him again.

He knew without a doubt that he was the luckiest guy in the world. And he was never letting her go.

CHAPTER EIGHTEEN

F ord slid his hand over Raegan's bare hip, squeezed once just to reassure himself she was okay. They'd been back at his place for hours and she'd long since crashed. He had a feeling she'd be sleeping a while. After such a scare it was only human nature to shut down, regroup. Sleep was sometimes the only way people could deal with shit. He knew that too well.

Unfortunately for him, sleep was elusive. Pushing out a sigh, he rolled onto his back. Part of him wanted to wake her up, but it would be selfish. He eased off the bed, headed into his bathroom. It was still dark out, but he wouldn't be going back to sleep anytime soon. Once the water was hot enough he stepped under the jets, let them pound against his back and shoulders.

It didn't do much to ease the tension as he relived everything. He'd barely thought when he'd tackled that guy, had simply reacted using all of his training. He rubbed his hands over his face, slinging water off as he dropped them to his sides.

When he opened his eyes he found Raegan stepping into the shower with him. He blinked, surprised by how quiet she'd been. "You're awake?" His voice was still raspy from sleep.

She didn't respond, just stepped right up to him, wrapping her arms around him as the water cascaded over them.

He held her close, savoring the feel of her full breasts against his chest as he rubbed a hand down her spine. "Sorry if the shower woke you up."

"It didn't," she murmured against his chest. "I've been having weird dreams."

Probably nightmares. "That might happen for a while."

She shuddered in his arms and pulled her head back to look up at him. Wordlessly she reached between their bodies and grasped his already hardening cock. It was pretty much guaranteed he was turned on if Raegan was naked and in his arms.

"We don't have to do anything," he said quietly as she started stroking him, once, twice... He groaned.

The grin she gave him was pure, wicked Raegan. She liked to tease him, he'd learned. "I know. I want to," she said right before dropping to her knees.

After everything she'd been through he thought he should be the one comforting her, but holy fuck... His hips rolled at the feel of her lips wrapped around his cock.

She made little sounds of pleasure as she ran her tongue up the length of him. When he realized she was touching herself between her legs, he about lost it.

"You stroking that pussy, baby?" he rasped out. He wished he could see her hand moving, her fingers dipping inside herself.

She hummed against his cock, kept sucking him. He clenched his jaw, focused on not coming as she gripped the base of him, squeezed once. The sensual woman might not talk much during sex, but hell, she didn't need to.

He could talk enough for both of them. Especially when he knew it got her hot. "Does sucking me off get you wet?"

She moaned against him now, her strokes getting faster, the grip on the base of his cock just a little harder.

He wanted to let her keep going, to find release in her mouth, but he wanted inside her tight body even more. Though it pained him to do so, he pulled his hips back. She made a protesting sound until he lifted her up, pinned her against the tile wall.

Feeling frantic with the need to get inside her, he crushed his mouth to hers as he cupped her mound. Stroking a finger against her folds he found out exactly how slick she was for him. In that moment, words eluded him.

He just needed inside this woman. She'd completely stolen his heart and today he could have lost her. That knowledge pierced him deep, sliced up a part of him he didn't even know existed. What he'd thought was love before, what he'd had with his ex, was absolutely nothing compared to what he already felt for Raegan.

If he'd lost her... God, he couldn't even go there. Not if he wanted to remain sane.

Raegan gripped his shoulders and lifted herself up, wrapping her legs around him as he thrust inside her.

Groaning, he paused, buried fully inside her as he looked down at her. Her blue eyes were heavy lidded with a hunger that mirrored his own. There was so much he wanted to say to her, but he wasn't sure he could find the right words, and didn't want to ruin this moment anyway.

He wanted to ask her to move in with him starting tomorrow but it was too soon. Or he guessed it was. Hell if he knew. All he knew was that he wanted to wake up to her face always, wanted to see her face every night before he went to sleep.

She gave him a teasing smile, rolled her hips against his once, a clear signal that he better start moving.

Reaching between their bodies, he rubbed his thumb over her clit. Her eyes closed and her head fell back against the tile on a sigh as he began stroking her with just the right amount of pressure. He'd learned what she liked quickly and she was so open with her pleasure and what she needed from him.

When her breathing grew erratic and her fingers dug into his shoulders with just a bit more pressure he knew she was close.

So was he. The base of his spine tingled, his balls pulled up tight as he held back from coming. Not yet.

He began thrusting in steady, even strokes, keeping her pinned against the wall. "Come for me, Raegan," he murmured, desperate to see the pleasure on her face, to feel her climaxing around him.

Her eyes opened at his words, her chest rising and falling more erratically as he continued stroking her clit.

When he pinched it oh so lightly, she jerked against him, burying her face against his neck on a cry of ecstasy. He felt her teeth barely dig into his flesh as her inner walls clenched around his cock, milking him harder and harder.

As she cried out his name, he let go of his own control.

Gripping her ass, he pulled her away from the wall and thrust harder, driving into her over and over as his own orgasm overtook him. He loved that he got to come inside her with no barrier. He never wanted anything between them, literally or figuratively.

She was his and he was most definitely hers. The woman completely owned him.

As he came down from his climax, he leaned against the opposite wall with her still wrapped around him. Jets of water still pounded down against them, but all he could focus on was Raegan. She laid her head against his shoulder, laughed softly.

"Laughing while I'm still inside you?" He nipped her earlobe.

"Just thinking that you've turned me into a total freaking nympho."

"That's a bad thing?"

She laughed again. "No. Not at all. I'm also thinking that you're probably going to have to carry me back to the bedroom. I'm feeling pretty useless right now."

He could hear the drowsiness in her voice, feel the laxness in her muscles as she wrapped around him. Yeah, she'd be ready to go back to sleep soon. Which was good. He wanted her to get the rest her body needed.

"That's not a problem," he murmured. "But first..." Though he didn't want to put her down, he set her on the small built-in bench and grabbed a bottle of body wash and lathered soap between her legs.

She squirmed slightly, watching him carefully. "You're the sweetest man I've ever met."

Uncomfortable with the praise, he didn't say anything. Just rinsed her off before grabbing towels for the two of them. He was surprised she let him dry her off and carry her back to bed, but he found he liked taking care of her like this.

When he tucked her back against his chest and held her close, he knew that he could get used to this. For once, he wasn't afraid of the future, wasn't worried that things would go south with the two of them.

He knew what type of woman Raegan was and he was damn lucky to have found her. Now that he had, he wasn't letting her go.

EPILOGUE

Three months later

"**H**oney, I'm home," Raegan called out, making Ford laugh from the kitchen.

"I'm slaving away over a hot stove." He turned at the sound of her shoes clicking across the tile floor.

"So, I'm guessing you ordered takeout?" She hung her purse on one of the wall hooks and slipped her heeled boots off, leaving them haphazardly where they fell. Which he'd learned was standard Raegan. It was a miracle she remembered to hang her purse up. Normally in the mornings she ran around looking for her purse and keys because she couldn't remember where she'd left them.

He just grinned, drinking in the sight of her. In bare feet and a dark blue sweater dress with a loose belt, she looked good enough to eat. He couldn't wait to strip her naked later. "You'll just have to come out on the patio and see."

"That sounds like heaven," she sighed.

Since the weather had started to slowly shift into fall it was cool enough to eat outside, so they'd been having dinner by the pool over the last week.

"Long day?" he asked.

She nodded, moving into him for a hug. She settled her face against his chest, just held him. "Yeah. Good, but long. We got a new client today and she's exhausting. Athena wants me to handle this job totally by myself."

"You'll do great."

"Yeah, maybe. It's still a little scary."

After everything she'd been through, he figured this would be a piece of cake for her. But he didn't say that. He'd come to learn that she simply liked to worry about work stuff, but always came through, always did a fantastic job above and beyond what was expected.

"I already know the answer, but how was your day?" she asked, pulling back.

He smiled down at her, amazed that this woman was in his life. He hoped to make it a permanent thing and was terrified he'd screw up tonight. "Awesome. The SF guys who did the training class really knew their stuff. And...we got to shoot a lot of weapons. The new guys were in heaven."

She just snorted. "That's why I knew you had an awesome day."

"Come on. Let's head out to the pool. Maybe we can swim after dinner?"

She lightly pinched his side as she stepped back. "I know that look and I'm not swimming naked."

He stifled a laugh. "My eighty-year-old and seventy-year-old neighbors aren't spying on us."

"You never know and I'm not taking the chance."

"I seriously love you," he murmured, kissing the top of her head.

"Well you're gonna love me more when you find out what I got for your birthday."

"What?"

"Nope. You don't get it until next month. I just wanted to torture you a little."

"I never realized you have a little mean streak."

She just grinned as he opened the back door. "Don't you forget it." She paused three steps outside, staring out at the transformed patio.

He'd had a little help with the idea—okay, a lot of help—but he'd set everything up himself. He'd moved all the patio furniture under the overhang into the garage and replaced it with a bunch of multicolored blankets and pillows. He'd hung up twinkle lights across the entire lanai and placed flameless candles in the shape of a big heart around the blankets. There were even different colored floating LED lights in the pool. He'd wanted to completely change the atmosphere so it was romantic but private.

Because he knew Raegan would have hated a public proposal. Hell, he just hoped she said yes.

It was pretty early in their relationship, but he'd given her a key to his place a week after the shooting, they'd said they loved each other two weeks after and she pretty much lived here now. She already took up half of his closet and he wanted her living with him permanently.

Raegan was it for him. He couldn't imagine a world without her in it. Didn't want to.

When she turned back to him, eyes wide, he was already on one knee, the box open. His hands actually shook as he held it out to her. "Marry me?"

She nodded, tears glittering in her eyes as she held her left hand out and cupped his cheek with her right. "Yes."

He loved how affectionate she was, how she never held anything back. Not her emotions, nothing. With Raegan, what you saw was what you got.

He slid the diamond on her finger, felt a weight lifting he hadn't realized he was carrying when he saw it glittering under the moonlight and twinkle lights. Hell yeah, she was his and he wanted the whole damn world to know she was taken.

Standing, he pulled her into his arms, brushed his mouth over hers lightly before deepening the kiss. Somehow he pulled back. "I got your favorite champagne." He motioned to the ice bucket in the middle of the blankets.

Smiling brightly, she practically dragged him to the bed of blankets. "If you do have pervert neighbors, they're about to get a show," she whispered, already making quick work of his belt buckle.

Laughing, he pinned her underneath him and captured her mouth again. He couldn't wait to spend the rest of his life with her. Raegan was the best thing that had ever happened to him and he planned to show her every day just how much she meant to him.

Dear Readers,

Thank you for reading the Red Stone Security Series box set: Volume 4. I hope you enjoyed it! If you'd like to stay in touch with me and be the first to learn about new releases you can:

- Sign up for my monthly newsletter at: www.katiereus.com
- Find me on Facebook: facebook.com/katiereusauthor
- Follow me on Twitter: twitter.com/katiereus
- Follow me on Instagram: instagram.com/katiereusauthor/

If you join my newsletter I promise to only send out emails for a new release, to let you know if I'm having a sale, or if I have a special giveaway going on. Also I hope you'll consider leaving a review at one of your favorite online retailers. It's a great way to help other readers discover new books and I appreciate all reviews.

Happy reading,
Katie

Complete Booklist

RED STONE SECURITY SERIES
No One to Trust
Danger Next Door
Fatal Deception
Miami, Mistletoe & Murder
His to Protect
Breaking Her Rules
Protecting His Witness
Sinful Seduction
Under His Protection
Deadly Fallout
Sworn to Protect
Secret Obsession
Love Thy Enemy
Dangerous Protector

THE SERAFINA: SIN CITY SERIES
First Surrender
Sensual Surrender
Sweetest Surrender
Dangerous Surrender

DEADLY OPS SERIES
Targeted
Bound to Danger
Chasing Danger (novella)
Shattered Duty
Edge of Danger
A Covert Affair

NON-SERIES ROMANTIC SUSPENSE
Running From the Past
Dangerous Secrets
Killer Secrets
Deadly Obsession
Danger in Paradise
His Secret Past
Retribution
Merry Christmas, Baby

PARANORMAL ROMANCE
Destined Mate
Protector's Mate
A Jaguar's Kiss
Tempting the Jaguar
Enemy Mine
Heart of the Jaguar

DARKNESS SERIES
Darkness Awakened
Taste of Darkness
Beyond the Darkness
Hunted by Darkness
Into the Darkness

MOON SHIFTER SERIES
Alpha Instinct
Lover's Instinct (novella)
Primal Possession
Mating Instinct
His Untamed Desire (novella)
Avenger's Heat
Hunter Reborn
Protective Instinct (novella)

ABOUT THE AUTHOR

Katie Reus is the *New York Times* and *USA Today* bestselling author of the Red Stone Security series, the Darkness series and the Deadly Ops series. She fell in love with romance at a young age thanks to books she pilfered from her mom's stash. Years later she loves reading romance almost as much as she loves writing it.

However, she didn't always know she wanted to be a writer. After changing majors many times, she finally graduated summa cum laude with a degree in psychology. Not long after that she discovered a new love. Writing. She now spends her days writing dark paranormal romance and sexy romantic suspense. For more information on Katie find her on twitter @katiereus or visit her on facebook at: www.facebook.com/katiereusauthor. If you would like to be notified of future releases, please visit her website: www.katiereus.com and join her newsletter.

59523632R00241

Made in the USA
Lexington, KY
11 January 2017